Just the Way You Are

Pepper Basham

Pepper Basham

To Granny Spencer
Whose stories inspired my creativity and whose life inspired me

What People Are Saying about Just the Way You Are

Laugh-out-loud humor combines with stick-your-head-in-the-freezer kisses in this novel of romance, faith, and a little historical mystery. Eisley Barrett is a positively delightful heroine, her Appalachian charm the perfect counterpart for Wes Harrison's British swoonworthiness. Secondary characters rich with arm yet unique personalities beg readers to pull up a chair and chat, while the family history subplot adds more layers of intrigue and romance to the plot. Above all, the theme of being treasured 'as is' rings true and full of grace. - 4 ½ *Star Top Pick from Romantic Times*

With a quirky heroine, a swoony hero, and a comedic collection of two unique cultures, Pepper Basham has crafted a romantic read full of personality, chuckles, and plenty of second-chance hope splashed in for good measure. – Jennifer Rodewald, author of *Red Rose Bouquet.*

Beautifully written, whimsical, and perhaps a little cheeky, Just the Way You Are grabbed a hold of me and wouldn't let go. – Janice Hanna Thompson, author of *Weddings* *by* *Bella.*

Chapter One

One step into the massive, glass-walled waiting area was all it took.

In a cataclysmic chain of events, someone bumped into Eisley Barrett, sending her purse and all its contents skittering across the glossy floor of Heathrow International Airport. Just as she regained her balance, her heel caught on her purse strap, forcing her off-kilter.

She liked comedy, but this was ridiculous.

In horrific slow motion, forward momentum merged with gravity, the crowd parted like the Red Sea, and she landed face-first on the floor.

Well, not exactly on the floor. Somebody broke her fall.

She gasped and the humiliating rush of heat in her cheeks soared throughout her entire body. *Somebody* broke her fall!

Eisley looked up from her unladylike position and peered through her veil of red hair at a pair of gray trousers and black Rockports. Her throat pinched air to a stop. The s*omebody* was male. Visions of a tall, dark, and deceptive ex-husband shifted through her mind. Post Romantic Betrayal Disorder, plain and simple.

A set of dazed gray-blue eyes with a tuft of silver brow blinked back at her. *Thank you, Jesus. It's a grandpa-aged male.* She choked on her relief as the thoughts rammed into place.

"Gracious sakes. I've squished a grandpa." Eisley pushed away from the man's crinkled dress shirt, then leaned in to grab his arms. "Oh my goodness, I'm so sorry. Are you okay?"

His lips quirked into an uncertain grin as she eased him up to a sitting position.

"I think I am well. It's the first time I've been assaulted by a young woman in an airport."

Eisley opened her mouth to protest, but the twinkle in his eyes gave him away. She offered her most daring smile. "It's my first assault. How did I do?"

"Brilliant, actually. First rate, I'd say."

She laughed but quickly sobered. Her first hour in England and she mows down a poor man in the airport. Fabulous start. "Seriously, are you okay?"

He winced. Eisley dropped her hold on his arms. "Oh, no. I *did* hurt you."

"Nothing serious. A sprain, perhaps." The man rotated his wrist, a strange expression crossing his face as he watched her. Most likely he was trying to figure out how much money he could get from her if he sued. "Per chance, would you be Eisley Barrett?"

His question clinked into place. She leaned back and *really* looked at him. She should have known him from his picture, but the whole squishing scene had been way too distracting for little things like recognition. He had one of those distinguished-grandfather appearances: dressed in a suit, salt-and-pepper hair neatly trimmed, with a sliver of moustache to add a sense of renown. Just like she'd expected, except the hair was a bit erratic after his near-concussion.

"Mr. Harrison?"

"Yes, Daniel Harrison. It's a pleasure to meet you, Eisley." Her name rolled off his tongue as if James Bond said it himself. Something inside of her melted.

"A pleasure to survive me might be more like it." She shook her head and groaned. "I'm so sorry about the fall. I knew I shouldn't have worn heels."

"Don't worry yourself, Luv. Accidents do happen. My wife has a habit of stepping on my feet."

Eisley winced at the memory of her coma-inducing footwork. "I bet she never tackled you in an airport."

He chuckled. "That wasn't a typical Appalachian greeting?"

She really shouldn't smile. After all, she'd nearly suffocated, possibly flattened, a senior citizen, but he was so downright charming it was difficult to maintain a guilty expression.

"Tackling is one of my family's traditions, but we usually call it *hugging*. It takes all the fun out if you clue strangers in on the attack." Eisley sighed. "Come on, Mr. Harrison, let's get you off the floor and into a chair. At least then, we won't add *trampled* to your list of possible injuries." She helped him to his feet. "And maybe we should pray for your wrist. That's what I do with my kids, anyway."

"Have you traveled without your children before?"

"Never more than a night or two, so this is definitely an adjustment." She placed her hand against her quivering stomach. Every inch of those four thousand miles pressed in on her heart like eating way too much of Aunt Tilley's Mastermind Meatloaf. She tossed a glance to the outgoing flights display. A fleeting thought to return home inched to mind.

No. She'd made a promise. *Uncle Joe.* She swallowed down the worry bubble in her throat and guided Mr. Harrison to a chair.

"But the kids are in great hands." She babbled on as if words would assuage mommy-guilt. "Christmas break's a week away and my parents are as excited as the kids. With my dad in charge, I'll be lucky if my seven-year-old isn't toting a rifle and my daughter isn't biting off bottle tops with her baby teeth within a week."

Mr. Harrison's sudden laugh pricked at Eisley's smile and curbed the mommy-ache.

"Yeah, it sounds pretty crazy, doesn't it? But my parents wouldn't let me turn down Cousin Lizzie's offer to come do research for Uncle Joe." She gave her eyebrows a playful wiggle. "And get a good dose of England in the process. The trip was their Christmas gift to me. Single moms need big holidays, they said."

His kind gaze held hers a moment. "No doubt."

She settled Mr. Harrison in a chair and detoured her high-octane emotions by gathering her various paraphernalia scattered across the floor. Her kids would be okay. They would still remember her name, and surely her Dad wouldn't have them chewing tobacco by the time she got home.

She stuffed her items back into her bag and sat down next to Mr. Harrison. "I can't thank you and Eleanor enough for letting me stay with you while I'm here."

"It's the very least we could do for one of our oldest and dearest friends. We were happy to offer our home. With Lizzie's father's ill health, it wouldn't have been suitable for you to stay at Lornegrave."

"Right." Lizzie's emails hinted about her father's dementia and psychosis, but everything else seemed as much a secret as Eisley's mysterious ancestor. Oh, this story kept getting better and better, nibbling at Eisley's lifelong obsession with great romance. Fictional, of course. The less painful kind.

Maybe hidden behind five hundred years of unsolved stories, she could discover what happened to Julia Ramsden, find the name of the man she married, and make her uncle's dying wish come true in the process. She drew in a deep breath of renewed determination. "It was very sweet of you to come to London for me."

"We were happy to collect you. We were already in town for our annual Charity Christmas gala. It is Eleanor's favorite charity and we never miss." He gave her hand a comforting pat. "Not one wit of trouble."

She peered around him in search of some elegant British counterpart. "Where is your wife?"

"Ah, yes. Eleanor felt peaked this morning."

Peaked? "Is she okay?"

His smile crinkled at the corners of his eyes. "I'm certain she'll be fit as a fiddle for the gala tonight. Social events always encourage her health. She's not fond of London morning traffic, I'm afraid, but she's quick to raise money for her cause at any given moment."

"Sounds like I'm going to really like her." Eisley shrugged. "As if there was any doubt about that. Do you feel ready to walk after I mauled you? I guess we're taking the Tube or maybe we can catch a taxi?

"Actually, my son is to drive us. Wes is quite capable. He lives on the West End." Mr. Harrison nodded toward the doorway. "And here he comes now."

Eisley followed Mr. Harrison's gaze across the expanse of the meeting area, past the red bucket chairs and rows of people, and right into the eyes of a Greek god. Her vision zoomed in like a camera, blocking out everything else – sounds, noises, her phobia of Prince Charming look-alikes.

A taller, younger version of Mr. Harrison walked toward them, as if directly from a Google search for swoon-worthy. His gray-blue gaze blazed through her, igniting fireworks in her chest and heat in her cheeks. Unfamiliar sparks burned through years of avoidance and splintered directly into her pulse. The emotion flashed into recognition with a harsh light. She held in a whimper. Attraction?

Lord, really? Are you joking?

She tried to adjust her expression. The last thing she needed was to look like a three-year-old in a candy store. Too much eye candy is bad for a wounded heart. Very bad. It might lead to thoughts of hope—or worse, possibilities.

She stumbled to a stand and bent to help Mr. Harrison from his chair.

"Eisley," he whispered. "It would be wise not to mention the falling incident to Wes."

She jerked her gaze to his. "What?"

"Wes." Mr. Harrison stepped forward and greeted his son. "This is Eisley Barrett. Our guest for the next few weeks."

Wes' gaze trailed over her, leaving a splash of warmth on her face and a knot in the pit of her stomach. *Calm. Distant. Glacial.* The perfect coolant for her overactive imagination.

The dutiful son offered his hand, somewhat reluctantly. "A pleasure, Ms. Barrett."

His hot-fudge smooth voice swept all words right out of her head and melted any images of icecaps. The perfect combination – fascinating eyes, a British accent, and chocolate. Yep, he was Ghirardelli in human form. She gave her wayward thoughts a mental slap.

Pull yourself together, woman. No man is worth a Marshall-sequel.

She peeled her tongue off the roof of her mouth, took his hand, and pushed all the giddy, junior-high feelings down to her pinkie toe. "It's nice to meet you."

A fake smile showed off his perfectly straight teeth. His taciturn expression proved he remained completely unimpressed with what he saw. Ah, the story of her life. Add a mile-high stack of comparisons to her twin brother and it was an instant flashback to high school.

She pulled her pink rolling bag to her side and shrugged off the sting of the disappointment she refused to embrace.

His smoky gaze skimmed down to her luggage. "Your baggage?"

"Pink is easier to find in the baggage check."

"No doubt."

Sarcasm? Daggone it, that just made him more attractive. Oh, what a pickle. Why here and now? The hopeless romantic she'd crammed underneath her busy-working-mother mask and three years of hardened resentment scrambled to the surface in full agonizing volume, hands opened wide to the daydream. The timing was horrible. There was nowhere to hide. No family excuses. Thankfully, Mr. Frosty-and-Fabulous curbed her lack of self-control with a solid dose of reality. He looked annoyed, maybe a bit bored, and definitely not carrying on an internal monologue to rival Bridget Jones.

Wes lifted her bags and started toward the doors. "Well, Ms. Barrett, Father's told me very little about you." A look passed between the two men, and Eisley stepped back from the glare. "You are from Virginia, yes?"

"Yes, a teeny tiny place in the Blue Ridge Mountains. Not too far from North Carolina and the Smokies. A great place to call home."

Wes remained stiff as a hardbound book binding, but – Hark! Was that a faint light of interest flickering behind his dull expression?

"The Blue Ridge Mountains? North Carolina?" His intense stare flipped to Mr. H.

What about either of those topics could possibly interest a handsome and aloof British guy?

She liked him better as rude and unavailable. Married would be even better. She took a quick glance at his left hand. Bare as the Jenkinses' table after a meal.

Hope plummeted to the heels of her unsteady shoes and self-control teetered in a frightening direction. *No, no, no – she couldn't afford daydreams with real possibilities.* Attraction held empty promises. All hormones – no heart. She'd learned the hard way how different those two were. She would not screw up her life again.

Wes led the way to the door, and even his stride was distracting. *Good grief.* She switched her attention to less distracting ground. Mr. Harrison. "Lizzie said your cottage is only a short walk from Lornegrave Hall, so I could take the footpath to her house each day."

"Of course." Mr. Harrison offered his arm, so she snuggled up next to him like he was Grandpa Jenkins and almost forgot about the Greek god toting her pink luggage through Heathrow. Almost.

"I can't believe I'll get to tour Lornegrave Hall. The same house Julia Ramsden lived in! My family has carried her legend down through generations, but the story always ended in a mystery. Somehow I feel like there are answers hidden there." She gave a helpless shrug. "Somewhere."

"And you hope to find them?" Mr. Harrison steered them toward the doorway. "Perhaps even write about them?"

"Uncle Joe's the writer, not me." A quiet nudge of defiance battled against her admission but she ignored it as usual. "I've been his researcher-in-training ever since I was a little girl. He knew a romantic when he saw one. He's like a second dad to me. Once he sucked me into his genealogical research, I was a lost cause. And he has an editor interested in Julia Ramsden's story as a novel retelling, so the information I find here will help him complete the book." She slowed her pace at the thought of her crazy and amazing uncle, who was dying from pancreatic cancer. "I'm determined to find out all I can since he's taking the elevator to Heaven instead of the stairs."

Mr. H nodded. "Lizzie mentioned time was essential."

"Yea, the doctors say five or six months...maybe." She took a steadying breath. "Funny, he wanted me to go on this adventure to uncover Julia Ramsden's brave story so she can be the heroine of his novel, but watching him face death with such strength and courage?" She shook her head and offered a shrugged smile. "He's definitely a hero in my book."

"I'm sorry he couldn't be here with you."

Eisley swallowed the football-sized lump in her throat and waved away his concern. "Oh well, Uncle Joe wants a grand and glorious finish. So this book is the capstone of all his research." The compassion in Mr. Harrison's eyes almost loosened her pent-up tears. She squeezed his arm, her voice softer. "Besides, it makes a difference when you know where you're going, right? Fear can't outshine God's love, and death can't, either."

They'd stopped walking, although people continued zipping past, and suddenly, a wave of peace rushed through her. God's love glowed brighter than her fears, too. Even if her kids were four thousand miles across a very large ocean. Even if the only grace she had was the grace of God. Even if the thought of any available man dug like a needle into her insecurities.

She chanced a glance at Zeus, and fell right into his stare. Gray-blue and intense. He blinked and cleared his throat, resuming his walk. "How long have you corresponded with Lizzie?"

"Uncle Joe met her at an online genealogy site about a year ago because they both had the same distant ancestors. I joined the conversations about six months later. Once we realized Lizzie actually lived in our ancestor's home, we all became great friends." Eisley grinned, but it didn't make a dent in Wes's expression. Was he purposely trying to intimidate or was it just a character trait? He sent off all sorts of Mr. Darcy vibes. She stammered on the thought. "She...she didn't even know about Julia's story until we met. So, this is going to be a discovery for both of us."

"What an interesting story." Wes's tone edged with suspicion.

A regular sweetheart. Jerks came in all shapes and sizes, even swoony.

"I hope it will be." She turned her attention back to Mr. Harrison. She wouldn't let Wes-Needs-Smiling-Lessons Harrison burst her sleuthing joy. "Tomorrow we travel to your cottage?"

"Yes, on the two o'clock train."

"Fantastic." She clapped her hands together like a little girl and sighed. "Oh, thank you for helping make this all happen."

"Well, I think we'll get on quite well, my dear." The twinkle returned to Mr. H's eyes. "And maybe you'll find a piece of your own story here too."

Eisley stared at him, trying to decipher the hidden message his elfish grin held, but his only answer was a gentlemanly gesture of holding the door for her. As his hand reached for the door, he winced.

"Careful, with that wrist, Mr. H. Don't want to hurt it worse."

"Hurt?" Wes stopped so suddenly she rammed into his back.

Uh-oh. *Open mouth, insert both feet up to the kneecaps.* She swallowed. Her cheeks flushed sunburn-hot. "Oh...well...um...we think he sprained his wrist."

"It's slightly tender, Eisley. Nothing serious, as I told you." Mr. Harrison looked to Wes. "No cause for concern."

Wes tightened like a banjo string. Concern? Oh, he didn't look concerned. He looked downright mad. At her. Did she have *guilty* carved into her freckles?

"How did Dad hurt his wrist?"

She opened her mouth to face her inevitable doom when Mr. H answered. "I tripped over an angel."

Eisley stared at him as if he'd confessed to seeing aliens. "*Tripped* over me? An angel?" A smile flashed behind his eyes. "Mr. Harrison, are you sure you didn't get a concussion from your fall along with a sprain?"

"A concussion? Fall?"

So much for subtlety. Might as well fully admit to her guilt, although running away in her near-homicidal heels seemed a more logical option. "I fell on top of your dad." She'd never been great at logic. "Squished him like a bug."

The words registered as fast as thawing water. "You did *what*?"

"Wes," his dad's voice firmed. "I'm fine. As you can see for yourself."

"You fell on him? You've been here a grand total of half an hour and you managed to fall on my father?" His gaze darkened to stormy gray and his bass voice added the thunder. "Or perhaps your actions are questionable. It appears terribly convenient to—"

"Wes, she knows nothing of your life." Mr. Harrison interrupted. "She's *our* guest. Not yours."

"Questionable?" Eisley pushed between them, any warm fuzzies in her stomach fizzed into sparks. "Are you saying I did this on purpose? You don't even know me. I have a bad habit of being clumsy, okay? And these new shoes didn't help, but that's it. An accident, pure and simple."

She didn't realize she was so close until she looked down at her finger poking his solid chest. And upon further examination, something seemed strangely familiar about that face and those fiery eyes. But why? She didn't know anyone from England, let alone the reproduction of a Greek god, but his temperament fit the description: arrogant, rude, quick-tempered, and ready to throw a lightning bolt at a person's first offense. Fine. She liked him even less.

Wes eyed her feet. "Perhaps you should learn to walk in them before wearing them."

The truth hurt, but she wasn't about to admit it. In fact, she wanted to growl and say something brilliant with Jane Austen wit. "Aren't you a charmer?" Lame. Far from Austen. "I may not be rich and sophisticated, but in the mountains where I'm from, we don't jump to ridiculous conclusions when we first meet people." *Well that's not exactly true.* "We usually give them the benefit of the doubt." *On most days.*

"Everyone is out for something, Ms. Barrett." His face inched so close she felt heat radiating off of him. Maybe a lightning bolt *was* in her future. "Meeting Lizzy online? A mysterious ancestor?" He raised that infernally perfect eyebrow of his. "Even *accidents* are suspect."

"Wes." His father scolded, and then turned to Eisley. "Please excuse Wes's reaction. He's not fond of strangers at present."

"Strangers?" Wes's gaze didn't leave her face. "Shrewd and quite devious strangers have caused a lot of trouble for us lately. It would take very little for Ms. Barrett to use her relationship with Lizzie to—"

"Listen here, Mr. Pleasant." She needled her finger a little deeper into his chest. Handsome or not, she'd learned her lesson about being a doormat. "This *was* an accident. I can't even understand why you're getting so angry. In my life, accidents happen all the time. I'd never hurt anyone on purpose." *Except maybe my ex-husband.* "What would I get from crushing a sweet man? A guilty conscience?"

His gray eyes widened, but she wasn't about to give him time to make more nasty accusations. *Jerk.*

"If it's any consolation, I would have much rather landed on you than your dad." *What?* Eisley pressed her eyes closed and almost groaned. "I mean, well...falling on *you* would have been much more gratifying." She was sure her cheeks deepened to carmine. "I mean...um...never mind."

She studied the sidewalk then the line of cars. Even Mr. Harrison's familiar Rockports. Anything to keep from looking at Wes. But he didn't say anything. Nothing. He just took a step forward, into her space, and brought a wonderful spicy scent with him. The heat in her cheeks shot down her neck. *Oh Jesus, please help me.* She bit her lip, took a deep breath, and lifted her gaze.

The look in his eyes held her in place without a single touch. Silence captured all competing noise. The world closed into a space where only the two of them existed and the strangest sense of 'right' settled over her for the briefest moment. *What was God thinking?*

Wes recovered first, because she was pretty much stuck in fatal-attraction mode.

"Forgive me, Eisley." His gaze softened for a moment and then probed far beyond comfortable. "Perhaps I rushed to a conclusion."

She stepped back and murmured, "At Nascar speeds."

He cleared his throat and began walking again, the hard edge of his expression a bit more pensive than grumpy. "Since Father's heart attack two months ago and then the incident with the paparazzi, I've been rather cautious of new people. Some *strangers* posing as family friends sold highly private photos of me and my father shortly after his attack, and it isn't the first time our privacy has been violated. I'm very protective of my family."

His sideways glance clearly stated he didn't trust her. Okay – maybe there still was a little grumpy in his expression. Well, she couldn't blame him really. His excuses were pretty good. Heart attack and paparazzi? If her father had recently had a -- wait. . .*paparazzi?* She caught her breath. Her throat tightened, so she swallowed. Her gum. Halfway.

A series of unladylike coughs doubled her over. Oh, how she wanted to sink into the sidewalk and never return. Wes touched her shoulder and leaned so close she got lost in the sweet scent of earth and spice and everything nice.

Death by bubble gum might not be so bad.

"Eisley?"

She sucked in a gasp at the sound of her name on his lips, but it was a bad idea. Coughing ensued, right in his face. *Come quickly, Lord Jesus. Preferably right now.*

Her coughing melted into a humiliated laugh. "I swallowed my gum." She shrugged, met that thought-blanking gaze again and a new explosion of heat lit her cheeks to the teary point. "Did you say *paparazzi?*"

Wes exchanged a look with his father and if possible, his posture straightened even more. He distanced himself with a step. "Well, yes."

Eisley's lips came unhinged and she looked over at Mr. Harrison. "Are you famous?"

Mr. Harrison grinned. "No, dear. The paparazzi were after Wes."

Wes? She examined Wes's face, which wasn't difficult to do at such close proximity. Somewhere in the deep recesses of her mind the fog began to clear. Wes Harrison? *Christopher Wesley Harrison.*

She grabbed his arm. "You're the actor, Christopher—"

"Shhh." He covered her mouth with his palm, his soft touch forcing a tingle through her. His eyes shot wide and he dropped his hand, apparently as shocked as she was. Maybe she *had* been struck by lightning!

"Pardon me." He looked away. "I...I prefer anonymity for now, if you don't mind."

Eisley stared, dumbfounded. Words, thoughts, and feelings crashed together inside her head. Christopher Wesley Harrison? No wonder she'd recognized him. No wonder she'd been attracted to him. She wasn't in danger of losing her heart. She almost giggled at the impossibility of it. He wasn't like a *real* person. Everything slowed down. Her breathing, her thoughts, her heartrate. Then the realization hit her. She was perfectly safe.

Chapter 2

A shock ran up Wes Harrison's arm, directly from Eisley's lips. Heat rifled through him, awakening his senses with every detail: the interlocking ribbons of green and gold in her eyes, the warmth of her breath against his palm, the scent of rosemary and mint. From the moment she told him she'd rather have landed on him instead of his father, her honesty set his cynical perspective into a spin. Whether it was the easy drawl of her accent or the feigned innocent look in her eyes, he was tempted to allow the suspicion of the past two years to fall from his shoulders.

To trust again.

The notion terrified him – and resurrected a stone-cold wall around his heart.

He dropped his hand from her mouth and forced the confusing emotions down until they knotted in his chest. Jane's face flickered across his mind, dousing the sweet aroma of attraction with the hard edge of bitterness. He was no judge of goodness or sincerity. With his reprehensible past, he couldn't even trust himself.

And he wasn't a big fan of surprises.

Everyone had an angle, and he worked hard to keep the sharp edges of that angle from digging into his family's lives. It was a hard lesson to learn, but he had enough scarred memories to keep the truth fresh in his mind.

He'd been in a foul mood ever since his parents had shown up in London the day before and informed him of their visiting guest. A complete stranger. Not six months earlier, pictures of his hospitalized father smattered the pages of a local entertainment magazine, confirming the truth his past engraved in his psyche.

Outsiders could not be trusted. Eisley Barrett was no different than those manipulative strangers or even his unfaithful ex-fiancée. His own experience taught him if something appeared too good to be true, too sincere, it usually was. He only needed time to call her bluff, so to speak. For example, which extreme reaction would she show at the news of his fame? Shyness or its cheap imitation? A coy smile or bold flirtation? *Women were all the same.*

Eisley finally released her kempt air and clamped her pink lips together until they formed a slight smile—a smile of uncertainty? Humor? Wes blinked. No, Eisley Barrett looked...relieved?

A nervous laugh bubbled from her. "No worries, Chris—" she slapped her palm over her mouth and offered a muffled laugh before removing it— "I mean, Wes. You're secret's safe with me. Completely surreal, but totally safe."

He studied her face, searching for any hint of her duplicity, but her wide eyes gave no indication except disbelief. So, she was an expert player, was she? The cautious edge fisted tighter for protection. He would not fall prey to his weakness with women. Not again.

"Thank you." He scanned ahead for his car, even though he knew exactly where he parked it. For his parents' sake, he'd maintain his politeness and keep a wary eye on their guest, but believe anyone could be as genuine? Never. Within an hour, she will have texted or tweeted everyone in her cyberworld with news of her encounter with a "famous" British actor. Or somewhat "famous". He had no desire to return to the high status and demands of his former life. "Not everyone is so obliging."

She nudged him with her elbow and wrinkled her nose in a grin. "Just one itsy bitsy request, though."

Cynicism burned a deep line into his counterfeit grin. "Yes?"

"Can I just share it with my mom? She's not only my best friend, but she's a huge costume drama fan."

"Your mother?"

"Mmm-hmm," Eisley nodded. "That's all."

"That's all, is it?" Unlikely.

Her eyes widened and she drew to a stop in the middle of the walk. "Okay, I thought we established I'm an honest person. That I have no intention of dispatching sweet elderly gentleman or ratting out handsome British actors." She pointed a finger and frowned. "And don't narrow your eyes at me like I'm some sort of criminal. I'm just clumsy."

"My father seems to trust you enough to invite you into his home." Wes shot his father a severe look but was promptly ignored. "How could I offer less?"

"I'm grateful for his kindness, and my Uncle Joe is too, but that's all I'm after – preferably without head wounds." Her hands followed the animation in her words. "Research *and* the opportunity to discover the history and romance of England. Nothing else."

He stopped in front of his car and crossed his arms, softening his stance as he leaned against its blue cover. Let the game begin. "Romance, is it?"

"I love romance." She sighed like a little girl at the end of a bedtime fairy tale. "I just like it tucked safely between the covers of a book or framed by the television screen. It's nice and predictable there." She raised a palm, forehead crinkling a bit. "I'm all for two-dimensional romance, thanks. *Real* romance scares me all the way to my knobby knees. My heart's not ready for a sequel to my past."

A twinge of guilt pricked at his conscious. *Her* past? With the joy pumping through each syllable she uttered, her past couldn't hold the same deep wounds as his. It all had to be a game— a ploy—and he was full-up of being a pawn by fame hunters.

"Oh no, I did it again. I spilled every thought in my head and jabbered away like a monkey with ADHD." She rubbed her fingers into her shaking head, the motion sending more of her minty scent his direction. "My mom keeps repeating that Bible verse to me—*we must be quick to listen, slow to speak*—but it hasn't stuck yet. I'm sorry."

Wes cleared his throat and forced out a hesitant reply, snuffing the slight spark of curiosity. "Not at all." Who was this woman? And what did she really want? "I'll place your luggage in the boot."

Dad ushered Eisley to the offside door. "Eisley, sit in front with Wes so you can have a proper view of the sites through town." His dad's eyes twinkled like Father Christmas. Not a good sign. "I should like to rest in back."

Rest? No, his father was busy scheming, and Wes had a sneaky suspicion he and Eisley Barrett were part of the plot.

Wes maneuvered through morning traffic, barely conscious of Eisley and his father's conversation regarding American and British driving. He couldn't shake the niggling of doubt she posed. In all his years around a variety of women, nothing prepared him for the apparent authenticity Eisley Barrett peddled. Add to the scenario his father's odd behavior, and he felt trapped outside his own story. Looking in – and confused about the next scene.

"So, Mrs. Barrett, when you're not traveling the world and accosting men in airports, what is it you do?"

He'd intended to slight her, but her smile bloomed and his chest constricted in a contradictory reaction. "Well, when I'm not torturing you and your father, I work as a preschool teacher. My adoring fans stand about yea-high." She measured the distance with her palm. "And pay me in kisses, snotty noses, and enough artwork to decorate the airport." She leaned closer and narrowed her eyes. "Jealous?"

A preschool teacher? It fit her to the sparkle in her eyes and curbed his inner critic with another clashing match. He wasn't certain how to respond. He focused his attention on the road ahead and tried to stifle a sudden urge to laugh. She had a well-thought-out story. He'd hand her that.

"And this bit about your ancestor? The ancestor you and Lizzie share." Dad interjected from his restful back seat. "Lizzie says her story is an adventure?"

"Well, from the little bits of information passed down through our family, we know she helped smuggle Tyndale Bibles throughout Derbyshire during King Henry VIII's early reign. I'm not sure how she smuggled them or who she helped, but more importantly"— her voice dropped to a mysterious whisper, nearly causing him to draw closer in anticipation. She was good. — "I want to know how she survived being burnt at the stake."

Wes nearly veered off the motorway. "What?"

"Isn't it amazing? Uncle Joe has spent about twenty years trying to unearth details from anyone who might know. Any tips or rumors. The family legend is, a local priest found out about Julia's secret work and tried to kill her. She was rescued, but no one knows how for sure, only that she disappeared afterwards. My grandmother thinks she was rescued by the man she finally married."

"And he was...?"

Eisley shrugged. "I'm hoping Lizzie and I can figure that out together. All I know are his initials—G. M.—from a torn letter that's been passed down through our family." She leaned forward in the seat. "Look at all these old buildings. Don't you just love living in a place so rich with history?"

The wonder in her face captivated him for a second before he turned his focus back to the road. Perhaps the wrong adult in the car secured an acting degree. Either that, or Eisley Barrett truly was as genuine as she seemed. His mind refused to wrap around the latter option.

"You know, Eisley," Dad said. "I hoped Wes might have the opportunity to speak with you. Your opinion will be invaluable to him."

Wes glanced in the rearview mirror. His father avoided the glare.

"*My* opinion? That sounds a little unlikely, Mr. H."

Mr. H? He'd heard it once in the airport, but now she used it like a nickname, and his father appeared to like it. This entire charade grew more questionable with each scene.

"Actually, he and his friend, Henry, have completed a screenplay based on a story set in your part of the world, I believe. It's some sort of historical adventure. Isn't that correct, Wes?"

Wes's reply came slowly. "Yes."

"You're writing a movie? That's great." Her entire expression brightened in awe. "Where is it set?"

He pulled his gaze from his father's incriminating grin. "I doubt you'd know it. It's a rather small community known as Summit."

"Summit?" Her palm flattened against her chest. "Summit, North Carolina? My mom's grandparents are from Summit."

"What a coincidence." His father's words hitched into the conversation.

Wes shot his dad another glance. "Isn't it?"

Dad raised his brows in declaration of innocence—to no avail. Lizzie Worthing and his father were playacting as matchmakers. No surprise on that score. His father had been guilty of it for years, with two strikes and a trail of disappointment. Father prattled on about second chances, but Wes neither wanted nor deserved one.

Eisley Barrett was not an option. Leave the woman with her two-dimensional heroes. They wouldn't lead to disappointment—for either of them. But his gaze lingered much too long on her face. A fruitless search for hidden agendas took a surprising slide into interest for a different reason. A sliver of warmth rivered beneath his skin. He stilled his wandering thoughts with an iron grasp.

"It's a beautiful place, Wes." Something about the lilt in her voice when she said his name, the familiarity of it, shook his pulse. "Way up high in the mountains. But you can't get there by main roads or anything. It's pretty remote. Why would anyone want to make a movie about Summit? I've heard my great-grandparents were characters, but not that kind."

Her easy humor caught him off-guard again. She kept doing that. It was unnerving. "Yes...well, it's based on a novel by Jonathan Taylor, the true story of a British teacher who left home—"

"Taylor?" A buzz at Eisley's side interrupted him, followed by the faint Kenny Loggins tune *Your Mama Don't Dance and Your Daddy Don't Rock and Roll*. She flinched forward. "My phone." She fumbled through her purse and pulled out a lime green mobile. The tune grew louder. "It's my mom's ringtone."

He felt his eyebrows lift.

"We're Baptist." Her crooked smile nearly provided enough distraction to send him veering toward oncoming traffic.

"Hi, Mom. Yes, I'm here, a little tired, but thrilled." Pause. "I'm in the car on the way to the hotel." Silence. "The flight was absolutely gorgeous."

Gorgeous?

"I've never seen the moon so big and close. And there was a storm underneath the clouds. It was amazing." Pause. "Yeah, I know. Isn't God awesome?"

Wes tried to keep his eyes on the road, but the more she talked, the more doubt crept around his excuses. Could she truly be this genuine? Experience told him *no*, but experience had never brought a woman like Eisley Barrett his way. His chest constricted and those knotted feelings in his heart tempted to unbraid. *Clamp them tight, mate.* She must have a well-hidden agenda at worst, and a need to steer clear of men with pasts like his, at best. Both options kept him at arm's length.

"Oh, Mom, you need to keep this information super-private. I mean you can't even tell Granny." Eisley shot Wes a wrinkle-nosed grin. "You'll never believe who came with Mr. Harrison to pick me up from the airport." Pause. "His son, BBC actor Christopher Wesley Harrison."

Wes exchanged a look with his dad, who was chuckling.

"No, Colin Firth played Mr. Darcy."

Another pause.

"That one was Matthew MacFayden." Pause. "No, Mom, Wes didn't play in any Austen remakes. That was Jeremy Northam."

So much for feeling famous.

She looked over at him and smiled her apology, and his responded, naturally. No acting involved. He tried to tame it, but failed miserably. It was official. He was barking mad.

Perhaps his safest option would be to steer clear of Eisley Barrett altogether. He looked back at his dad and old fears stifled the fresh interest.

"Wes played in the newest version of *Wuthering Heights* that came out last year and he just finished staring in the amazing movie *A Ransomed Gentleman*." Eisley suddenly gasped. "Oh, my goodness, it's Big Ben. Mom, can you believe it? I'm staring at Big Ben in London, England." Excitement tinged every syllable.

No clock held that sort of interest, surely. Not even Big Ben.

"That means we're crossing Westminster Bridge." She let out a little squeal and took a deep breath. "I know, I'm acting like a preteen girl...Of course I'll take pictures. Loads. How are the kids?" Tenderness quieted her voice and its authenticity wiggled further into his protesting heart. "Tell them I love them, okay? And give Emily a big kiss for me." She clipped her mobile closed and sighed back into the seat. "They're so far away."

"You have three children?"

"Yeah." A touch of sadness quieted her reply. "Nathan— he's eight and a mastermind. Pete is a six-year-old daredevil. And Emily is a little over two and kind of looks like a cuter version of Gollum—ya know, hairless and big blue eyes."

What a mental image! Coupled with her animated expression, it was difficult to keep any emotional distance whatsoever. What had his father done? He met his dad's gaze and knew...*he* knew. This did not bode well for his single-minded future at all.

He brought the car to a stop by the hotel, determined to halt his father's nonsense before it strayed any further into the ridiculous. "Dad, might you help me with the luggage?"

Once Wes was safely hidden behind the boot, he turned to his father. "Is Mum aware of this matchmaking scheme of yours?"

Dad fumbled with one of Eisley's bags. "I have no idea to what you are referring."

Wes placed his hand on top of the bag in his father's grasp. "Dad, there are too many coincidences. She even has family from Summit, North Carolina?" He narrowed his eyes at his father's profile. "As I've told you before, I have more important pursuits at present than building a romantic relationship."

"I'm not responsible if you feel an attraction to our guest."

"Attraction?" Wes lowered his voice to a harsh whisper, and peeked around the boot of the car to see Eisley shaking the valet's hand. "I never said I was attracted."

"*If* you were attracted to her, then I would say it showed good sense on your part, and the coincidence? Nothing more than luck, I should think."

"Luck doesn't hand-deliver with such accuracy, as a rule, and I don't need your matchmaking games, Dad." He crammed a hand through his hair. "I'm trying to focus my career in the right direction. On the *right* path."

Dad jerked the bag from the boot and leveled his son with a stare. "Who says she isn't standing directly in the middle of this right path of yours?" He shrugged Wes's concern away. "Think what you will. I suspect you'll have little time to set your mind to it, as your schedule usually keeps you busy, doesn't it? She's really none of your concern."

"When she's a stranger in my parents' home, she's of great concern to me."

"Rubbish." His father growled. "If you'd remove your suspicion for half a moment, you'd see she's charming. A perfect match, if one *was* thinking of such matters."

"What does Mum say about your ploy?" His father tinkered with the handle of Eisley's bag. Hesitant. "Mum *does* know Eisley is coming, doesn't she?"

"Of course, perfectly aware." His father raised a brow and averted his gaze. "You are in a mood for accusations, son. Bad habit, that."

Wes peeked around the boot of the car. Eisley was engaged in an animated conversation with the valet, and the valet seemed to enjoy the attention a bit too much. Wes lowered his voice. "As I recall, Eisley isn't interested in pursuing a relationship either, so your attempts are futile."

"Codswallop." Dad slid Eisley's duffle from the back. "If you're worth your salt, you won't let a little thing like that stop you. Not if you thought she was worthy of the second chance?"

His father's voice reverberated through him as if from the mouth of God. It wasn't her worthiness he was questioning. Or was it? He'd done nothing but interrogate her motives since the first glance. And why not? He didn't know her, but the way her humor burrowed its way through his defenses proved warning enough. *He was in trouble.*

Eisley popped her head around the back of the car. "Is there anything I can do to help?"

Wes moved aside so the valet could take the bags, and Dad turned to Eisley. "All you need to do is settle in. We meet Eleanor at ten for tea, after which we are off for an afternoon tour of Westminster. Then there is the Christmas gala, of course."

Wes pulled his gaze from Eisley to zero in on his father. She was going to the Christmas gala?

She grinned up at him. "Will you be there too?"

"Wes rarely attends these parties, though he is between films at the moment." His father lifted a brow to him.

Eisley touched Wes's arm, the gentleness in her expression tugging at the twist of his emotions. "After your time out of the limelight, it seems you're taking a slow and steady reentry. Besides, you've never struck me as the flashy sort." She laughed. "Not that I know you or anything. Not the real you. Only the fictional you."

"Ms. Barrett, in this case, the fictional Christopher Wesley Harrison is much more appealing than the reformed and somewhat introverted Wes Harrison." He stared down into her face, uncertain and interested. For the past two years, he'd been more of a hermit than a "famous" actor. Two years of depression turned to healing, with a fair amount of bitterness to slow the process.

Her green eyes glimmered with curiosity. "I'm from Appalachia. Fact is *always* stranger than fiction." Her grin twisted crooked. "And usually a whole lot more interesting too."

"The Gala is quite posh. Perfect for the season of fresh beginnings, I should think." The glint of mischief twitched the edge of his father's moustache. "Music, food, dancing."

"Dancing?" Eisley's face paled and she waved her hands as if to wipe away the word still floating in the air. "Oh no, I thought it was one of those parties where you stand around, eat, drink, and maybe criticize other people's clothing. You didn't say anything about dancing."

"Not to worry. We'll have a lesson or two this afternoon."

She gave her head a fierce shake. "Mr. H, don't you remember my questionable footwork in the airport? The kind that nearly broke your ribs?"

"Eisley, the fall was not as bad as that." His dad pulled Eisley's arm through his. "We shall go inside, get freshened up, and then enjoy our afternoon."

She looked over Dad's shoulder, her eyes pleading for rescue. "Could you please jump out of that fictional world of yours for a minute and come up with a great excuse to get me out of this?"

Wes closed the boot. "Weren't you the one who touted how fact was much more interesting than fiction?" *He'd teased her? He barely knew the woman and he'd teased her?*

She sighed. "Fact in this case is certain to be more humiliating, I'm afraid." Her shoulders rose in a shrug and the smile returned. "Well, what's the saying? Hope springs eternal."

No, Eisley Barrett wasn't like anyone he'd ever met, or even imagined meeting. The curiosity about her first English Christmas gala was too much for him to miss. If she was hiding something, he wanted to discover it before his parents felt the sting. If she was as genuine as she appeared, then maybe a closer acquaintance might be the perfect medicine for his skeptical heart.

Wes snuck through the doorway of his office merely long enough to retrieve the screenplay on his desk. When he'd returned from his sabbatical, he'd chosen a smaller office in a quieter part of the West End, a safer distance from the life he once knew. Eisley Barrett's apparent authenticity somehow forced his past into his thoughts with new clarity. He'd been selfish and blind. Lost.

He closed his eyes, the rush of memories drowning out the hum from the office machines in the next room. The women, the parties. Vivian and Jane. Betraying others...and being betrayed. He had so much for which to atone.

The past year he'd begun the process of reinventing his professional life with his two newest movies, small films of substance. *A Ransomed Gentleman* defined the changing point, almost prophetic in title. Though, he wouldn't have considered himself a 'gentle' man. The last year bathed in his family's love made him stronger and more determined to choose God's way instead of his own.

He stepped across the dim room, blinds drawn to pinch out distraction leaving the office space gray and sleepy. With his back to the hall, he searched the papers on his desk and checked his watch. He had an hour to get back to the hotel to catch his parents before they left with Eisley to explore Westminster. He wouldn't leave them alone with her for too long until he felt certain they were out of harm's way.

He scanned the working title of his script: *A Sea of Mountains.* If Eisley Barrett was typical of the people in the Blue Ridge Mountains, this story would provide the part he'd been hoping to play for years. A story with true meaning – a story to mirror the change in his life and provide his own agenda of inspiration to a world he'd previously given sex and paltry romance. He wasn't the same man anymore and he'd prove it to everyone.

Something warm and soft glided around his waist and smoothed against his chest, awakening his nerve endings and shocking his spine pencil-straight. Long slender fingers skimmed across the buttons of his shirt. Red nails. The scent of lilacs. *Vivian Barry.*

Wes turned around. Her arms tightened against his back, trapping him against her. She inched forward, face angled for a kiss.

"Vivian?"

"It's been a long time since our last visit, Mr. Harrison." Vivian's husky voice purred through full lips that drew temptingly close. "Haven't you missed me a little?"

Wes jerked back so quickly, Vivian lost her balance and would have toppled to the floor if he hadn't caught her. *Missed her?* Not in his heart, but his pulse reacted with a very different answer. Even after two years of celibacy. Would his sin forever haunt him?

"What are you doing here?" The office door was closed.

"I sent Grace out for a long coffee break so we could"—she lifted a carved ebony brow, coupled with a twist of her scarlet lips as her arms linked around his neck— "talk."

"Talk?" Wes repeated, hating the way his body responded to hers. Everything about her screamed to be touched, from the dark curls framing her face like a pixie to the supple dip at the base of her neck. Her body moved in an intoxicating dance against his senses. Warmth swelled in his stomach. He knew her body well. Too well. And the familiar ache began.

"I think a continuation of our last conversation will be sufficient," she crooned, pulling him closer until her lips covered his, warm and urgent. Taking control.

Her body melted against his and the carnal part of him wanted to take what she offered. All of it. Indulge in the hunger that used to consume him, the pleasure. The familiar sensations battered his infant faith. The empty pleasure. He'd brought this on himself. A few romantic dinners, a couple of unexpected kisses at her initiation, and a regrettable past bound him like a malefactor for execution.

God, be my strength.

"Vivian, no." He kept his voice soft and took her hands from around his neck. "No," he added with more conviction.

"No? I don't think you mean that, darling. Not really." Her bare leg rubbed against his knee, sparking heat upward. "We're perfectly safe."

"Safe?" He was nearly suffocating under the temptation. *So easy...so willing.* "No, I don't think so."

She grinned like a cat closing in on its prey, her arms sliding around his waist and drawing him against her. "Well, not *too* safe."

He gripped her shoulders and put her at arm's length, forcing words from his dry throat. "Step away, Vivian." He walked to the door and jerked it open. The cool air from the lobby blew against his hot face. He drew it into his lungs to remove the scent of her perfume clouding his mind.

"I thought you'd be happy to see me." Vivian's cerulean eyes rounded into innocent sapphires, beating against his fragile wall of self-control. "Three months abroad is such a long time."

Not long enough. The realization arrested his thoughts. Exactly. There had been a sense of freedom at her absence. He wearied from being on full alert every time she neared, anticipating a war of worlds between the past and present. He'd distanced himself from her after his grievous decision two years ago, but her father's work as Wes's agent kept Vivian in his life, and guilt bound him all the more.

"Vivian, it is always a pleasure to see you." He raked his hand through his damp hair and moved behind his plush office chair a physical barrier. "I do appreciate all the work you and your father have done for my career, but—"

"But?"

Regret softened his voice. "Our relationship ends with friendship."

Her eyes slid into slits and the manufactured pout dissolved into a snarl. "You don't know what you want. Three months ago you gave me a parting kiss which spoke of more than friendship." A kiss *she'd* given *him* in front of a crowd of onlookers. Almost as if she'd staged it. A new and unnerving idea pushed forward. Could Vivian be trusted?

"Two years ago, you wanted *much* more." Her grin slid wide. "And the news on the street is I didn't travel to Venice alone."

Gossip columns and tabloids spreading their usual lies. He rubbed the back of his neck, his jaw firmed against the anger of her hint. Being back in the limelight, as Eisley Barrett called it, came with its price, exaggerations and lack of privacy at the top of the list. "Vivian, that kiss was a–" He almost said *mistake*, but thought better of it. "Regardless of what the papers say, I can only offer my friendship."

"It's been two years. Two." She rounded the chair and pressed her finger into his chest. The manicured nail edge dug into his skin. "We used to share the same passions, the same dreams. Ever since Jane's death, you've been teetering on the brink of throwing your career away. First, you blamed yourself and disappeared for an entire year, spending your days like a hermit back home in your little hamlet, and then you found religion. From bad to worse." She rolled her blue eyes, a grimace contorting her features. "And now you're refusing certain career opportunities on the basis of scruples?" Her brow bent. "Oh yes, I heard about your refusal of the lead in Canmen's suspense thriller. I can't believe you declined a certain box-office success. What is wrong with you?"

"I won't compromise my standards, Vivian. I shouldn't have with Jane, but I did, and look what happened."

"Jane made her own decisions, and they were unfortunate. You must make yours. You have this one life to live, these few opportunities for greatness. Take them instead of squandering your time on this worthless—" She picked up the script on his desk and glanced at it in disgust.

Wes steadied his expression, but his jaw tightened. Past or not, guilt or not, with God's help, he would start over. *All things are made new.* He clung to that truth like the last breath of a dying man. "I think our definitions of greatness may differ."

She shook the screenplay at him. "Something like this will lead you nowhere quickly. A third-rate, small film disaster? Father and I are concerned for your future." Her eyes and voice softened, and he stepped back, away from her searching hand. She didn't take the hint. "You're brilliant, talented, and gorgeous. Think of where you were before. On the edge of stardom. I want to see your career blossom. And see you happy, my dear."

Wes took the screenplay from her and held it as a barrier between their bodies. "And what if this does make me happy? What if an inspiring true story makes me happier than I've been in years?"

"As I said before, you don't really know what you want." Her eyes glimmered and she pressed her words into a seductive whisper. "Trust me. I do."

His foot hit the wall behind him. "I'm not the same, Vivian."

"Words, words, words." Her smile curled again and her palm slid up his chest. "Actions speak louder. Deep in your virtuous heart, you want me. I've felt it in your kiss. Besides, I'm perfect for you. I know all your little secrets, with no strings attached."

"Vivian, we ended things a long time—"

She placed a finger over his lips. "When you realize you want me back, on those lonely nights in your flat after a long day working with beautiful women, let me know. I'll never stop reminding you of what we once had." She pushed away from his chest and took languid steps toward the hall, making every movement of those elegant legs count.

He squeezed his eyes closed.

"I'm very patient." Stopping at the door, she turned and ran her fingers down her neck, her eyes darkening along with her smile. "But I've waited a long time...and I want you."

Her words simmered with warning.

"You *will* want me again, Wesley. One kiss is never enough, even for you." She blew him a slow kiss from the doorway, the shape of her lips and the look in her eyes branded in his mind. Desire and determination. "Cheers."

She prowled down the hallway. Wes tried not to watch her disappear out the door, but his disobedient eyes admired every step she took. A breeze from her exit cooled the beads of sweat on his face and neck, igniting a shiver.

He closed the door and slammed his fist against it. He was such a fool. Wasn't it enough that his past haunted his dreams, did it have to haunt his waking moments too?

I can't be trusted.

But Father, you can. He massaged his hands into his aching forehead. *Please, free me from this hold of my past and give me the strength to choose the right path.*

And if actions spoke louder, as Vivian said, his next conversation with Carl Barry would secure his fresh start. God would see to his future. It was time to put the past far behind him.

Chapter Three

"*That* young woman is Ansley Barnett?"

Eleanor Harrison nailed her husband with a look, daring him to answer in the affirmative.

"Eisley Barrett, and yes, she's —"

"Not even forty years old." Eleanor attempted to keep her voice calm. After all, no amount of shock should disrupt her demeanor, but this was far beyond acceptable. "I assumed she'd be closer to Lizzie's and my ages, not some *young* woman."

"You never specified an age requirement, Luv."

"She's closer to Cate's and Wes' age." Her gaze zeroed in on her husband, who kept his attention firmly planted on his teacup. *Coward.* "I see the way of it, Daniel Harrison. Haven't you toyed with such fancies long enough? Wes doesn't need your meddling hands rummaging around in his romantic affairs. He is old enough to manage them himself."

"Eleanor, the opportunity arose in such a providential manner—"

"Don't blame this catastrophe on God." She released a puff of air from her nose to contain her frustration. What a preposterous notion. An Appalachian? A single mum? The man was utterly off his trolley. "You and Lizzie Worthing have schemed behind my back, haven't you? I assumed a friend of Lizzie's to be one of our contemporaries, and here comes a woman half our ages. A *single* woman, at that. How could you have lied to me?"

"Ellie." He reached to touch her hand resting on the table but she pulled away, refusing to soften at the endearment. "I never lied to you, Luv. I merely failed to contradict your false assumptions."

"Quite. And I suppose the other tidbits of information were true? She's a mother of three? From some place in Appalachia, wherever that is."

"When you meet her, you'll understand. She's perfect for him."

"Daniel." She rapped the table with her napkin. "You and this matchmaking have to stop. I see how Lizzie might amuse herself in such frivolous fashion, but you? How many does this make? Let me think."

"Ellie, this is the one. I know it."

The earnestness in his eyes nearly convinced her. As usual, his intentions were in the right place. "Of course, you do." She tossed her hand at him and turned to sneak another peek at Ansley...Eisley. Whatever the girl's name was. "So, the dancer from London didn't work, nor the teacher down in Portsmouth." Eleanor grimaced her opinion. "And to top it off, he has to contend with the lecherous Vivian Barry, who lurks about Wes like a"—a slight cringe tightened her shoulders, but she managed to keep her teacup steady— "vampire."

"But Eleanor..."

"Now you've resorted to some foreign divorcée with three children whom Lizzie met through the Internet?" She rolled her eyes and felt a sudden ache develop over her right eyebrow. "Really Daniel, what are you thinking? As I've told you many times before, our son is quite capable of finding a wife on his own without your interference. He's thirty-three years old."

"But she's perfect for him, Ellie. Genuine. Kind. The two of you will get on splendidly. I'm certain of it."

"As certain as you were of the previous two young women?"

"She's nothing like the other women. In fact, she's everything for which we've been praying the past six months. Besides, Lizzie just knew from the start—"

Eleanor shushed him. The ginger-headed woman was moving toward them, scanning the room. She'd give Lizzie Worthing a large piece of her mind, as soon as she sussed out this catastrophe. The last thing Wesley needed was a single mother hunting a husband for herself and father for her children.

Eleanor steadied her shoulders for battle and stood just as Eisley's gaze found them among the tables of the hotel's restaurant. Her lips bloomed into a lovely smile, and Eleanor's skepticism faded slightly. *There's a mercy, anyhow; her teeth are white and a complete set.*

A wave of exhaustion wearied her to her bones. Two weeks with an Appalachian?

"Hello again. Long time no see, Mr. H." Eisley's voice rang with welcome as she took Daniel's hand. Eleanor felt her brows skyrocket. *Such familiarity.* Highly inappropriate.

"An entire hour, I believe." Daniel chuckled and sent a glance over Eisley's shoulder to Eleanor. Good heavens, the man was half in love with her already. "This is my wife, Eleanor."

Eisley released Daniel and before Eleanor could prepare, she was clasped in the grip of a complete stranger, arms trapped at her sides. Her entire body stiffened. *This is a fine kettle of fish Lizzie's cooked up.*

"You are so kind to have me. Thank you, Mrs. Harrison." Eisley stepped back, her green eyes filled with as much animation as her words. "I really can't express how grateful I am to you."

"Well, Eisley, I am certain there are many things Daniel hasn't told me about you, but I..." Eleanor drew in a deep breath for strength. "I look forward to furthering our acquaintance."

As they took their seats, she speared Daniel with a glare, but if the look she sent left a mark, he didn't seem to notice. He was completely satisfied in his madness.

Eisley leaned over and whispered, "You have the sweetest husband on the planet."

To her own astonishment, a smile invaded her face. She managed to control it. *Sweet* wasn't the term she'd use to describe her husband at present. Other days, most assuredly, but not today. *Mischievous? Misguided?* "Yes, he is dear."

"We have a few surprises in store for you, Eisley." Daniel winked at Eleanor and a flush erupted in her cheeks. Already the little Appalachian was influencing him. He hadn't winked at her in years, and she wasn't certain how she felt about it. "Eleanor's planned a full schedule for this afternoon since we leave for Derbyshire tomorrow."

More time with the young Appalachian? The pinch of pain in her forehead deepened. *What do to? What to do?* She forced a smile. "While we are on the West End, we thought you'd enjoy a visit to Westminster Abbey, and, perhaps. St. Paul's."

"That sounds wonderful!"

Eleanor stumbled over her assumptions at the look of sheer gratitude on Eisley's face. Genuine. Her eyes held such fascination, it was almost contagious. A voice deep in her heart posed a question. What if Daniel was right? Eleanor closed her eyes and sighed, releasing control for yet another thing in her life. *What's done is done, I suppose.*

"Daniel speaks as if he's known you for years. You've made quite an impression on him."

Eisley grimaced. "Oh dear, with my reckless driving in heels, I might have more likely made a dent."

Eleanor's lips quivered with the effort to keep her decorum. She wanted to dislike, or at the very least disprove of, Eisley Barrett, but she found herself warming to her a bit. Not enough to wish her into the family, of course, but the girl seemed harmless and much too transparent for her own good.

"And tonight is the gala." Daniel added into the silence.

Eisley's body slumped forward until her head rested in her hands. "I don't think attending the gala is the best idea for me." Her smile didn't reach her eyes and Eleanor felt somewhat disappointed. "I packed one of my poshest dresses. Isn't that what you called it, Mr. Harrison? Posh?"

Daniel coughed through his laugh.

Eleanor's rebel lips twisted into a grin. "Yes, though I'm not certain if 'poshest' is the word he would have used."

Eisley leaned closer, her voice dropping to a whisper. "You know what? When he told me to be sure and pack some Wellies and a Macintosh, I was completely confused. First of all, I had no idea what Wellies were and had to look them up on the computer. Praise God for Google."

Eleanor didn't dare make eye contact with Daniel for fear of losing what little control she held over the laughter locked in her throat. Daniel had been right about one thing: Eisley was absolutely nothing like any of Wesley's former interests. She held a category all her own. For the good or the bad, Eleanor wasn't certain yet, but more improved than Vivian Barry, at any rate.

"And the Macintosh? I wondered why you preferred Apples to PCs and then I had to look those up, too. Who would have thought rain boots and rain jackets have names of their own in England?"

Daniel's coughing crecendoed into full laughter.

Eisley wagged her finger at him. "You think it's funny now, but what if I royally screw up? Are you sure you want to take *me* to a party? If I had to look up three of the first words you wrote to me, what will it be like for an entire evening?" She raised her palms in surrender. "I think I should stay at the hotel."

"You'll be fine, dear. You don't have to dance, and you have your natural charm." Of course, Eisley's variety of charm was a bit out of the ordinary.

"Right. I don't *have* to dance. I can just observe from the safe distance of a doorway or closet or something."

Releasing Eisley Barrett into the high society of the Darlington House might be more than any of them could manage. As Eisley launched into conversation with Daniel about the differences between British and American words, her smile returned. This meeting was not an accident, and Eleanor almost shuddered at the thought of what God's plans might be. Eisley and Wes? No, of course not. But if they all survived the gala, it might be the beginning of a lovely friendship. And the best part of it all? Vivian Barry would be positively furious.

∞ ∞ ∞

"It looks like a Ferris wheel from outer space." Eisley tried to focus on the London Eye but was already feeling dizzy from her glimpse at the transparent egg-shaped tubes rotating in painfully slow motion. She and heights shared a hate-hate relationship. Her exploits in heels set a clear precedent.

"It has a spectacular view." Daniel took her elbow and escorted her toward what she feared was the capsule of death, with Wes close behind.

"And we're fortunate to have a clear day," Wes added.

Something caught in her throat. *Fear, pure and simple.* Well, at least she'd die with a spectacular view on a clear day, right? She sent a glance to Heaven, but she had to look past the horrific wheel of terror to do it.

Hadn't the airport scene been enough to kick her pride into submission? "Maybe I should sit this one out." She hugged her shaky stomach and shot Wes a warning look. "You know, I just finished that chocolate trifle at lunch."

"Afraid you'll lose it?" A glint lit his eyes.

Gee whiz, the guy was teasing her? Unbelievable. He'd shown up just before she left the hotel with his parents and stayed with them from Covent Garden to Westminster Abbey and now here, at the wheel of doom. At first, he oozed as much suspicion as he had in the airport, cloaking his expression with stiff politeness but within the last few hours, the edge had left him and cut a clear line into her comfort level.

She caught little glimpses of Tollhouse cookie sweetness beneath all those movie posters and acting lessons, and chocolate marked a certain weakness for her. She inwardly groaned and shook off any concern. Mr. Movie Star didn't pose a threat, so she shrugged the tension from her shoulders and played along. "Who would ever want to lose perfectly good chocolate? Sounds like a crime."

Wes nudged her forward. *Turncoat.* "Chocolate is a weakness of yours, is it?"

Had he jumped inside her head? Oh dear, she hoped not. "I'm a sucker for sweets, but nothing tempts me like chocolate." She took a deep breath and let Wes help her over the threshold of the glass pod. Eisley stumbled with stiff legs to a seat in the middle of the capsule. "About how high do we go?"

"Over four hundred feet. Isn't that right, Dad?" Wes slid beside her and draped his arm over the back of her seat.

She offered him a wobbly smile. Maybe. She couldn't be sure because her mouth was so dry, her teeth were getting stuck to the backs of her lips. An embarrassing moment loomed ahead of her. She practically felt it biting at her spine – or maybe that was the tingle from Wes's nearness. Either way, it spelled trouble.

She drew in a shaky breath and caught the slightest scent of his woodsy cologne again. Well, if he was going to be a passing acquaintance, she'd always preferred good-smelling ones.

"Four hundred feet?" Eisley's voice squeaked and she cleared her throat. "Over water. In a glass bowl?"

"Eisley, darling, you're not afraid of heights, are you?" Eleanor took her seat and comforted her with a gentle look.

"Well, maybe just a little bit." Eisley drew her gaze from the closed doors, her lifeline, and forced a smile. "But I'm sure this is completely safe, right? I mean, no major accidents or *deaths* reported recently?"

"Relax." Wes's gaze softened a little more, perfectly polite from dark mane to cleft chin. *No harm in handsome acquaintances, either. Easier on the vision, of course.* "The view will distract you and if you want, Mum could talk to you the entire half hour without stopping."

"Christopher Wesley," Eleanor started, her eyebrows creased, then her expression returned to neutral. "Eisley, after this flight we'll return to the hotel and have a few hours to freshen up for the gala."

The gala? Oh boy, her stomach started hurting for a whole new set of reasons.

"Perhaps you could save me a dance?" Wes's voice tightened like his father had to prod the request out of him.

Painful.

Of course, when she finished dancing with anyone tonight, that description would most likely fit her partner's reactions. The ground disappeared out the windows. "You mean if I survive this ride?"

"Lizzie mentioned that Lornegrave is key to your research," Eleanor said. "What is the connection?"

A thrill spiraled through Eisley's middle and pushed most of her fear right out the glass doors. *Oh, if only Uncle Joe could be here.* "Lizzie lives in the Ramdsen family estate, our ancestor's home. I have a letter passed down from our family which tells of Julia's work with the Tyndale Bible and her engagement to an Edward Lattimer, but the rest are just rumors and legends. Lizzie seems to think there is something to discover in the attic of Lornegrave, so she's started her sleuthing up there in anticipation of my arrival." She grinned and Wes responded with his own smile, the kind that lit his eyes. *Really nice acquaintance.* Eisley glanced over his shoulder and saw nothing but blue skies. Heat drained from her arms down to her fingertips. "Oh dear...."

He dipped his head close. "You ought to take a look while you're here, or you'll regret it." He stood and offered his hand. "Ready?"

A hand? Was he nuts? She grabbed his whole arm, holding tightly enough to feel the muscles flex beneath his jacket. Dizziness spun a kickstart in her head, but the confidence on his face nudged her a step forward. A shaky step. Well, if someone like him believed in her, then maybe she'd survive.

The view spread all the way to the fading horizon. Lights glittered below, reflecting millions of golden stars, while rows of buildings formed an uneven patchwork of dark and light patterns below. The Thames's fluid 'S' sliced through the middle, speckled with a myriad of boats and bridges.

"It's beautiful." She glanced over at Wes, trying to steady her gaze. A well-chiseled chin provided a good focal point. "Pete would call this a God's-eye view."

"Pete sounds like a smart lad."

"Yeah, they're all pretty smart. Emily's type of smarts is a little tricky, though. She's an exhibitionist."

"What?" His offered a slight grin, the kind he displayed in his best movie, *A Ransomed Gentleman*, when he was guarding his laugh.

She'd replayed the final kiss scene in his movie about fifty times when it came out three months previously. If taking a year break from acting brought out that kind of skill, other actors could benefit from a reprieve. She pulled her attention back to the window in a dreamy daze and murmured, "She likes to run around naked." She closed her eyes to gain her balance and take control of the heat soaring into her face. "It probably doesn't help that she's adorable, from bald head to bald bottom."

Wes chuckled beside her. "Is everyone from Appalachia like you?"

Eisley's gaze zoomed back to his. "Oh gee, I hope not." She gave her head a little shake to dislodge the dizziness. "Other people have to make better personal choices than *me*, Appalachian or not. And I'm certain both of my sisters are less homicidal in heels."

His full laugh, so free and unreserved, shocked her and settled into a double dimple on his face. A strange flutter like hummingbird wings twitted to life in her stomach. What a great sound! She had a feeling it didn't happen as often as it should. A teeny bit of pride wiggled up her spine. There was something incredibly satisfying about bringing a smile to Christopher Wesley Harrison's face. A huge success in her book – and that was saying something.

He was just being nice, though. One day some woman would find a fairy tale in him, for sure.

She turned to the window to break her stare and gasped as the sunlight hit the golden tip of one of the most recognizable buildings. A white dome rose from the shadows and caught the last few rays of sunlight. "Isn't that St. Paul's Cathedral?"

"Pardon me."

Eisley turned to see a woman staring at Wes as though she might fall prostrate any minute. Brown hair curled into a pleasant fluff around her face. Her rounded eyes glowed in wonder and Eisley held her laugh in check. That's probably the same expression she had on her face about five seconds ago when she was pondering his Superman appeal.

"I absolutely adored you in *Wuthering Heights*, and your most recent role in *A Ransomed Gentleman* was quite splendid, really. Your best movie yet."

Wes bowed his head in humble acceptance of her compliments. "Thank you. It's nice to hear after my sabbatical, so to speak."

She offered a timid smile. "Might I trouble you for"—the woman's voice dropped so Eisley barely heard— "an autograph. My daughters are over by the glass there." She tilted her head to the left where two teenagers tried to ignore their mother. "And they're a bit narked over their mum's behavior at the moment."

Wes lowered his voice to match hers. "I'd be happy to oblige, Mrs...?"

"Markson, Charlotte Markson." She pushed a magazine and pen in his hands. "I saw your photo in *The Post* this morning and never imagined I'd have a chance to meet you." She glanced down at the newspaper, now in his hands. "I was so delighted to see you and Ms. Barry back on. You make a splendid pair."

Ms. Barry? Eisley looked more closely at the magazine. The center of the page displayed a glossy photo of Wes embracing a dark-headed beauty. The heading read: **A Rematch of Romance?** *After two years of uncertainty, are Christopher & Vivian taking the next step? Did their recent excursion to Venice reignite their relationship?*

Reality hit. Her entire body relaxed from the effort to ignore the tingles of attraction surging through her like a seizure. No need to worry. She could just enjoy his company for now and save her twitterpated heartbeat for the safe distance of a movie screen.

His composure and suspicion proved he wanted distance. After all, he was an actor. She had plenty of experience with actors. Her ex-husband played the role like an Emmy Award winner.

"Thank you." A look of sadness curled his lips into a frown as Mrs. Markson walked back to her daughters.

Something was definitely wrong. She placed her hand on his arm. "Are you okay?"

He pulled in a deep breath and met her gaze. "Part of the job."

Was he saying that more for himself or for her? "Well, you handled it like a gentleman, like you've been about everything today."

A twinkled resurfaced in his gray-blue eyes. "Right. When I criticized your footwear, and accused you of trying to harm my father?"

She hitched up one shoulder and turned back to the observation window. "We'll take that as a commercial break in your otherwise pristine gentlemanly behavior. Besides, I'm a redhead. We send off all the wrong first impression vibes."

A lovely dimple peeked from his cheek and pierced a vulnerable place in her heart. Her breath hitched. *Ignore the glitch. Ignore the glitch.* She turned away and looked straight down hundreds of feet into the black waters of the Thames as two boats passed underneath, and her stomach waved like the trail of bubbles behind them. Her vision kept moving even when the boats passed from view. She touched her head in a vain attempt to slow the spinning and pressed a hand to her stomach to keep the trifle securely in place.

"I think I need to sit down." She turned toward her seat and saw Eleanor moving. For a proper older British lady, she could move fast. No wait. Eisley was the one moving, falling.

Arms tightened around her. Her voice thickened, like her thoughts. "I'm sorry, I don't think a God's eye view of London is the thing for me." She tried to straighten but only fell back against something solid and warm. It felt nice after all the spinning. She collapsed into her seat and kept her eyes closed, partly from necessity and partly from humiliation. The familiar warning tingle of a migraine buzzed across her forehead. *Oh, no.*

"Dear child, are you all right?" Eleanor's voice came from her left.

She slowly opened her eyes and peeked to her right. That nice soft landing involved the strong arms of a movie hero. Perfect. *Swept off her feet* took on a whole new meaning, in an embarrassing shade of country charm. From one calamity to another.

But he did smell really nice. Earthy and spice, and everything nice. *Oh, good grief, Eisley, pull yourself together.*

"Eisley?"

Her foggy brain focused back on Eleanor. "I think the heights induced a migraine. Usually, my headaches follow barometric pressure changes, but after a full seven-hour flight in an airplane today, plus this little taste of London space travel, I might need a nap after all."

"Eisley dear, why didn't you tell us?"

"It only started now." Eisley tried to reassure Eleanor with a smile, but since her lips were going numb she couldn't be sure. "They're worse in winter, for some reason, and they usually mean snow is coming soon."

Mr. Harrison's eyebrows shot high. "Snow, is it? You're an adventurist, amateur sleuth, world traveler, *and* meteorologist, are you?"

Eisley tried not to laugh. Movement encouraged the newborn pounding in her skull. "And astronaut, if we include this little tour." She waved a palm around the capsule. "I'm really sorry about all this."

"It's quite all right, Eisley," Eleanor said, her cool fingers wrapping around Eisley's hand. "Daniel took me to a festival once and forced me to ride some monstrous, spinning machine."

"I never forced you," he interrupted, and Eisley could imagine his fluffy brows shocking north.

"Hmmm, as I recall, you lowered those attractive eyes of yours, offered your most tempting grin, and asked if I'd like to join you. Yes, quite forced." Eisley peeked through her lashes at Eleanor, whose manicured brow shifted in challenge. "Of course, I was ill-prepared for such a ride and ended up getting sick all over his shoes."

Eisley sniggered, the world coming back into focus, but the unpleasant sparkle of aura made everything look kind of fairy tale-ish. She tried to ignore it. "And you married her, anyway. It *had* to be love."

An endearing look passed between the older couple and Eisley's heart replied with a sharp pang much sharper than the one crossing her line of vision—the same wistful longing she felt each time she caught her parents in an affectionate moment. Such a deep part of her craved a love like that, but at what cost? No reward was worth the risk. And she'd proven she had no business trying to pick a happily-ever-after. She'd failed so miserably the first time.

She drew out of Wes's arms and blinked him into view. "Isn't that sweet?"

His eyes twinkled, or maybe it was the aura. Who could be sure? "Getting sick on Dad's shoes?"

"No silly." She gestured toward his parents. "The way they look at each other. That forever kind of look."

"You mean the kind that doesn't exist anymore?"

"Your parents and mine are a dying breed. Everybody's into fast food consumerism. Give it to me now and it better make me happy or I'll get a cuter, younger upgrade."

The sudden awareness in his expression sent her thoughts into replay mode. Daggone it. She'd slipped up and mentioned too much *again.*

"Hmm." As he examined her face, something beyond the well-honed politeness inched into his expression. An understanding. "I don't sense a hint of bitterness hidden behind those freckles, do I?"

Eisley forced a grin, thankful he didn't probe any further. "A hint? Gee, I thought it was an entire color spectrum."

He let her sentence disappear into silence. Thankfully, Mr. Handsome Harrison lived in a realm all his own and much too far for her glass slippers to travel. Whether in fairy tales or baseball, she had learned the hard way: *three strikes and you're out.* Marshall used up two. Eisley wasn't interested in a strike number three.

Chapter Four

*E*isley wasn't in Pleasant Gap anymore. If the accents and expensive food didn't convince her, then the white Christmas lights sprinkled about a magical fourteenth century manor house clued her in. She stopped in the doorway and closed her eyes to steady her nerves. *Lord, don't let me embarrass Mr. and Mrs. Harrison, or fall flat on my face, or have another stupid migraine...*

She sighed and stepped across the threshold.

Voices murmured in a quiet hum with the music from a string quartet, crystal and silver tinkled like Christmas bells, and the soft breeze from the dance floor whispered against her warm cheeks, carrying the scents of cinnamon and berries. *Magical.* A smooth parade of couples glided across the dance floor, moving to the music like a misty dream. A rivulet of envy spliced her middle. She'd practically lamed poor Mr. H during his brief dance instructions before the gala, proving one thing: Two lessons doth not a dancer make.

The couple in the middle of the room caught her attention. Wes danced with a goddess to match his Adonis persona. Long, smooth legs. Thin freckle-free arms. A Scarlet O'Hara look-alike wearing a red...*towel*? From the flow of it, it couldn't really be a towel. Maybe an oversized red scarf.

Vivian Barry in the flesh – enough visible, wrinkle-free flesh to model for Victoria's Secret. If possible, Vivian was more stunning in person than the magazine photos. Oh, to have curves and a waistline like that! Eisley sucked in her stomach and stood up a little straighter. No use. She groaned. Chocolate ice cream was such a traitor.

Daniel Harrison nudged Eisley out of her stupor and whispered, "Would you care to dance, Luv?"

She pressed into his shoulder with her own, curbing a touch of homesickness with his camaraderie. "No thanks, you sweet man. I'll just stand here and do my dad's kind of dancing." Eisley pointed to her black heels. "Tap my toe, nod my head to the beat, and smile as if I know something no one else knows. Believe me, it's less catastrophic this way."

Daniel chuckled. "I've a mind to like this family of yours."

Eisley pushed a mock shudder through her body. "And you think *I* make a lasting impression? Just wait until you meet my dad and brothers." She whistled low. "You'll never be the same."

Her attention drifted back to the couple on the dance floor. Wes's hand rested on the small of Vivian's back, the awareness of it sending sparks skidding up Eisley's spine. *Stupid hormones.* Vivian's palm touched Wes shoulder, their poise a perfect match. They looked beautiful.

"Like the cover of a storybook."

"Pardon?" Daniel asked, leaning closer.

Eisley nodded toward Wes and Vivian. "The two of them look perfect together, like a fairy tale."

Eleanor made some noise resembling a growl and murmured something that sounded suspiciously like "wicked witch."

Eisley bit the inside of her lips to keep from asking, but curiosity unlocked her jawbone. She reached for a glass of water, feigning indifference. "They've been together a long time, haven't they?"

Eleanor closed her eyes, wearily. "I'll not deny they've had a past, but I certainly hope he's outgrown her shallow ploys. If he doesn't have wits enough to steer clear of her, he deserves a sound slap."

The thought of Wes Harrison receiving a sound slap tickled a grin and drew her attention back to the dance floor as the music drew to a close. Just then, Wes's gaze caught hers. His smile started from one crooked corner and spread all the way across to a dimple on the other side.

Oh, what a smile. The kind to send embittered women out of their self-imposed spinsterhood. The kind to shatter the singleness of the resolute celibate. The kind that made her knees a little too shaky to *ever* consider dancing.

He walked toward her, his James Bond appeal growing with each step. Open-collared white shirt and black slacks added to the pure attraction. She pinched herself to make sure her imagination hadn't gotten the better of her. Tall, dark, and dreamy belonged to the lady in the red-towel, right?

A trail of model look-alikes littered his past, and the glamour of brilliant stardom glittered in his future. He lived totally out of her league and danced with a past which mocked hers. But why didn't the man from the papers match the guy she'd hung out with all day?

She released her clutched breath and offered him a smile. A shared smile for a friendly acquaintance. And *only* a nice safe acquaintance, with swagger.

"It's a pleasure to see you again, Ms. Barrett." Wes took her cool hand into his warm one. "Are you feeling better?"

The candlelight haloed his face, giving his eyes a golden glow and inviting an intimacy she ignored like the electricity traveling up her arm. She pulled out of his hold and waved away his concern. "Yes, thank you. Please don't use anything I said during my aura-induced state against me, okay?"

A dimple flickered in his cheek. "And where's the fun in that?"

Heat skittered up her spine at the theatrical combination of charm and good looks. Oh, how she loved fiction. "Right. Well, I'm sure your day with a crazy Appalachian provided lots of entertainment."

He closed in and all sorts of strange fireworks shot off in her stomach. Okay, so admiration from afar may not be far enough, but this was the wonderfully impossible kind of admiration. She could enjoy it while it lasted since it was perfectly safe and deliciously one-sided. *Very* movie-like.

"I haven't had such a pleasant afternoon in a long time. It must be the company I keep." He winked, controlled grin honed to perfection. *The actor emerges.*

Yep, totally fictional.

"Are you anxious?"

She followed his gaze to the jittery movements of her hand against the dark green satin covering her stomach. The last time she'd worn this particular dress had been pre-Emily and post Mama's Marshmallow Cookies. Now it gave a firmer hug around her middle before cascading to the floor in a pretty rain of her favorite color.

"Of course, I'm anxious." She released her hold on her gown and stood up straighter. "How many times do you think someone like me visits a place like this? Three guesses, and they all end in 'never'." She smoothed her palm over the wrinkles her jittery fingers made against the fabric. "Actually, I'm trying to hold my breath. I haven't worn this dress in years and I don't want to show off my baby roll." She looked up and her mouth dropped open. She didn't voice those thoughts out loud to Christopher Wesley Harrison, did she?

She snapped her eyes shut and prayed for the rapture. "Never mind." Heat coursed into her cheeks with such vibrancy, she had the sinking suspicion her face color matched her hair. Red face, green dress. Perfect for Christmas. She bit back a whimper.

"Eisley."

She peeled open her eyelids with a subdued wince. Wes worked those perfect lips of his like he wanted to laugh. Who could blame him? She sighed. It didn't matter. Soon she'd be miles away from dashing actors and safe within the folds of Uncle Joe's research. Maybe then humiliation wouldn't be an every half-hour occurrence.

"I can't even blame a migraine on that comment." She groaned. "Can you just pretend I didn't say anything?"

"You don't have one wit of pretension, do you?" He chuckled, a sound that somehow made her think of freshly baked chocolate chip cookies. "I appreciate that more than you know."

"Really?" She gave a mental eye roll. "So, you appreciate me humiliating myself with country girl flare?"

"I appreciate sincerity. The country girl flare is merely a charming bonus."

Yeah, right! "That line was sweet as pie."

"Chocolate pie?"

"Well," she drew out the word. *Oh heavens, talk about charming.* "That's a pretty prestigious rating. Give me some time and I'll let you know if you reach chocolate-status, but you'll have to work for it. Only the cream of the crop, so to speak, need apply."

A dimple flickered like a temptation, which might have made the little dialogue worth the heat planting in her cheeks. "Is that a challenge?"

The sweet banter teased a new addiction. Oh, she could really like this guy.

"Pardon me. I don't believe I've met your guest." The cobalt glare of Vivian Barry burned into view.

She wrapped her arm around Wes's with red claws clutched tight. From the snarl on her lips and the fire in her eyes, every pale piece of her very visible skin screamed one message loud and clear: Stay away from Christopher Wesley Harrison.

"You must be Estley Ferret?" Vivian raked her gaze down Eisley's body, her tone in unison with her frosty expression.

Eisley's smile froze in place and Polyanna died a painful death. Yep, mean people live everywhere, even jolly ole England.

"Her name is Eisley," Wes interrupted, his quick reaction meant to lessen the blow. He withdrew from Vivian's clutches and placed a bit of distance between them. "Eisley Barrett. Would your middle name be as unique as the first?"

Vivian's blood-red lips took a dive toward a snarl.

Eisley's grin resurfaced with full force. "I'm afraid so. My family has this crazy tradition of naming the first two grandchildren after grandparents from each side." She placed her palm on her chest. "I am named after my English grandmother, Eisley, and my Irish grandmother, Honora. Neither of which are fun to spell in Kindergarten."

Wes's eyes lit with a smile. Vivian's lit with something less inviting. Well, for the sake of her lovely hosts, she'd look for the silver lining around Ms. Barry's heart.

"It's a pleasure to meet you, Ms. Barry." Eisley offered her hand, but Vivian barely acknowledged it with a look. Ah, a silver lining made of steel. *Fabulous.* Eisley's teeth gritted.

"Vivian?" The crinkle just beneath Wes's Superman curl deepened, clearly surprised by her blatant rudeness. His stare locked with Vivian's until she produced a reluctant palm, slow enough to prove his influence wasn't touching her will.

"A pleasure."

Eleanor Harrison emerged into the conversation. "Eisley has come to stay with us for a few weeks as our particular guest. We hope to make her stay as pleasant as possible." Her gaze fastened with potent accuracy on Vivian.

Now that was a well-honed mama-look. Eisley shivered from the sheer perfection of it.

"Of course, you've always been so kind to"—she peeked back at Eisley— "strangers."

"I'm grateful for their kindness." Eisley turned to the welcome warmth in Mrs. H's face. Maybe Eisley was growing on her a little. It was hard to tell under all the properness.

"Eisley is doing a bit of research with Lizzie Worthing." Wes was trying to bridge the glaciers in the conversation and looked pretty stunned from the process. *Poor guy.* "She's visiting from a small town in Virginia, in the Blue Ridge Mountains, no less. Lovely country, from what I understand."

"And what is it you do in this small place?"

Eisley didn't even blink from the disdain in Vivian's voice. "My family runs a private preschool in town and my younger sister and I work as a team with kids who have special needs. She's a speech-language pathologist. We stay pretty busy, so this visit is a wonderful break."

"Your sister is some sort of teacher for *proper* English?" Her smile flamed into a wicked grin. She lifted a challenging brow as her glass touched her lips.

Vivian's attempt at intimidation rolled right off of Eisley's bare shoulder. *Seriously?* She worked with preschoolers who were more mature. "Proper where I come from, I guess, but to be like you I imagine I'd need a totally different education."

"Hmm, I'm not certain you would be allowed into my circles, dear." Vivian's voice dropped words like ice cubes.

Eisley forced her snarl and fists into submission. *Well, you'd fit right into mine.* She'd worked with brats before.

"Eisley, perhaps I could encourage you to dance with me?" Wes stepped past Vivian and offered his hand. "It seems Vivian is somewhat unfit for pleasant conversation at present."

Vivian's gaze brightened with enough sparks to celebrate the Fourth of July and her syrupy smile took a menacing turn. Fine. Getting away from Vivian deVille was worth a temporary agreement to dance with Wes. Once safely out of earshot, she'd politely decline. She wasn't tempting her or Wes's fate by dancing with him. No matter how adorable his dimples.

∞ ∞ ∞

Wes barely noticed his steps as he moved toward the dance floor. Vivian's behavior secured the decision he'd considered for months – to sever his relationship with all of the Barrys. He'd spent nearly a year trying to build emotional distance from Vivian, even drawing away from her father in an attempt to make a fresh start.

Carl Barry had recognized Wes as a twenty-five-year-old dreamer, hungry for a challenge. Wes had craved success, bathed in it, and followed Carl's suggestions regarding his professional and private choices. Hindsight highlighted Carl's subtle involvement in the romance between him and Jane. Somehow, in the middle of it all, one sister pitted against another. One seduced him, the other destroyed herself. Arrogance married ambition and birthed jealousy. A hateful trail of pain followed. It took months of reaping the unconditional love of his parents to save him from the same fate as Jane, even as story-hunting paparazzi thrust Jane's unfaithfulness and his promiscuous lifestyle into the tabloids.

He never wanted to return to those shadows. Those haunting choices and empty pleasures. His past sealed his fate. He was no judge of women.

He glanced down at Eisley at his side, the comparison between her and Vivian proving as different as chalk and cheese could ever be. If Eisley was all she seemed, he certainly didn't deserve a chance with her.

But what was it his father said? If men got what they deserved, they'd be a sorry lot indeed.

Ginger hair rested in ringlets on her head and spilled down her back, settling against the shiny green material of her gown. Her soft palm nestled on his arm, warm and right. One bare shoulder boasted a sunburst of freckles, an alarming distraction since he'd first seen her from across the room. Freckles. His grin inched up a notch and the room became hot for an entirely different reason. It felt good. Too good. Warning stirred deep in his chest. What if he was wrong again? Fatally wrong?

"I'm sorry for Vivian's behavior. I'm not certain why she's—" Wes stopped. "Please accept my apologies."

Eisley tilted her head up to him. "It's fine, Wes. But it's pretty obvious Vivian could benefit from some double-barreled country charm and a little of my Gran's advice."

"Advice?"

She scanned the ballroom ahead of them, lips twisted in humor. "You know the old saying, 'you catch more flies with honey than vinegar'?"

"Yes."

"Well, my Gran adds, 'some people are spiders, so you have to make the honey thick.'" She lowered her voice and squeezed closer, unaware of the flint igniting at her nearness. "And in Ms. Barry's case, I'd say extra thick. No offense, of course."

"I believe you're right." His chuckle brought a light to her eyes, something he found particularly satisfying. "So, are you ready for this dance?"

She shook her head, palms splayed in the air. "No, Wes. I only agreed so we could get away from Lady MacBarry. It's not a good idea for me to dance with you. With anyone. In fact, I can't."

He captured her wrist in a light hold, lingering a moment in the tempting trace of mint accompanying her. Perhaps the dance would prove her duplicity? Surely, she wouldn't flounder if it was all a game. "One little dance? You've already agreed to it, you know. One try won't hurt."

"There are some things in life that really aren't worth trying. Not even once. One is sky diving. The other is giving a pack of bubble gum to a two-year-old." She looked out over the ballroom, worry lines deepening. "I'm pretty sure dancing with me might be a third."

A hunch, or perhaps his spirit, nudged him to toss aside his fear. See her as the person she portrayed, true and genuine. In fact, he almost *needed* to believe it. "I'll guide you."

She studied him for a full fifteen seconds as if measuring his sincerity as much as he was hers, then a timid light flickered in her eyes. Faith. In him. His chest expanded with purpose.

"I won't let you fall, Eisley."

"Are you sure you want to risk these." She pointed to the black heels on her feet. "Chopping off a few of your toes?"

"I have ten of them and they are at your disposal. You may bruise them all you like, but I ought to warn *you*." He leaned close and glanced down at his open palm in invitation. "I'm a very good teacher."

Her eyes grew as wide as a two pence, hand paused in the air as if she wouldn't commit. He forced every ounce of confidence into his expression. Why did helping her somehow feed the wounded man inside of him?

She stared at his outstretched hand, bottom lip caught between her teeth. His airway tightened. He'd wait for five minutes, palm outstretched like a beggar, if she'd agree. For some reason, his faith depended on it. Faith in the new man he wanted to be.

She put him out of his misery soon enough. Her hand slid into his and a sudden calm fell over him. Like the final cut to a movie. He led her to the middle of the room and placed his hand to her waist.

She dutifully cupped her left palm on his shoulder, clasped her right hand in his, and raised an eyebrow in challenge. "Ready or not?"

His grin spread wide and the dance began. After the first twenty seconds, he was pretty certain she crunched all ten of his toes at least once. During the second twenty seconds, they both almost tripped. Wes caught her in his arms and started laughing. No one could pretend this type of fumbling about, and certainly not in a room filled with people. His doubts took another fatal blow. Eisley Barrett was for real.

Her cheeks colored to terra cotta. It was the most endearing thing he'd witnessed in years.

"Well, this is a first."

"I'm so sorry, Wes. I bet you've never heard of homicidal dancing before."

She tried to pull away but he held fast. He couldn't remember the last time he'd laughed this often. "You have the right technique. You only need to relax."

"Okay...hmm...relax?" She looked at him like he was daft. "I'm dancing in the middle of a ballroom with Christopher Wesley Harrison, along with a hundred other people whose shoes probably cost more than my house. Besides those things, I'm an Appalachian in London and I don't know how to dance. *Relax*?"

"I need to think of something to distract you?"

"Good luck. I think I'm—what would you guys say? —sufficiently diverted trying *not* to fall flat on my face." Her lips pouted for a moment. "And this is one of my favorite jazz standards too."

There was an idea. Certainly, God wouldn't object to some wooing with Sinatra. Wes splayed his hand across her back and leaned forward so his lips grazed her ear. "I know this song too."

Softly, he began to hum the melody.

She drew in a sharp breath, her body tensed, but then slowly released a sweet *mmm* as her body relaxed, allowing him to guide her steps. Her tangled legs caught the pattern his set, as if taking her mind off of the motions gave them freedom to follow. Her hand slipped from his shoulder down his arm, and a sigh brought her cheek against his. Mint coated the air around him in a delicious intoxication.

"Will you marry me?" Eisley breathed the question out on a whisper.

He drew back a few inches to view her face.

Her eyes were closed. "I think I could live off this moment for a good five years."

Perfect. She'd forgotten all about Vivian's spikey mood or their previous dangerous dancing. He drew her a little deeper into his embrace without missing a beat.

She looked up at him. Islands of gold floated in the emerald sea of her eyes. "You're really working on that chocolate pie status, aren't you?"

A surge of tenderness squeezed his voice to a whisper. "How am I doing?"

"I think you've moved up to strawberry with whipped cream." Her gaze searched his. "You're so...so nice."

"You sound surprised."

Her cheeks darkened. "Well, besides the fact you're sort of fictional and all, you do have a history of being the bad boy type." Her smile turned apologetic. "But this entire time you've been...well..."

Their breaths mingled in the silence.

"I'm not who I used to be."

She studied him, taking her time to digest his statement. "A change of plans?"

"Well, more appropriately, a change of heart."

She tilted her head and stared, her curious gaze boring deep. "Nice line." Her nose wrinkled in thought. "You're such an anomaly."

"Now you're trying to flatter me, aren't you?"

She grinned. "Yeah, I bet you get compliments like *that* all the time." Her gaze turned thoughtful. "But seriously, what puzzle piece am I missing? You're charming and kind, not to mention famous. How can you *not* have a date or something?"

He caught Vivian's glare from the crowd, her eyes narrowed. Almost a warning. They hadn't arrived together, but she'd made a point to attach to him fairly quickly. No wonder he'd avoided social gatherings for so long. How had he not seen it! It was time for a fresh start with an agent who held Wes's new vision, career choices with meaning beyond dollar signs, and a romance...

He wasn't quite ready to commit to the thought, even with the beautiful inducement in his arms, but the idea was growing on him. "Fame certainly brings people, but not love. And I'm far from perfect." He glanced at his parents dancing nearby. "You've met my parents. I want what they have."

A sliver of pain creased her brows for a second. "That kind of love is worth waiting for. Don't settle for less, Wes. You'll regret it."

Her wounds ran deep. Perhaps as stark and scarred as his. Was her joy an act, a defense mechanism, or a hint toward her faith? "You seem to speak from experience?"

"I've used up my happily-ever-after." She shrugged her beautifully freckled shoulder and produced a hard-won smile. "But I love dreaming them up for other people. And yours would be such a fun dream."

He felt his brow shift with his grin. "So, you're saying you want to dream about me?"

She stumbled, but he tightened his hold to keep her steady. "No, not in *that* way." She snickered. "But after meeting you, my overactive imagination can certainly dream up a perfect match."

"Really?"

As she observed other dancers nearby, he allowed his gaze the freedom to roam her face, her hair, even the brush of freckles across the bridge of her nose. Yes, his father had been right – attraction burned like wildfire through his veins, but he wasn't a fool anymore. Attraction lit quickly and died with the same speed. This...this felt new, fresh and somehow, pure. "And what would you choose?"

"Someone beautiful, of course." Her pointed look brooked no argument. "And smart, because, well, that's kind of a no-brainer. Having lived with a man whose idea of conversation consisted solely of monologues on basketball teams, his fading high school popularity, and the woes of life as a married man, intelligent *conversation* is vital."

Some bloke took a bludger to her confidence. *Idiot.*

"Oh, a sense of humor is necessary. It's almost impossible to face all the hard stuff in life without one, and a gracious heart." She grimaced and looked back up at him. "Because we all screw up, don't we?"

"And need a second chance?"

She topped off her smile with a nod. "Keep your eyes open, Mr. Movie Star." She scanned the room and lowered her voice to a whisper. "Your second chance could be anywhere. Even in this room."

The edge in his caution dissipated. *Precisely.*

"Well, if Christmas is the season of miracles, you've renewed my faith in them." She stepped away from him and smiled through her curtsy. "We both survived my first dance."

The music had ended?

"You seem surprised at your success."

"Are you kidding? I've spent the last eight of my life with preschoolers as my primary conversational partners. I feel accomplished if I use more than two syllable words in a sentence and don't end up with kid stains on my clothes. This is definitely a storybook moment for me."

Her look of appreciation fed him to his core. The sweetness in her unpretentious joy poured over his raw soul with a healing touch. Somehow by the light of the Christmas glow, he almost believed in miracles again. Even for a reformed scoundrel.

Chapter Five

hat an evening! Eisley pried off her shoes and rubbed her sore heels, blinking her focus on the bedside clock. 2:07 a.m. Crazy end to a crazier day. After Wes brought her back to the hotel from the gala, they'd sat in the lobby and talked for two more hours. It had been an oddly easy transition from their fun dance floor banter to a longer conversation. Almost like a friend.

Which was pretty impossible. But sweet and encouraging a sort of comforting feeling to settle right around her heart. Of all the possibilities she'd conjured up about her once-in-a-lifetime trip to England, she'd never imagined anything like the past eighteen hours.

As she unclasped her hair, the weight of it fell around her shoulders, surrounding her with the full potency of rosemary and mint. She threaded her fingers into her aching skull and massaged out the kinks, reliving each scene of her evening with growing morbid clarity. Oh no!

She sighed back into the folds of the comforter. "I can't believe I teased him," she murmured into the blanket and blindly stretched her hand to the nightstand, fumbling for her phone "And I nearly broke his legs. Idiot. Why on earth did I dance with him?" She flipped open her telephone. "His whole family has to think I'm-" She stumbled around in her head, searching for the perfect British word. "Crackers. That's me. Blooming crackers." She pressed a pillow up against her chest and listened through three rings. *It's a good thing I'll never see him again.*

"Hi, Mom."

"Good morning, honey," Mom's voice drew out the words with a syrupy just-woke-up sound. "How are things going?"

"Oh, wonderful. And horrible." Eisley buried her face into the pillow and released a moan. "I've got to learn to control my tongue. I'd sin a lot less and wouldn't look nearly as stupid." She cringed before unloading the full nightmare. "I mentioned the baby roll to Christopher Wesley Harrison, and I nearly lamed him when we danced, and..." Eisley whimpered, remembering. "I asked him to marry me."

"What?" Mom burst into laughter. "You've been busy for your first day."

Busy. Humbled. Completely mortified.

"You have no idea." Eisley rolled on her back and stared at the ornate moldings on the ceiling. The entire evening's events bubbled out of her in humiliating detail. She'd taken her one chance to feel like Cinderella and instead transformed into Lucille Ball...with an Andy Griffith accent. "But he's nothing like I'd expect him to be. Not arrogant or impersonal." She cleared her throat. "He's nice."

"Nice?"

"Yeah, nice." A vision of his double-dimpled grin flashed to mind. *Really nice.*

Silence greeted her from the other end before her mother broke in again. "It sounds like you two spent a lot of time together."

The look of tenderness he'd given her while they danced flickered forward. He'd lowered his perfect profile long enough to show off the sweet creamy middle of his personality, and the delicious temptation tickled her hope- bone. *Stop. Right. There.* "Very weird."

"No romance, though?"

A cackle burst out before she could stop it, probably loud enough to shake the nerves of the Harrisons in the room next door. She caught the rest of her laugh with her hand. "Are you crazy? No way. Not him and definitely not me. It's impossible."

"Eisley," her mother's tone held a brief reprimand.

"Nope. Don't even go there, Mom."

Her mother heaved a sigh, which probably curbed a long diatribe about second chances and happily-ever-afters...two very dangerous things. In fact, she was able to relax around him because he *wasn't* a threat. No possibility for mutual attraction, romance, then years of heartache and self-flailing. Any sweet nothings she conjured up in her head were exactly that – nothings, for her imagination to enjoy.

"When do you leave for Derbyshire?"

Eisley rolled on her stomach and picked at the corner of a blue satin pillow. "Tomorrow morning. We should arrive there in the evening, after we've made a few stops along the way. How are the kids?"

"Great," Kay answered. "You haven't been gone a long time. Emily's asked about you the past two nights before bed and the boys make sure to pray for you,

50

but..." She paused and her voice sounded distant. "Eisley, I'm going to have to get off here. Emily just woke up and is..."

"Naked?"

"Of course. At some point, you're going to have to glue that girl's clothes to her body."

A giggle in the background floated through the receiver and clenched Eisley's heart. She took her wallet from her bag and flipped out the long row of pictures. "They'll be okay, won't they, Mom? I mean if you need..."

"They're fine. Relax and enjoy yourself. And don't be afraid to believe the impossible. God specializes in the impossible, you know."

Eisley snapped her wallet closed. "Mom, I'm not interested, remember? How much heartbreak do you think I or the kids need?"

"Your kids are fine, Eisley. The only one having heart issues is you."

Eisley bit the inside of her lips to keep from firing off a sarcastic reply. "I love you, Mom. Give Dad and the kids kisses for me."

"Love you too, honey."

Eisley exhaled a long breath and closed her eyes. Thankfully, one tall, dark and handsome distraction was out of the way so she could place all her focus on Julia Ramsden's story. Wes had returned to London's movie scene with auditions or something else with 'famous' tagged behind it, and she was free to rewatch his films with a little more 4-D understanding of his smell and touch. Safe and fictional.

Besides, she was in England for a totally different purpose than distractible dimples and a heart-stopping smile. She had a job to do. A promise to keep. A mystery to solve. Jenkies, she sounded like a script from Scooby Doo.

Wes's smile emerged in her mind and she embraced the warmth dancing over her skin at the memory for just a second. Maybe, just maybe, she'd enjoyed a Cinderella moment after all.

Eisley yawned and blinked her room into view. Rose Hill Cottage, Derbyshire. The evening darkness had obscured most of the view the night before, but she'd recognized the wonderful lack of street lights as a certain clue she'd entered familiar territory. Country life.

And country folks were country folks everywhere.

She swished back the mountain of covers and tiptoed on bare feet to a veiled window, holding her breath for the great 'reveal'. Heavy layers of cloth peeled back to frame a vast view of green patchwork hillsides swathed in a dawn–hewn blanket of mist and a light sheen of snow. Her smile pulled against her cheeks, nudging a ridiculous giggle. For once, her migraine was worth it. Snow had never looked more beautiful or inviting. A perfect morning for a mystery, and Julia Ramsden's house was only three miles away.

She danced a happy jig and scanned her room. It reminded her of home. Overhead beams of dark wood created a ladder effect across the low–lying ceiling and gave the room a rustic feel which belied the elegant furnishings. Wingback chairs covered in embroideries, and even a massive wardrobe decorated with painted vines, added to the enchantment. Embers winked through charred wood from the rock fireplace, sending a whiff of roasted oak. It was perfect.

With quick work, she jerked her wild mane into a somewhat controlled ponytail and tugged on a pair of jeans and a sweatshirt. She topped her sleuth ensemble with a ball cap and peeked from her bedroom door, tucked at the end of a small hallway. The dim light of morning gave the hall a vacant look, probably because the Harrisons were still snug in their bed. She hedged past two closed doors and made it to the top of the stairway before a massive creak from the boards underfoot broke the silence. She cringed and shot a glance over her shoulder. No movement. No sounds.

At the foot of the stairs, the narrow passage opened into a long sitting room. Windows lined the eastern wall and allowed fresh morning light to decorate the oak floors with a golden haze. She followed hot tea's savory aroma to a wooden door beyond a stone fireplace alive with flames.

With a careful push, the door opened and ushered her forward into a fresh breath of English Breakfast. Eleanor sat at the table, wrapped in a pink robe, a steaming and dainty cup in her hand.

"Good morning," Eisley whispered.

"I see we share a love for mornings." Her cup clicked into the dainty saucer. "Did you rest well, duck?"

The affectionate term tipped Eisley's grin. "Yes, very." It was another room of character. Copper pots hung from the exposed beam ceiling, reflecting the pebble-colored walls. Two giant windows bordered the view of a rock–walled garden yielding to a mossy countryside and a distant row of trees. A fireplace stood behind the country breakfast table, blinking with dying flames. "This place is beautiful."

"Mother would have been pleased with your compliment." Eleanor's focus faded into memories. "Her haven, she called it, and my childhood home. Daniel and I are from two very different worlds." She blinked back to the present. "Would you care for some coffee?"

"No, thank you. I don't want to disturb your reading." The soft twitter of birds from beyond the window tempted her. "But I'd love to take a walk before breakfast." She wiggled her brows. "Maybe toward the Ramsden place?" She scanned the kitchen again. "Unless there is something I can do to help?"

Eleanor chuckled. "Margaret, the housekeeper, will see to it, but all should be prepared within the next hour and a half." She stood and moved to the counter to pour herself another cup. "I do hope you've recovered enough for another busy day."

"We're back in the country. I *know* country." Eisley snatched a banana from the counter and peeled it. "Besides, it's pretty obvious I don't mesh too well with high-class city girls."

"Vivian Barry is a beastly woman." Eleanor shuddered. "And don't group all of Vivian's class into the same lump. She's of her own mold, my dear. Daniel was born to privilege and opportunity, similar to Vivian, and you can see quite plainly how unaffected he is."

Eisley sighed against the counter. "He's absolutely adorable."

"Yes, he is." Eleanor ducked her head, cheeks rosy and voice soft.

The admission tossed the typical emotional salad inside Eisley, endearing and heart wrenching, dangling a carrot she wasn't sure she wanted to snag.

"And my son is much like his father. He feels things deeply. Cares deeply." She walked back to the table and placed her cup in its saucer with a frown. "He must keep Vivian around as an obligation to her father, Carl Barry, no doubt. It's the only logical reason she's still involved in his life, if logic is involved at all."

"She's drop-dead gorgeous with enough curves to shame a pretzel. Logic has nothing to do with it." Eisley frowned at the thought of Vicious Vivian. "Besides, she does seem pretty sneaky."

"Precisely." Eleanor offered a pointed look. "And the men in my life appear oblivious."

"Don't they always? The good guys fall for the temptress, and the good girls end up with the jerks." She waved the half-eaten banana at Eleanor. "See why I prefer fiction? Reality is terrifying and too unfair."

Eleanor's lips quirked just enough to hint at a smile. "And I suppose you are one of the good girls?"

"Well, I'm certainly not a temptress. I guess if I had any seductive bone in my body, my husband might have stuck around a little while longer." The familiar weight of failure nudged her shoulders forward. "No, that's not true." *It feels true, though.* "He made his choices too, but my failures seem to sting worse. Maybe it's because I actually have a conscience." Eisley slapped her palm over her mouth. "Sorry. I'm trying to stop that."

Pardon?"

"Saying bad things about Marshall." Eisley sighed, a pinch of conviction inching to the surface. "It just comes so easily. I remind myself of his bad habits to strengthen my resolve against a second failure." Eisley worked up a grin and donned her best British accent. "Regret is the perfect tool to ensure my eternal spinsterhood."

The woman stared at Eisley for a long moment, blue-green eyes peering deep. "Regret is a poor substitute for love."

Love? A second time? *Yeah, when Dad shaves his moustache.* "Which is another fantastic reason to go in search of Lornegrave Hall this morning." She tossed the banana peel into the trash and tilted her head toward the door. "It's a much more positive way to use my energy instead of wallowing in self-pity, right? Besides, I think Julia Ramsden might have her own love story hidden somewhere in all those mysterious years."

"You are incorrigible, my dear." She walked to the back window and Eisley followed. "I will introduce you to Elizabeth Worthing this afternoon, but since you are so excited..." She gestured outside. "See the footpath there, stretching through the wood?"

A thin path cut a well-worn line from the backyard through a sheep pasture and disappeared into the forest. Excitement quivered up from Eisley's stomach, squeezing her voice into a higher pitch. "Yes, I see it."

"If you follow it through the wood, it will lead to a lovely prospect of Dethicks' countryside. Should the fog cooperate, you might see Riber Castle. Not a true castle, but impressively situated nonetheless. Lornegrave is nestled near a small pond in the distance between your location and Riber."

"Okay." Eisley shrugged into her coat.

"Mind the bridge at the bottom of the hill. Some days it freezes and is none too easy to cross." Eleanor tapped Eisley's cap. "'Tis a nippy morning. It would be wise to return soon after you reach the view."

"Thank you." Eisley leaned over and kissed Eleanor on the cheek. "You are so sweet." Eisley rounded Eleanor and opened the back door. "See you in an hour or so."

"Eisley, dear."

Eisley halted her forward momentum and turned.

"Perhaps it is time to start seeing your life from the present rather than the past. I believe it would be a lovely view, filled with many more possibilities than regrets."

The tinging of tears moved from the bridge of Eisley's nose into her watery vision...or maybe it was just the chill in the morning air. Yeah, that had to be it because what Eleanor Harrison spoke of resembled a leap of faith...in heels, and though she had plenty of faith in God, he wasn't the one who made all the wrong choices.

"Thanks, Mrs. H."

Eisley brought the door to a close and turned toward the footpath. Keep her eyes on the present? Her smile spread wide. Perfect. *Lornegrave, here I come.*

∞   ∞   ∞

Eleanor lowered back into the chair. She touched the cheek Eisley had warmed with a kiss and unleashed a full smile. Eisley Barrett broke any mold Eleanor could have concocted or predicted. Genuine from crooked cap to joyful heart.

Yet her joy distracted people from noticing a deeper pain which hovered a skin's depth and haunted soul-deep. But there was no doubt why Daniel took to Lizzie's preposterous matchmaking scheme. Wes and Eisley fit perfectly – whether they realized it yet or not.

Providential?

The notion found a nestling place. Another glimpse out the window afforded her a view of Eisley spinning, arms lifted in the air, while the morning breeze tossed her fury of ginger hair. Eleanor covered her broad smile with her hand, stifling a chuckle.

She settled back into her chair with her tea and opened the paper. The curious paparazzi wasted no time in featuring a small photo of Wesley and Eisley outside The Darlington House. They stood side by side, waiting for the car, Eleanor next to Daniel, Eisley's head tilted toward Wes, and Wesley...laughing. How long had it been since she heard her son laugh? Eisley certainly brought it out in him. The caption of the brief article posed the question, *A New Romance for His New Roles?* and prattled on about whether Eisley was a family friend or a newfound romance.

Eleanor never became accustomed to her son's popularity and lack of privacy, but perhaps the paparazzi might get a story right for a change instead of connecting Vivian Barry to her son at every available moment. Almost as if someone handpicked the opportunities.

"Good morning. It looks as though Eisley brought the snow with her."

Wesley entered the kitchen, gray trousers hanging loose around his legs and a white t-shirt clinging to his chest. *How much he resembles his father.* He yawned, raked a hand through his unruly hair, and walked over to kiss his mother on the same cheek Eisley had kissed.

55

"I thought you had an audition this week. When did you arrive?"

Wes rubbed his eyes and took a cup from the cupboard. "It was past midnight. After the voice-over, I had no interest in staying in town." He scanned the kitchen. "Besides, the audition isn't for a few days."

Eleanor tempered her smile. Actor or not, her son's behavior since Eisley's entrance into his life blazed with interest, especially after their long conversation after the gala. "You decided to join us here rather than return to the country house?"

"Now, I wouldn't have seen my parents if I'd gone to Harrogate Park." A mischievous glint marked his true intentions, but his hapless shrug meant to send her off his trail. "Everyone still asleep?"

Eleanor took another look out the window, a lingering sip of coffee, and decided on a noncommittal, "Hmm."

"I suppose Eisley's knackered after all of her traveling." He peeled a banana, sat down at the table, and stretched his legs out in front of him to expose his bare feet.

This interest in Eisley Barrett opened a door to a world he'd bolted closed two years before. Was he ready? Eleanor had spent months, if not years, praying for another opportunity for Wes. Hope trembled to life in her pulse. His year of spiritual growth prepared him to return to his profession but acting flaunted his weaknesses in front of him daily. It couldn't be easy. And Vivian's pursuit didn't help.

She waited through the silence until Wes looked up. "Wesley, I'll not have you trifle with that girl's emotions. If you have intentions for Ms. Barry, then you should—"

"Mum." Wesley flattened his palms against the table. "There is nothing between me and Vivian." His jaw twitched. His words released with a growl. "However, because of our shared pasts, she's plagued with the same pain and memories as I am. She misses her sister."

"Codswallop. The only thing that woman misses is a conscience. She's devious, Wesley. I see it written all over her face and she's using your guilt against you." She softened her words, splaying her fingers out to touch his. "You are not the man you once were, darling. God has forgiven you, yet you are bound by this guilt. Don't continue to work for a debt which has already been paid. You are free to start anew."

Wesley's hands fisted and opened, a sign of his inward struggle or his exhaustion with her plea. "I know, Mum. And I rang Carl about it yesterday to schedule a meeting with him once he returns from Venice." He met her look with a confident one of his own, sending a clear message he could manage his own affairs now.

Pride, and a precious pound of peace, eased over her previous anxiety.

"My past is a part of me." Wes stared into his coffee cup, his brow tightened. "A fading part of me. I can't change the choices I've made or the people I've hurt, but

I've learned from those mistakes. Those losses." He sighed and lifted his face. "And a fresh start has only looked better since Eisley arrived."

She busied herself in the silence by topping off her tea and staring out the window, giving Eisley a bit more time. "I hate to admit it aloud, but your father was right from the beginning. I'm glad she came."

"So am I."

Eleanor studied her son for a moment and then leaned into his gaze. "Mind some advice, duck. The greatest romance is born out of friendship. She's been deeply wounded. As have you. Take some of the patience you've learned through your profession and in the injuries of the past few years and practice it now, with the care of a friend. Be gentle and slow, for both of your sakes."

His smile held no promises, as he slid into the chair across from her. "You make it sound as though I'm impetuous, Mother."

Eleanor ignored his sarcasm and took another sip of her tea her lips tempting to unbraid into a grin as she watched him over the rim. "I do hope Eisley finds her way on the footpath this morning. The fog is quite thick, don't you think?"

Wes had just taken a large bite of his banana and almost choked at his mother's words. "Chee wan bu duh woo?"

"Wesley, I think you are old enough to remember one doesn't speak when one's mouth is full. Hmm?"

Wes grimaced through a painful swallow of the half-chewed banana. "She went through the wood?" He stood from the table and took a quick drink of his coffee.

"Why didn't you tell me she was out already?"

"I wanted to give her a head start...and clarify *your* intentions." Eleanor offered a noncommittal shrug. "She doesn't know what you've been through – how pain has changed you and given you a proper perspective. She sees you as an impossible dream, and impossibilities are safe for wounded hearts. She'd be terrified if she knew you harbored interest in her."

Wes drew his anorak off the hook and slipped it over his t-shirt. He pulled on his wellies. "What happened to all that renewed faith I saw in your eyes earlier? Doubting me already?"

She ignored his teasing grin. "She's in desperate need of a tender hand, and you are in need of the hope. Take care, Wes."

His expression sobered. "I'll take my time." He hurried to the door in complete contradiction to his words.

"Obviously."

He shrugged as if helpless, a fresh spring to his step. She'd missed it.

With a wave of cool air, Wesley disappeared into the morning and Eleanor finally finished her tea *Matchmaking did hold an element of fun, didn't it?*

Chapter Six

*E*isley drifted into the fog, mesmerized as if she'd entered the magical world of Narnia. A cool mist sprinkled across her face and heightened the otherworldly feelings already dancing across her skin. London was interesting, but this landscape...this vast, iconic countryside? Breathtaking.

Her presence interrupted the morning routines of the furry natives, who skittered through the underbrush before she caught a solid glimpse of them. A hush of breeze whirred above and cooled the droplets kissing her cheeks and eyelids. She drew in a deep breath of the air, scented with wet soil and the faint hint of something sweet. A rock wall guided her path down the slope and up ahead, a wild vine of pink winter blossoms clung to the ledge of a stone bridge.

Daphnes? A few sprigs of snowdrops pushed up in a sparse frame. Her granny said they were God's reminders that spring was never too far away. Eisley fingered the soft petals and smiled. *Hope.* Eleanor's gentle reminder tugged her thoughts in a frightening direction. Love? Yeah, she'd thought it would be enough, but even after almost three years. fear fought the same war between the little girl who wanted to believe and the woman who knew how painful rejection burned.

Hope? Regret was so much safer.

A familiar sound arrested her attention and yanked the mother-strings of her heart. A child, crying. Eisley quickened her pace toward the sound, her feet hitting the bridge with such force she slid halfway across it, barely keeping upright.

A small creek ran beneath the bridge and standing on an island-rock in the middle of the brook was the source of the cries: a little girl. Tears trickled down her pale cheeks from a set of round dark eyes. One hand wrapped around a rag doll and the other clung to the pocket of her little brown coat. Golden curls spilled from beneath a mousy cap. Oh, poor baby! Eisley crossed the bridge and skimmed down the steep bank.

"Hi, sweetie." She squatted to eye level with the little girl, the gentle flow of water separating them. "How did you get all the way out there?"

The easy gurgle of the stream mingled with the girl's sniffles. Her bottom lip wobbled, and then she wiped her nose on her sleeve. *Go figure! British kids do that, too?* Her rosebud mouth pinched closed. Eisley offered her friendliest smile.

"My name is Eisley and I'm visiting Mr. and Mrs. Harrison just on the other side of the woods. Do you know them?"

hesitated and then the blond curls bobbed up and down with a nod.

They've sent me on a special journey this morning. I'm supposed to make it to the top of that hill over there and look for a castle." Eisley scooted a pace forward, toes at the water's edge. "Do you like to explore in the mornings too?"

Curls bobbed, followed by a tremulous sniffle.

"Would you like some help to get back over here? I can carry you."

The little girl looked from Eisley's face back to the flowing water on either side of her and shifted from one bright orange Wellie to the other. Good girl. Be cautious with the whole 'talk to strangers' thing.

After a moment's hesitation, she nodded her reply.

Eisley scanned the creek for the simplest place to cross, the narrowest passage. The girl stood in the middle, a little over a van's distance away, and the only stepping stones available were meant for kiddie-sized feet.

Why hadn't she packed her waders?

With a resigned sigh, Eisley stepped to the first rock and her foot made an unladylike slip right into the cool stream. Her body tensed as the freezing water seeped through her tennis shoes, clenching every muscle, even her voice. Geeze Louise, she didn't even need to be in heels.

"I guess you'd better tell me your name." Eisley's words pitched high from the chill running up her thighs. "So, I'll know you're a real girl and not a pixie trying to trick me."

The pout disappeared, and the little girl jutted out her round chin. "Mary, and I am not a pixie."

The light airiness to her voice contradicted her statement.

"Mary? Well, that's a wonderful name and very un-pixielike, so I guess I'll believe you."

"Pixies aren't real." Her sweet voice took a hard edge, too hard for a maybe six-year old.

Eisley tilted her head upward as if pondering Mary's statement. "Oh, I'm not too sure about that. The storybooks have a lot to say about them."

Mary's frown deepened. "Fairy stories aren't real either. There is no such thing as magic."

Tough crowd and a bit too cynical. Even if Eisley didn't believe in 'once upon a time' anymore, this six-year-old damsel in distress shouldn't slam it. Fairy tales went with childhood like rainy days and mud pies. You couldn't have one without the other.

Eisley rallied to defend the daydreams and dispel the much too hopeless look on Mary's young face. "Oh, but I know a few *true* ones. Fantastic and as near to magical as anything else I've ever read. There's one about a young boy who killed a giant with a slingshot and stone, a magical moment when an entire sea split in half, and another one about a fairy-like creature who brought an amazing message to a young girl."

Eisley tried to move her hands as she walked but kept losing her balance. "The coolest is about a real-life prince who fought a dragon named Death and crushed his head without using one sword."

The spark of interest in Mary's eyes brought her mom's words back to her. *God specializes in the impossible.* Maybe faith, trust, and a little pixie dust wasn't such a bad idea. Even for grown-ups—especially grown-ups who knew about the wonder of God's love. Somehow it always held a magical quality to it, vast and beyond understanding yet close enough to wrap around her.

Eisley reached the island and put her arms out for Mary, stashing those musings for later. "There now, let's take it nice and slow to the other side. Are you ready?"

Eisley scooped her up, wobbled on her turn, and started back across the creek. "Do you have any brothers?"

Mary nodded and held up one chubby finger.

"One? Wow, I have three and they weren't always so nice. Is your brother nice?"

Mary frowned and shook her head. "He's loud."

"Yeah, that's boys for you. Loud and mischievous." Eisley shrugged. "Once when we went camping, they pulled me out of the tent while I was sleeping and set me on a rock in the middle of the creek. When I got up the next morning.... whoa..." Her foot slipped a little, but she caught herself. "When I got up the next morning, there I was in the middle of the creek in my pajamas. I got so mad I pushed my sleeping bag down into the water, walked through the cold creek to the tent." She placed Mary down on the pebbled shore and tugged the little girl's coat more tightly around her. "And put my dripping bag on top of their sleeping heads."

Mary's brown eyes grew wide and then she giggled.

"They never did anything like that to me again. Lots of other things, but not that." Eisley placed her hands on her hips and peered around them. "Do you live nearby?"

Mary turned her attention toward the right. Faded field stone and hints of a black roof filtered through the shroud of trees.

Suddenly the little girl released a gasp. "Maggie."

Eisley looked in the direction Mary's pointing finger and there lay the little rag doll, on the same rock from where Mary had just come. *Perfect.*

"No problem, sweetheart. Dame Eisley to the rescue of another damsel in distress." Eisley wiggled her cold toes. "Besides, my shoes are already wet."

∞ ∞ ∞

Wes sprinted through the pasture and wound his way into the canopy of trees, no sight of Eisley. Had he ever had the opportunity to pursue a woman? His father's wealthy status coupled with his own prominent profession blared like signage to interested women. But most of them wanted the millionaire's son or the famous actor, not the somewhat insecure, rather bookish, introverted Wes Harrison, with a newfound faith guiding his choices.

And wooing God's way? With patience and gentleness? The thought humbled and energized him at the same time. A challenge with the right purpose. The memory of his dance with Eisley, the hurt in her eyes as she spoke of love, firmed his patience. Their post-gala conversation encouraged a kinship he hadn't expected. Was it too perfect? Her sincerity? Her kindness? He glanced heavenward. Could God really bring someone like her into his life? It seemed too good to believe.

As he rounded a bend and the rock bridge came into view, he slowed his pace to mind the slippery hazard. Over the beating of his pulse, he heard a voice drifting out of the wood, a strangely familiar voice with the lilt of Appalachian undertones. He grinned and started across the bridge. *If she was talking, then all must be well with the world.* Her voice brought a smile with it.

Mary Wright caught his attention first, her hands jammed into the pockets of her coat, a pout waiting at the corners of her mouth. Wes followed her stare to the middle of the creek where Eisley stood, reaching down to retrieve Mary's doll. Her ginger hair flared on the breeze beneath her cap. A cap? Was it possible for her to be any cuter? Her words chattered on the breeze, something about talking vegetables and a bad pickle. Wes ignored it. *Must be a bizarre Appalachian idea.*

As she straightened, a triumphant smile lighting her face, her gaze locked with his.

"Oh." Her eyes shot wide and her free palm slammed against her chest. "You're here?" She opened her mouth to say something else, but her words dissolved into a puff. He watched in horrified silence as Eisley doddered and attempted to steady herself.

Pushing away from the bridge railing, he ran to the other side in time to see her lose her battle with gravity. She fell back into a splash of mud and water, arms flailing in a wild attempt to remain upright. His chest collapsed with a groan. Perhaps she wouldn't be too narked.

He stood at the water's edge in a moment.

"I saved the doll." Eisley snickered and wiggled the threadbare toy in the air while the rest of her remained seated in the middle of the brook. "There were casualties, however. My pride was slain."

A laugh of surprise jolted from him. No ploys. No pouting. Only laughter at herself. He'd never recognized how badly he *needed* her joy, how distorted his expectations had become.

His wellies guarded his feet from the chill of the water as he waded through the brook and peered down at her. One patch of mud stuck to the side of her cap while little dots added darker spots to her pert nose. She lifted humor-filled eyes, her face wreathed in smiles, and he lost all sense of words, time, and space. He'd held on to his heart with both fists, terrified to release it into the unpredictable hands of another, until now. Until her. Nothing else felt so right.

"If you've come to rescue me, you're too late. Wait." She wiped her empty palm against her jacket. "I suppose I *am* a damsel in distress." With a look over to Mary, she pointed at Wes. "Look, Mary. Here is a great example of a real-life fairy tale. I needed help." Her gaze met his again, expression expectant. "And here comes a knight to rescue me." She held out her hand to him, completely unaware of the heat vibrating in the air from her declaration. "Seems pretty magical to me."

He pulled her to a stand, feeling very much like a hero. *Magical? Without a doubt.* He drew in a breath and reminded himself to keep a steady heart. Patience. "Well, your rescue of Maggie was quite impressive."

"I bet." She snickered and slipped her hand from his. "If I'd flapped my arms any harder I'd have shot into orbit."

Funny, his pulse launched as soon as he took her hand. He cleared his throat and steadied her with a palm to her shoulder, while he dug into his pocket for his handkerchief. "Here, let me see to your face."

"My face?" It took a moment for her to decipher his meaning, until she noticed his handkerchief. "A handkerchief? You mean that's not just in the movies?"

She closed her eyes and lifted her face for better access. "I thought it was only another prop to enhance the lovely refinement of England."

He hesitated. She probably shouldn't trust him, but her simple act spotlighted his desire to change. Could God recreate him into a new man? A true hero? Was there even a hero left? He was determined to find out and prove to his cynical heart that Eisley Barrett wasn't like Jane or Vivian or any of the others. That he *could* see clearly now.

He cupped her cheek and wiped at flakes of mud, even pretend ones— anything to study her longer and sort out his sudden fascination with freckles. She'd realize her mistake of dropping her guard soon enough, but not yet. Her baseball cap sat lopsided, and loose strands of her hair caught the faint lights of morning glittering through the trees in flames of red and gold. *Striking.* The cool air grew thick and lodged his breath in a stranglehold. Would her skin taste as minty as she smelled? His attention slid over to her mouth. Her lips lured him, full and round, like the other temptingly curvy parts of her. A blast of heat scorched his throat and he swallowed. *Don't look at her lips. Look at her ridiculous cap. There's a chap.*

Her eyes flickered open, bewitching him with their wonder, humbling with their questions. By slow degrees, her smile faded and a breath of apprehension tinted her countenance. *I won't hurt you.*

He slid his thumb against her cheek before releasing her face. "Do you give a wit about yourself?"

She moved away, dusting at her jeans and jacket, and if his gift of observation was still intact, avoiding eye contact. Which meant his heart rate might not be the only one at a gallop.

"Sure I do, when it matters. Cold water and jeans?" She blew air through her lips and started walking through the water. "That's nothin' a warm fire and a good washing machine won't fix. Otherwise, I'm the queen of self-preservation. When it comes to my family, or my heart, catapults and dragons wouldn't stand a chance."

She wavered, so he jumped to the rescue, steadying her with an arm to her waist. This 'rescue' bit was growing on him and taking up residence. Eisley Barrett needed a rescuer, whether she'd admit it or not, because she was the most trusting person he'd ever met. Possessiveness gripped him with purpose, and his gnarled doubts gave way to something much better. Hope. Even a knight with tarnished armor could still bear a hero's heart, couldn't he?

"I did warn you about my clumsiness, right?"

He tapped the tip of her cap. "We must get you home. Your bum is soaked through."

"My bum?" Eisley repeated, trying to peer over her shoulder. "Oh, *that* bum."

She stepped onto the pebbled beach and leaned down to Mary. "Here you go, Miss Mary. You know what? I think a little bit of daydreaming wouldn't hurt you one bit."

Mary's eyes danced. She snatched the doll and disappeared into the forest without a glance back.

"She's forever getting into trouble, that one." Wes nodded toward the little disappearing figure. "Her mum died about a year ago. It's been difficult, but her dad's a good fellow and she's resilient."

"She's also adorable and her voice is so sweet." Eisley pressed her hand against her chest. "Straight to my heart."

Ah, he knew the feeling.

"Let me see you home." Wes took her arm and steered her to the bridge.

"No way, buddy." She pulled away and placed both hands on her hips. "I sacrificed my lovely, five-year old jeans *and* practically all of my pride to see this spectacular view of Lornegrave Hall and I plan to march my soaking bum up the next hill and do just that." She pointed ahead of them and lifted a playful brow. "Of course, I wouldn't mind company if you want to escort a soggy American." She took off her hat and sunlit strands of hair fell around her face. "With mud on her favorite baseball hat."

"You're going to freeze, Eisley."

She wrinkled up her nose and waved away his concern. "Nah, I'm a country girl, remember?"

Without another thought to his words, she started up the footpath, her easy strides accenting her long legs. Energy lit his pulse. Might this be the most important scene of his life, with a God-appointed costar? He rubbed a palm over his chin, gratitude tightening his throat. He wouldn't miss this take.

"Stop smiling at my muddy bum and come on." She gestured with her arm. "Who knows what other trouble I'll get into? Aren't there crags in England? Can you fall off a crag?"

Her voice drifted ahead, and he ran to catch up with her, each step a little lighter than the one before. Rescue her? No, it was quite possible she'd be the one to rescue him.

"Oh wow, there it is." Eisley relaxed against the rock wall and stared into the distance, assigning the memory a special place. Gray stone emerged from the pale blanket of morning fog, as mysterious as the haunting tales of Julia Ramsden. A few buildings of the same stone scattered along the hillside behind the manor house, all the way to a vine-covered hunting tower. It was ten times better than she thought. She snapped a few pictures with her phone and wondered if four hundred years had smudged Julia's story into the shadows of history.

She took in a deep breath of winter morning. Had Julia ever climbed this hill to breathe in the cool air or watch dawn's sunbeams filter through fingers of mist? What waited to be discovered behind those stone walls?

Birds broke the silence in chipper conversations. One, in particular, chirped with a loud staccato sound, like the high end of a violin string. Wes stood beside her, gaze focused on a horizon of clamoring morning hues painted over hills of layered emerald. A gentle smile parked on those creamy lips like he pondered some humorous thought. Maybe it was an inner chuckle at her poor ballerina skills in the creek. She cringed as the scene skidded back to her mind in humiliating brilliance. But Wes's presence, and a fresh wave of spicy man-scent, wafted a pleasant distraction from her embarrassment.

His friendly conversation, his gentleness, slipped beneath her caution like Pete's hand under the cookie jar lid. And all her grand and glorious spinsterhood self-talk landed at the bottom of the creek with her soggy backside.

Why had he come? Sure, she was hanging with his parents, and he might want to see them too, but didn't he have movie star stuff to do? Far away? And definitely out of smelling-distance?

He caught her staring and raised a brow in question.

She shifted her attention back to Lornegrave, a scratchy heat climbing up her throat. "So...um...what brings you to Derbyshire?"

"I'll travel back to London tomorrow for an audition." He tilted his face to the sky and drew in a deep breath. "But Rose Hill settles me. It affords a peaceful contrast and lovely views."

"It is beautiful. Uncle Joe would love it. The scenery, culture, and history." She hugged her arms tighter around her shoulders. "The rolling hills are a lot like home."

"I should like to see the Blue Ridge Mountains sometime, especially for my research."

She grappled with her smile, but the thought of him with her big and crazy family set it loose. "I'm pretty sure it'd be an adventure, if nothing else."

He lowered next to her, hand inches away. If she moved her pinkie over just a teeny bit, it would touch his. Hands and feet. Her crazy fascination. There was just something about his large hand next to her smaller one. Firm and protective. Tough but gentle. Hands told stories—strong enough to wield a weapon or slam a hammer, yet soft enough to caress the cheek of an infant or trace a woman's face. The tactile memory of his thumb against her cheek, a tender stroke of skin on skin stirred a tremor.

"You think I can't manage your..." He tipped his head. "Is it five or six siblings?"

She held up the appropriate number, if nothing else to move her numb fingers. "Six, but Rachel and Rick are my cousins. They came to live with us after their parents died in a car accident." A trauma which sent Rachel into rebel mode. "They've been with us so long; I just refer to them as my siblings."

"And they all live in Pleasant Gap?"

"All except Brice." Eisley rubbed her arms to warm herself and take the edge off the mention of her brother. Somehow, even his presence in a conversation made her feel inferior. He'd always been the perfect twin. "He has the Midas touch—smart, great at sports, brilliant at managing people. He moved to Charlotte after college and is co-founder of a computer software company there."

"Is Charlotte far from your home?"

"About two hours, but Brice isn't a frequent visitor." Occasional might be pushing it too. "He stays pretty busy in his job."

Silence enfolded the moment, with occasional interruptions by the violin-bird thrown in. Maybe Wes couldn't hear the disappointment in her voice about her twin. She was proud of him, really, but somewhere in the middle of all his perfection, he'd lost sight of his faith and his family—and she'd never quite measured up to him.

She studied Wes again, a bit in awe of the experience. "Do you think it's weird you and I are sitting here in the middle of nowhere talking like we're friends?"

He chuckled and crossed his arms in front of his chest so his jacket pulled taut over his shoulders. "Not at all. In fact, it feels comfortable."

"Yeah." She dropped her volume, talking to herself. "I think I like you even better as a *real* person." Eisley's breathing snagged. *Oh no, no, no. Not a real person.* She couldn't think of him that way. *Real? Attraction? Available?* "You really should have a girlfriend, you know."

"Should I?" He nudged her with his shoulder.

She closed her eyes and smacked her palm to her forehead. Yep, she'd said it out loud. "Sorry, that thought just popped right out."

"Maybe I'm waiting for the right girl."

What little warmth had been hovering in Eisley's legs drained right out of them. "Wise man." She rubbed her arms methodically to keep her heart steady. "I jumped in with both feet and didn't even check for snakes."

"Perhaps I should clarify. *Now* I'm waiting." Sorrow flickered across his face and settled in his stormy eyes. "But I haven't always."

Right. She'd seen the tabloids. A lady's man for sure—and quite the variety. "Did you fall in love with any of them?"

Wes winced and massaged a hand into his chest as if the statement hurt. Ack, there she went again, kicking the filter to the curb. She was clearly an Englishman's worst nightmare.

"Sorry, I shouldn't—"

"No, it's a fair question, isn't it? And another consequence of my choices."

His penitent expression spanned the gap between them and wrung Eisley's heart.

"I could blame a host of things, but they all boil down to pride at the center. After I watched my elder brother die of cancer when I was a teen, I rebelled against everything I'd been taught. Wealth, a sharp wit, and the wrong people fed my pride until I wallowed in choices to shame my parents." He paused, his Adam's apple bobbing from a swallow. "When I started university and my acting talent became clear, the attention fueled my inflated conceit all the more. A lethal combination."

Sounded like her sister Rachel's story, except for the acting bit. Had God changed Wes's heart like he'd done for Rachel? She wasn't the same—except for the wicked sarcastic streak.

"I fancied myself in love once, but the more time separates me from the situation, I realize it was a devastating pairing of arrogance and naiveté. I had the image, she had the connections." He shook his head, his shoulders dropping forward. "We used each other to get what we wanted, and in the end, we both lost."

The poor man looked like he was drowning in his memories.

She threw him a lifeline. "God rescues lost things, you know."

His gaze fixed on hers. "Yes, indeed he does."

"I'm sorry." Eisley touched his arm. "Hindsight can slice as deeply as a harsh word, can't it?" She watched the path of a bird gliding on a breeze across the valley, pain stinging deep. Hateful memories, bad reruns of all the stupid things one does. Yeah, she knew what it felt like to drown in them.

His silence whispered an entreaty to open her heart, his presence caressing her scars and encouraging more trust. She drew in a breath for strength. "I know all about naiveté and arrogance." She forced a bitter laugh. "I *believed* in fairy tales. Thought a guy would love me for me, ya know?"

"As he should."

The confidence in his quick reaction shot a shimmy down her spine. "At twenty-one, I wasn't quite as clear on all the "shoulds" and "dids". I equated passionate kisses with glass slippers. Don't get me wrong, I'm all for passionate kisses."

Without thinking her attention drifted to his lips. They twitched. Heat soared to volcanic proportions in her cheeks. She shifted her gaze back to the view.

Pepper Basham

"But they're all smoke and mirrors if you don't have love. I'm not a halfway person, as evidenced by my grace and poise." She laughed away a little of the former embarrassment. "If I'm gonna fall, I'm gonna fall hard. Marshall was handsome, charming, and we had fun together." Her cold nose began to tingle with the warning of coming tears. "But once Nathan came along and I had to divide my time between Marshall and a newborn, everything changed. The first *incident* happened when Pete was about six months old. Marshall found a commercial break from the 'noose of marriage' in the arms of a college girl."

"*First* incident? There was more than one?"

His compassion melted over her bruised spirit like butter on a hot biscuit. "Yeah, I picked a winner." Her sigh came out as more of whimper. "I wanted my kids to see how important marriage was, to understand it wasn't something you promised for just the good of it, but for all of it. God had forgiven me, over and over again... and as badly as it hurt, couldn't I forgive my husband?"

"You took him back?"

Wes's look of admiration spurned her forward. "I'm an eternal optimist I guess or used to be. He was gone two weeks and crawled back, repentant and broken. Oh, how I wanted to believe he meant it. Things seemed to be working for a while." Eisley massaged the tension in her neck, but nothing erased the memory burned into her mind. "One day, I came home early from work and found him in bed with a woman from my bible study. Another redhead. Younger, cuter, and from what I could see, she had nary a stretch mark on that perfect little body of hers."

Wes released a low moan.

"He left and never tried to return. The next month I found out I was expecting Emily."

Wes's warm fingers slid over hers for a brief embrace. "And all of the hurt hides behind your lovely smile?"

And red-rimmed eyes at present. She flicked a tear off her cheek and worried her bottom lip through an apologetic sniffle. "You asked."

"I did." He gave her fingers another squeeze, a sweet reassurance. "I meant it."

She narrowed her eyes with her smile. "I thought Brits steered clear of personal questions."

"Until the subject becomes interesting enough to ask personal questions."

Interesting? Charm, thy name is Wesley.

She wanted to believe him but couldn't. It didn't make sense. "Why? Why would you care to know anything more about me than the fact I'm not going to steal your parents' money or kill them in their sleep? In two weeks, I'll disappear back into my normal world and you'll return to your glitz, glamour, and hundreds of

68

adoring fans. Why take the time?" She narrowed a look at him. "Unless you're going for some old-fashioned comic relief, because I can give that in spades."

He leaned back and examined her with his thought-stopping gaze. "Perhaps I'm looking for a friend."

"You're some rich and famous British guy. I'm a clumsy Appalachian single mom. It's not exactly the first friendship pairing people expect."

"Others expectations don't concern me." He gave her another measured look. "And at the heart, we're not so different. Both healing from past wounds, both hoping for something with more certainty in the future." His grin teased her. "And if we're honest, both a little curious about true love and all of that nonsense."

She looked away, nowhere close to admitting any curiosity of the sort. "You've been making movies too long, mister. True love nowadays?" She graced him with an exaggerated eye roll. "There are no special effects in the real world, and we've both learned the hard way the rewind button doesn't work."

"Ah, but there are sequels."

"You *are* an optimist." And she liked him better for it. *Daggone it.* She pressed her finger into his shoulder. "Here's the deal. I'll pray God sends you a Kiera Knightly look-alike to blend into your high-profile world and you pray." She sobered. "You pray God helps me accept his possibilities."

He pinched his lips closed in thought. "Here's a better deal. I'll pray God heals your heart and perhaps sends a friend to help you." He tapped the end of her cap. "If you'll push aside the whole actor part of my life and let me practice being that friend?

"You and me? Friends like regular people?" He *had* to be nuts.

"Acting is my job, not who I am." He leaned in and stole her breath like a pro. "I could use the practice, and perhaps you could use the friend?"

Her pulse hammered a 'yes' in Morse code. Her brain screamed 'beam me up, Scotty.'

Wes stood and offered his hand. "Would you be my friend, Eisley Barrett of the Blue Ridge Mountains?"

Her gaze moved from his face, to his hand, and back again. Sincerity? Confidence? A flutter of hope lodged like a football in her throat. *Run Eisley, run.* She swallowed down the lump and slid her cold hand into his warm one. "Friends."

And nothing more.

His touch grabbed her all the way to her heart and hit the panic button. What was the point of self-talk if her body didn't listen to it?

He pulled her up to her feet. "Fantastic. Now let's get you home, my friend, before you freeze."

He started his decent down the path, while Eisley tried to move her numb legs. *Friends?* An emotion kindled inside her, floating just beyond recognition. Wes waited up ahead, crooked grin in place, even the dimple poised in challenge. Somebody needed to slap a disclaimer on that smile—Warning. This *man is dangerous.* Especially for women who are trying their best to steer clear of knights in shining armor.

Chapter Seven

"Eisley, darling, I'm so happy to finally meet you in person." Lizzie Worthing wrapped her slender arms around Eisley's shoulders and pulled her into a hug. "Is all that red hair natural, Luv?"

Eisley repressed a laugh and peered over Lizzie's shoulder at Eleanor, who only shook her head with a 'you gotta love her' smile.

"Every last bit of it."

Lizzie stepped back, hands steadied on Eisley's arms, caramel eyes brightened. "Simply lovely. If I'd had children, I wished for one with red hair. It's so unique." She fluttered her fingers towards the chairs. "I hope you've come with an appetite for adventure."

Eisley kinked a brow. "Are you baiting me?"

Lizzie's tilted lips continued Eisley's playful banter. "Hook, line and sinker."

"She's always been the daring sort, Eisley dear." Eleanor said, the closeness of the two ladies almost palpable. "She's pulled me into many an adventure."

An immediate kinship linked her to Lizzie Worthing, and since they were forty-fifth cousins, or something like that, it was perfectly natural. She was the British equivalent of her baby sister Sophie, plus about thirty years. Glowing golden eyes, dreamy expressions, all housed within a mind wandering from reality to fantasy and framed within a head of sun-kissed hair.

"I must admit I am invigorated by a good scheme."

Eleanor's gaze fastened on her friend. "I believe you've involved Daniel in your most recent plot, haven't you, my friend? With a match or two?"

An undercurrent passed between the ladies, a message Eisley was a little afraid to ask about.

Lizzie's eyes widened in response. She cleared her throat and stared past Eleanor in the doorway. "Speaking of your darling, where is Daniel today?"

"He felt a bit ill this morning, so he's lying in. Wes will collect Eisley in a few hours." Eleanor quirked a mischievous grin. "I'll leave the two of you to your discoveries."

Lizzie's eyes darted from Eleanor's face to Eisley's with enough excitement to send them all on a search for the Lost Ark. "Precisely. Discoveries and the hope for more discoveries. Uncle Joseph will not be disappointed."

The house was enormous. Lizzie spent an entire hour giving her a tour and sprinkling in tidbits of history. Impossibly large rooms with ten-foot, twelve-foot, and sometimes taller ceilings lined with ornate crown molding and windows reaching to the floor. Reminiscent of all those lovely Regency movies Eisley watched after the kids were in bed the house inspired a posture switch. Tall and straight.

With every new room, each centuries-old portrait she passed, questions about her mysterious ancestor singed deeper. Had Julia walked these halls? Which of the bedrooms had been hers? How did she manage to escape the same fate as other Protestants of the time? When and how did she meet her mysterious husband? Uncle Joe waited on the other side of the Atlantic for the truth, and she needed to know the end of this story too. She wanted to solve this. Prove she wouldn't fail at something else.

"Now I bring you to the pinnacle of my discoveries." Lizzie bounced up the narrow stairway like a woman half her age, leaving a chuckle in the air. "I only discovered it three days ago, hidden away behind centuries of rubbish in the attic."

Lizzie was a kindred spirit. From their first contact on an ancestry website, they'd developed a sweet relationship of shared stories and interests in their British-American histories. Chatting with her every week took out the awkwardness of a first meeting, since it seemed to be a simple extension of their six-month-long conversation.

Lizzie pushed open a tiny door at the top of the attic stairs, its old hinges squeaking in protest. "No one's investigated this place for years. Who can say how long these old trunks and boxes collected dust before you alerted me to our family mystery? I even found letters exchanged during the English Civil War." She tossed a look over her shoulder before she disappeared into the pitch darkness of the attic space.

Eisley stopped in mid-climb, hand braced against the wall. English Civil War? Wasn't that in the sixteen hundreds? She crept the rest of the way up the stairs and bent to peek into the dimly lit corridor. The doorway forced her to hunch like a bell ringer and the view sent her imagination reeling into a Nancy Drew book. Chests, bookshelves, papers, and boxes stacked on either side of a curved attic space, barely allowing a thin path through the gray light. Dust swirled in the faint glow of a desk lamp placed on the floor in the middle of the room where Lizzie stood, hand to the hip of her petite tailored pants.

"Come on, then. You traveled across an ocean for this." Lizzie snatched a small box from a bookshelf and plopped onto a blanket draped across the old floor. "I had no idea who Julia Ramsden was until your uncle contacted me—had never heard mention of her name, and now, I've discovered all sorts of intrigues and treasures."

"Should we find a place with better lighting?" Eisley lowered herself onto the blanket beside Lizzie.

Lizzie's grin curled with an impish tweak. "It's all about atmosphere, Luv. The first time you see this, it must be here, where I uncovered it." She placed the box between them and leaned close, the air prickling with as much anticipation as Eisley's thumping heart. "With your help, we're certain to find out even more." Lizzie unhooked the latch to the tin box and kept her eyes fastened on Eisley as she lifted the lid.

"What is it?" Eisley whispered, staring down at the papers tied with red ribbon.

Lizzie kinked a brow. "Letters."

"Letters? From the English Civil War?"

"Even better. And there's more." She pushed the papers to the side and fingered a small, round object which looked like a...

"A picture?"

"Miniature," Lizzie corrected, her hand palming the treasure like a priceless vase. "And in oil so it lasts much longer than other forms of paint." She opened her fist. Inside rested a faint painting of a young woman.

Eisley dared not breathe. It couldn't be, could it?

"Eisley Honora Barrett, meet our ancestor, Julia Ramsden."

Eisley's fingertips trembled as she reached toward the golden frame. Impossible. How on earth could a portrait survive almost five hundred years? Her eyes burned, but not from the swirling dust in the room. "How?"

Lizzie's grin softened with understanding. "Well-packaged, is all I can say. I'm certain we have brilliant people in our family history who thought about such things." Her brows gave another wiggle. "And there are three more trunks I've not investigated yet, as well as another room attached to the back of the attic. I have high hopes for more answers."

Eisley cradled the miniature in her hand and examined the face staring back at her. Ebony locks framed the pale face of a young woman who looked barely sixteen. Her eyes, so blue they appeared purple, knocked a chill from the mid-sixteenth century all the way to Eisley's skin. She was beautiful, but those indigo eyes held sorrow—a weight of grief beyond her youth. Her pink lips turned downward, her chin out, as if she was fulfilling a duty. "How can you know it's her?"

"The letters." Lizzie gestured toward the papers in the box. "One is torn with no signature, but the other is a simple missive from her father regarding the painting of a portrait for her fiancé, Edward Larrimer."

"But they didn't marry—or at least that's what the family story says." Eisley slid her thumb across the glass cover of the miniature, unable to pull her gaze away.

"Precisely, but we're to discover who she *did* marry."

"Her eyes remind me of my mom's and my sister Julia's—the same interesting blue." Eisley's voice barely warbled above a breath, as the face of the woman in her family's stories materialized out of the past. "She's beautiful, but her expression is ...." Eisley looked up.

"Sad." Lizzie finished.

"Because of the broken engagement?"

"Or her father's harshness. His short missive speaks of a forceful personality. No endearments. No requests. Only demands and orders."

Eisley reluctantly handed the miniature back, her gaze riveted to the pages in the box. Surely Lizzie wouldn't just dangle those letters in front of her. Kindred spirits did not leave kindred spirits hanging.

Lizzie placed the painting back in the box and snapped the lid closed. "I'm having dinner with Richard Larrimer this evening. As you know, we Brits remain in our family homes for centuries, and Richard is no exception. We've corresponded through email for the past month and he wishes to meet to discuss our little investigation, but I'm ever hopeful he'll fall madly in love with me." Lizzie sent a flirtatious wiggle through her shoulders. "He's scandalously wealthy, I understand, and if he doesn't propose marriage, I'll return with further information about Edward Larrimer."

"I can feel the romance vibes blowing off you in torrents."

"One never knows," Lizzie steadied her grin. "I wager he'll cock a snoot at me since I haven't the posh pedigree his family possesses, but no matter." She firmed her chin. "What is it you Americans say? A girl can dream."

Eisley burst out laughing with Lizzie's contagious giggle joining in.

"Wes will be here to collect you soon. Take these with you this evening and peruse them for clues." Lizzie pushed the box into Eisley's hands. "The letter is written as if it's giving off hints of some sort, but I can't make it out."

Eisley clutched the box with newfound respect for ring bearers. "You...you'll let me take them?"

"They're part of your family, as well." A doorbell echoed in the distance.

"Could that be Wesley already?" She twisted her wrist to peer at her watch. "Early?" She shrugged and started toward the door. "Father is undergoing an evaluation until tomorrow afternoon, so we must see to as much as we can before his return. Could you come early tomorrow? Perhaps we could search through a few more trunks."

Eisley clutched the box to her chest and rushed to catch up with Lizzie.

"The letter in the box is written in a familiar style to someone named Thomas. I wager he was a friend, a close friend, since the form is in no way romantic. It is a strange letter, and I think your extra set of eyes might be just the thing we need to uncover what it might mean."

Eisley doubled her pace to keep up and managed not to stumble down another flight of stairs. Clues within the letter? A tingle shot from her toes to her nose. Could this adventure get any more breathtaking?

As if God was trying to prove a point, Wes met them in the entranceway, grin spreading to boast a dimple. The song "Someday My Prince Will Come" rose unbidden in her mind. Fantastic. Even her thoughts were treacherous.

"Wesley, dear. So good to see you."

"Lizzie." He leaned forward and placed a kiss to her cheek. "Lovely as usual."

She gave his cheek a little pat. "You dear boy." She sent a glance to Eisley. "Have you had the opportunity to become better acquainted with your parents' guest?"

Wes's playful gaze found Eisley's. Her throat tightened.

"Yes, I believe we are to become great friends."

Lizzie's attention volleyed between them and she seemed a bit happier than the simple conversation warranted. "Friends? Lovely. We can use as much help as we can muster to solve our mysterious family romance. Are you up for the challenge of a good romance?"

Eisley swung her attention to Lizzie, hoping genetic telepathy might advance her plea. Heat scorched her cheeks until she was pretty sure her freckles were smoking. Surely Lizzie didn't realize the double entendre in her question.

Maybe Wes didn't either.

"Help Eisley with romance?" The second dimple flickered into view. "What are friends for?"

Wes steered the car toward his parents' cottage with Eisley nestled in the seat next to him. She'd spent four hours with Lizzie, only four, and he'd arrived at Lizzie's half an hour early just to see her again. He'd promised himself and his mother to allow this possibility with Eisley to unfold with a gentle and patient hand, but he was already fumbling it.

She was a lovely temptation, almost as if God had handcrafted her for him. Who else could have come into his life and shocked his cynical nature with such an accurate dose of compassion and sincerity? He drew in a deep breath and offered a quick prayer for added patience. She needed time. He needed practice.

It was painfully right.

She squeezed the little box in her lap, her wealth of auburn hair pinned back from her face to show off her cheekbones. Her teeth skimmed over the bottom lip of her smile like a little girl with a secret. Hang it all, she was adorable.

"Eventful day?"

"You have no idea." She squeaked out her excitement as if she'd been waiting for him to ask. "It's an amazing mystery, Wes. And Lizzie thinks there's even more to discover. She just needs some sleuthing help."

He liked the sound of his name on her lips. "Does this mystery have anything to do with that little box you're clenching like the ring of power?"

She giggled. "Okay, I'm a little excited."

He lifted his brow and she hung her head in mock shame for half a second.

"*A lot* excited. It has a letter in it and a miniature of Julia Ramsden. Lizzie wonders if the letter holds some clues to more information, but she hasn't figured it out yet."

"What do you think you'll find?"

"I don't know, but who cares? How often does someone find a letter that dates back to the fifteen hundreds?"

"In England?"

She tilted her head in consideration. "Oh yeah, I forgot. Old in America is like newborn in England."

"And the letter—what did it say?"

"I haven't read it." She jolted pencil-straight in her seat, her voice ratcheting up a few notes and gaze locking with his. "I haven't read it?"

Wes stopped the car in the cottage drive, killing the engine and turning to face her. The glow of excitement sparkled in the hazel hues of her eyes.

Her slender fingers trembled as she opened the box and drew out a small miniature. "Julia Ramsden," she whispered with reverence.

"She's lovely."

"Yeah." She rubbed a finger over the glass of the miniature. "I wonder what she was like."

She pulled a ribbon-wrapped bundle from the box and unraveled the yellow-tinged papers so carefully he thought she might never open them. "Okay." She flattened the pages against her knee and peeked up at him. "Do you...um...want to hear what it says?"

The poor bird second-guessed everything about herself. Even his obvious interest. "I don't think I can help you with your discovery of romance unless you give me some clues."

She narrowed her eyes to study him. Would she pick up on the hint? Her lips unhinged in uncertainty, then she snapped her attention back to the letter. "Oh...well, to the letter."

Thomas,

I am trapped and trust no one, save thee. Until my beloved can come to my rescue, I must persevere, God willing. I beseech my heart to arm against bitterness toward Edward. He chose the path of his convictions, as I have chosen mine. Father has secured plans for my departure on the morrow. The pain in his punishment is acute and I must bear it. But how can I? I am to marry the man whose heart is as withered as his skin. Yet I cannot.

Father Martin has won the ear of my father. Pray for God's guidance on my behalf, as my friend according to God's word. My plight is known by Him and none other need know.

I will take my wine at half past ten and soar to the heights of memory, never to return. Thou wilt see me there, my friend, and we can fly together.

Footsteps on the hall....

"That's it?" Eisley turned the page over and scanned its blank back for any further information, but the writing ended rather abruptly.

"Might I see it?"

She offered him the letter, their fingertips brushing during the exchange. Every fiber of his skin attuned to her movements.

"So that must have been when she was under house arrest."

Her bottom lip pouted as she thought, inviting another opportunity for his errant thoughts to consider a taste or nibble of those lips. *Pull your mind from the rubbish bin, Wes.*

"And Lizzie seems to think that Thomas was a friend. Not the guy she ended up marrying."

He read over the letter again. "Or the hideous fellow her father wanted her marry, it seems."

She grimaced her opinion. "But this *one* letter already gives a lot of information. Father Martin is most likely the priest who discovered her secret distribution of the Scriptures, and possibly the same priest who tried to burn her at the stake. Maybe her father was trying to marry her off to the withered guy because her engagement to Edward didn't work out."

"Edward?"

"Edward Lattimer, Julia's former fiancé." Eisley stared at the letter. "He was Catholic and was persuaded by his family to dissolve the relationship, but surely he cared about her, right? My grandma says it must have been a love match, not a betrothal – or at least that's the story in the family. I'd like to believe it was love, at least."

Ah, the eternal optimist still lived – even if she wouldn't admit it. He was relying on that good heart to see beyond the similarities his past held with her ex-husband's. "Trials are a solid measurement for sincerity, are they not?"

"And endurance. I think a lot of people can have sincerity for the short haul, but time weeds out the fakers. Throw in some trials, and it just speeds up the process."

Worry lines formed in her brow, scars from mistreatment. It was unfathomable to imagine any man capable of wounding such a tenderhearted and honest woman. If God allowed him the opportunity to win her, he'd treat her carefully. His trials had taught him well to appreciate his treasures.

"This bit about the wine. It doesn't fit, does it?" He offered her the letter, which she folded methodically and placed back in the box, lost in thought.

"Sounds as though she's setting up a place to meet, doesn't it? A clue."

Wine? Half past ten? The puzzle pieces snapped together. "Has Lizzie examined the wine cellar?"

"The wine—" Her head came up, eyes wide. "Maybe something's hidden there?"

"The only way to know for certain is —"

She snagged his arm, grin sliding from cheek to cheek. "Wanna join us tomorrow? Who knows what might be down there."

Close quarters? Dark spaces? With Eisley? Sounded like a dream come true. His hope collapsed. "I must leave for London tomorrow morning for my audition." He covered her hand with his. "Might I take a rain check for when I return, friend?"

"The more help we have, the more info we're bound to find for Uncle Joe." Her shoulders lifted in an excited scrunch. "Oh, my goodness, I'm tingling with the possibilities."

Possibilities? His thoughts exactly.

Chapter Eight

*E*isley grabbed her Bible and made the same tiptoeing route to the kitchen she took the day before, careful to keep her clumsy feet from stirring the monster-creak on the steps. She pressed against the wall, gaze fixed on the closed bedroom doors, and eased down, step by step. *Success.* Hopefully, Wes would stay sound asleep while she grabbed a coffee, read some Scripture, and tried to wrap her mind around these new interlocking pieces of Julia's story. She didn't have time to fantasize about actors and nonsense. Besides, her bedazzled response to a movie star was perfectly natural. She was simply star struck.

Right?

Her mind spun back to dinner with Wes and his parents the night before then skipped through to their family game of charades that followed like a scene from some Hallmark movie. His boy-next-door appeal slung feel-good vibes like Spidey's webs, tangling her words and thoughts. She craved his easy friendship, even felt a weird kinship to him as if she'd known him for a long time, and not from a film either.

She'd slipped into friend mode with a scary ease yesterday, trusting him with her history, asking him to help her solve the mystery. Haphazard choices reminiscent of her past. She needed him to stay safely in the fictional realm, among the two-dimensional heroes littering her DVD case at home, but he kept emerging as a real-life good guy. Someone her family would love. Someone she could snuggle up by the fire with and....

Good grief, as if....

Her quick call to Uncle Joe, relaying her meeting with Lizzie, was a reward in its own right and firmed another solid hold on her purpose. She could practically see his hazel eyes sparkle with interest as he sat in his recliner and slid his thumb across his chestnut moustache. His voice sounded strong. Alive. No hint of the poison eating away at his body, but it reminded her why she'd come. Her goal did *not* involve Wes Harrison.

She rounded the corner to the kitchen. Time to give cute distractions a nice swift kick in the.... Her feet tripped to a stop and her brain stuttered three seconds behind.

Wes sat at the table reading the newspaper. His black hair stood in adorably confused directions, his lazy green t-shirt hung around his baggy blue sweatpants, and his bare feet stretched out before him, crossed at the ankles. A blitz of pure awareness quaked her body like an eight on the Richter scale. *Oh...bare feet and that smile.* Kryptonite to her suddenly unguarded heart.

"Well, good morning." Wes glanced up, those practically-perfect-in-every-way lips arching with a heart-stopping welcome.

God? This is not funny.

"Did you rest well?"

Eisley stayed by the doorway, fidgeting with the sleeve of her shirt and desperately searching for another grown-up in the room. The blistering warmth coursing through her veins might need a chaperone to ensure safety of all those involved.

She cleared her throat. "I had a lot on my mind."

"Adventure, no doubt?"

She hoped she smiled, maybe, but her body wasn't listening to her brain very well. She gripped the back of the wooden chair for support. "Definitely."

Wes stood and walked over to the counter to retrieve two pieces of toast. "Care to read devotions with me?

She squeezed the chair until her knuckles went numb. The smile she clenched tight dropped into a gaping 'oh'. An absolutely gorgeous, barefoot, British man reading the Bible? *Lord, isn't there something about not being tempted beyond what one can stand?* Her knees protested. Maybe she should sit.

She slid down into the chair. "You...you're reading the Bible?"

One side of his mouth twitched as he nabbed a jar from the refrigerator. "Actually, I pray too."

She shook her head and groaned. "I didn't mean—"

He set the jar on the table, leaned close, and all his wonderful scent made a mad dash for her weak senses. *Cowboy cologne, all spice and leather.*

"I'm a firm believer in miracles, pet. Even for someone with a reprehensible past such as mine."

Eisley caught herself swaying into the scent, into the endearing look on his face, drawn like a fly to the flame. She startled straight up in her chair. *Actor. Actor. Actor.* "I'm sorry. Of course, God changes people. Even without experiences as—" she searched for the right word– "eclectic as yours, I still fight a mean battle with bitterness and anger."

"And fear?" His whispered question somehow brushed like a caress against her cheek.

No use trying to answer. Whimper, maybe, but forming words seemed pretty impossible. *Fear?* The ghosts of her past nipped at her heels like the Baskerville Hound. She never wanted to live through the hurt, shame, anger, and utter self-doubt of a betrayal again. Afraid? She was terrified. But evidently not terrified enough because Wes's closeness, his kindness, opened up a need for *something* sweet. Her face warmed. And maybe a little spicy too.

Ugh. If she were alone she'd slap herself. As it was, she held on to her flimsy smile and prayed he couldn't see through the mask to her ridiculous swoon and man-candy delusions. Star struck? By Wes-lightning. Definitely.

He gestured toward the plate on the table. "I have two pieces of toast, some homemade strawberry jam, and we both came downstairs to read devotions." His ebony brows did the mamba to match her pulse. *Another grin. Daggone it!* "Quite providential, don't you think?"

From the heat waving through her body, she was pretty sure Providence might be the wrong one to blame.

"I'm in Proverbs right now." The words worked their way through her tight throat. "Chapter three, actually. How about you?"

"Proverbs three is perfect. Perhaps we could read from Ephesians tonight. I've been studying it over the past month."

Studying Ephesians? Who was this guy? Maybe this was one of those Wizard of Oz moments and her previous black-and-white life just turned to full color...and smell.

He flipped open his Bible and absently ran a hand through his hair, upsetting his disheveled black mane even more. Eisley wrestled with her smile. *Talk about surreal.*

He met her gaze and tried to pat down his errant hair. "I suppose I could have made myself a little more presentable this morning." A slight hint of pink flickered up the side of his neck into his cheeks.

His boyish vulnerability drew her in. "Are you embarrassed?"

He rolled his eyes, his smile spreading along with the deepening shade of crimson. "I'm an actor, not an alien. I do get embarrassed on occasion, the very human part of me."

"You look...well...you look endearingly disheveled. I'd pay good money to look as adorable as you in the mornings."

He placed his arm on the back of her chair and inclined his head, closer, examining her. "Embarrassed and complimented at the same time. There's a first." His voice, his scent beckoned her toward a headlong plunge into complete and utter lunacy. "Seems you inspire a great many firsts, Eisley Barret."

Oh brother, who wrote that line? Reality doused the daydream. It was an act. Remember... a nice display of his degree in performing arts. She slumped back in her chair and grappled the attraction into obedience, determined to keep her inner conversation away from dimples, eyes, and other tempting options. "There's nothing wrong with early morning spider hair. You should have seen mine this morning."

"Thus, the reasoning behind these cute plaits." He tugged on one of her braids.

I'm not cute and stop smiling at me like that.

"I'm sure you'd prefer Anne of Green Gables to insane-looking frizz woman."

Wes burst out laughing.

"What a pleasant sound to begin the day." Eleanor sashayed into the room and offered a pristine smile, pink robe hugging her petite frame. "The plaits suit you, Eisley." Her attention drifted to Wes. "Darling, did you even consider combing your hair this morning?"

Wes sent Eisley a wink. "I've been told I look endearingly disheveled."

"Oh, is that it, then?" Eleanor poured a cup of coffee and joined them at the table. She surveyed his appearance, her smile softening. "I suppose one could call it that."

"We were just beginning to read a bit of Proverbs together."

"Were you?" Eleanor's gaze danced between them in an unsettling sort of way. "Might I listen as you read?"

"Oh yes." Eisley seized the chaperone idea with her quick reply.

Wes watched her for a few seconds. Maybe those handsome eyes caught her desperation because he drew his attention away before she lost all control of her senses and ran a hand through that endearingly disheveled hair.

"Proverbs three, it is." His honey-coated tones smoothed out the words as he began reading.

Eisley lost all sense of time and place while he read. Within the twenty seconds it took him to croon out the verses, she had envisioned their marriage, honeymoon, and twentieth wedding anniversary. So much for her subdued inner monologue. *Major fail.*

A verse filtered in through her daydream. "Would you read verse five again?"

"I think six goes along with it. *Trust in the Lord with all your heart and lean not on your own understanding. In all your ways acknowledge him, and he will make your paths straight.*"

Trust. Eisley paused a smile. Faith, trust, and a little bit of fairy tale pixie dust? If God was trying to get her attention, He was doing a splendid job. God called her to trust him – even in matters of her hyperventilating heart. "I'm not too sure my heart is very trustworthy." Her lopsided shrug added a visual to her uncertainty.

"If you are trusting God," Eleanor's voice cooed. "He'll guide your heart and you needn't rely on your own understanding, as it says. Yes?"
God would guide her? Like He'd guided her downstairs to Mr. Bare Feet and Sexy Hands? The muscles in her throat pinched down a very big swallow. She was in so much trouble.

Daniel rambled into the kitchen just in time to save her from further introspection.

"Good morning to the lot of you." He walked to Eleanor, tipped up her chin, and touched his lips to hers in an attitude of a *gentle*man. "Good morning, Luv."

The utter tenderness of the distraction pearled all over her longing heart. Daniel Harrison was a class act, and the way he looked at his bride easily encouraged thoughts of happily-ever-after. What would if feel like to have someone cherish her? She tried to dislodge the thought from her head, but the way Daniel's thumb caressed Eleanor's chin dug the ache a little deeper. She was a glutton for punishment. Maybe she and little Mary had more in common than she wanted to admit.

"Would you like to read from..." Wes stopped. He looked from his parents to Eisley, a tender smile softening his eyes. "I thought you would have become acquainted with their affections by now."

"How can anyone become familiar with something as beautiful as that?"

"Surely your parents are affectionate?"

Eisley snorted. "Yeah, my dad's affectionate, but nothing like yours. He lumbers into the kitchen, grabs my mom in his arms, and brands her with a kiss to last her the rest of the day."

"There's an idea." Daniel's eyes took on a dangerous glint. He pulled Eleanor up from the chair and leaned her into a dip, kissing her all the way down and back up to set her on her feet again.

Daniel Harrison," Eleanor shot the name out with a squeak. She balanced against the table and looked at her husband as though he'd transformed into Dracula, smoothing back her hair with a shaky palm.

Eisley grinned like a complete idiot. It was the best scene she'd witnessed in years.

Daniel's step got a bit lighter as he walked to the refrigerator. "Well, that shall do me for the rest of the day."

"I should think so." Eleanor lowered herself back into her chair. "Perhaps an entire week."

Wes leaned by her ear. "Kisses are powerful things."

Every muscle of her body screeched to a stop. The warmth of his cheek brushed hers. His smell already shot like venom to her grand resolve, and now he had to go and mention kissing? As if the smile, feet, and hair thoughts weren't enough? If she turned her head ever so slightly, her lips would be in close proximity to his. Yea, this friend idea wasn't sticking quite as well as she'd hoped. Or maybe it was a little too sticky. Very web-like.

"So, Eisley." Daniel's interruption saved her from doing something really stupid, like giving in to that little turn. "Off to Lizzie's this morning, then back to enjoy a bit more sightseeing with us for the afternoon? Chatsworth House is not fifteen miles away."

The normal workings of her brain started moving again. "Chatsworth? How do I know that name?"

"The Palace of the Peaks, it's called." Daniel answered. "It was featured in a popular movie, wasn't it, Luv?"

"Yes, *Pride and Prejudice* of 2005," Eleanor added. "Have you seen—"

"Are you kidding me?" Eisley slapped her palm against the table. "The place with the sculpture room? My sister Sophie is going to be so jealous."

"I'm to miss two adventures today?" The sad look on Wes's face almost had her believing he meant it. "I'm tempted to blow off the blasted audition."

"Come on." Eisley patted his arm. His strong, muscular arm. "You have an audition? That's amazing. I mean, how fun could sneaking through a pitch-black tunnel be, compared to auditioning for a movie?"

His gaze held hers, disclaimer smile emerging slow and easy. "There's plenty of recent incentive to give it healthy competition."

She was pretty sure she couldn't lean any further back in her chair without tipping over. Competition? Her brain worked to sort out his obvious underlying meaning but stopped right before a possible reference to *her*. Maybe country life? "I'd want to stay in the country too. Not a city girl, obviously." She winked and stood. He *couldn't* be talking about her as an incentive. The idea sent prickly spider tingles crawling through her middle. No way. "And speaking of life, I'm gonna head upstairs and get ready for my day."

He snatched her hand before she could escape, the rough ridges of his palm skating over hers. "Save some exploring for me, will you?"

She slid her hand from his and distanced herself by taking a few backward steps, her heartbeat galloping at full retreat. "I'll do my best." She caught herself from a little stumble. "Have a safe trip, and good luck with your audition."

Eisley spun around and took off up the stairs at the same speed as her pulse. Maybe, just maybe, he'd stay away longer than a day. But for some frightening reason, the thought didn't make her as happy as it ought.

Chapter Nine

*E*isley insisted on walking the three miles to Lornegrave. The solitude gave her time to talk some much-needed sense into her thick skull. Only yesterday, Wes had topped the hill with her, shared little pieces of his painful past, and asked her to be his friend. *Reality check, Eisley.* You shook on friendship...that was all. Besides, she barely knew the guy.

She followed the footpath down the hill toward Lornegrave, scanning the verdant countryside along the way. Gray clouds hung overhead, inviting more fog. A mysterious and obviously unused hunting tower clung to the side of the hill behind the house, almost hidden within a tangle of trees and ivy. She passed below it and grinned at the thought of Julia taking this path. Had she met her mysterious suitor along this road or had Father Martin chased her here to catch her sneaking another copy of the Scriptures to some local peasants? Who had she married? Did she find love in the arms of her second romance? Uncle Joe's novel didn't need all those details, but a deep craving stirred inside Eisley for answers, as if her heart might benefit from them.

She studied the gray sky, cool mist sprinkling her forehead. "Lord, I'm trying to give up this fear, but it's so hard. I don't want to go through that type of hurt again. And I know you use unexpected ways, but don't you think this is a little...crazy?" God coming down to save the world being at the top of the grand and glorious craziness list. "Besides, it's not really you I'm having trouble with." Her confession slowed her pace past the vine-blanketed hunting tower. "Well I guess if I doubt your plans, then it's you I'm having trouble with." She cringed. "You said, you...ahhh!"

One minute she was praying. The next minute she clung to the sides of a hole which devoured half her body. Her ankle gave a twitch of pain but nothing serious. A laugh bubbled through her as she tossed another look to the sky. "Who says you don't have a sense of humor, right? Aren't you the one directing my path, Lord?" Eisley pushed herself out of the waist-deep pit and dusted the dirt from her pants. "Or maybe you're trying to get me to watch where *you're* going?"

She snickered but the idea nicked at her conscience and then her spirit. She'd focused so much on her own fear and mistakes, she'd forgotten to open her eyes to what God wanted for her, just as she'd acted with Marshall. She'd closed off God's voice in her life and only listened to her desires, and now? *God, help me listen. "Trust in the Lord with all your heart and lean not to your own understanding...."* A heavy sigh shook her. What if it *was* God's way?

The idea hadn't occurred to her. Not once. Because it was way too ridiculous. Two very different people in two completely different countries with two polar opposite lives? Nope. That seemed too weird even for him, didn't it?

She shrugged the thought away, weaved around the towering garden wall and knocked on the door to Lornegrave.

"Ah, Eisley, right on time, Luv." Lizzie swept her into another hug and ushered her inside. "Tea? Cakes? Scones?"

The counter boasted a plate overflowing with a variety of delectables, but Eisley ducked her head sheepishly. "I'm okay for now, thanks. Kind of distracted." She bit her lip and started tapping her foot in an attempt to keep her anticipation in check.

"Very well. Tea can wait." Lizzie grabbed her arm and started out of the kitchen. "After you phoned last night with Wesley's brilliant notion about the cellar, it all made perfect sense." She pulled Eisley down the hallway, lifting a backpack off the table as she passed. "Brilliant. Absolutely brilliant. I can't believe I didn't think of it." Lizzie turned another corner in the maze-like house and tossed a glance behind them. "Wesley isn't coming along today?"

"Wesley?" Why would Wesley come along? "He had an audition in London."
Eisley bumped into Lizzie who had screeched to a halt in the middle of the hallway. "Peculiar." Then she resumed her frenzied pace, leaving Eisley lost in the dust of her confusion.

Maybe Lizze had lived alone with her father for a little too long. "What do you mean, *peculiar?*"

"Here." Lizzie stopped at the cellar door and rummaged through her backpack. "One torch for you and one for me. It's incredibly dark and cavernous down here. We mustn't get lost." A burst of cold musty air blew from the reluctant cellar door.

She started down the stairs without another word, darkness enfolding her like a cave. Eisley placed a palm to the cold stucco wall and followed, shallow breaths keeping step with her descent. Gracious sakes, her throat was as dry as an overcooked turkey. Five hundred years? What would they find?

Lizzie bent to clear the low-lying ceiling at the bottom of the stairs. Eisley imitated her. A vast room of darkness stretched as far as the eye could see. The cavernous feeling closed in with a creepy catacombs prickle, raising the hair on Eisley's neck. The pale glow of the flashlight disappeared far ahead of her into the thick pitch of the endless cellar. Yep, this gave off all the right sleuthing vibes, maybe even a few thriller ones too.

"Wow, this place is huge."

Lizzie stepped ahead to the wine racks. "Who knows what is down here? I've only been to this front room to store our wines and never cared to search beyond. The blueprints show the cellar is almost the same size as the house, so it must be enormous."

It may take much longer than two weeks to find anything down here then and she'd return home a big, fat, freckled failure. No way. Not again. She resurrected her inner Sherlock.

"Now the half past ten bit of the letter, yes? Wait... let me get his blasted torch to work." She shook the flashlight and its beam flickered a disco pattern against the earthen walls, causing the shadows to dance along with the beat. "There are ten wine racks housed in this cellar, I believe. Over here—yes, at least ten."

Lizzie flipped a switch and a shallow glow fell upon a line of black shelves pressed on either wall. The single bulb gave more light than their flashlights but not much. Only the closest shelves were visible enough to see rows of dusty bottles. The rest sat like dark sentries framing a narrow walk of earthen floor.

Eisley shuddered. "So, what exactly are we looking for down here? Another letter? Maybe one in a wine bottle or something?"

Lizzie's finger danced in the air, counting each shelf as she passed. "Ten, as I thought." She stepped around the final shelf and slid a hand over the wall behind it. Eisley followed, but the flashlight's golden glow revealed only the dimpled wall.

"Nothing." The pinch of disappointment curbed Lizzie's tone. "I'm not sure what I expected to find, but at least something."

Eisley scanned the row of shelves and replayed the words from the letter. *Take my wine at half past ten. Half past ten?*

She counted back five. "Lizzie, what if it was a twist on the phrase? Maybe half of ten?"

Eisley's beam sliced like a spotlight down the wall over the previous five shelves, the sound of her breath a whisper in the silence, her hope even smaller. Another crazy delusion of hers? What was she thinking? Her beam smoothed passed a dip in the wall and she stopped. "Lizzie?" Eisley brought the light back to the indention, her breath dropping out altogether. "Lizzie!"

"I see it, Luv." Lizzie came to her side and directed the flashlight's rays between the shelves.

A wooden slab door, perhaps three feet tall, wedged in the shadows, tucked in an unusual curve of the wall. The old door's faded brown slabs matched the wall color so well it was easily overlooked, especially without the convenience of electricity, and the angle at which the door fit into the wall obscured it from view. It was a perfect hiding place. Maybe even a secret room?

Lizzie moved first, squeezing between the shelves to the wall. "This most certainly isn't on the blueprints." She crept along the wall until she touched the ringed handle of the door. "A subterranean passageway, I'll wager."

"A...a subterranean passageway?" The words stuck in her tight throat. "Underground?"

Lizzie shoved at the latch. It didn't budge. She took her flashlight and beat against the metal handle until it moved. "We shall see, shan't we? Come, give us a hand."

Eisley rushed forward and pressed against the door. With a clank loud enough to rattle the wine bottles, the door lurched open, sending a screech into the shadows surrounding them. Creepy. Eisley stumbled forward into the murky passage, the scent of soil and stale air another proof of its long-kept secret.

Was it an escape route? Julia's escape route?

Scenes and conversations unwound inside Eisley's imagination, waiting for a keyboard and a touch of fiction to tie it all together. Her ancestor came to life in her mind, her story itching to be written. Oh heavens, this had to go in Uncle Joe's book.

The cool air from the midnight-black passage moved over her skin and took her body heat with it. Nothing but darkness stared back. Her stomach wobbled a response. "Do you think Julia was meeting someone?" Eisley's swallow made an audible click. "Through here?"

Her question hung as thick as the damp air. Lizzie's golden eyes glimmered in the flashlight's beam. "There's but one way to sort it out."

Their eyes met and despite a healthy warning shudder, a grin pried open Eisley's lips. She shoved her fear aside and embraced the adventure. "I'm ready if you are."

"Follow me." Lizzie stepped into the darkness without hesitation.

The narrow tube of shadows snuffed away Eisley's angst, drawing her deeper, further toward the discovery of a lifetime. This was ten times better than anything she'd expected. Did God love her or what? She smiled. Why didn't she recognize that truth more often? It shouldn't take a subterranean passageway and a family mystery to remind her of God's big love.

Darkness enhanced the weird shuffling sound of their steps as the pale light from the cellar faded behind them. The narrow passage only allowed for single file. They crept along, the wisps of breaths and shuffle of feet on dirt their only companions. She hoped.

She looked over her shoulder, but the cellar was too far behind them to give any light. Julia had been here? But why? Sneaking out to deliver Bibles? Fleeing from someone? She paused. Or *to* someone.

Which reminded Eisley....

"Lizzie, what did you mean about me and Wes? You know, when you said it was peculiar that he didn't come today."

"Oh, yes. Well, I might be an old spinster, but I know sparks when I see them." The tunnel caught her voice and smoothed out her tones so the words didn't register as fast as they should. "In fact, I am more aware *because* of my spinsterhood. It's a marvelous diversion, when one has no romance oneself, to meddle, even prophesy, of others' romantic futures. Quite dry down here, isn't it?"

"Romantic futures? Sparks? What *are* you talking about?"

"Your interest in Wesley." The cave turned to the right, the flashlight's beam slicing the darkness ahead like headlights through a moonless night.

"What?" Eisley stumbled as the path took a sudden incline, or maybe because Lizzie's assumptions finally started clicking into place.

"The passageway is in good order so far. I'm surprised it hasn't collapsed by now."

"Interest in Wesley? I...you...he...."

Lizzie craned her neck to look behind her, blinking as if Eisley's protest belonged in a straitjacket. "If you have eyes, a brain, and half a heart you should set your cap at him. He's a fine catch with a good family and in need of a kindhearted woman. Your faith and your happy spirit would be a good match for him, especially since his disappointment. It broke him and changed him for the better."

His disappointment? Broken? Okay, she'd argue about her 'interest' and 'match' options later. "What do you mean?"

"They were both trying to make their way in the acting-world when they met, he and Jane, of course. Her father became Wes's agent, and both of his daughters wanted a part of Wes too."

Knowing what the tabloids said about Wes's previous life as the famous and shameless, she could only imagine what Lizzie meant. She cringed, trying not to bring any visuals to mind with those implications. It was hard to match the guy she'd chatted with over dinner with the playboy painted in the papers.

"I met the ladies at Eleanor's house parties. And I've not met a pair of more fickle or conniving women in all of England. It was clear what they wanted from him." She slowed and turned to look over her shoulder. "But Wes is a better man now, a man worthy of a good woman. That's why he needs someone like you, dear."

"Someone like me?"

"Exactly. You're perfect for him."

Clearly, the woman was going mad. "Whoa there, Lizzie. I'm no match for the likes of Christopher Wesley Harrison. I eat food with my fingers. I only wear clothes that are stain resistant, and possibly flame retardant." Her voice grew a bit louder with each statement to pin her argument into place. "I shop consignment."

Lizzie turned and stared at her with a raised brow. "Shallow arguments are all you have? I'm certain you're cleverer than that, Luv." She shone her flashlight ahead and left Eisley in the wake of guilt and frustration. "Hmm, looks as though we've come to the end of our path."

Eisley lifted her light and her heart sank a little more. A wall of earth blocked their way. Dead end. As blocked as the probable conclusion to Lizzie's ridiculous suggestion.

Lizzie moved forward and shone the light on all sides of the mound. "'Tis sealed closed, I'm afraid." She cushioned her words with a sigh and turned around. "No matter. It is still quite the discovery."

"That's it, I guess." Eisley's head drooped, matching her voice. But why? They'd already discovered more than she'd expected, especially with the letters. This would have been icing on the chocolate-covered cheesecake, but definitely not a deal-breaker. "What could we really expect, Lizzie? A secret room or—"

"Shh." Lizzie raised a palm to quiet Eisley. "First of all, your insecurities keep you in a constant state of doubt which blinds you to God's work in your life. In other words, you're wrong." Her pointed look gnawed an exclamation mark at the end of her sentence. "And secondly, another glance from a fresh perspective might afford a clearer view." Lizzie gestured toward the dead end.

Eisley lowered her beam and the light reflected off the clasp of a small box. Like the one Lizzie gave her yesterday with the miniature and the letters. It lay tilted on the ground, as if thrown at random. Eisley knelt and took the cool metal into her hands. "How did it get here? I wouldn't have noticed it."

"A more careful look is always a wise choice."

Eisley really wanted to ignore the I-told-you-so implication, but she couldn't. It stung with a truth she needed to hear.

Lizzie slid past her and gave her shoulder a gentle pat. "Any good adventure is worth a risk or two, don't you think? Especially the adventures worth a lifetime." Her smile sent all sorts of hidden messages. "We may not have found the end point of our passage, but we made a discovery nonetheless. Let's take it back to the house and see what we've uncovered. This collapsed tunnel business is merely a slight disappointment, and disappointments always inspire my appetite." She started back toward the way they'd come. "I should think tea is in order, wouldn't you agree?"

Talk about incorrigible. Lizzie Worthing held the award. And food as a goal? Yep, they were definitely related. Eisley shrugged off her own deprecation and tried to breathe in some courage. Maybe it was time to start praying for God's way instead of running from her fears. "Excellent idea, *Luv.*"

"Ah, now you sound British, too. I shall peel back the generations in you and draw out the blue blood."

They walked in silence a few minutes before Eisley hazarded a question.

"What happened, Lizzie? With Wes...and his...."

"Suicide."

Eisley's quick intake of breath split the darkness.

"Pitiful, really, and nearly Wesley's undoing. But for his father, he might have followed in Jane's path. Guilt ate at him until he was only a shadow of a man. Blamed himself, he did. It was Wes and the girl's sister who found the body."

A shiver passed over Eisley's skin. More silence gave time to digest the new information. What a price tag to place on poor choices. Guilt? Fear? Yeah, Wes might understand a little better than she thought. Maybe there was much more to him than an actor and a pretty face. "How did Wes recover?"

"Faith and family." Lizzie glanced over her shoulder, eyes amber in the beam. "Daniel stood by Wesley, supported him, and finally led him to God. As far as I know, he's not entered into a relationship with anyone since." Lizzie slipped back through the doorway, her voice tense as she squeezed between the wall and wine rack again. "But for the viper who continues her pursuit of him."

"Vivian?" Eisley pulled the door closed and followed Lizzie up the cellar steps to the main house.

"Hateful woman. Wants what her sister had, I suspect."

"Vivian is Jane's sister?"

And people thought Appalachia held some convoluted stories!

"There are many threads to this history I don't know, Eisley." Lizzie entered the kitchen, holding the door for Eisley to pass. "But of one thing I'm certain. Sparks as bright as Roman candles flew between the two of you yesterday, as they should." Lizzie touched Eisley's cheek, a nudge of sincerity to accompany her words. "I've emailed and phoned you for half a year. I've known Wesley since he was born. You're a beautiful match of strengths and needs. A lovely complement. When I saw you together, all these wonderful points converged at the same place, like—"

"The Bermuda Triangle?"

Lizzie stepped up to the counter in the kitchen. "Blind girl. Open your eyes and stop doubting. Fear will steal something beautiful, if you let it."

Eisley studied the kitchen counter, battling the urge to shove Lizzie's words away, a habit she'd developed to move forward in her life. But she'd closed off God's possibilities by doing it. Her head knew God loved her. Why didn't her heart act like it? Had she really let the hurt from her past distort her view of God's love too? She squeezed her eyes closed and rested her face in her hands.

"I understand fear more than you realize. There *are* reasons why I'm a spinster." She leaned across the counter, pulling Eisley's hand away from her face. "Time and experience have made you wiser." She lifted her brow. "Use that wisdom. Let go of your fear and follow what you've learned to be true. Look where your wisdom and a bit of adventure led you today."

She nudged the box into Eisley's hands and a little hope followed suit. Maybe it was time to start dreaming again.

∞　∞　∞

"Are you going to cast me off like you did to Jane?" Vivian curled up on the lounge in his office, her eyes red and swollen from crying, pink lips trembling. "Get rid of me and Father after all we've done for you, after our patience and support?"

Vivian had barreled into his office in tears, not half an hour after he'd returned from his audition. After he'd buzzed her father, it produced an avalanche of anxiety. He'd not openly discussed relieving Carl from his contract, which in turn would remove Vivian, but the implication laced their discussion. Familiar guilt snaked through Wes.

He shoved his hand through his hair, exhausted. "Vivian, this has nothing to do with Jane or the gratitude I have for you and your father."

"You never loved her, did you? You used her like you're using me. To get to my father. Now you're going to leave for that little Appalachian boiler." She moaned and buried her face in a pillow. "Perhaps my life is as worthless to you as Jane's was."

Wes sat down across from her and braided his fingers together. Her tears and her unpredictable nature added mass to the guilt he thought God had removed. Didn't He promise a clean heart? How could Vivian's presence rake across his faith and steal his confidence. "Your father's business hasn't been my chief concern in a long time, even before Jane died. I have a new vision, one that is certain to disappoint both of you."

Her azure gaze flooded with a fresh swarm of tears. "You're going to sack us? I knew it! Ever since that ginger-headed—"

"Vivian." Just the reference to Eisley pulled up his defenses. He'd not have her slandered. "I plan to discuss things with your father when he returns from Venice and decide on the best course of action for all involved."

Her sobs grew. There was nothing else to be done. He stood and made for the door, but she caught the sleeve of his Oxford and jerked him toward the sofa. He pulled free, stumbling back, but she met him and buried her wet face into his shoulder.

"You can't do this, Wesley. Please. After all this time, after all we've been through together."

He stiffened and attempted to pull away, but her grip tightened, kneading her hands into his back. Heat made a steady climb to his face and carnal descent through his body. His skin responded with rebellious heat and almost suffocated him. *God, help me.* He pushed her away with the effort of prying apart Velcro® and stepped toward the door.

"There is something wrong here." The words chopped between breaths. "Perhaps you should see your doctor."

"I don't need my doctor. I need you to come to your senses." She marched to the window, then swung around.

The disappointed, worried woman evaporated like the click of a switch. It was all a game? He'd been played by his co-conspirator? The picture cleared slowly and with painful clarity. She'd manipulated him for years, and he'd let her. What a fool he'd been.

"What happened to us, Wesley? I've waited for you to move past your grief, regret, your religious experience. I'm through with patience."

"I've finally come to my senses." The edge in his voice caught her attention. "For the first time, I see very clearly, and it's made my decision much easier."

"Has it? You're not the best at decisions, my dear. Should I remind you where you were the night Jane died?" Her ebony brow curled upward. "Or rather, with whom?"

Wes flinched. His gaze flickered down Vivian's body, the two-year-old burden a leaden weight. "I know the damage I caused. The pain." He straightened, fighting against the despair her accusation unearthed. God told him otherwise. He clung to the truth. "There isn't a day I don't hate my betrayal of her."

"Her? I've stood by you these years and you mention *her*?" Vivian crossed to him, eyes narrowed to viperous slits. "You've always been naive. You weren't her only lover, you know. The baby could have belonged to one of the others."

The declaration splashed like alcohol on an open wound. Jane's lovers. Yes, he'd found out about them the month before she died. Punished her by ignoring her pleas of forgiveness, distancing himself while she grieved for their child. *Her* child.

He'd remained faithful to her before then, devoted himself to her alone, especially after the baby. But then Vivian came. His arrogance coupled with his base need had triggered the executioner's accurate swing. Agony spilled through him, consuming the fire and leaving the hiss of shame as thick as the perspiration on his skin. Could his forgiveness have saved her life?

Vivian met him at the door and captured his face between her hands, her voice a whisper. "Why fight so hard, darling? We can drown our hurt within each other. Jane never appreciated you, loved you"—her voice mellowed, inching closer, breath mixing with breath— "as I do."

Eisley's words made a mad dash to his thoughts. *It's all smoke and mirrors without love.*

Love. That's what he wanted. And that's exactly what God promised. He breathed in the freedom and pushed Vivian away. He was not a slave to his sin any longer.

"No more, Vivian." He shook his head to clear it from any of her lingering influence. "I am bound to you no longer. Everything I've done, you've contorted it into some sick game." He slicked back his damp hair with his shaking hand. *God, forgive me.*

She started forward but he swung open the door, separating them by the threshold and nodded to Grace, who had returned to her desk. "You used my past and my guilt to seduce me. And you call it love? You don't know what love is." He leveled his full attention on her, furious at himself, at her. "I cannot change my past. God knows I would, but I *can* change my future. Starting right now."

Her voice dissolved into a whimper. "But if you leave—"

He lifted his hand to silence her. "Do what you will. I can't rescue you. And I'm finished trying." He turned to his secretary. "I'm departing for Derbyshire, Grace. Would you lock up after Ms. Barry leaves?" He faced Vivian. "We won't be seeing her again."

Chapter Ten

Chatsworth House, the Palace of the Peaks, created a dramatic backdrop behind Eisley as she walked toward the gardens, casting a magical promise of pixie dust and princesses. Gilded by the last rays of afternoon light, the edifice rose like a beacon of wealth and creative architecture.

From the magnificent painted hall, with its masterpiece ceiling and immaculate great staircase, to the sculpture gallery of alabaster stone, it detailed a world fit for daydreams and movies. In fact, every room in the house was a work of art, from paintings with scenes of Greek gods to those portraying Christ in his glory, as well as furnishings of varying dates and designs, even a pair of thrones. It was mind-boggling, and she'd taken one hundred and seventy-five pictures to prove it to the folks back home.

Dusky hues filtered through an overhang of trees and the sweet melody of birdsong serenaded her steps up the gravel lane toward the gardens. How could she return to normal life after this? With a solid dose of the Regency magic in her thoughts, along with Lizzie's conversation from the morning, Wes's movie *A Ransomed Gentleman* came to mind. He'd played the part of a reformed scoundrel, charmed into a new life by the love of a woman. It was easily the best acting of his career thus far, probably because he'd lived it.

Snippets of past web searches revealed a long display of model look-alikes on his arm, in his arms. The tabloids had a field day guessing who would end up with him next. And Eisley refused to watch one of his films because the movie trailer showed more skin and hailed more curse words than a football team's locker room.

Even if Lizzie had spinster-induced delusional expectations, she was right. Wes wasn't the same man he used to be. The new Wes seemed to know the power of grace. The reforming hand of love. The beauty of forgiveness.

Forgiveness. A stark reminder of the newest letter she and Lizzie had discovered. No matter how many sermons she'd heard over the past three years, none of them struck the basement of her soul like the forgiveness threaded through

Julia's newest letter, one to the man who had broken their engagement. Its conviction pierced her spirit's bull's-eye and drilled a death blow to the bitterness knotted deep. Forgiveness was the only true remedy. Forgiveness of Marshall. She shuddered and squeezed her eyes closed, her shoulders tense with the last remnants of her fear.

Forgive one another, just as in Christ, God forgave you.

"God." Her voice sounded small in the open air. "I can't do this on my own, but I can with your help." Peace began a sudden course through her, steadying her nerves. "Please help me forgive Marshall." A tight thread around her heart loosened.

And yourself, Beloved.

The whispered words caved her last strip of pride. She wiped a hand across her misty vision, the words souring in her mouth a little. "Okay, Lord. I give." Divine strength and pure will fisted her emotions and wrestled them into submission. Forgiving Marshall might be a lot easier than forgiving herself. She looked up at the gray sky. "Help me trust you to guide my choices and open my heart to your path for me."

Prayer was the first step. But already she felt the welcome ease in her spirit, the comfort of doing things God's way, as contrary to her human nature as it might be. She drew in a deep breath of the crisp evening air and increased her pace down the long pathway between the trees, her feet crunching on the gravel. Maybe she could find a nice guy back home, like a schoolteacher or carpenter—someone who fit into her world.

A path to her left brought her to the goal of her walk, the garden maze. Thumb-shaped bushes lined the footpath to the perfectly squared maze, which spiraled into a labyrinth of hedges leading to an open space in the center, marked by a weeping willow.

Her maze history consisted of the corn maze at her Aunt Tilley's farm, created for Halloween every year. So, this clipped, pruned, and beautifully-crafted maze was a new type of puzzle. And after her excursions in a subterranean passageway, she should be a pro at solving mysteries, right?

She walked through the hedge-arched entryway and immediately had to make a choice between left or right. She chose right. The chilly air rustled by, hushing the leaves inside the ten-foot verges like a whisper. This shouldn't be too hard. A few more turns resulted in a dead end and then another. She growled and doubled back, arriving at the entrance again.

Seriously? No way was she giving up. Dried leaves crunched underfoot as she started again, her walk speeding to a jog through the narrow pathway between the towering bushes. Left, then right. Another dead end? Good heavens, she could see the tree rising above the hedgerows, pointing its crooked branches at her like fingers, but apart from vaulting over the hedges, she couldn't figure out the way.

She twisted around another corner and caught a glimpse of the tree, even a bench underneath, through gaps in leaves. *Aha!* Increasing her pace, she made the next turn and rammed directly into someone. She steadied against him and looked up.

"Wes?"

"I hoped to find you here."

Words straight to a girl's heart. *Find me? Keep me?* She ignored the stupid flutter and studied Mr. Gorgeous. He steadied her with hands to her shoulders and then stepped away, almost cautious. His eyes looked tired, weary even, and his smile faded too quickly.

"Are you okay?"

"Of course."

Big lie.

He shook his head and forked his fingers through his lovely hair, avoiding her gaze. "Mum and Dad told me you were coming to the maze."

"How is your dad feeling?"

"He's still recovering, but better." His lips drooped in a sorrowful sort of way. No light in those eyes, which looked suspiciously red from...crying? Her heart twisted tight. She didn't have a lot of experience with a man who cried. "The tour overtaxed him, but Mother said he is doing much better. He's still having trouble breathing."

Eisley laughed to lighten the mood. "No shocker there. The tour guide said something about seventeen staircases. And I've never seen so many near-naked bodies in all my life. What would you say? Eighty-five percent of the statues in the house are naked or very close to it? That's enough to cause anyone to have trouble breathing."

His grin almost reached his eyes. Well that was progress, but she was hoping for a dimple or two. She waited, and he finally looked up, his expression raw. Vulnerable. She shifted closer.

"Looks like you could use a friend. Just so happens, we shook on it." Her comment drew out a dimple. *Score.* "Do you know how to get to the bench just over this hedge? Maybe we could sit and talk in there. Nobody is around and it seems like a pretty secluded spot."

He tilted his head, studying her, and then took her hand, guiding her around the next turn to the center of the maze. *Hmm. Well, she'd almost made it on her own.* The tree's trunk crooked upward with barren winter limbs weeping downward like an umbrella. They were surrounded by the maze, a little haven. Eisley settled onto the wooden bench, but Wes paced in silence.

"Bad audition?"

He shuffled from one foot to the next and stared up at the sky, hands in his jean's pockets. Poor guy. Whatever it was, it hurt. The pucker of his brow and tension in his jaw proved it was deep. She waited, wind brushing her cheeks and bringing little hints of spice in her direction.

He cleared his throat and finally sat beside her, bending forward so his elbows rested on his knees, his gaze to the ground. "Have you ever felt trapped by your past, defined by it?"

"You know I have."

He shook his head, a sigh pressed out. "Sometimes it seems no matter how much good I do, I can't escape the reputation I left behind."

"Our pasts will always be there, but they don't have to define who we are now." Her declaration pinched into her recent conviction. *Beloved*, he called her. A wave of relief poured over her. "They show us where we've come, and give us hope to believe in something even better."

Exactly. She wasn't doomed to make the same mistake. Not if she focused on God instead of herself.

"Vivian found me and practically forced herself on me." His brow creased into a 'V', probably for Vivian. "I'd hoped to show her kindness, but she's manipulated me with the guilt from the past. I was an idiot. How could I have been so foolish and blind?"

"We're all foolish and blind sometimes, Wes. It's what we do when we learn how to *see* that makes a difference." Eisley's gaze roamed his face. The mere mention of Vivian Barry should have fueled her *look but don't touch* mentality, but Wes's openness, his vulnerability, pricked at her stupid heart.

Christopher Wesley Harrison might be bulletproof, but Wes Harrison could use a friend, maybe even a rescue. Her palms ached to brush back the one loose strand from his hair which fell over his forehead, to lay her head against his shoulder under the haven of this tree and offer her comfort, to.... *Whoa, thoughts. Stop. Right. There.*

She covered his hand with hers, clearly rebelling against the warning signs. "God loves you just the way you are. It's amazing and humbling, and oh so wonderful for those of us who fall flat on our faces most days." She squeezed his hand to punctuate her words. "And he forgives completely. We're the ones who hold on to things. That realization hit me like a linebacker this morning when I read over the new letters we found."

A small smile upset his frown. "You found more?"

She pressed her shoulder into his, trying to draw him away from his darker thoughts. "I can't wait to show you."

He stared down at her hand and gently covered it with his own, allowing silence a moment's place. "Your past is spotless compared to mine. I've made ruthless decisions that altered the courses of other people's lives and left mine in shambles."

"Don't bet your money on my past. You weren't a Christian when you made your choices. I was. I should have known better, but what did I do? Went against my parents' advice, my grandmother's advice, and the sting of my own conscience because I was selfish and listened to my hormones over the Holy Spirit. Now who hurts from my rash decision? Not just me, but my kids and my family." She nudged him again. "The truth still remains, God forgives completely, no strings attached. And our lives aren't in shambles anymore. You can't blame yourself for Jane's choices, any more than I should blame myself for Marshall's."

"Who told you about...?" He rolled his eyes and almost relaxed his expression into a full smile. "Lizzie." Wes's face sobered, his gaze distant and a bit misty. "I should have been with Jane the night she died. I could have stopped her. I was weak."

"But you're not controlled by those things anymore. Remember, you belong to God. He's forgiven you. He gives you strength to do what you couldn't do before. You're a *new* man."

"*I once was blind, but now I see?*" He folded her hand up against his chest and stared into her eyes. His look of tenderness trapped her breath like his palm trapped her fingers. *What was he seeing right now that brought a sparkle to his eyes?* "I am a *new* man."

In that moment, some seal connected her to him with Tupperware suction. She couldn't look away from the search lights in his tempest eyes...and she didn't want to.

"And don't you forget it, buddy," she whispered, since she couldn't really breathe to add volume.

"Can you see me as a new man, Eisley? Not the man I used to be, but who I am right here, right now."

He didn't seem to need a reply but brought her fingers to his lips and exhaled a kiss over them. Her skin absorbed the warmth of his breath with a honey-coated heat to her veins, arousing a sleeping hope. Wes kept his lips pressed against her fingers, eyes closed and grip tight, as if holding on to her mattered. As if *she* mattered. To *him.*

Silence whispered between them, as delicate as the last rays of sunlight streaming through the trees. She lowered her head. Tenderness brought tears of her own. Who was she to someone like him?

I know you by name. You are mine.

The divine prod nudged a reminder. She belonged to God. He loved her. He had a plan. But fear reared its pointy finger, touting a list of failures and comparisons to give hope a swift kick.

All things are possible. The voice, soft and firm, shook through her like a gentle warning. *Warning?* She glanced toward heaven. *He will direct your path.* In the haven of trees and sweet friendship, her fascination began to slide into something more, something wonderful and terrifying, and completely impossible.

Except, just maybe. She shuddered with a different truth. Could the God of impossible things have a happily-ever-after for her?

Chapter Eleven

es stumbled to catch up with Eisley as she forged like a bullet down the path toward Lornegrave. Lizzie's call last night revealed another attic discovery and prompted Eisley to compose a three-page e-mail to her Uncle Joe about her current exploits. She read a few lines of a scene she'd composed for Uncle Joe's benefit and the rich detail of her words exposed a talent Wes wasn't sure Eisley even knew about herself. The animation in her expression was fascinating, each emotion as clear as if engraved in her freckles for all to see. No pretense and absolutely endearing.

His heart squeezed tighter. He'd known beautiful women. It was part of his profession, but Eisley's brand of attractive emanated from a genuinely stunning heart. And another unexpected delight? She remained unaware of how sexy she was—no use of physical ploys to derail his good intentions. The curve of her pink lips, the playful glint in her round jade eyes, her carefree and sincere laughter, the freckles across her collarbone....

So much for the acting degree. He couldn't keep from staring. Chatsworth sent him over the edge, 'round the bend, and barking mad for her. She was everything for which he'd prayed, with a few unexpected charms added in by a loving Father.

He lost all defenses in the gentleness of her expression. Her joy and inner glow opened an addictive interest for more. He couldn't exactly put a name to the feeling, but it started with the scent of attraction and burned much deeper. Soul-deep. He smiled down at the paper in his hand, careful to guard it against the gentle breeze wafting up from the dell. "So, this is one of the letters you found yesterday?"

She slowed her pace to move in step with him. Her hair bounced a rhythm around her face and hung in waves down her back, begging for a sweep of his fingers. The tight hug of her jeans accentuated her curves in a distracting way. He grinned. If she could see what he saw, she'd never doubt herself again. Or perhaps it would frighten her all the way back across the Atlantic. She'd given no indication of affections beyond friendship. Her open personality and generous compassion made it difficult to suss out whether she was attracted to him or merely expressing her usual care. It was a peculiar quandary.

A toss of wind afforded him a double dose of her minty scent, sending him a step closer for another drink. *Sweet.* Oh yes. At the maze, she'd flung aside her apprehension and comforted him as his friend. His dear, sweet, wonderful friend with the hope of so much more. It was too much. Too good. And something he didn't deserve.

"And there's the painting, of course." Her profile turned thoughtful.

"Would the glimmer in your eyes hint at more, pet?"

She liked the endearment. Every time he used it, she'd rake her top teeth over her bottom lip in a pleasantly embarrassed smile. *Ace.*

"You guessed it, handsome. I think Julia might be the artist behind all of the paintings, which makes her story even more interesting." She nodded at the paper he held. "And the letter in your hand is from Edward Lattimer, when he broke off their engagement. There is another from Julia, evidently the one Edward returned with her miniature." She creased her face in disgust. "Julia's is simply beautiful—full of forgiveness—but Edward's is pretty short."

"Hmm." He scanned over the note. "Would you have wanted to waffle on and on about the reasons for breaking an engagement?"

Her quirked lips tugged into a full-blown smile, with a one-shoulder shrug tagged on as an afterthought. "Why not? I waffle on and on about everything else."

He was falling as hard as her creek scene and the teasing glint in her eyes tempted him to nick a kiss out here in the middle of the fog-fingered daylight.

"Would you read the letter out loud while we walk?"

"Aloud? You want me to read the nasty heartbreak letter aloud?"

Her laughter settled in his heart like the perfect line. "It's by a guy, a British guy at that." She looked up at the sky and sighed. "And I just love to hear you read or talk. Either is lovely."

Ah, another weakness? Reading he could do. He cleared his throat and focused on the page in hand, his pace slowing to keep from stumbling down the path.

"Miss Ramsden,

After thoughtful consideration of our differing dispositions and attitudes of mind, I have been persuaded to discontinue our engagement and return the

miniature which thou bestowed unto me. I cannot—nay, will not—bend my
convictions under the weight of my affections.

I am unwilling to recant the principles which claim credence of my soul and
pray that thou wilt become like-minded, for fear of thy life. Julia, these are
oppressive matters. If thou wilt not renounce thy convictions, and I cannot,
then our affections meet an impasse.

May God keep thee safe and awaken thine heart to his truthe.

E. Lattimer

"He started out with the right intentions, but when trials came, he wasn't cut out for it. It hit close to home, you know?" A struggle to maintain composure wrestled across her features. "But then I read Julia's letter, and realized something. Not all guys are that way. Your dad, my dad, you."

She resumed her walk. "I think maybe Julia's forgiveness gave her freedom to open up her heart again, and I want to believe her mysterious husband was that second chance. The letter, or piece of a letter, passed through our family was written to Julia by a man who really loved her." Her gaze came up to his and she worried that distracting lip of hers. "We're only here for two more days before we go to your parents' country house."

"And?"

"I really want to find out who he was."

The morning light filtered over her profile, a golden halo bathing her face and hair. There was longing and hope mingled in her voice. A need to know love was worth the risk. His father had been right again. Eisley needed someone to rescue her, and her heart was ready, even if she didn't believe it.

"You have over a week left in England." One week to change her heart from terrified to his. Patiently? Curious how God might work this one out. "Even if we're not at Rose Hill, we can do research from Harrogate Park. Or drive back over if Lizzie needs you. It's not far. An hour at most. I'll do all I can to see you find your answers, pet."

She tossed him another smile. "You are wonderful." Her lips pinched closed as if she hadn't meant to divulge that particular information. "A simply wonderful friend." She looked ahead, face paled. Hmm, perhaps her sweetness wasn't all indifferent friendliness after all. *Brilliant.*

"And thanks for helping me pick those gifts out for the kids last night. That remote-control dragon was phenomenal, and Nathan will *never* expect it."

"Perhaps I should invest in duct tape for Emily?"

Her laugh bubbled toward him. "Duct tape? Now there's an idea. Do you think it'd work?"

"How determined is she to disrobe?"

"As stubborn as her Mama, I'm afraid." She smacked her hand over her eyes and almost lost her balance. "I...um...mean, she's stubborn like me, not that I'm determined to disrobe." She shook her head. "Ugh. I'm a nightmare." She murmured, a crimson blush sweeping across her face.

He started to object to her self-deprecation when without warning, she slapped her palm against his chest, stopping him in mid-stride. "Watch out. There's a big hole there."

"A hole?"

"It's pretty deep, too." She stepped to the left and nodded directly ahead at a three-foot depression in the ground. "I fell in it yesterday."

"What?" He turned and took hold of her shoulders, turning her to face him.

A quick inventory of her body, and her bewildered expression, didn't indicate any injury. He softened his grip and enjoyed the view. Her navy jacket cinched at her waist brought added attention to all the ways God blessed her genes, and her ginger hair hung in windblown disarray around her shoulders. Fit. Lovely. His palms slid down her arms, tugging her a step closer. He ached to prove to her how wonderful she was, to cherish her, to skim the curve of her jaw with his lips, to taste the soft skin at the juncture of her ear and neck—and though the sweltering heat spiked desire, a deeper burn of protectiveness melded to his soul. A blistering passion to take care of this gift God offered him.

Did she feel it?

Her shallow breaths pulsed in answer. Surprise, and a touch of fear, winkled into her eyes, quieting his impulse. She beat herself up with her failures. Insecurities read a twisted script to her every day and pummeled her with doubts. But there was no denying the attraction. She swayed forward, her gaze flickering to his lips and back to his eyes, almost dazed. Was she even aware of it? His chest expanded with a relieved sigh and then he set to work forming his strategy. He could show her all the reasons why opening her heart was a fantastic idea, starting with a kiss to leave her gobsmacked, but that wasn't what she needed, was it?

She needed to trust herself to make the first move. He relaxed his touch on her shoulders. Give her time, gentleness. The Holy Spirit breathed calm over him. He stepped back. "Were you hurt?"

She blinked out of her stare and took a full ten seconds to answer. He *was* getting to her.

"Um...nope, just clumsy." She made a slow, mesmerized turn and continued her walk to the back-kitchen door of the manor house.

Lizzie answered on the first knock, shadows beneath her pale brown eyes. She ushered them inside, voice crushed in a whisper. "Father arrived from the evaluation in bad spirits last evening. Attempting to get him back on his schedule has proved discouraging. He's attempted to set fire to his room once already, so you're on your own today. The nurse should arrive tomorrow." She gestured toward the counter where another box sat.

"The new letter and painting are there. What a treasure, Eisley dear. Exactly what you've been hoping for, I'd wager."

"I'm sorry, Lizzie. For your father—"

"No worries, dear. Two more weeks, then he'll be removed to a more permanent facility where they can care for him much better than I can. It's beyond me any longer." A crash echoed through the hall followed by a string of profanities. Lizzie released a long-suffering sigh. "He's never been one to control his temper and he's going off about spies again." Her gaze flitted to Wes. "The loft of the barn has some old rubbish you can explore and perhaps check the garden house as well." The sound of shattering glass burst from upstairs followed by a battle monologue. "Hurry along, for there's no knowing what he might do." She took a few steps toward the stairs and turned, a new twinkle in her eyes. "And have fun."

∞ ∞ ∞

Eisley relaxed in her chair, her stomach satisfied by the large supper, but her curiosity still craved more information. The morning's treasure hunt didn't unearth any new findings about Julia Ramdsen. However, it sparked all sorts of feelings about Wes.

She inched a glance over at his profile, studying him while he spoke to his mother. His Superman-wave fell over his forehead, bouncing a bit when he nodded his head. He'd been a sweet friend to her all day, sharing in intimate conversations, teasing or laughing with her. Each glimpse of this 'new' man tripped her deeper into a fall, directly into the intoxicating aroma of romance.

She grimaced. The undeniable connection at Chatsworth coupled with the tender look he'd given her that morning awakened a longing she desperately wanted to ignore but couldn't. She was an idiot.

"So, you discovered another piece of your little puzzle today, did you, my dear?" Daniel folded his hands and leaned forward.

Eisley pulled her rebel gaze from boring a stare into the side of Wes's head. "Actually, Lizzie found it in the attic. Another portrait, which confirms Julia *was* an artist, and possibly the artist for all these paintings we've found so far. Then there was a torn letter, but I haven't had a chance to study it much since we got back from our excursion in the Dales." She propped her chin on her hands. "And then at the bottom of the metal box, we found strips of paper with Scripture written on each in old style. Julia's era." She looked at Mr. and Mrs. H's encouraging faces. "Wanna see them?"

"Of course." Daniel's moustache twitched with his smile. "Gives us a bit of being a part of the adventure, doesn't it?"

"You should have seen her at Lizzie's, scouring the barn for clues." Wes's voice brought her head up. "She was like a little girl at Christmas."

"Or rabid squirrel in autumn." What had she looked like scampering from one place to the next? The endearing twinkle in his eyes stilled her reach for the metal box. Maybe she hadn't looked as rabid-squirrely as she thought.

She shook her head. Daggone that man! Daggone her soft heart! *God, will you help me be brave?* Her fingers trembled as she opened the box. "It's been amazing, the preservation of the paintings and the letters. Who would have thought it possible?"

She drew out the small painting first, another landscape but not of the smooth hills of Derbyshire. Instead, the dangerous and breathtaking edges of cliffs stood as sentries against the crashing waves of the gray sea. A towering castle blended in with the rugged hillside, setting up a foreboding fortress and sending off all sorts of Bronte motifs.

"Neither Lizzie nor Wes could pinpoint where this was taken. See the bottom." She gestured toward the bottom right corner. White words scratched against the canvas. *Eskin Fel – J. Ramsden.* "Any ideas?"

"Northern England has mountains known as Sca Fel and Sca Fel Pike." Eleanor added. "The terrain reminds me of it. Some of my people are from that part of the world and we'd holiday there as children."

"A possible geographic location?" Eisley bit her lip and studied the painting again. "There's a starting place for more research, anyhow. I wonder what she was doing all the way up there and if it had anything to do with her rescuer."

"The accompanying letter might give you a hint, pet."

That nickname Wes used flowed through her like melted chocolate. Sweet…and leaving a wonderful warmth. Oh, how she *loved* chocolate.

Eleanor tapped her lip. "Please, Eisley dear, would you read it to us?"

"Sure, but it's only half a letter." Eisley's throat tightened as she smoothed back the fragile paper and began to read.

Should your sight fail thee or your thoughts waver, do not discount the truthe in thine heart. We have persevered to this point, we shall not fail now. I will not have thy father destroy thy hope nor thy future. There is no place within all Britannia from which I will not rescue thee, my love.

Until I come, find thy courage. Hold fast to hope in Providence. Mine affections do not waver, nor dost mine purpose.

I will come for you.

My heart is in thine hands.

G. MacLeroy

"How beautiful," Eleanor whispered into the reverent silence.

"Sounds to me like he loved her," Eisley said, the careful guard to all her fears slamming against the words on the page. *Oh, to know such a human love as this!*

She read over the elegant calligraphic words again. *My heart is in thine hands.* She breathed in the sweetness of it. What kind of man even feels something like that, let alone writes it? *My heart is in thine hands.* Her pulse ratcheted. "I've seen this handwriting before. That phrase."

"Have you?" Eleanor's posture straightened even more. "In one of the other letters?"

"In *my* letter." Her gaze shot to Eleanor's. "The one passed down from my family. Holy moly, this was Julia's husband. G. MacLeroy." She reread the name twice more. "G.M."

Eisley jerked her backpack from the floor and took out the plastic folder in which she stored her research. "It's him. Wait until you see. We have a name." She giggled with every ounce of giddiness of a little girl at Christmas, Easter, and at least three more holidays. "Look."

She stood and placed the paper on the table near Mr. and Mrs. H. Wes came to stand behind her as she started to read.

155--

Beloved Julia, my friend,

At last, I have liberty to call thee, Julia, though my mind whispered thy name a thousand times before. Three weeks have passed since our parting, yet not one hour without thy memory visiting me. The portrait which thou left in

*my care has found a permanent home by my heart, but it will not satisfy
without the warmth of thy touch or light of thine eyes. I will come soon and
rescue thee.*

*My words cannot rehearse these feelings but know my heart holds affections
my pen cannot explore. I send thee my love, which thou must hold 'til thou
canst hold me in flesh, or I hold thee. To possess thine affections is an honor
second only to God's grace, and a treasure meant for kings. Do not say true
love strikes once and never again. For we have both forgone the romance of
youth and found mature love lingering even amidst sorrow's touch,
impassioned with truthe. My heart is in thy hands.*

G. M-----

"The handwriting is the same." Eleanor's dainty fingers touched the corner
of the paper. "And that phrase?"

"I know." Eisley laughed. "He has a name. Oh wow, I can't wait to tell
Uncle Joe. Can you believe it?"

Wes posed behind her, settling his palm against her shoulder and kindling a
surge of awareness down her spine. "A happy ending in her second chance, you
think?"

His voice vibrated heat at the base of her neck and his mere existence
radiated strength. She'd gripped her independence close just to survive, terrified to
risk giving to another person, but in one simple act of intoxication, she leaned back
against his chest, reveling in the quiet sanctuary his presence slam-dunked her
fears. It lasted less than five seconds before her numb brain registered what her
errant body decided to do, but in those moments Wes's cheek settled against her hair
and his arm tightened with gentle pressure.

It felt like coming home.

And the glimpse into that world jackknifed her doubts like nothing else. She
couldn't run to her job as a distraction right now. No kids to hide behind. No family
appointment to use as an excuse. All those wonderful things in her life kept her
mind from thinking, her heart from hoping for any romance beyond the binding of a
book. Her future lay stark naked and frighteningly vulnerable. And she trembled.
Was she willing to find some courage? The longing ached through her muscles like
the soreness of a ten-mile hike. She wanted a second chance.

"Since we travel to our home in Bakewell day after tomorrow, do you feel
you've discovered enough to appease your uncle's curiosity?"

She stepped out of Wes's arms, her emotions raw. "Oh yes. From everything we've found so far, I'm sure he can plot out his novel without any trouble. I still don't know how she smuggled the Scriptures, but I think this painting gives me a new place to start looking for clues about G. MacLeroy." She picked up the letter and folded it into its careful pattern. "And I've been reminded of the main reason I got caught up in Uncle Joe's research in the first place. Julia's faith. God's work in our family's history started with Julia and threaded down to me and my kids. What a beautifully humbling thought." Her vision blurred a moment. *And a reminder He still worked in her life. He still had a plan.*

Eisley stepped from the kitchen after dinner and walked into the sitting room. Daniel sat on the cozy red couch, a newspaper in hand, the golden glow of the fire flickering across his features. He looked up and a welcome smile crinkled the corners of his eyes. "Finished washing up?"

Eisley nodded, sitting beside him, the tension from her inner drag race lifting. "Wes told me he'd dry the dishes, so I came in here to have a..." She tried one of her new words. "Chin wag with you."

"I fancy myself in the perfect mood for a chin wag."

Adorable man. Probably a picture of Wes in twenty-five years. A gentleman. A caring father. Faithful. Still holding on to a large dose of 'swoony'. "I don't suppose when you offered me a place in your home you thought I'd spend every dinner monologuing about underground passageways and five-hundred-year-old romances, did you?"

"I don't think I imagined with such detail as that, but I suspected you'd bring a great deal of joy."

Suddenly homesick, Eisley snuggled in beside him, like her own dad, and rested her head against his shoulder, hoping wisdom would seep through into her brain. "Joy?" She stared into the fire, red flames surrounded with golds and yellows, licking up through the mouth of the stone fireplace. "You've been so sweet to me. Like I was part of your family."

"Quite right." Daniel patted her hand, his vague response shooting a question mark to her mind. "I am very glad to know you, Eisley Barrett. You have been an answer to an old man's prayers."

Eisley twisted her head to view his profile from the comfort of his shoulder, a smile itching for release. "You prayed for a chatty, clumsy American with a history of making poor personal choices?"

He chuckled. "I prayed God would bring someone with a generous and genuine heart. He always gives more than we ask."

Emotion stole her voice, so she rested her head back on his shoulder and listened to the crackling fire. *More than she asked?* "I was afraid to come here at first. Leave my kids? Possibly come back empty-handed? But I'm so thankful I came. Your family and Lizzie have touched my life in so many ways, and we've fulfilled a wonderful man's dying wish."

"I've learned over these many years of my life that letting go of our fears is difficult, but when we do, God brings more than we imagined possible. We can't grasp what God has for us if our hands are holding to fear, can we? Besides, nothing worth having is without risk. It makes the treasure more precious."

She stared up at him, wondering if he'd jumped inside her head. Her focus drifted back to the fire. "You're right."

"What was it you read yesterday? *Trust in the Lord with all your heart and he shall direct thy path.* You are precious to him, and he holds your heart in his hands, as surely as the words you read in the letter. Yet much more secure."

A tingle burned her eyes. Knowing it and believing it fought a battle of wills. Her head and her heart played a dangerous race of 'chicken' with the Holy Spirit refereeing wisdom here and there. Wasn't this entire romance impossible? "And He'll keep me from falling?"

Daniel tapped her chin. "He'll give you exactly what you need, Luv. What if you *need* to fall?"

He continued without noticing her little intake of breath. "My dear girl, God knows the best goal for you. Who better to trust as your guide, even if you must dodge occasional holes along the way?"

"Yeah...." Eisley sniffled, then replayed Daniel's words. In a slow and steady climb, they congealed into a bing of certainty. Her head shot up. "Mr. H! That's it."

"What?"

"The hunting tower." She smacked her palm over her open mouth and then waved both hands in the air. "It's perfect."

She jumped to her feet and ran to the kitchen, grappling the possibility into words as she slid on the rug in front of the kitchen door. Wes turned at her entrance, towel tossed over his shoulder, plate in hand. How on earth could that look so sexy?

Ahh! She shook the image from her head—okay, dislodged it—but it was sure to visit her later. "Wes, I've figured it out, I think. *Heights of memory?*"

He twisted his brows in question.

"The hunting tower, where I fell in the hole. It's on the same side of the house as the collapsed tunnel?"

He frowned and then he got it. "Of course, it's brilliant."

She squealed and clapped her hands like a caffeinated cheerleader after a touchdown. "I just know there's something else just waiting for us to find. Something special in that tower. I won't sleep a wink."

"Might I join the expedition?"

111

Warmth spilled through her, with a little bit of hope sprinkled in for good measure. "Sure. Who wouldn't want to get involved in a treasure hunt?" And perhaps it was time to find her courage for a second chance.

Chapter Twelve

izzie met them at the door, golden eyes brighter than the day before. "Good morning, d—."

"Lizzie, I think I know where the tunnel leads," Eisley interjected, unable to contain her excitement.

Lizzie shifted a startled gaze between Eisley and Wes. "Yes?"

"The hunting tower. It's on the same side of the house as the tunnel. I mean, it would make sense, right? Two mornings ago, I fell into a hole in the ground up near the tower and in Julia's letter she wrote, "I'll take my wine at half past ten and go to the heights of memory." That's the tallest place on the property."

"Clever, dear." Her expression clouded a moment. "The building is so overgrown with rubbish, I've never thought of it. In fact, I haven't a clue where the door is." She drummed her fingers against her chin, eyebrows almost touching. "I'll collect the older keys and you can see if there's a winner."

"How's your dad?"

Lizzie offered a soft smile. "Well enough and I plan to join the two of you once Father's caregiver arrives."

She disappeared into the house and Eisley rolled back on her heels. She smiled at Wes as they waited in awkward silence and his reassuring grin speared her in all the soft spots his tenderness had awakened. *Trust him, Eisley.*

This was the day she'd find her courage. Maybe. If she didn't die from hyperventilation first.

Lizzie returned, an iron ring of keys in hand. "If you can find the door, perhaps one of these keys will fit. I'll join you when I can." Her brows jiggled an obvious love dance. "Have fun."

She was surrounded by traitors. She shook her head. No, she was surrounded by God's little encouragers, right?

"I can't imagine anything else, dear Lizzie." Wes stepped back so Eisley could pass in front of him toward the tower.

He drew close to her side as they walked. She liked it and ached for a deeper closeness in a barren place she'd closed off after Marshall ripped her heart out and danced on it with another partner. Maybe the yearning burned deeper because of the hurt.

The very presence of the tower, its atmosphere, breathed with enough mystery to distract her inner paranoia. From the faint fog twisting through the trees, revealing and concealing hillsides, to the cool wisp of morning dew, it told its own story of time and age. Broken stone walls camouflaged by green ivy shrouded in fog juxtaposed a physical world of hand-hewn rock and some other mysterious place built in daydreams.

"What if you search one side of the tower, and I take the other," Wes offered, nodding to the tower's right side.

"Good idea." *Just dandy. More time to work on her plan.* She bit her lip and rounded the other side of the tower, fastening her gaze ahead.

She pushed her hands into the tousled mass of vines and began spreading her fingers through it, feeling for the indention of a door or a window. The overgrowth braided into a knotted layer, as protective as the wall underneath and surprisingly symbolic of the tangled net her emotions spun in a fight-or-flight battle. Her palms pierced through the damp vines and slid across the cold stone, wetness soaking into her skin and adding extra chill to the moss-scented air.

Minutes, possibly an hour, passed as she worked in silence, occasionally passing Wes or catching the faint aroma of spice and leather nearby. She'd nearly talked herself into an absurd plan to ask him on a date. Utterly ridiculous, but hey, she had a fabulous track record at ridiculous already, so why not keep up appearances.

Her searching fingers slicked across stone for the hundredth time and then bumped over an edge in the wall. She fell forward, snagged by the twisted branches. *What in the world?* She righted herself and thrust her hand back through the overgrowth again, fingers dancing across the wall until she found the depressed area again and traced its rectangular edge. A doorway?

An adrenaline rush pushed volume into her words. "Wes, I think I found something."

Eisley tried to pry the vines from their possessive hold on the wall, and though they clung like weight gain, her efforts weren't in vain. They loosened.

"What is it?" Wes ran to her side.

Just the thought of him running to her had her grinning like a dope. *Stop it, Eisley.* She needed to convince herself she was content with friendship, just in case he laughed at her crazy date offer.

"I think I found a door." She grabbed his hand and guided it through the vines, leaning with him and his solid body. Good gravy, she was practically spooning the guy! She ignored the immediate fireworks erupting at lightning speed inside her chest. He didn't so much as flinch, despite the fact he could probably feel her heartbeat drumming into his spine. Content with friendship? *Liar, liar! Skin on fire!*

She was crazy. To prove it she rested her cheek against his shoulder for a millisecond. Oh my, how intoxicating. His solid strength pressed against her, encouraging her plot of lunacy.

He shifted and looked down at her, his lovely dimple close enough to taste. She released his hand, stepped back before she reacted to her maddening impulse, and trained her attention on the tunnel they'd made through the overgrowth. "Oh look, there's a keyhole."

Wes fumbled for the keys while Eisley held back the vines. The first two keys were too small. The third fit but wouldn't turn. The fourth slid into the hole, and with effort, eventually clicked under Wes's determination.

They exchanged a wide-eyed stare and then looked into the darkness of the doorway. "Mind your head." Wes felt it too, the need to whisper.

How long had it been since human feet violated the space within these walls? Decades? Centuries? A shiver moved her closer to him. He slipped his hand around hers, as if it was the most natural thing in the world, and tugged her behind him through the doorway into a dark corridor. Yeah, there was pretty much nothing natural about her circumstances at present. She was walking through a five-hundred-year-old passageway, *holding Christopher Wesley Harrison's hand.*

"Did you pack a torch in your rucksack, pet?"

Rucksack? Torch? The close quarters were one thing, the darkness was another, but his scent chasing her around the passage and the croon of his bass voice had her stomach crunched in a continual Pilates hold. Maybe she should just give up and let that cowboy cologne catch her. "Oh flashlight. Right."

She reluctantly released his hand and swung her backpack around to find her light. With the flip of a switch, a faint golden glow cast a haze into the circular room, giving hints of a fireplace, a simple wooden table with two chairs, and a large chest near another door across the room. They'd entered Sleeping Beauty's tower – everything powdered with a layer of dust and waiting for a spell-breaker. This was single-handedly the coolest moment of her life.

The drifting beam of light landed on the round-topped chest, so they followed the glow.

Wes leaned down and ran his hand across the top of the chest. "It looks to be iron."

"And pretty stinkin' old."

His grin curled crooked. "Quite." He finagled the hook of the chest with those magical hands of his and, after a snap, lifted the lid.

"Books?" Wes pulled out a red-covered one and blew the dust off, a thin wisp floating through the flashlight's glow. "Robinson Crusoe. A first edition, I believe." His gaze met hers over the book binding. "Certainly, something one doesn't see every day."

"That tells us someone's been in here within the past few hundred years then, huh?" Eisley peeked into the chest, her arm brushing his.

He nudged her shoulder and offered a boyish wink. "Care to see what else awaits?"

She smiled her reply and without hesitation, he grasped her hand again and opened the other door. Its grating creak announced its age. A stone stairway twisted around the curve of the tower leading to...the heights of memory? Only one way to find out.

As they moved up the stairs, her innards did the shuffle right along with her pulse. She experimented with a little boldness, braiding her fingers through his instead of palm to palm. He didn't jerk his hand away, which was a good sign, and the touch gripped with more security. Certain. He even squeezed her hand to add a note of confidence.

She held her breath. *Lord, I know this seems small in the grand scheme of things, but would you give me a clear sign of what to do?*

A narrow metal door with a latch from the dawn of time topped the stairs. Wes released her hand and worked to turn the door handle, his voice tense from strain. "This is remarkable. I imagine you know a bit of information about the history of Lornegrave, then?"

"Lizzie said this house fell into disrepair until the end of the eighteenth century, when Michael Richard Worthing inherited it from his grandmother Moriah Ramsden." She pressed her back against the door and watched him. A dark lock loosed from the others and dripped forward as he worked on his knees, shadowed chin tight with focus. Could a guy like him care about a girl like her? "I can't believe we're the ones who get to discover all this."

He looked up at her through hooded lids, long lashes framing those piercing eyes. "There's no one I'd rather share it with, pet."

Her palms pressed to her chest. "Words straight to a girl's heart, handsome."

His brow angled a half-inch, and he stared long enough to thicken the air around her with a heat wave in December. "As I recall, the way to your heart is chocolate and Sinatra."

Evidently a British accent and spicy cologne work too. She dove deep for a scrap of courage. "Wes, um...you like the country, don't you?"

He went back to work on the door. "Of course."

"And its simplicity and sometimes quirky charm?"

He gripped the latch tighter, his voice pinched with concentrated strength. "Yes."

"And country people can be pleasant and...um...attractive, can't they?"

He tilted a brow along with his head, eyes dark and piercing. "Without a doubt."

Her throat went dry.

"Well, what would you think of—" Something clicked followed by a pop and the door gave way. Eisley fell back, flashlight flying, and landed on her backside in the middle of a window-lit room.

Wes was at her side, kneeling and sliding his palms down her arms. "Are you alright?"

She ignored the flash of embarrassment as he helped her to a stand. "Yeah, I landed on my softest spot."

His gaze did a shimmy over her body, leaving a few more flashes in its wake. "You are certain—"

A sudden *boom* cut off his words and the door from the stairway slammed closed.

"The door!" She ran to it, taking the ring handle into her hands and pulling. "Uh-oh. I think it's locked."

"Let me have a go."

She stepped aside, her stomach knotting, a sudden fear crippling her thirst for adventure. Alone? With Wes?

After a few attempts, Wesley confirmed Eisley's fears. "It appears you're right. We are locked in."

"Do you have your phone? I left mine charging back at your house."

Her hope went the way of his shaking head. "Mine is home as well."

"What do we do now?"

"We wait." His dimple emerged like a challenge.

Trapped? She didn't have an escape in case her crush-confession turned one-sided. Which seemed most likely. In fact, she literally fell on her bum during the first attempt to open up to him.

She turned toward her prison room. "Well, I guess while we're here, we should look around, right?" *While I work up a new dose of courage.*

Three windows allowed more visibility than the windowless room below, but there wasn't much to see. Dust cast a hazy glow into the gray-gold rays of morning light filtering in through the vine-draped windows. A few sconces lined the walls—one cross-shaped and three ovals—a bookshelf, and the remains of an old bed.

Wes checked the door across the room, bringing in a blast of chilly wind. "It's the balcony and overgrown with vines like everything else." He stepped out and looked up at the tower wall, pushing back the snatching ivy. "It doesn't seem right. The tower's taller than this, but there isn't another doorway to lead higher?"

He closed the door, retrieved her errant flashlight from the floor, and handed it back to her.

"Thanks." She swept the room another glance. "Do you think there's a secret door or something?"

"Where would it be?" Both hands rested on his hips, his steeling gaze taking inventory of the room. His stance drew attention to the lean sweep of his legs, tapered waist, and the firm chest she'd so deliciously leaned against last night. *Out. Of. Her. League.* But she'd never been good at baseball.

He caught her staring and raised a brow along with a corner of his mouth. Nope, she didn't have answers yet, but she was working on it. She jerked her attention to the walls, staring at the sconces as if her life depended on them. The cross-shaped one caught her attention, different from the other three in the room. "Well, sometimes if you turn a lever, it will open a secret door."

"Did you get that notion from Indiana Jones?"

She didn't have to turn around to hear the smile in his question. "Actually, I was thinking more along the lines of Scooby Doo, but Indiana Jones works too." She lobbed a grin over her shrug.

Double dimples rewarded her. Yep, she could get used to a side of that with breakfast every morning. "Sorry, I don't have the magic of animation at my fingertips today. Or a talking dog."

Eisley already had the cold metal of the sconce in her grip. "You're hilarious. Are you sure your ancestors weren't from the jester line?" The sconce loosened under her hold, inflaming her determination. A secret door would be the culmination of all her amateur sleuthing.

She gave the metal a little twist. It shifted and then shot through the air like a bullet, zooming an inch from Wes's head and imbedding into the bookshelf across the room.

Wes ducked just in time.

"Goodness, Wes." Eisley ran to him. "I'm so sorry." Without thinking, she took his face in her hands and attempted to scan every hair for possible scalping evidence. "I guess my Scooby Doo vibes aren't working today. I almost decapitated your beautiful head."

His eyes lit with an interesting glow and if her romance radar worked, she'd say attraction. He covered her hands with his, sandwiching her palms against his cheeks and rendering her absolutely frozen in place. His thought-numbing stare produced an electric current spilling like hot java on her nerve endings.

"I know that was the habit of the sixteenth century, pet, but let's not regress, shall we?" His voice swooped low taking her breath with it. "I surrender."

Oh, heaven and all its angels! His lips drew temptingly close and she couldn't quite pull her attention away from them as fast as she needed. *What would kissing friends be like?*

"Um…you'd better surrender. I'm pretty dangerous." She shuddered through quake-like tingles, but otherwise didn't move. Or couldn't move. She wasn't quite sure which one. "Aren't you afraid?"

He tilted his head and searched her gaze with tenderness enough to drag every secret in her heart she clamored to contain. *Time to find her courage?* From the fear tickling up her dry throat, she was pretty sure her courage was stuck on the other side of the slammed door.

Chapter Thirteen

*W*es felt like a cat locked in a room with a nervous canary. The heat simmering beneath his skin bordered on predatory, so the description might be appropriate. When Eisley had taken his face in her hands, her concern and close proximity unraveled his discipline like little else. An odd combination of desire and some unexpected bond merged deep into his spirit, pulling him further into an intoxication to which he'd happily indulge. He wanted her. In a way, he'd never wanted anyone. In every way. From the sweep of her ginger waves to the heel of her bright yellow wellies, he'd never been more certain in all his life. His *new* life. There was no going back.

"Why are *you* afraid?"

"Afraid?" Her eyes grew wide and she sent a glance to the closed door as if for escape. "Wh...why am I afraid?"

Her hands slipped from his hold. At first, he thought she might try to retreat as she'd done before, but surprisingly she didn't go far. Her palms settled on the front of his jacket, fingers fidgeting with his buttons, gaze fastened on her task.

The simplicity of relaxing his pursuit somehow unknotted her fear in little stages– leaning against him last night, her head touching his shoulder this morning, her fingers threaded through his on the stairs, and now, keeping close to him and spiking his internal temperature to volatile proportions. *Breathe slowly, in and out. And keep your head, mate. Her heart and yours are worth it.*

Her gaze flickered to his and she nibbled her bottom lip. "Um...I asked you a question first."

He raised a brow, sending a signal he could be as stubborn. "I asked you a question second."

Her hopeful expression plummeted into a crinkled-nosed frown. "Humph!" A deep sigh, as if pulled from her soul, blew out a long whiff of the chocolate granola she'd eaten for breakfast. "I'm...I'm not good with this kind of thing." Her attention went back to his buttons. "You know, attraction and interest and infatuations that

120

reach Disney proportions? I'm much better with fiction and no touches or smells, so I..." Color flooded her cheeks and she leveled him with a serious expression. "Okay, look. Jerks, I can handle. They're predictable and safe. No risks. I learned about them the hard way." She lifted an animated finger, as if pushing a stubborn button in midair. "But you?" Her voice quieted into a whimper, almost as pleading as the look in her eyes. "You're not a jerk."

Poor beautiful bird. "And that is frightening?"

She steadied her expression, trying to regain some fight, but the hint of a smile was counterproductive. "Exactly. You're charming, handsome, gentle, and...and." She released a helpless groan. "And incredibly romantic." Her gaze roamed his face with such wonder it smoothed like a caress. "Did I say handsome already?"

He nodded, biting his lips to steady them.

"How about charming?"

"First one."

"Oh." She drew her brows together and looked down at his buttons again, obviously having a little inner war with herself.

Such vulnerability. Such honesty. For him? He couldn't keep the smile from forming and placed his heart in her fidgeting hands without one more hesitation.

"This...um new man gig. You're doing a great job at it. I want to believe you are exactly who you say you are. But all the hurt with Marshall—" Her voice broke and she drew a step back, dropping her hold on his buttons. "I don't even know how to believe what I see anymore." Her words ended and then she drew in a deep breath. When she looked up again, tears floated in the golden-green of her eyes. He closed the gap with another step. Her bottom lip quivered and he nearly drew her into his arms on the spot. *Let her guide you.*

She shifted another step back and cleared her throat. "For someone who's trying to keep her heart safe, you're a knight and a nightmare all wrapped into one."

A cloud of silence filled the space between them. He took a step closer to her. She slid another foot away.

"There you go, complimenting and insulting me all at once." He dipped his fingers into his jacket and offered her his handkerchief, closing the gap between them once again. "Isn't faith being certain of what we can't see? Trusting in something greater? Having hope for more?"

Eisley took the offered handkerchief. "Oh, I'm not *complaining* about what I see. Are you kidding?" Her gaze swept over him with such appreciation he almost groaned with the need to reward her. "But...but that's just the thing. I've started to care about you. Not just the sweep-me-off-my-feet infatuation, but something real. I know it's crazy. You're *you.* I'm...just *me,* and we've only known each other a week, so well—" She fisted the handkerchief and held it against her chest, sniffling. "What am I doing? I knew I'd screw this up." She pressed the handkerchief in his hands and stepped back, bumping against the stone wall. "And I'm trapped," she whispered, more to herself than him, and sent another frantic look toward the closed door. "Look, we shook on friends, and that's fine—"

"Eisley." He tightened the gap with another step and swept a rebel tear from her cheek. "I'm falling in love with you."

"Somehow, I've trip-wired my brain to see things that weren't there and now I—" She stared up at him, eyes as wide as that lovely mouth of hers. "What?"

He caught her hand and brought it to his lips, watching disbelief move across her features. "Friendship is the beginning of any worthwhile romance, but I want so much more, pet." The pulse at her wrist escalated against another touch of his lips. He allowed his gaze to roam her body to emphasize his words. "And I like everything I see, just the way you are."

She blinked a few times and then a hint of fire lit her narrowed eyes. "That's not funny."

"I would not play sport with your heart." He held to her hand, though she tried to pull it away. "You're beautiful. Inside and out. And the more I know you, the more I'm in awe of how perfect you are for me."

"Perfect for you? Oxygen levels are definitely low in this place."

"I'm quite lucid, pet."

She looked up, face contorted into adorable confusion. "But...but I'm not looking for some temporary fling. I'm not that type of girl."

"I'm not that sort of man." His words barely reached a whisper. "Not anymore. And temporary is the last thought I have in my mind." He slid another palm up to frame her face, watching the morning light wave over her features as hope and doubt vied for a victor. "You've awakened my heart as no one ever could. I can't go back to a life without you in it."

Her teeth snagged her bottom lip from another quiver and she snatched back the handkerchief. "Is that a line from a movie?"

He pushed a ginger tendril from her damp cheek. "This isn't pretend."

"But easily the best date offer I've *ever* had." She raised a timid palm to his cheek. He leaned into her touch. Soft and warm. Mint lingered in the air. He turned to kiss her palm and her quick intake of breath encouraged him to chase a few kisses up to her wrist.

"But...but how can this possibly work?" The worry crinkle formed between her brows again. "We live an ocean apart."

His thumb slid a curve from her cheek to the corner of her mouth, prompting a smile. Her eyes swooped closed, face turned upward in trust. "I believe there is a verse in the Song of Solomon which says, *many waters cannot quench love.*"

Her eyes flashed open and her breath eased out a long sigh, sending a whiff of chocolate with it.

"Poetic and perfectly placed?" Her free hand slid up his chest to hook on his lapel, gaze studying his mouth, focused and a bit diverting. "No wonder you can write lips...er...scripts."

He would have smiled at her misnomer if her nearness and solid grip on his jacket hadn't sent his thoughts into predatory territory. "Oh, pet." He breathed in her closeness, her heat. "If you could see what I see—"

One second, he was trying to express his admiration and the next her hold tightened on his collar, drawing him the short distance to the object of his previous distractions. Her mouth. Soft, inviting, and shocking his system with the potency of a perfect match. Gone was her uncertainty, as her lips explored his. He delved in with the same enthusiasm, tasting a rare combination of mint, chocolate, and Eisley. Quite Christmasy –and he loved Christmas.

She released a satisfied moan and ran her hands up his arms to link about his neck, offering fully as she'd said she'd do. *Trusting him.* A fierce protectiveness tempered desire with a deeper burn, not enough to quiet the flames licking the inside of his chest or shooting predaceous thoughts through his head, but enough to garner sensible control. Her mouth proved the best discovery in the entire tower. Pliant, curious, and delicious. A delicacy to last a lifetime.

"Whoa." She pulled back with a little stumble, hand to her chest. "I didn't mean to—" Her breaths pulsed in shallow puffs. "I'm... I'm...um...not quite sure what happened just then."

He tightened his hold against her waist. "I am."

He drew her lips back to his, lost in her scent and taste, warmth shuddering through him with a sweet sense of *home.* They stumbled together, all of those soft curves trapped against him and the unyielding wall. Two years of waiting? No, he'd been waiting a lifetime for this. His palms itched to explore her body, but he shoved the urge aside and threaded his hands under her wealth of hair instead. Tilting her head, he deepened the kiss until another sweet moan escaped her. Her hands clenched and unclenched his shoulders, massaging him deeper into the kiss, until her fingers moved to entangle in his hair.

She kissed with as much commitment as she did everything else. Fully. And he didn't harbor one complaint. He tasted her cheekbone and brushed a few kisses against her hairline before returning to her chocolate-flavored lips.

"Wesley? Eisley? Are you there?" Lizzie's voice drifted up through the stairwell just beyond the locked door.

He drew back only enough to feel her mouth stretch into a smile against his. *Lizzie who?*

The door shook with a clank. "Christopher Wesley? Eisley?"

Eisley unwound her fingers from his hair as her lips grazed the edge of his jaw in sweet benediction. "I personally recant every ugly word I've ever said about happily-ever-after."

He tipped her chin with his forefinger. "That's smashing, because I couldn't make it happen without you." His thumb skimmed over her swollen lips and then he leaned in to take another taste. She encouraged him to linger. He happily obeyed.

His body pulsed with awareness of every piece of her pressed against him, supple and warm, and perfectly fitted. Yes, it might be wise to proceed with caution and a great deal of prayer. He breathed out the inner predator and touched his forehead against hers. "Eisley Barrett, you are one remarkable woman."

"I'm certainly one astonished woman." She exhaled. "Oh wow, I'm numb from the brain down." She leaned her head back against the wall to expose the pale skin of her neck. He kissed the spot below her earlobe, just as he'd wanted to do. "I lied." She drew in a quick breath. "I'm not numb." Then without warning, she flinched and looked down at the bookcase. "Wes, do you feel that?"

He nuzzled her neck, saturating his lungs with mint and chocolate. "In all the right places, pet."

"Oh, my goodness." She grabbed the front of his jacket again and pulled him flush against her, tilting her head for his better access. Suddenly, she straightened. "No, wait. Really. There's air coming from this spot in the wall."

"Wesley?" Lizzie's voice broke in again, a bit more frantic. "Are you in there? Are you alright?"

He groaned and buried a kiss into Eisley's hair before turning toward the door. "We're locked in."

"Well, *there* you are." Lizzie's voice muffled from the other side. "Did you see the books downstairs? I'm over the moon. There's a second edition *Pride and Prejudice* among them. Come now, how do we open this door?"

"Lizzie, turn the latch." He grabbed the door ring and pulled.

A resounding click ushered through the room and Lizzie bustled in, black hat in place, and hands flapping a rhythm of excitement. "This is too fantastic to believe. A trunk filled with dozens of antique books. Old furnishings. It's a treasure trove."

"It's certainly been an amazing morning." Wes caught Eisley's gaze from her bent position by the bookshelf and the embers in his body lit to flame. Her cheeks glowed from their previous and heavenly diversion. Perhaps he should shove Lizzie out and lock them back in for a bit longer.

"Well, it's a mercy I came to collect you. What would have happened if you had been locked up here without..." Lizzie's voice trailed off and Wes snapped his attention away from Eisley.

She looked from Wes to Eisley with hawk-like acuity. "Ah, I have an inkling more discoveries than antique books were made this morning." She offered an exaggerated sigh. "The two of you shall be worthless now. Frightfully romantic, though. Inside a five-hundred-year-old tower. What will Eleanor think?" She slapped her hands together. "I say it's about time."

Wes laughed, heat spreading into his face at her obvious knowledge. "Lizzie, the way you talk, we've been struggling for years, instead of a week."

Lizzie tilted her chin up and huffed, examining them both as if they were specimens under glass. "Struggling for years? It may describe you more than you realize. Perhaps being prepared for this time?" She turned toward the door, her gaze growing distant. "For some people, it only takes a moment and if you wait you may never have another opportunity. Seize the moment." She drew in a long breath and smiled, hand on the door. "As I said, it's about time."

$$\infty \quad \infty \quad \infty$$

Eisley pulled her attention away from Wes's smile and back to the bookshelf. Every hair on her arms tingled. Her legs wobbled from her trip to heaven and back, and her thoughts moved as if weights were attached to each one. She was drowning in pixie dust and daydreams, except she wasn't dreaming. She slid her tongue across her numb lips, reliving each moment in body-warming detail.

One minute he was whispering sweet somethings near her ear and the next minute she'd sprung to the attack, taking his mouth and half his face with her. *Hot Mama!* And boy, was she. Oxygen levels definitely dropped to an all-time low, which might explain some of her behavior.

She slid her glance to him and caught him staring, without paying one bit of attention to Lizzie's happy spiel about the books downstairs. A dimple dipped with his smile and her body splashed with a fresh wave of heat. Okay, men did strange things in five-hundred-year-old towers, probably.

It was a new experience for her.
And once they stepped out of this magical wonderland and oxygen became abundant, would it shock him back to his senses? Hope squeezed against worry. Gorgeous, sweet, and senseless worked for her.

"Eisley, what are you doing?"

Lizzie's question grounded her, and she recapped her reasons for staying at the wall, besides the desire for an instant replay of two minutes ago. She turned back to the bookshelf and another rush of stale air touched her face.

Air. Coming from behind the bookshelf. Right.

"I think I've found something." She lifted her palm to the juncture of the wall and bookshelf, at the place the sconce embedded.

Wes brought the full enticing aroma of spice with him to her side and her brain spiraled right back into daydream, Song of Solomon mode. "Um...feel right here."

"Another discovery, pet?" He ran a palm over the crease and a grin perked. "Let me try to move this shelf." Those broad shoulders took the brunt of impact against the shelf, but in only a few shoves and with a little help from Eisley, the shelf slid away to reveal another curving stone stairway.

"I say," Lizzie breathed, her hand covering her mouth.

Eisley's palms came up and she laughed. "Okay, that's it. My life has to officially end right now. What can possibly top this day?"

"I wouldn't give up just yet." Wesley offered his hand, his gaze sending a dangerous flicker down her body.

"As I thought. Positively useless." Lizzie stepped past them and through the doorway, shaking her head and making a poor attempt at holding her smile in check. "Come along when you can. I have no interest to observe any treasure hunts between the two of you."

Eisley took Wes's hand and followed. The stairs, much narrower than before, disappeared into darkness above them. Lizzie flipped a switch and a beam of light from her flashlight slid through the pitch blackness. Eisley brought out her light to join Lizzie's and their twin beams brought a small doorway into view at the top of the stairs.

Maybe it was just her imagination, but memories crowded Eisley as she ascended the stairway. Memories that weren't hers. Thoughts of a young girl rushing through the subterranean tunnel, candle in hand, as angry voices pursued her through the shadows. Fantasies of her dropping to her knees at the base of these uneven stairs, her breath puffing against the candle's flame while she frantically searched for a letter or a rescuer....

Or...just maybe...

All these wonky feelings were due to the side effects of *post romantic kiss disorder.*

Through the small doorway, Lizzie's flashlight cast a cheerful glow into the dark recesses of a tiny room, stone-framed walls rising to a dome shape. No windows. No apparent entry except this one. Small, dark, and empty.

Suddenly Lizzie's light landed on a flash of white. She gasped. "Eisley, your torch!"

Eisley lifted her beam to join Lizzie's and every shred of air congealed in her throat. The double beam revealed a row of paintings of various sizes and shapes, one row in front of another, about ten of them.

"This is remarkable, simply remarkable." Lizzie edged closer with Wes and Eisley on her heels. The beams drifted over the closest four, all landscapes, one showing a replication of Lornegrave in the snow. Shared silence held the moment in reverent wonder.

She had been here. The knowledge tingled up Eisley's spine like fingertips and heat whooshed from her limbs in a rush of shock. Julia Ramdsen. Here is where she hid her paintings. But why?

The shadows pressed closer, almost like a presence nudged at Eisley's shoulders, but when she turned to look, only the silence of vacated space followed. The paintings weren't Van Goughs or Monets but well-done despite their simplicity: A hillside, a lake, a tunnel of trees—all in oil, like the others. Painted to last a long time.

Eisley started breathing again, her voice shaking. "Should we touch them?"

"Touch them?" Lizzie knelt down to the floor, her hand grazing the corner of a landscape. "I plan to wrap them in my arms and examine them from corner to corner. Look at them. They're so well-preserved."

"Let's see the one of Lornegrave." Wes placed his hands on either side of the rectangular canvas and drew it from the others, but the painting behind it hooked Eisley's attention like a grip to her throat.

It was a portrait. A man's face. Intense emerald eyes housed within a sharp chiseled face stared back through the dim light...and beyond hundreds of years. His raven black hair jutted in all directions, a deep cleft dimpled his chin, and the ghost of a smile softened his otherwise commanding features. Maybe *ghost* was the wrong word to think about at present, with shifting shadows surrounding her. His rugged good looks were both attractive and a bit intimidating if viewed in different ways. He was mesmerizing.

"See here, Eisley, it's as we suspected. They are all hers."

Eisley pried her stare away from the portrait and focused her light on the landscape painting of Lornegrave Wes tilted toward her. "In the bottom corner."

In white paint, as on the others, was the signature *J. Ramsden*. It was too good to be true, too perfect, a beautiful story waiting to be written. She had scenes popping through her head at hyper speed. Uncle Joe's novel was blooming into an amazing true story.

The portrait's stare pulled her back and she reached to touch the corner of the frame. "Do you really think it's possible they survived this long?"

"I suppose with the right conditions..." Wes began, running his hand along the canvas edge.

"They're perfect conditions." Lizzie wedged the flashlight against her shoulder and brought the painting of the lake into her lap. "Dry, dark space. Professors at university would know, wouldn't they?"

Eisley bent closer to the portrait, a faint line of words trailed at the bottom left. What were they? She peered closer. *My heart is in thy hands.*

With a gasp, her thoughts unraveled along with the strength in her legs. She bent to her knees on the hard floor, tears stealing her volume. "It's him."

Wes knelt beside her and studied the painting. "What did you find?"

"G. MacLeroy."

Lizzie crowded to her other side. "Do you think? Is it possible?"

"I'm starting to understand a lot of impossible things are more possible than I think."

Lizzie's hand flew to her neck. "I'm a romantic at heart, but my nerves can't afford any more surprises of this sort at present." She flashed her light around the room and stood, taking a canvas in her arm. "Treasures atop treasures within half an hour." Her beam glided to the stairs, followed by her body. "I daresay I need a few moments of reflection after all these fantastic events. I find extreme elation encourages my appetite."

Eisley stood on her shaky legs, a grin pulling at her lips. "I thought you said disappointment did that."

Lizzie stopped at the entryway and furrowed her brow, a painting beneath one arm. "Did I?" Her expression cleared. "Ah yes, I should think any intense emotion encourages my appetite. Excitement, disappointment." She sighed. "The best remedy for heightened senses is a superb strawberry trifle with fresh cream."

Wes's voice whispered by Eisley's ear. "A dessert to compete with love and chocolate."

Eisley turned ever so slightly, her nose almost touching his. She could only blame her bold reaction on the intimate and mysterious atmosphere—and maybe the pleasant hum of warmth from his earlier kiss. "Oh, chocolate and true love never compete. They live in perfect harmony. You know, some people are as sweet as chocolate?" She leaned close enough to offer him a light kiss. "Yep, just as sweet."

She thought she heard a growl rumble from him as he followed her to the stairs. "Do I obtain similar incentives if I continue with this sweetness rating, as you call it?"

Eisley tossed a grin over her shoulder and winked. "Chocolate *is* a temptation for me."

Chapter Fourteen

urreal was the only word to describe the last forty-eight hours. Another day of investigating Lornegrave, then a trip to York, all the while reveling in the attention of a dream guy. And it came so easily. The conversations, the laughter, even the times they'd held hands to pray. That's the first thing that had gone wrong between her and Marshall. *Too much kissing, not enough praying.*

Speaking of kissing. Kisses had been extremely scarce since the tower. Oh, those kisses remained clearly imbedded in her psyche, but like the best chocolate, one could always do with a little more. Since the tower, Wes seemed perfectly satisfied with the whole handholding, cheek-kissing, occasional cuddle sort of thing, but brain-numbing kisses? Of course, in his line of work, kisses were probably a common occurrence, not near-extinction like they were for a divorced mom of three. After attacking him in the tower, maybe he was a little afraid she might cause permanent damage next time. She sighed. Besides, she reminded herself, she wanted much more than kisses from him. She wanted happily-ever-after. Who wouldn't be a little cautious about an expectation like that?

So here she sat. Eyes closed. Driving to Wes's home near Bakewell, pouting about brain-numbing kisses, and drowning in residual doubt about God's current, crazy plan for her life.

"All right, pet, you can open your eyes."

She blinked the view into focus and stopped breathing. A grove of trees split in half and opened to a vast grassy lawn, manicured to NFL status. Harrogate Park sat in the center of the lawn, its three-story, Georgian sandstone walls painted a golden hue from the late-afternoon sun. She barely kept from smashing her face against the passenger window as they continued up the gravel drive toward the Harrison's country house. House?

"Um...Wes, this isn't a house." Eisley couldn't look away as they rolled to a stop before the double glass doors and three thousand windows. "Houses don't have butlers coming down the front steps to meet you."

A tall, rather thin, elderly gentleman with posture to impress a wax figure made his way toward them. It was going to take a while. There were a lot of steps.

"That is Jacobs. Been with the family for years and is a good chap." He winked and reached for his door. "They're going to love you here."

Love me? She was as out of place here as her bright yellow wellies. She was grass stains and gravy. He was cashmere and caviar. Every single thread of the courage she found in the tower slid right out her car door as Wes opened it.

He took her hand and weaved it through his arm, gaze fixed on her face. "Is something wrong?"

"Are you sure...um...having a relationship with me isn't an experiment of some kind?"

His brows shot all the way under his Superman curl. "An experiment?"

"Your world and mine?" Worry fisted in her stomach. She swallowed the sudden tennis ball-sized lump in her throat. "We're pretty much as different as chalk and cheese."

Wes brought their braided hands to his lips, drawing her close. "All this?" he gestured toward the house. "It's merely stone and mortar. You provide joy, companionship." His gaze dropped to her lips. "And other delightful benefits."

"Two hundred years ago, I would have been the person living in your Gardener's Cottage. Oh Wes, how can I compete?"

"There is no competition. You win, freckles and all." His gentle reprimand secured her attention. "A relationship is not about *things*, it's about *people*." He placed their clasped hands against his chest. "And our hearts."

"But..."

He covered her protests with his finger. "Don't create a chasm that doesn't have to exist, pet. Be who you are."

She drew some strength from the confidence in his eyes. A sliver of delight wiggled around the utter panic shocking her spine as straight as Jacobs'. *Easy for him to say. He was practically perfect in every way.*

"I can't wait to show you my home. Take you to my favorite spots. And you'll get to meet my sister, Cate."

His sister? His rich, probably aristocratic, beautiful sister.

"Jacobs." Wes stepped forward, hand. "I'd like you to meet Ms. Eisley Barrett, my particular guest for the next few days."

Jacobs bowed his head in perfect BBC order. "Welcome to Harrogate Park, Ms. Barrett. Might I take your baggage to your room?"

Yep, surreal. "That would be wonderful, Jacobs. Thank you."

He inclined his head again and Eisley shared her wide-eyed expression with Wes.

His eyes lit. "I believe introducing you to Harrogate Park is going to be more fun than I anticipated."

The first step through the front door jolted Eisley to a stop. Two levels above her towered a white vaulted ceiling filled with carvings, creating an almost tunnel feel through the entryway corridor. It was a very open tunnel feeling, since the ceiling soared at least twenty feet above them. Just below it, Grecian statues peered down from their heights, questioning her entrance as much as she was, and almost guarding the balcony wrapped behind them.

"There's been a house on this spot since the early fourteen hundreds, but Harrogate wasn't built until 1723 by Sir Robert Harrison. This is called the Vaulted Hall."

Obviously. Exactly what she would have called it.

Wes was almost breathless as he tugged her down the gilded corridor and talked about a French designer or something like that. His excitement held a boyish appeal which curbed the actor bit into an every-day sort of normal. And surprisingly, more charming. Wow. She probably wore a dorky smile to go along with her gooey internal emotions.

"This is the floating staircase to the first and second floors. And there's a tennis court in the back garden."

Was it even possible to like him better? His voice rung with pleasure, his reservation replaced by comfort. He seemed *happy* to have her in his home and for the first time in this crazy daydream, she believed he actually was. From the healthy growth of all the ferns in the vaulted Plant Room they passed, oxygen was abundant, so senseless wasn't as much an explanation her as in the tower. Maybe, just maybe, he really did like her, for *her*.

He looked down then, gaze softening with the warmth in her stomach. He bent and took her mouth in a lingering kiss she felt all the way to her toes and back. Slow, gentle, capturing not only her lips, but all the sweet tingles ping-ponging in her chest. *Yes. I do. 'Til death do us part.*

When her breathing returned, she ventured a comment. "You seem different here. I mean, more at ease and happy."

"I've never known freedom like this. I haven't brought someone special here in years, and never anyone like you."

Of this, she was sure.

He stared at her as if *she* was the famous one, as if *she* could make him star struck. A verse slipped into her muddled thoughts with a slice of clarity. *To him who is able to do immeasurably more than all we think or imagine, according to his power within us, to him be glory.* She couldn't cram these massive emotions into coherent words, so she just smiled and tugged his hand to encourage him forward.

They walked down the massive hallway and took the first flight of the floating stairway, ending up in a library. Floor to ceiling bookshelves stood laden with thousands of bindings, framed by dark red walls with stark white trim. Family pictures stretched the length of a dark mahogany fireplace.

"Here's Cate." He touched a silver framed photo of a dark-haired beauty holding a laughing baby boy, her hair streaked with hints of brown, unlike Wes's midnight do. "That's Simon, her son."

"She's beautiful." She leaned close and peered up at Wes. "She has your eyes – stunning and somewhat mesmerizing, you know?"

"Mesmerizing, are they?" He tipped her chin up and showed off some flickers within those smoky eyes.

Yep, her brain pretty much collapsed into a puddle of goo. This had to stop. She was a smart, independent, creative woman, not an automaton whose electronics sparked into shutdown mode with one gray glance of some fantastic eyes.

She grinned and snapped from the hold, a teeny tug of pride at her self-control straightening her spine. The next photo was a picture of Wes and another guy, an obvious relative from the resemblance. They stood with their arms around each other and both in mid-laugh. "Who's that cutie-pie?"

"My brother, Mark."

Loss softened Wes's words. Time shifted the weight, but a cloud hung over tragedy no matter how sunny the rest of the thoughts. It was a reminder of Heaven and mortality and why our souls were in constant ache for something else, something greater.

"Well, your dad's genes certainly took dominance, didn't they?"

"I hope my father's likeness will run much deeper than appearances." Wes raked a hand through his hair and tipped a grin to the photo. "Mark was the one who introduced me to Jonathan Taylor's biography, *Summit.* While he was confined to home during his illness, he read incessantly. It wasn't until my break from acting that I rediscovered it and realized I needed to bring it to life on the screen and relaunch my acting career in the right direction."

"Speaking of Jonathan Taylor." Her gaze met his over her shoulder and she tossed in a little brow wiggle to increase the suspense. "I knew he was in our family, but I wasn't sure of the connection, so I asked Uncle Joe about him. Jonathan Taylor was Uncle Joe's great-grandfather, and since no one else in the family was interested in Jonathan's notes and things, it all passed to Joe. You should totally pick his brain for research."

"And the pieces come together." Wes's grin spread wide, dimple to glorious dimple. "I see how it all worked. Lizzie met your Uncle online, they discussed family history, Jonathan Taylor's name surfaced, and they realized the familial connection. Lizzie heard me or Father speaking about it, and the matchmaking mayhem began."

"You think they planned this?" She waved a hand between them.

"Most definitely. They must think we're fairly useless on our own."

Lizzie's questions and statements? Uncle Joe's persistent prodding? Her mother's gentle nudges to open up her heart? It all made sense. The whole group had conspired like a flock of yentas. It was the sweetest thing anyone had ever done for her. She covered one of his palms with hers. "Or they must really love us."

He gave her hand a firm squeeze. "I've never been so happy for meddling in all my life."

"I'm starting to realize their benefits too."

A flash of color on the desk near her caught her attention. Was that a photo of her and Wes? In the paper? She leaned closer, pulling Wes with her. "Wes? You might not be so happy about meddling hands when you see this."

The snap mocked him, another chink in his well-placed armor of privacy. Perhaps a photo at Chatsworth or during their tour of Bakewell might have been expected. Any passerby could have taken one, but this photo had been taken directly outside his mother's secluded family home of Rose Hill Cottage – an extreme breach of his privacy, almost betrayal.

The caption read: *Is Wes trading in class for country charm?*

How could anyone have known about their presence at the cottage this week? Most of the regular photographers and story-hunters knew of Harrogate, but Rose Hill? "How did someone take photos of us there?"

Eisley twisted the paper around so they could see it more clearly. "Aren't people always trying to get pictures of the rich and famous?" She winced. "Ugh, the camera really does add ten pounds. I am never wearing those slacks again."

"I can't believe this."

She started reading to herself. "From the London Eye to Darlington's Christmas gala and finally snogging in the country, Christopher brings his newest conquest home to meet the family." Her lips twisted with humor. "We snogged? Shouldn't I remember doing something like snogging?"

He would have grinned. Taken her into his arms and reminded her exactly what snogging was, but those photos and the information posted with them revealed personal details very few should have known, or even found interesting. *A Ransomed*

Gentleman proved a solid film, but nothing to warrant renewed interest from the tabloids, unless someone encouraged the interest – planted the information. He skimmed over the introductory sentences. *Is she after the man or the name? Who is his mysterious American?*

A sliver of doubt snaked its way through his chest as he lifted his gaze back to Eisley. The slight shake of her head and chuckle seemed to suggest she wasn't even concerned about this violation. She was a single mum, *pinching pennies* as she'd mentioned when they'd purchased those Christmas gifts for her children. "Did you tell any of your family about Rose Hill?"

"My mom and Uncle Joe know about it, of course, but the rest of my family doesn't even know where Derbyshire is, so why confuse them even more?"

It couldn't be a ploy, could it? Not with Eisley. "But in your excitement perhaps you revealed more?" The doubt slithered deeper, down the familiar path to suspicion against his will. "Did you make any contacts in London? Talk to anyone at the gala who would have extracted information from you?"

She looked up at him, confusion wrinkling her brow. "If you recall, you're the only person I nearly debilitated that night. I might be a foreigner, but I'm not stupid. Why on earth would I ever want people printing pictures of me for the whole world to see? Besides, I care about your family and you. Why would I...?" She picked up the magazine and grimaced, then pierced him with a narrow gaze. "Wait a minute, are you back to the whole 'suspicious strangers' thing from day one?"

The hurt in her rounded eyes slashed a knife's blade through his middle.

"I've tried to be careful to guard my private life and I couldn't imagine anyone knowing unless—"

"Unless I was after you? Or money for information about you?" She blinked and when she stared at him again, fire burned in those golden-green hues. "If you think just a minute instead of getting up on your crazy rant, you'll remember *you're* the one who came after *me* in London. Not the other way around. And then *you* followed *me* to Rose Hill. I never tried to convince you to come."

He squeezed his eyes closed and massaged his fingers into the back of his neck, guilt weighing against him like another set of shackles to carry. "You're right, Eisley. I'm sorry. The betrayal is still so fresh and painful, I'm not certain why I immediately came to that conclusion."

"Maybe because you have a chip on your shoulder the size of the leaning tower of Pisa?" The flames in her eyes died. She slapped her palm over her mouth. "Oh, I didn't mean to say that."

He was a complete and utter idiot. She didn't even have the heart to insult him. And he deserved an insult or twelve. "Eisley, I can't—"

"But I thought we'd established a mutual trust here. You know, that relationship thing?" Her hands landed on the hips of her dark jeans, her brows jutting high. "I shouldn't have to keep proving my honesty."

"My life is a bit more complicated on the trust factor. It isn't as simple for someone whose life is under constant scrutiny—"

"Whoa, just a minute." Her palm rose to stop him. "Are you saying you shouldn't have as much faith in me because I'm not famous? Or are you saying the fact I trust you isn't as big a deal as you trusting me? That I'm not taking risks for this too?"

Her questions slammed all the air from his lungs. *Imbecile.*

"I knew it. I knew it was too good to be true. Kiss a woman in a tower and she loses her touch on reality." She slammed a palm down against the paper on the desk and shook her head. "You? Me?" She jerked the paper from the desk and slapped it into his chest. "Maybe I'm not the only one creating a chasm, Mr..." Even her search for an insult proved her innocence. "Mr. Actor."

She marched past him out of the library, thumping the door closed behind her with a finality that clamped his breath. Suspicion had become a hardwire in his veins, an instant reaction to any inconsistency with new people. But not with Eisley. What was he doing? He flung the paper to the desk and raced after her. She was already halfway down the stairs to the main level.

"Eisley, wait. Please."

She doubled her pace, taking a right turn at the bottom of the stairs in the opposite direction from the front door. In ten seconds, she'd be lost. The house proved a puzzle without the proper guide. How could he have been such a fool? Was he ever to learn from his mistakes and recognize truth and authenticity when it was plain before him?

The first two rooms at the bottom of the stair were empty, but then he heard...laughter? He groaned. The sweet sound drifted from the small chapel. Its dark mahogany walls rose to the white-domed ceiling, giving her laughter a pleasant echo.

"You have a chapel in your house?" She shook her head and buried her face into her hands, her chuckle dissolving into a whimper. "This was doomed from the start."

"No, Eisley." He stepped close enough to tease one of her hands from her face. "Please, don't give up on us because of my idiotic paranoia."

She peered up at him, eyes squinted as if in pain, pain he'd inflicted. "Yeah, I think your paranoia hit mine with the domino effect. Not a good match, handsome. I don't need someone else to measure up to." She wagged a finger at him. "And just because you're an actor who lives in a mansion and speaks in an accent to make my knees weak, doesn't mean I'm—"

Pepper Basham

"That's exactly right." He grinned, proud of her little declaration in herself. He caught her wagging finger and drew both of her hands to his chest, so naturally her body followed suit. "I shouldn't have said those things. You deserve my trust and I'm sorry I doubted you."

Her hands remained limp in his and she stared up at him without an ounce of confidence. He deserved it. "Maybe it's just another hint that this little fairy tale isn't going to work. I'm better at Scooby Doo mysteries than Cinderella stories."

"You do realize if you run away like Cinderella, I'll pursue you. None of this waiting back at the castle like Prince Charming."

The hitch in her breath and her widening eyes had him drawing her all the way into his arms, trapping her warmth against his. "You're worth a thousand quarrels and chases through the house." He ran a kiss over her forehead and then steadied his gaze on hers, unflinching like his resolution to make it up to her. "And I'll keep coming after you, all the way across an ocean. I'm sorry I allowed my fear to blur my vision."

"I know what that's like." She sighed but didn't meet his gaze. However, she did rest her hand against his chest. "At least I know you can be imperfect like any other human. It makes the playing field a *little* more level. It's hard to compete with demigod status when you're a mere mortal."

"Eisley," he whispered, tipping her chin up and waiting for her to look at him, hating the hurt and doubt resurrected in the lines around her eyes. "I have a long list of imperfections and as we get to know one another better, I'm certain you'll see more than you like. In fact, my many imperfections might lower me to pauper status within a month of our acquaintance." Her expression softened. How could he have doubted her? "I imagine I'll need a lifetime of refining."

She patted his chest and peaked a brow rather sheepishly. "That makes two of us."

"Please forgive me, pet?"

"It's a pretty appropriate place to find forgiveness, isn't it?" Her smile bloomed with the slightest hitch. He'd renew her confidence. She gestured a large wave as if to encompass the room. "What a great thing to use a chapel for, right? Forgiveness?"

"Well, we have used it for weddings on occasion, too."

"Smooth reply, Prince Charming." She tried to pull her hands free but he wouldn't let go. Her gaze flitted to his, a question in it.

"I'm broken, Eisley. Imperfect. See me as a flawed human like everyone else, or you'll only continue to be disappointed in me over and over again." He kissed her fingers. "I have every intention of keeping you in my life for a long time, so we're certain to make it into the papers again."

136

She cringed and stepped out of his arms. "Oh, the idea of photos like that one forever branded in print. Ugh." Her hand went to her stomach. "I know what my New Year's Resolution is going to be."

He took his time scanning over her body and didn't see any need for one change, which turned his mind to a very pressing matter of clarification. "About this snogging business."

Her grin etched a slow and adorable curve into her cheek. "Smart guy. You're going to use distraction? I'm impressed you already know me so well."

"I'll use every advantage I can to make sure you stay right here." He placed his palm over his chest.

She wrestled to subdue her pleasure but couldn't. And he gave a mental *thank you* to God. "Besides, I couldn't have you not recall snogging." He rubbed the palm on his chest as if massaging a wound to his heart. "It's criminal."

"We snogged at the London Eye?"

"No." The inner predator shot a fire-warning up his chest. He took a step toward her.

She studied him, her lips pulled into a pout. "Was it something we did at the gala?"

He took another step closer. "I thought about it, but no."

"Is it a game we've played?" Eisley narrowed her eyes, oblivious to the direction of his thoughts.

He took her hand and pulled her back toward him. "I assure you, *I* take it quite seriously."

"The name isn't very attractive—"

He caught her statement with his mouth. Her body jolted from shock, and then she sighed into him, one arm sliding up his back while the other clenched the lapel of his jacket, pulling him closer. His mouth possessed hers, roving over her jaw and back again. His hand combed through her hair and fanned a trail down her neck, triggering a gasp. She released his jacket and skimmed her way up his arm and into his hair, deepening the kiss until he drew back with a reluctant groan.

"Snogging?" Eisley's voice emerged in a rasp. She shook her head sending a delicious aroma of mint in his direction. "That word is about as appropriate as calling this castle a house."

"We'd better not encourage too many of those right now." Wes's grip eased, and he pulled her into a hug, his chin resting on her head, his pulse pounding nearly loud enough to block his words. His palms itched to sweep down her curves and abate his curiosity in a way his old self would have indulged without hesitation. But not now. "I'm tempted to enjoy it a bit too much, pet, and I refuse to make the same mistakes of my past."

Eisley nuzzled her head against his chest. "I was worried that because you've had all this experience and my kissing practice has been pretty much pinned to one or two guys that I...I'm not...."

"You are perfect for me, Eisley Barrett." He breathed into her hair. "And I like kissing *you* very much. Only you." He smoothed his palms over the soft threads of her hair. "How I wish I could offer you the same innocence you offer me. It's beautiful." He skimmed his finger across her cheek. "You're beautiful."

"Okay, you're totally forgiven," she whispered, her mossy eyes pooled with unshed tears. "For things you haven't even done yet."

"I'll need the grace." He chuckled. "Because I'm playing for keeps."

"You know this isn't the real world, right? Towers, tunnels, brain-numbing kisses, privacy?" She shook her head. "In my regular life, I do well to get a shower every day and keep my house from looking like the inside of a toy bin. No towers, and practically no privacy, especially with my family."

"Brain-numbing kisses can happen anywhere, with or without the towers, you know."

The buzz of Wes's mobile vibrated from his jacket pocket and into the heat-strummed silence. "I think those ideas began when you offered to fall on me instead of Dad." He perked a brow at her grin and drew out his mobile from his jacket, scanning the number. "It's Mum. They must be arriving with Cate soon."

"I probably should have said fall *for* you instead of fall *on* you." Eisley murmured and clasped her hands behind her, stepping back to examine the room while he took the call. Either scenario worked for him. Or both.

He brought the phone to his ear, keeping his gaze fastened on the lovely woman staring up at the ornate ceiling in the chapel, a look of wonder on her face. His grin inched wider.

"Hello, Mum."

"Wes?" His mum's voice trembled out his name and then she cleared her throat. "Wes." Her breathless voice spiked his pulse. "Thank God you answered."

"Mum, what is it? What's wrong?"

Eisley turned, a question in her eyes.

"I can't-" Muffled voices followed by a sob broke into the conversation. "We're on our way to Accident & Emergency." Wes held his breath, his gaze fastened on Eisley's.

"Wes." Cate's voice came to the other end. "It's Dad. We believe he's had a heart attack."

"No, Cate."

Eisley stepped back to him, palm rested against his arm. He covered her hand with his free one, his breath gripped to a stop.

"He's unresponsive, but we're almost to the emergency now." Cate's voice quivered. "Wes, it doesn't look good."

"I'm on my way."

He ended the call and looked at Eisley.

"Dad's heart—"

"Do you want me to come? I'll be happy to go with you."

He paused and ran a hand through his hair. "I've no idea what will be expected. It may be family only and a great deal of waiting. Would you mind staying here until I know more?"

"Of course not. I'll pray. You go." She nudged him toward the door. "Don't worry about me." She offered a comforting smile and squeezed his hand. "Go."

He kissed her head and without a look back, ran for the door, taking in enough air to feed his weak lungs. *God, please don't let my father die.*

Chapter Fifteen

"Can I get you anything, Miss?"

Eisley looked up from the page she'd been staring at for the past fifteen minutes, not reading a word. It was even Jonathan Taylor's book, but not even the wild tales of her Appalachian ancestors could keep her mind from spiraling into the worry zone. She'd talked to Lizzie, who couldn't leave to drive to the hospital until the nurse arrived to care for her dad, and she'd even pulled out her laptop to try writing a few lines for Uncle Joe. It was useless.

Jacobs stood with an expectant expression in the library doorway, tea-laden tray in hand, waiting for her response.

"Aw, Jacobs, thanks. I think I am starting to get a little hungry." The nice butler kept checking on her every thirty minutes or so. She needed to say *yes* this time to give him something to do. "Doesn't good food and English tea make everything a little better?"

She thought the corner of his mouth twitched, but she couldn't be sure. He seemed pretty unflappable. "Quite right, miss."

"Do you want to have some with me?"

His brows skyrocketed.

Eisley leaned forward and lowered her voice. "I won't tell. Promise."

The tightness around his eyes softened but she failed to win a smile. "Thank you, Miss, but I must attend to other matters. Should you wish for company I can fetch one of the maids."

One of the maids? How many did he have? "Oh, that's all right. No need to bother one of them with my quest for distraction. I've walked up and down that floating staircase about five times to help with the...waiting, you know?"

His eyes glimmered, but otherwise his expression didn't change. "I happen to be quite efficient at waiting."

The turn of phrase nudged her smile. "An occupational hazard?"

The glimmer moved to his lips in the touch of a smile. "Precisely."

The phone nearby rang again. Probably the fifth time in an hour. She glanced to the desk and back to Jacobs. "I know it's not my place, but I've heard the phone ring a few times since Wes left." She bit her lip and hoped her expression looked pleading enough. "Any news?"

Jacobs placed the tray on the table in front of Eisley and raised back to his pencil-straight height, though it seemed a little more relaxed than before. "No, Miss. Not a word."

Eisley popped a piece of a cookie in her mouth and grimaced. "Is that normal, then? All those constant phone calls? That would drive me crazy."

"No, it has only become a common occurrence over the past week. It seems to be a hoax. A crank caller, I believe, is the term with which you are familiar." Oh, he was definitely softening to her. "Both Ms. Craven and I have answered it to find no voice on the other end, but we have someone looking into it. Highly peculiar for Harrogate." The phone rang again. He gestured toward the tray. "Might I get you anything else?"

"No, thank you, but please let me know if you hear anything."

"Of course."

Eisley went through the ceremony of fixing her tea, using way more sugar than any good Englishwoman should, but she'd lost her appetite. She stood from her plush green roost and started another round of pacing. Wes's text an hour ago had said his father was having some sort of procedure and was unconscious. That was it. Nothing else. Guys really didn't get a woman's need for information.

She took another bite of cookie and moved her pacing out into the hallway for a different view. Her steps led her around the balcony overlooking the entryway, past the floating staircase, and deeper into the bowels of the great house with its ten-foot ceilings or higher, ornate crown moldings, and enough hidden rooms and corridors to put the Chatsworth maze to shame. Halls of portraits with serious faces stared down on her, as if wondering how on earth someone like her belonged there. She had the same questions. And her kids? She cringed. Good grief, they'd have this place torn apart in an hour.

Harsh whispers brought her to a stop at the intersection of two hallways, one of which led back to the main part of the house. She peeked around the corner to see Jacobs in close proximity to a young lady dressed in some sort of uniform. The girl was in tears. Jacobs didn't seem the mean sort.

"You are never to give personal information about the family, do you understand?" Jacobs' words bit into the air. "It is unacceptable."

"Please, Mr. Jacobs. I'll not do it again. She kept wafflin' on about needing to get in touch with Mr. Wesley about his job, so I thought it was important." The girl buried her face in her hands. "I didn't know."

"She's using her past connections to gain information, and we can't be party to it. She is quite forceful, Ms. Osbourne, but Mr. Wesley has ended his relationship with the lady and her father. If Ms. Craven and I could have notified the staff of Mr. Wesley's decision sooner, we would have avoided this difficulty. However, we were only made aware of the change this morning."

"I remember seein' her here a few months back so I just thought it would be all right. I didn't mean nothin' by it, Mr. Jacobs. Oh please, don't sack me."

Jacobs gave the girl a stiff pat on her shoulder. "She's the persistent sort and not too keen on being told *no* either. I spoke with her earlier in the week and she was quite put out that I refused to give the Harrisons' whereabouts." He cleared his throat. "However, I expect better choices should another occasion arise. Is that understood, Ms. Osbourne?"

"Yes, sir. Thank you, sir."

Jacobs turned then and spotted Eisley before she could sneak behind the curve in the wall. "Ms. Barrett? May I help you?"

"I'm sorry, Jacobs. I didn't mean to eavesdrop, but since I did," Eisley shrugged and took a few steps forward, palms out in surrender. "Sounds to me like the Harrisons might be getting an unwanted guest at the hospital."

Jacobs looked as though a fifty-pound weight landed on his shoulders at the declaration. "I'm afraid so."

Eisley offered a slow nod, filling in the pieces from the conversation she'd heard. She brought her hands together and narrowed her eyes up to him. "And I think the caller might be a certain sneaky, dark-haired beauty who works, or perhaps I ought to say *worked*, with Wes's agent."

Jacobs gaze locked with hers. "For certain."

"And a red-lipped sneer ready to unfurl at any moment?"

His brow arched. "Precisely."

"Wes isn't responding to texts right now, but someone needs to warn him Vivian deVille is on the way."

The firm line of Jacobs' mouth inched up on one side. "Very good, Miss. I shall have the car brought around."

∞   ∞   ∞

The nice elderly lady at the desk had just turned to check her computer for a room number when someone bumped Eisley out of the way.

"I need Daniel Harrison's room at once."

Vivian Barry didn't even acknowledge Eisley's presence but tapped her red nails against the counter with the impatience of a hungry toddler. She sported her usual top-dollar attire—trim and snug black suit, coat draped over her arm, and ten-inch heels that made Eisley dizzy. She must have been staring, because Vivian's dark head swung around and froze her with a cobalt glare.

"Do you need something?"

Eisley opened her mouth to answer when the desk clerk interrupted.

"Stroke unit. Fourth floor waiting. For the both of you."

"Thank you." Eisley extracted a smile from the clerk, who proceeded to ignore Vivian and return to her work at the computer.

Vivian's head turned slowly back to Eisley and studied her, recognition dawning with the downward turn of her ruby lips. "Eisley Barrett." She hissed the *s* through her clenched teeth as her gaze skimmed over Eisley's much less classy ensemble.

Call it being related to Nate Jenkins, but Eisley's anger roiled against people who put on airs. She stood to her full height, proudly a good inch taller than Miss Prancy Shoes. "Vivian, I don't think the family knows you are coming."

"I don't need an invitation, dear. I am connected with the Harrisons intimately."

At the word *intimately*, the curl in Vivian's snarl twisted right around the confidence in Eisley's spine. She wouldn't let Ms. Nasty get under her skin. She tilted her head and gave Vivian's body the same type of condescending glare. "Forcing a poor maid to give you private information says you're more of a bully than a close friend." Eisley sweetened her smile. "Or maybe just desperate? I think for the sake of the family you should leave."

Vivian's ebony brows tipped upward. "*You* are telling *me* to leave?" A joyless laugh crested. "Don't start a battle you can't win. You are woefully unprepared and have no idea with whom you are dealing. I will always find my way back into Wesley's life because I *know* him and, despite what he may tell you, he needs me."

Eisley didn't even try to hide her eye roll. She turned and started to the elevator. There was no use trying to talk to her. Two-year-old boys listened better. Unfortunately, the quick clip of Vivian's death-heels nagged as constant as a headache. She passed Eisley on the right, chin up, and attempted to cut her off at the elevators. However, as a woman with six siblings, evasive living was a necessity. Eisley easily sidestepped her, leaving Vivian nearly tumbling to the glossy hospital floors from her misstep in defensive walking. Vivian pushed the Up button, lifted a saucy smile as if to gloat, and then almost mowed over a poor nurse on her sprint through the elevator doors. Yeah, Eisley was dealing with a real grown-up here.

And her initial intimidation over Vivian's beauty and elegance? Well, looks certainly weren't everything. The doors closed on the two of them. Alone.

Fantastic.

"You're wasting your time, you know." Vivian's warning sliced through the match point tension.

Eisley feigned ignorance. "Yeah, I know the elevator takes longer in a hospital, but I wasn't up for the stairs."

The elevator stopped, doors opened, and two people entered.

Vivian's eyes narrowed to chilling slits, very serpentine, as her words even slid into a snaky slither. "You're a mere distraction in his life, a harmless flirtation. He will be done with you in less than three months and leave you heartbroken. You're not the first, nor the last."

Eisley lifted a brow and felt one corner of her mouth twitch. "Well, then, if I'm a mere distraction then you should have nothing to worry about, right?"

The elevator doors opened again, adding three more people. Eisley's arm brushed against Vivian's suit jacket and the woman recoiled, elbow jabbing into Eisley's ribs and buckling her over. Some of the contents of her bag spilled onto the floor. She bit back her anger and bent to retrieve her things.

"I see you're well prepared for a man of high class and sophistication. I don't even give you three months. Maybe one." Vivian's voice dropped to a hiss and she unexpectedly lowered to Eisley's level at the floor. "It's a useless dream, darling. You'll never fit into a life of his caliber."

The thick sarcasm in her voice lit a fuse in Eisley's chest. She snatched up a few more items and stood to her full height. "However, Vivian, I do fit into his heart just fine without ugly threats, manipulation, or perfect makeup."

"You think yourself quite clever, don't you?" She pulled in a breath through her teeth. "Do you suppose a few walks down a country lane and a handful of family dinners give you a future with someone like him?"

Eisley tilted her head. "No, I don't." Her smile itched wide. "But they might give him a future with someone like me."

Vivian's eyes widened. "You can't be so naive to believe it could ever last. His roles with tantalizing women, long weeks away in exotic places filming, and an expectation of wealth and class will dig into all your insecurities and expose you as the poor, simple country girl you are."

"Well, that argument is anticlimactic. I *am* a poor, simple country girl, but I'm also smart, brave, and completely unconcerned about your opinion. If that's the best insult you've got, I think you ought to give up altogether."

"Oh, I can do much better." She tapped her finger against her chin and the look in her eyes started a chill on Eisley's skin. "Are you willing to accept a man who is as much a betrayer as your ex-husband?"

Eisley's newfound confidence quivered, and Vivian saw it. "How did you know about—?"

"I have connections in many unexpected places, my dear. I know how to find information when it's useful to me." A smile crept onto her face, slow and wicked, like the Grinch whose heart was three sizes too small.

The doors opened and three people exited, leaving space for Eisley to take a few steps back from Vivian's venom.

"I suppose your sweetheart didn't tell you where he was the night Jane died?"

Eisley couldn't look away. The moment unfolded in slow motion, no way to stop the certain disaster. One more floor.

"Or with whom?"

Eisley steadied her palm against the elevator wall, refusing to buckle under Vivian's scrutiny. Wes? A betrayer like Marshall? Her lungs squeezed through another breath. With Vivian? She closed her eyes, blocking Vivian's sardonic expression, and pressed her hand against her stomach to push back the swelling nausea. Flashes of memories shot in quick succession through her mind.

No!

Eisley barely found her voice, forcing more confidence than her shaky knees felt. "Desperate threats again, Vivian?" She shook her head as if sorry for the vicious woman. "You had to reach back two years for that one. Wes doesn't live there anymore. He's outgrown you."

The elevator door dinged. Vivian's presence shifted closer. "He'll always belong to me. No matter what he may say or do, how charming he may act, he'll always come back to me in the end. I *know* him." Her words slithered to a whisper. "Intimately."

If Eisley hadn't been so close to tears, she would have knocked Vivian's triumphant declaration right back down her throat, but at the moment her heart beat an uneven rhythm in her ears and her legs barely kept her upright.

The Wicked Witch's theme from *The Wizard of Oz* played in Eisley's mind in time with the annoying click of Vivian's heels as she disappeared down the hallway. She snatched up the rest of her items from the floor, but the elevator door closed before she could catch up with Lady Red Claws.

Tears stung her eyes and tingled the bridge of her nose, warning of showers to come. She leaned her head back against the wall, pressing the tears into submission, thankful for the privacy. This was ridiculous. She didn't care about Wes enough to cry over him, did she? She'd known him a grand total of a week. How could this news sting so badly? Besides, it was in Wes's past. Done. Forgiven.

Just like Marshall?

The ugly whisper beat the bruise of her failure like a heavy metal drummer. How could God want this for her? A man with a past like Marshall's? A man with a world so far removed from hers? What was God thinking?

Did she really believe all those things she'd told Wes? That his past was in the past and he was a new man? She squeezed her eyes closed and sighed. *Help me, Lord.*

She shook off the voice of insecurity, which sounded a lot like Vivian's, and pulled herself together. If nothing else, she cared for Wes and his family enough to push her inner turmoil behind her and find a way to comfort them. It was not time to bathe in a pity party. But later? Maybe—or at the least, bury herself in a heavy indulgence of great chocolate.

She pressed the elevator button to return to the appropriate floor and focused on her goal. Directional signs pointed to a waiting area down the hallway, so Eisley followed them. A bowed head in the waiting area looked strangely familiar. Dark brown, shoulder-length hair with stripes of bronze nestled on bent shoulders. A smaller, darker head appeared over her shoulder, laugh in full bloom and a giggle to squeeze her weary heart with girdle strength.

She shoved her own hurt to the side and walked to the couch. "Cate?"

Cate jerked her head up, gray eyes red-rimmed. A tired smile broke into her pale face. "You must be Eisley." She gave Simon a little bounce. "Wes will be glad to see you."

"I'm sorry we're meeting under these circumstances." Eisley took a seat next to Cate.

"I only came to warn you that Vivian is here."

"Vivian? What is she—" Cate closed her eyes and released a long sigh, pinching the bridge of her nose. "How did she learn about it?" She lifted a palm and tossed a wearied shake of her head. "Never mind. Vivian Barry finds information out better than Lizzie Worthing and Mother combined."

Eisley offered a sad grin, still a little unnerved by Vivian's awareness of her personal information. Everybody knew everybody in Pleasant Gap but rarely shared it with outsiders. "How's your dad?"

"The doctors took Mum and Wes back to speak with them." She nodded toward Simon. "I'm afraid Simon wanted to talk to the doctor in baby speech, which wouldn't make the conversation easier to hear, so we stayed in Waiting."

Eisley ran a finger across Simon's round cheek. He reached up to take her finger and she nibbled on his hand until he giggled. "Would you feel comfortable leaving him with me so you can be with them? My resumé with kids is pretty extensive."

"Oh, I couldn't."

"I don't mind one bit, and then you won't miss out on too much of what the doc says, plus you can warn them of the coming storm in heels."

Cate even had her brother's dimple. "I think you and I are going to get on quite well, Eisley Barrett."

"It's that mom connection, right? Insanity loves company." Eisley repeated her munching motion on Simon's hand until it produced another giggle and he reached for her to do it again.

Cate perked a brow. "I've never seen Simon respond to a stranger so quickly."

"I bet he knows I'm a mom. I probably have some sort of residual spit-up on me, or something comforting like that."

Cate's laugh rang out. "I see my parents weren't exaggerating about you. One can't be certain with Dad. He's fairly extravagant with exaggeration."

"Your dad is wonderful." Eisley covered Cate's hand and the woman's gaze shot wide with a second of surprise. "Why don't you go ahead? I have some sort of weird kiddie game on my phone if he wearies of my other games."

"I didn't believe Wes at first, you know, but you are exactly as he described."

Eisley grimaced. "What was the description? Uncouth and classless?"

"Charming and utterly lovable, I believe is what he said." Cate's smile softened, and those stormy eyes misted over. "Are you certain you wouldn't mind?"

Eisley teased Simon into her arms and he didn't even whimper. "I'm really just being selfish, you know. I get to have some much-missed baby cuddles, plus when you get back, I can find out how your dad is doing, too."

"Thank you, Eisley. I'll not be gone long."

The dark-headed boy rolled his big blue eyes to her, his butterball cheeks so squishy Eisley was pretty sure he held at least three hundred calories in each one. Tasty.

She played a game of peekaboo until his little giggle became so loud it distracted the nurses at the desk behind them. Oh man, he was a cutie-pie. She reached over in her purse for the stress ball she kept for Emily to play with when they were out. After digging she handed it to him and he promptly said, "Ball."

Probably most boys' first word. It had certainly been true for Pete.

A sudden surge of homesickness had her diving in her purse for her phone to look at her kids' pictures, and possibly show them to Simon, but her phone wasn't there. *Weird.*

She hadn't used it since texting Wes at Harrogate and she was certain she put it back in her bag. Simon threw the ball across the room, so she snatched him up on her hip and danced with him over to it, giving him another reason to share a contagious giggle.

Oh wait! The elevator crash.

A quick recap of her steps revealed nothing, but the visit back to the elevator had her reliving Vivian's unnerving declaration. *The past is in the past, right?* Wes wasn't the same man he used to be. Besides, scenes from his personal life had been splattered all over the media, so it shouldn't be a surprise—except that it was with Vivian, his fiancée's sister. What sort of man betrays like that?

Can you see me as a new man, Eisley?

His heartfelt query came to mind as if nudged in place by God. Her newfound faith in fairy tales tripped on all the what-ifs. Their argument back at Harrogate, his assumptions, and this recent information slammed against her need to believe. Everything within her wanted to run like a coward whose heart couldn't take the familiar grip of betrayal. *Oh Lord, help me trust you with my heart again...today. Give me courage to believe.*

Chapter Sixteen

A remnant of fire burned in the pit of Wes's stomach. Vivian? Here? When he saw her in his father's room, evidently allowed in by some unsuspecting nurse, he was barely able to contain his fury enough to keep from upsetting his mother.

Mother.

Her face had paled at Vivian's unexpected and unwanted presence in their fragile moment. Wes pinched his eyes closed. The nurse hadn't removed his father's breathing tube from the previous procedure yet, and there was the simple courtesy of respect for his father's privacy.

He made certain Vivian left with a clear understanding of his anger and disgust in her astonishing disregard for his family and of the simple fact she was no longer welcome in his life.

He'd expected more of a fight from her, perhaps even a few crocodile tears, but she turned without an apology and stalked away. Perhaps, she accepted it, but clearer hindsight with Vivian Barry gave him little hope in that notion. She seemed to be the embodiment of his past in relentless pursuit of his newfound freedom. Her selfish conceit—and perhaps something darker—drove a dangerous persistence, and he wasn't certain how far she might go to get what she wanted.

But what did she want? The thought knifed another jab into his peace. He returned to the room. His father slept painfully still, his appearance too close to death to allow Wes's breathing to relax. The surgeon cautioned them that the next twenty-four hours would prove crucial.

"I wonder if Eisley is weary of Simon yet." Cate's attempted to lighten the mood with a tired smile. "You were right, Mum. I liked her at first sight." Her gaze flickered to Wes. "I think she might be a keeper, brother dear."

The mention of Eisley's name pulled a smile. "I'll be certain to take your brilliant advice, as always, Cate."

Cate exaggerated her widened eyes. "Liar, liar. And if Dad hears you, he'll start up from the bed to set the record straight."

His dad's only response was the release of a long, steady breath. Wes's chest constricted. *Not yet, Lord. Please, don't take him yet.*

"You've been here a long time, Wes. Why don't you take a little break," his mother's voice pulled his attention away from his father's pale face. "And I can't think of a better distraction than the one in the waiting room."

"Two brilliant women setting me right, I see." Wes's smile resurfaced. "I'll be back in a trite."

He slipped from the room and heard Simon's treble giggle before he turned the corner into the waiting area. Eisley knelt to one side of a chair playing peekaboo with Simon. He leaned against the wall, watching her face light with a wide-eyed smile to encourage Simon's laughter. Her long hair waved behind her in a ponytail. Occasionally she glanced under the furniture or fumbled about as if she was searching for something.

When she looked up and met his gaze, the tension of his father's condition and sting of Vivian's presence dwindled. Somehow, her joy and compassion reminded him how close God was, even now. He stepped up behind Simon, snatched him off the floor, and gave him a little toss into the air.

Eisley came to stand beside him. "I can see him and Emily plotting to rule the world with their cuteness."

He settled Simon on his hip and took her hand. "Thank you for being here, Eisley."

"How's your dad?"

"The next twenty-four hours are crucial, but the doctors are hopeful. They said he's strong."

"And he is." Her eyes took on a glint. "He's survived me so far, and that's saying something. Besides, your dad still has to meet my dad. His life can't be complete without the moment when charm meets quirky. The cataclysmic encounter will probably result in a national holiday of something or other."

He laughed, giving in to the need to kiss her with a quick touch. "Now, were you in search of something when I spied you a few moments ago?"

Her brows pinched. "Oh yes." She spun around and lowered to her knees. "I can't find my cell phone. Ever since I spilled my purse in the elevator with Vivian the Vain, I haven't been able to find it."

"You had to talk to Vivian?"

Eisley grimaced and kept up her search. "I'd hoped to beat her here so I could warn your family, but we arrived at the same time. Spilling my purse—or rather Vivian knocking it out of my hands—in the elevator slowed my progress." She turned her head but didn't meet his eyes. "Did she find you?"

"Unfortunately, yes."

"Oh, great." She stood and dusted her hands against her jeans. "All you needed was her unexpected presence in the middle of everything else. I'm sorry."

"No wonder you didn't receive my call. Just before Cate arrived, I buzzed you to express my appreciation for your care."

"Aw, how sweet." She placed her palm on her chest and then seemed to remember something. She took a step from him and gave the room another glance. "It has to be somewhere close, right?"

"Perhaps I could ring it." He handed Simon over and drew his mobile from his jean pocket.

"That's a great idea."

The phone rang once, then a nurse from the hospital identified herself as she answered. Wes thanked her and turned to Eisley. "Your mobile is at the nurse's desk. Someone reported they'd found it."

"Well, that was nice of them." She nodded toward the desk. "Let's get it so I won't miss any more of those messages."

Wes called Eisley before bed and apologized for his absence, but she encouraged him to stay at the hospital. The fear in his voice proved he needed to be there and miss nothing, should the worst happen. She prayed it wouldn't and tried to keep her mind as far from Vivian's revelation as possible. The grand distractions of touring Harrogate, chatting with Cate, and going over her research helped, but doubt hovered like a shadow.

Her midnight stroll through the house did little to allay her fears. The corridor nearest her room opened to reveal the massive Entrance Hall. From her perch on the balcony encircling the room, she had a better view of the domed ceiling and ornate cornicing, centuries of elegance and wealth hauntingly pale in the moon's glow. Even the statues appeared more lifelike and foreboding.

A voice splintered through her soul. *You don't belong here.*

She glanced down the hallway. No one. But the words spilled a chill over her spine. She sighed. Suddenly life had become much more complicated.

Oh Lord, please help me trust you today...and again tomorrow....and the next day.

In the middle of all the craziness, one thing remained constant: She was loved completely by a God who held her in his everlasting embrace. She'd trust him with her heart and let tomorrow bring what it would.

∞ ∞ ∞

The next morning, Wes greeted her at the bottom of the stairs with a good-morning kiss that left her with a grin to match his.

"I'll take that smile as good news?"

"Dad woke early this morning. By the time I left to fetch you, he had eaten and was speaking in short sentences." His gaze skipped down her body and he searched her face. "Have you eaten yet? Want to come with me to hospital?"

That welcoming grin, paired with his good looks, had her gravitating right into his arms and pushing aside all those itchy fears. "No and yes. I'm so glad to hear your news." She stepped back on the stairs. "Let me grab my purse. Are you sure you want me to come? Would he want it?"

Wes's palm settled on his chest. "And miss more time with you? You leave tomorrow. Besides, Dad's already asked where you are, so you'd best oblige him."

"Well, in that case. I'll be right back down."

∞ ∞ ∞

The sight of Daniel Harrison nearly brought a shock wave of tears. His pale face, purple hue under those smoky eyes, worked to welcome her with a weak smile.

Wes ushered her forward. "Thought I'd bring someone to brighten your day, Dad."

His lips parted as his smile grew. He made a futile attempt to adjust himself into a sitting position. Eisley and Eleanor rushed forward.

"The doctor said you need to remain still, Daniel." Eleanor's tone warned more with worry than anger.

"Besides." Eisley rounded the bed and took his other hand. "This is your golden opportunity to use everyone's concern to your advantage. You can sit back, relax, and revel in the service of your adoring fans." She winked up at Wes. "Get a taste of life in the limelight."

He gave her hand a light squeeze and, with effort, worked his mouth to speak. "Already had the fans."

Eisley slipped into the chair beside him and sandwiched his hand beneath her other palm, then scanned each family member's face in the room, ending with Wes. The soft look in his eyes glowed…for her. Vivian's words wound a serpentine threat to Eisley's future with the poison of forbidden fruit. Would he get tired of her? Would the tenderness fade over time, and would he leave her heart even more broken than Marshall? No! She wouldn't let those doubts cloud the last day she had to spend with this lovely family. After all, she'd have plenty of time to torture herself with the thoughts once she was all alone again, across the pond. Then she'd see if Wes was the man he seemed.

She rallied her unraveling attention and smiled back to Daniel. "They do seem to adore you, Mr. H."

"Daniel," he whispered. "Call me Daniel."

A smile warmed her heart. He was welcoming her friendship and by golly, with or without Wes, she'd take his offer. Though she'd really like to keep Wes around. "All right, Daniel it is, and you can add me to your adoring fans list, okay?"

"He asked if you were still here, Eisley." Eleanor patted Daniel's hand. "He was afraid he'd missed your departure."

Eisley looked back at him. "You don't think I'd leave without saying goodbye, do you?" She shook her head and exaggerated a grimace. "Even if I had to sneak into the room to leave a note, I'd have found a way. No worries, Mr.— "

His raised brow stopped her.

"I mean, Daniel."

"They've scheduled another procedure for this afternoon." Wes stepped forward and placed a hand on his father's covered foot. "Nothing as serious as the one yesterday, but vital, nonetheless."

Eisley squeezed Daniel's hand. "Then it looks like I'll have to say my goodbyes today, huh?"

"I'll come visit *you*." His voice took a hue of tease.

"Well, you'd better make sure your heart's ready for a trip like that one. All the craziness involved in the Jenkins family will either strengthen you or send you racing back across the Atlantic."

His smile creased the corners of his eyes.

A fresh wave of tears stung. "And I'm honored you used your matchmaking skills on someone like me."

Both his brows shot high and his gaze flickered to Wes. Wes came to stand behind Eisley, his palms warming her shoulders.

"That's right, Dad. We've unearthed your scheme." His hand threaded into her hair and she almost leaned back against him from the wonderful tingle that followed. "I foresee an extended trip in our future very soon."

Eisley glanced up at Wes, clinging to the hope she saw in his eyes. "Well, Wes Harrison, one thing is certain. It's going to take every ounce of fairy tale magic for you to survive the Jenkins family and *still* want to continue this relationship, so bring on that pixie dust."

∞ ∞ ∞

Wes blinked the bedside clock into view: two thirty. There would be no sleep. He yawned and snatched up his robe. He'd stayed longer at Hospital than he'd planned to ensure his mother was comfortable, only to miss spending time with Eisley.

And she had encouraged him to stay. The importance of family was a clear link between them. But he'd missed her, and even though she spent the entire afternoon rummaging about Lizzie's house, she'd called him just before he left hospital to check in on him and his father.

As he passed by her bedroom on the way to the library, he grinned. How long would he be able to wait before traveling to America? What would it be like bring her kids back and introduce them to this house?

His pace slowed as he neared the library, wondering what her children might think of him. How would he fit into their world? The sound of a page turning brought his head up. His sister sat, book in hand, in one of the wingback chairs that bracketed the fireplace.

"You're awake?"

Cate met his gaze and brought a finger to her smile. "Simon is nocturnal." She sighed. "I finally got him down but had worked myself into such a flap I couldn't go to sleep." She gestured her head toward the chair opposite her. "Come join the party."

Wes stepped around it and there slept Eisley, wrapped in a blue dressing gown, legs curled underneath her and ginger waves framing her tranquil expression. Sleeping Beauty, indeed.

"I see she can't sleep, either."

Cate caught her chuckle in her hand. "I was in the far corner of the library searching for a book when she stumbled in, praying aloud." Her smile tilted impishly. "It seemed rude to interrupt her heartfelt conversation with the Lord.

Before I could make my presence known, she'd mumbled herself to sleep. Oh Wes, I can't help but adore her."

"I know," Wes whispered and knelt beside Eisley's chair. He skimmed his fingertips against a few stray strands of hair and pushed them away from her face. "So, you eavesdropped on her prayers, did you?"

"Unintentionally, I assure you." Cate's brow angled. "However, as I was listening —"

"Eavesdropping?"

Cate's smile flickered. "She's preoccupied with making the same mistake twice or wounding her family again." Cate placed a palm on his arm. "The trust she's offering you is a treasure. Take care."

Wes's fingers slid down Eisley's soft cheek and a new depth of tenderness bound him to her all the more. "I plan to."

Eisley murmured something unintelligible and tilted her head into an uncomfortable-looking position.

"Perhaps I should take her to her room."

The elfish glint returned in his sister's fire-lit eyes. "Be good then, brother dear."

Wes studied his sleeping beauty, trying to sort out the best way to lift her. Once in his arms, her head plopped against his chest and her murmurs grew. "Naked statues...in...the church?"

Wes cast a glance to Cate for interpretation.

Cate's grin etched wide and she turned her attention back to her book in hand. "Chatsworth certainly leaves an impression, doesn't it?"

Wes tightened his lips to keep the laugh under control and exited the room, his feet barely a hush upon the rug. He breathed in a pound of delicious mint and pulled Eisley's warm body closer against him. She snuggled in as if it was the most natural thing. Here she was, in his house, in his arms, at night. He kissed the top of her head. *Right where you belong.*

She nuzzled her cheek into his chest and talked through a yawn. "I...said chocolate...."

His smile broadened. Somehow the sweet timbre of her constant chatter brought peace to his heart. He pushed the door to her bedroom open with his foot and felt her shift in his arms.

She stared up at him through half-lidded, sleep-glazed eyes, a soft smile on her lips. "I love dreams like this."

Her tousled auburn tresses and the warmth from her soft curves against him, combined with the slight slip of her dressing gown from her bare shoulder, teased awake a rumbling desire. He drew in a shaky breath and trained his full attention on those disarming eyes instead of the soft wealth of skin exposed from her neck. Dracula didn't experience temptation like this.

"They happen often, these dreams?" Was that his voice? Breathless and raspy?

She murmured some unintelligible response and her eyes flickered closed again. He lowered her to the bed and hovered a moment, drinking in the sight and reigning in those distracting passions from the Dark Side. Love garnered new control over his senses.

Love?

The feeling settled deep and secure. Love. Could he love someone he'd only known for two weeks? Each steadied beat of his heart confirmed it. He loved Eisley Barrett, the adorable, Appalachian American, single mum with a smile to wilt him at the knees.

An overwhelming sense of gratitude produced a smile. He was swimming in the afterglow of God's goodness and hoped he'd never lose sight of it again. What a wonder! Had it taken all of his pain to recognize the importance of a grateful heart?

His mind knew the answer. He'd have never given Eisley Barrett a second glance four years ago. Never benefited from the freedom of love for love's sake. Yes, he was grateful.

He slowly bent closer, his fingers sliding across her cheek until his thumb teased the corner of her mouth into a faint smile. He brought his lips to hers, trying to touch them as gently as the moonlight filtering through the windows onto her face. Her lips gave a faint response to his, causing him to linger a moment longer. She sighed in her sleep.

Were her feelings as intense as the ones filling his chest? If his father had taught him anything by example and through hard experience over the past two years, it was to cherish the ones you love. Wes drew the duvet around her shoulders and placed a gentle kiss against her forehead before leaving the room. Whatever it took, he'd prove to Eisley he would not treat her heart as lightly as her ex-husband, and she'd learn to love him too.

Chapter Seventeen

"Wes, are you sure about this?"

They walked through the Manchester airport, Wes pulling Eisley's bright pink bag behind them. He hated the thought of her absence. Necessary? Yes, but his life would feel the emptiness worse than Christmas without snow. "You leaving?" He shrugged. "No, not at all."

She slowed her pace and Wes matched hers. "Ha. You know what I mean. There are so many challenges ahead. Distance, our real worlds, distance, my family, distance. You might want to rethink this whole..." she waved her hands between the two of them.

"Relationship?"

A smile rushed into place and lit her entire face. "It sounds so much nicer when you say it."

"You doubt my ability to meet the challenges?" He stepped closer, his gaze searching hers. "Your children, perhaps?"

"You won't have trouble charming those little elves of mine. There is a whole herd of other people to worry about." She sighed. "It will be an act of God if you're still interested after you meet my dad and my aunts and uncles and cousins and grandparents. Then there's the overall weirdness of everyone, and the cultural differences and the oh-so-ugly distance. And my dad is really protective since all this mess happened with Marshall." She drew in a deep breath. "You have an opportunity to change your mind right now without any hard feelings.

"I have no plans to let you disappear from my life, pet." He tipped her chin up with his thumb and forefinger and brought his lips to meet hers in a gentle touch. "I'm determined. Quite determined." He tugged her into his arms and rested his chin against her head, praying she'd believe him. "I know you must return home but leave with a clear understanding. I have no intention of ending this relationship, no matter how large an ocean separates us."

She stared at him a long time as if gauging his sincerity, but as he expected, her smile won over her doubt. "Me, either."

He pushed his palm through her hair and tilted her face up to his. "Then let me give you a proper goodbye." His wiggled his brows. "One to tide us over all of the distance."

Which he proceeded to do for much too long, finally releasing her—three times—before she had to break from his hold to make her flight. He watched her fumble through the security queues, caught a view of the top of her head from a distance, and then she disappeared behind the crowds. Whatever part her presence carved in his life, it suddenly hollowed in his chest with vacated space. He missed her already and nearly vaulted over the security ribbon to beg her not to leave. He massaged the ache in his chest and turned from security toward the way out.

His mobile vibrated.

Miss you already. How is that possible? Here is the pic I took right after that lip-numbing goodbye kiss.

It was perfect. She held the phone up, snapping the shot and staring up at it with eyes sparkling and smile wide while Wes buried a kiss into her hair. Their arms wrapped around each other as if they belonged together. He could still smell the mint in her hair.

He texted back. *They appear to fancy each other.*

He pictured her grin as she read his note, then he continued his walk. At least he could ring or text her. That allowed for some connection. His mobile alerted him to another message.

The redhead is definitely smitten.

He shot off a quick reply. *I'm certain the brooding Englishman is too, pet.*

He passed a few paper stands on his way out, giving them an indifferent glance, but a tabloid headline snagged his attention.

HARRISON'S FATHER NEAR DEATH. Was romance with a penniless American too much for Christopher Harrison's father to bear?

Wes snatched the magazine from the stand and flipped through the pages. A picture of his father in his hospital bed ignited his fury. Who would do such a thing? And how? His thoughts replayed each scene in the hospital. Each nurse or doctor's face. Each moment by his father's bed. Vivian?

No, she wouldn't risk her profession for this, would she?

Without another moment's hesitation, he rang Andrew Chesterton, one of his closest friends who held intricate connections. "Drew, I'm in need of your resources. I need you to investigate an article and a photo to locate the source. Can you do that for me?"

"I'll be glad to try, Wes. Send me the details and I'll get some of my best men to work on it."

Wes finished the conversation and walked to his car, more determined with each step. No matter what it took, he'd find the person responsible for stripping his family of their privacy. It was one thing for him to bear the brunt of his professional choices, but quite another for his family. Whatever the cost or the consequences, he'd catch this mole and set the record straight.

"Papa let me fire his rifle!"

Neither a 'hello' nor a 'we missed you, Mommy' greeted her, but Nathan's hazel eyes glimmered with more excitement than Eisley had seen since the first time he'd beaten her at checkers. She tried to reign in her annoyance at her father's testosterone-driven grandparenting skills, but her overprotective mother instinct reared its ugly head without warning.

Eisley walked into the kitchen and scanned the room for the barrel-chested culprit. There stood her father, dark brown hair in a shaggy mess with a chocolate chip cookie halfway to his mouth.

"I'm home a grand total of five minutes, and I find out my seven-year-old has been firing a rifle?"

Nate, her stubborn-as-a-mule father, shrugged his wide shoulders and sniffed at the comment, his walnut-colored moustache quivering from the rush of air. "*I* was shooting a rifle by the time I was six and practicing on squirrels. Ain't no reason why he can't start." Her dad puffed his chest out like a proud rooster and took a giant bite of his cookie. "Besides, you can trust your dear old daddy. I wouldn't let nothing happen to my grandboy."

Eisley glanced over at her mom for help.

"Don't look at me, Eisley." Mom placed a squirming Emily in her arms. "There was no talking to him. Did you get any rest on the plane?"

Eisley kissed Emily's head and breathed in the sweet fragrance of baby shampoo. "I did something a lot better than sleep. I spent almost the entire flight writing down every memory and scene I could for Uncle Joe's story. He's going to love it."

"I don't see why everybody thinks Nathan can't handle a gun. He did a fine job." Dad slapped his grandson on the back and Nathan nearly stumbled across the room. "A real fine job. Takes after his Papa."

Nathan grinned up at Dad as if his papa was encased in gold and perched on a pedestal.

Eisley groaned. "Oh great! Has Emily started biting bottle tops off with her baby teeth yet?"

"Shucks." Dad grinned and lightly chucked Emily's chin. "I knew I forgot somethin'."

"Look, mama." Peter brought a paper for her investigation, his blue eyes sparkling with wonder. She knelt down beside him, bringing Emily with her. Pete's usual Spiderman mask sat on top of his red head, with the rest of the costume covering from neck to cloth-webbed feet. "I drawed a picture of Santa Claus comin' to our house."

"You *drew* a picture of him?" Eisley gently corrected. "Oh yeah, that's a great picture –well done, buddy." She squinted and looked closer. "Hey, Pete, who is this with—is that a gun?"

"Yeah." Pete nodded, his round chin lifted with pride. "It's Papa trying to shoot one of Santa's reindeer."

Eisley released a long stream of air through her nose and squeezed an eye roll to a stop before it started.

Dad peered over Eisley's shoulder at Pete's paper. "Yep, I see." He jabbed the page with his finger. "I'm aimin' for that one right there. He's an eight-pointer."

Nathan pushed in between Pete and Eisley. "Did you get any cool presents over in England, Mom?" His golden brows danced a jig. "For your adorable children?"

"Hmmm." Eisley ruffled Nathan's sandy-blond head and smacked a kiss on his cheek. Boy, had she missed them. "My adorable children will have to wait until Christmas to find out."

"Aw, come on." Nathan pleaded, his hazel eyes rounding into puppy-like orbs and his lower lip quivering with well-trained precision. "How can you say no to this face?"

She paused as if to consider the actor—after all she'd developed a certain fondness for actors lately— and then gave her head a shake. "Nope. Even with the most pitiful look in the world, these presents are too awesome to see before Christmas."

"Did you hear that, Nathan?" Pete nudged his brother, his voice rising into a near shout. "Too awesome, mom said. Oh wow, I wonder if she found the remote-control Green Goblin glider."

"Mama go bye-bye." Emily's sweet voice rang with the angelic lilt of a two-year-old. She touched Eisley's cheek with her soft padded hands, her dark blue, round eyes searching Eisley's face as if to bring it back into memory.

"Yes, I did, honey." Chocolate pie and strawberry trifle couldn't stand a chance to this sweetness. "But now I'm ready to find a Christmas tree. What do you say we talk Papa into going with us on Saturday? Only three days away?"

All eyes lifted to Dad. He heaved an exaggerated sigh and patted his slightly extended tummy. "Oh well, I reckon I'll have to *find* some time."

"Yay!" Nathan, Pete, and Eisley cried in unison, with Emily responding two seconds behind.

∞ ∞ ∞

"Thanks for staying with the kids." Eisley tossed her dad a smile as she entered the living room, all three kids snug in their beds. She collapsed into a nearby rocking chair.

"Well, of course we don't mind watching our grand young'uns." Dad braided his fingers behind his head and leaned back on the couch, feet propped on the coffee table and a light of pure mischief twinkling in his expression. "Somebody's gotta keep 'em straight."

Eisley leaned her head back and closed her eyes, her own grin tempting her lips. "It's a good thing I got back home then, isn't it?" She didn't have to open her eyes to know her dad was smiling. She could feel it. "Dad, words can't describe how good this trip was for me." She looked over at him. "Much more than discovering amazing things about our ancestors or fulfilling Uncle Joe's life wish, but some real time for my heart."

"Your mama said you've met some British fancy pants." Dad crossed his arms in front of his broad chest, his nose curled into a snarl.

"Nate Jenkins." Mom glided into the room and smacked her husband's thigh before sitting down. "I never said such a thing."

"Dad, he's not a fancy pants." She leaned forward, elbows on her knees, her smile stretching to the hurting place. "He's a great guy. Solid. Good."

Dad's accusing finger popped back into the air. "You need to find somebody who can understand where you come from, Eisley. Who's a *real* somebody, not fake as your grandpa's hair. I think you'd have learned from the low down, sorry man you called a—"

"Nate, honey." Mom placed her hand on Nate's knee, a laugh in her eyes. She turned to Eisley. "I think your daddy's concerned you don't make the same mistake twice. We want to see you happy. That's why we've been praying God would bring someone to you." Mom leaned forward and touched Eisley's knee. "You've known Wes for fourteen *days*. Time and space will tell whether you're meant to know him longer."

"You are absolutely right." Eisley sat straight up in the chair. "He told me he believes I'm God's gift to him for a second chance."

"That's a bunch of—"

"Nate." Kay warned.

Eisley shook her head, unexpected tears warming her eyes. "Believe me, I don't want to make the same mistake twice, either."

Her dad's jaw twitched and he cleared his throat. "Girl, I just want you to get somebody who's worth somethin'." Dad stood to his feet and patted his hands against his jeans. "I ain't gonna be around forever to teach your boys the things they need to know. If you marry some namby-pamby, then who's gonna show them how to hunt and fish?" He nodded his head in a self-satisfied manner. "You need to think 'bout those things."

"Number one, Dad." Eisley lifted to her full height. "*I* can teach them how to hunt and fish like you taught me, right?" She poked his belly and watched his grin expand. "Besides, what if Wes can hunt and fish...and other very *manly* things? He may be your equal, even."

Her dad exhaled air between his lips in a raspberry sound. "I'll eat my words if some hotshot English actor knows anything about real-life stuff. Hard work? He probably don't know his hammer from his chain saw." He pointed his finger at Eisley. "And if he comes over here—"

"*When* he comes," Eisley corrected.

"*If* he comes over here," he repeated more loudly. "I ain't gonna make it easy on him. He's gonna have to prove himself. If he can't stand the heat, I'll send him back home like a sissy boy to his mama." He took a pose that reminded her of the Tin Man in *The Wizard of Oz*. "I'm still your daddy. I still have some say in who's gonna mess with my grand-younguns, and no prissy pants actor is gonna sweep in here and try to—"

"You talk a mean game, but I know you. You're really mush in the middle." Eisley rocked up on her tiptoes and kissed him on the cheek.

"Hey now, don't you go talkin' about my mushy middle." Dad pursed his lips together. "What on earth can an actor do besides act and talk pretty?"

"I feel sorrier for Wes all the time." Mom patted Dad on the back. "Come on, Mr. Optimist, let's get you home before you turn into a grouchier bear than you already are."

"I ain't grouchy. I've been in a good mood today." Dad feigned an offended glare, tucked one hand in his jeans, and patted Eisley on the shoulder with the other. "Eisley knows her daddy loves her."

Eisley eased into her dad's arms. "Yeah, I know. But just wait till you meet him, Dad." She lifted her head, her grin exploding anew. "Hey, if you really want to see him, I can let you borrow his latest movie. It's over here on the bookshelf somewhere."

"Naw." He shook his head and grimaced like he'd eaten a lemon whole. "I ain't watching one of them movies you and your sisters sit down and 'ah' over. 'Specially the ones where they talk with them accents. No siree." He thumped his fist against his chest. "I'll be just fine with Indiana Jones and Rocky. You can keep Fancy Pants at your house."

Eisley's mind jumped over to Fancy...er...Wes at her house and her pulse wiggled up a beat, but her Dad seemed to catch his slip of the tongue.

"Naw, Fancy Pants ain't staying at your house. Keep your friends close and your enemies closer, right? *If* he comes, that boy's staying at *our* house."

Eisley's spine straightened with a tremor of faith, a dash of hope, and maybe a little bit more of that pixie dust. "Well, then you'd better get the guest room ready, Dad, because Wes Harrison is a guy who is true to his word. He'll be here soon."

∞ ∞ ∞

Wes retired to his room after helping his father, who had been home for an entire day, to bed. Relief chased sleep but couldn't battle the worry rolled into a stone in Wes's stomach. The dark marks beneath his eyes and his pale complexion reminded Wes of his father's frailty at each glance. Another close call. His thoughts shifted to the photo in the tabloid and enflamed concern into a simmer. His friend Andrew reminded Wes that following a lead like this could take a while, but Wes was nearly full-up of waiting.

The buzz of his mobile redirected his weltered thoughts. Eisley's name played across the screen and pushed some of his anxiety to the background. He opened her message and a photo of her and her children trying to fit a tree through their small front door inspired his grin. A broad-shouldered man, recognized as her father from previous photos she'd shown him, held the base of the tree, a laugh captured on his face. Cherub Emily rode on Nathan's back, her small arms squeezed around her brother's neck, and Pete trailed behind, pointing some sort of red box he had fastened to his arm at the tree, while a Spiderman mask sat atop his ginger-head. Wes studied the box a moment. Ah, must be some sort of web device.

He couldn't help smiling. Everything about this photo turned his heart inside out. His gaze moved to Eisley, who guided the top of the tree through the door, her head back in a full laugh. Pressure built from a pinpoint in the center of his chest and branched out, filling up every space between his shoulders. *Home.* He belonged there – precisely in the midst of all the chaos and laughter. Somehow, the weight of his father's recovery became lighter, knowing she waited on the other side of the world for him. Her note followed the photo. *Ready for something crazy like this?*

He typed back a reply. *Without a single doubt.*

A few moments passed before the mobile buzzed again. *I miss you.*

The size of the ocean tripled. *I miss you too, pet.*

Off to decorate the tree. Talk to you tonight.

Tonight. They'd begun a routine of video calls every other night, and though they were both distracted by various other things, his feelings for her had only grown over the past few days since she'd returned home.

When would his father be well enough for Wes to take a trip? His father refused to cancel the annual Christmas party, which proved a good sign toward his recovery.

If all worked out as he hoped, and his father recovered in good time, Wes would be sure to make a surprise visit to Virginia for Eisley's birthday. One month, and all those challenges she'd warned about with her family would come. He couldn't wait to prove to them, and to Eisley, that his heart was hers to keep.

Chapter Eighteen

ncle Joe's house welcomed Eisley with the aroma of pipe tobacco and leather, almost convincing her mind to forget her uncle's illness until she passed by the wheelchair, motionless near the door. She paused in the foyer, closed her eyes, and breathed in strength. She knew the statistics. The average life span of most people with advanced pancreatic cancer was six months, and his diagnosis had come two short months ago.

The doctors had said the end usually came quickly. He could live his life as usual until a month, or even a few weeks before the end, and then he would experience a fast decline. *Please, Lord, keep him with us for a little longer. Please.*

"Are you going to stand around in there all day or actually let me see the excitement on your face?"

Even though her mom had warned her he wasn't as spry, an immediate weakness almost buckled her to the floor. She bit a smile tight and turned the corner. He sat on the old leather couch right where she'd left him before her trip, and nothing had changed. She released her breath. He looked the same.

He peered over his wire rim glasses, his dashing smile etched with the mischief of someone much younger than sixty. "I saw you walking across the field. Did Greg steal your Jeep again?"

She laughed. "No, I've learned how to keep my Jeep safe from my crazy brother."

He gestured toward the window, concern in those pale blue eyes belying his lighthearted tone. "It looks like rain, Pippy. You ain't gonna walk all the way home in a winter rain, are you?"

A rush of warmth enveloped her at his familiar endearment. She cleared her tightening throat. "Dad's coming to pick me up in a little while. Mom took the kids Christmas shopping and Dad had to drop a few items off at Julia's bakery, but then he'll stop by and help you move your trunk downstairs."

"Good. I need to get out a few items for you to send to Wes, and I don't think I can bring the chest downstairs on my own. It's falling apart."

Eisley settled down beside him on the couch. "For Wes?"

"Didn't you say he was working on Great-Grandpa Taylor's story?"

Eisley blinked from surprise. Her answer came slow. "Yes."

"Good, I thought I'd make copies of Grandpa's journal, add some other items I've collected over time, and send them off to him. They'd help him, wouldn't they?"

"He'll love it, Uncle Joe." Eisley clapped her hands together. "Oh wow, we could send it as a Christmas gift, couldn't we? Is there time? He's going to be thrilled."

"I reckon if we pay extra." He patted his knee as if the decision was final. "I'll send a copy off to him and you can keep the originals."

"That's your life's work."

"And nobody else has cared about it like you have. Seems right that you should have it now."

Eisley grew quiet, his implication shoving reality into her face again. She perked back up for Uncle Joe's sake. "You'll love Wes's interpretation of Jonathan Taylor's story. He let me read a few scenes and it sounds like such an adventure."

"It *was* an adventure. It will make a great movie."

"I can't wait to tell him. He'll be *over the moon*, as they say in England."

He studied her, his smile softening. "You like this Wes fellow, don't you?"

She offered him a sneaky grin over the thumbnail she nibbled. "Yea, a little."

His raised brows probed for a full confession.

"Okay, I like him a lot, but I'm being careful. Smart, this time."

"Seems our little plan was a success, then?"

"Your little plan?"

His eyes sparkled like the trickster he was, and for a few seconds Eisley forgot about his illness. "When I first contacted Lizzie through that genealogy chat room, it was to get information. But then we started talking about other things." He released a low whistle and shook his head, his eyes softening to a distant look. "If I wasn't a dyin' man, I would have crossed an ocean and snatched her up."

Eisley grinned. What a match they'd have made.

His eyes focused back on Eisley. "But when I told her about my assistant and shared your story, she became *real* interested in doing a little matchmaking. We talked a long time about you and Wes, your pasts, your hurts, your dreams. One day she asked me what you needed."

"What I needed?"

He relaxed back into the couch and stretched his palms down his legs. "Yeah, what your heart needed most."

"My heart?" Eisley blinked, trying to follow Uncle Joe's line of thought. "What did you say?"

He snuck in a grin and settled his piercing gaze on her. "I said you needed a fairy tale."

Eisley pulled in a quick breath. "A fairy tale?"

"And Lizzie said she had one to provide."

She stood and began pacing. "So, you got Daniel Harrison involved and the plan was set? Well, you picked the right kind of movers and shakers to set your harebrained scheme in motion. Me and somebody like Wes Harrison?" She laughed. "Maybe a combination of your medication and some powerful daydreamers can work the impossible."

"I think he got the best end of the deal."

She sat down next to him and nudged him with her shoulder. "You chose well. He's amazing."

"No one else will do for my best girl." He tapped her nose with his finger. "There's one more thing I'd like you to do, Pippy."

"After creating my little fairy tale? I'll do anything you want, Uncle Joe."

He chuckled. "That's music to my ears, girl." He turned to the table at his right, grabbed a giant notebook, and placed the bundle on her lap. "I want you to write Julia's story."

"What? Me?" She shook her head and pushed the notebook back toward him. "I'm not a writer."

"Stop it. Those excuses you keep wielding are nothing but lies. Living with a brother as talented as Brice is tough. Your Uncle Cob was like that for me. But stories have been brewing in your heart for years, waiting for the right time."

"I can't write a novel."

"The pages you sent from England have been as good as anything I'd write, probably better, because they came straight from your heart. You have a natural skill few people are given."

Eisley jumped to a stand and stepped back, shaking her head and arms up in defense. "A novel? I'll admit I love Julia's story and this trip to England has inspired a lot of creative thinking, but I'm not up for something this big. I haven't had training or read all those writing books."

"I know your writing. I've read all your articles for the preschool's newsletter, heard your crazy kids' stories you created for your classroom, and now these chapters about Julia. You have what it takes, and my editor will give your work a solid edit before he publishes it."

His smile bloomed with a whole lot more confidence than Eisley felt, with maybe a little crazy hovered in there too. "Those articles were little things like the kids' stories. Fun and simple. I can't write something as good as—"

"That's a bunch of hogwash." He slammed a palm down on the arm of the couch. "You let one hurt in history steal your gift, and it's a cryin' shame. I don't care how much you think Brice is better than you. There's no one else I'd trust with this story, and there's no one else who can write it with the same passion as you, girl."

"Uncle Joe—"

"Oh," he breathed and placed his hand on his chest as he pressed back into the couch. "You've got me all worked up."

Eisley jumped forward and fell at his knees. "Are you okay? Uncle Joe, do I need to call the doctor?"

"No." He waved her away. "All this worrying. And after you promised to help me...."

"Don't worry, okay? We'll take care of it. I'll do whatever you need me to do."

He pressed the notebook back into her hands and moaned. "Take it."

Eisley made a hesitant movement and then wrapped her hand around the book. "I'll try."

"Good." Uncle Joe suddenly jolted back to life. "Could you run over there to the kitchen and grab me one of them delicious chocolate chip cookies your mama brought over yesterday? She's quite a sis to have."

Eisley's mouth dropped and then she smacked him on the shoulder with the notebook. "Why you little trickster! Some people will do anything to get what they want."

The twinkle in his eyes dimmed into a sober look. "And some people need to figure out what they want, find the courage to do it, and shoot for their dreams. You've got the wrong picture of yourself in your head – a picture of some failure. But God don't see you that way."

She glared at him as she grabbed two cookies, letting him know she wasn't quite over his sneaky manipulation.

"You're a sweet woman who loves her family and brightens the lives of everyone she meets. Somehow, you've listened to the wrong voices about who you are, but God sees you as someone beautiful and precious. Someone worth dying for." He took the cookie with one hand and held on to her arm with the other. "God knew all the sorry stuff I'd do. How much I'd mess up my life! And still, before I was born, he loved me." His gaze rested on hers and she sat back down beside him. "He loved you." His nod punctuated his words. "Maybe you should remind yourself of that more often, Pippy, and celebrate His love for you." He tapped the folder in her arms. "The gift is in you."

Eisley's vision blurred. "I do love this story."

"And God loves *your* story. I think it's past time you left your failures in God's hands and trusted him to your future. He wants to do something great through you. Take the life you have and live it for today and tomorrow —not for yesterday."

The truth of his circumstances added gravity to the intensity of his gaze. He was right. She'd spent the last two years wallowing in her past instead of looking for God's work in the present. It was time to let it go.

"Anybody home?"

Nate Jenkins's voice broke into the room. He tugged off his ball cap and gave his dark hair a forceful ruffle. "Looks like the two of you are up to no good."

Eisley shared a smile with Uncle Joe and patted him on the knee. "Why start changing habits now, Dad?"

"Ain't that the truth." Dad shot a frown to Joe. "She been moonin' over her Mr. Fancy Pants, Joe?"

Joe adjusted himself against the cushions of the couch. "Less moonin' and more talk about dreams and stories and such." Uncle Joe's gaze needled his point further into her conscience. He was right. She could do this. Or she could at least try.

"Well, I reckon she'll want this instead of leaving it in the front seat of my pickup." Dad raised the carefully wrapped painting to her. "You made such a fuss about showing it off, it's a wonder you forgot."

She nearly ran across the room. "Oh, my goodness. Uncle Joe, you're going to love this." She pried the rectangular package from Dad's teasing grip and walked with careful steps back to the sofa– as if her very movements might shatter the precious parcel.

Uncle Joe's eyes grew wide and he shot Dad a look. "This seems pretty serious."

"You remember the paintings we found in the tower?"

His grin stretched full. "Now how can I forget such a tale?"

She peeled back the paper inch by inch. "Lizzie let me bring one of them back with me and I chose this one because I thought you'd want to meet someone." She turned the portrait of G. McKelroy toward her uncle for the grand unveiling, her smile so broad it tensed her whole face. "Uncle Joe, meet G. McKelroy, the guy I believe is Julia Ramsden's husband."

"Who's Julia Ramsden?" Her dad's voice barreled into the almost solemn quiet.

"Dad." She breathed out a forty-pound sigh. "Do you ever listen to me?"

"Of course, I do. I'm the one who helped pay for that ticket to Scotland."

She stared at Uncle Joe, who did nothing to hide his humored smirk. Her dad. There was such a big heart hidden under all the gruff, you just had to search for it. She chuckled. Evidently her sleuthing practice started earlier than she thought.

Uncle Joe let out a low whistle and pushed forward on the couch. "G. MacLeroy, eh? I'm surprised the painting's stayed in such good shape after all this time."

Dad stepped closer, hands on his hips as he gave the portrait a thorough examination. "It's a shame it's broke, ain't it?"

Eisley looked up at her father, his words registering a few seconds slower. *Broken?* She whipped the portrait around and noticed a diagonal tear sliced a few inches from a lower corner to the man's shoulder. "Oh no!"

"Eisley, it's only in the bottom corner." Uncle Joe's quiet voice soothed.

"But it was in perfect condition before the flight."

Her heart sank. After she'd been so careful. So gentle. Her thumb trailed the ragged canvas, pushing back the open gash. The unfortunate results of air travel. She should have learned her lesson from the airport scene in *Toy Story 2*.

"I bet Charlie Ross down at the photo shop can patch it right up. He's worked on all sorts of pictures before, even some of the paintings from Drew's Antique store."

Well, at least her dad was trying.

"Thanks, Dad, but I don't think Charlie's had a lot of experience with five-hundred-year-old paintings." Eisley smoothed over the rip and noticed something within the tear. At first, she thought it was another touch of black paint or a trick of the light, but after closer investigation, she realized it was writing.

"What?" Uncle Joe leaned closer.

Eisley lowered herself beside him and placed the portrait on the coffee table in front of them. "I'm not sure."

She carefully peeled back the loose canvas to allow more overhead light into the torn space. Her fingers trailed over a loose scrap of paper tucked within the tear. Was it a message? She caught the corner of the strip with her fingernail and pulled it forward. "I think it's a note or something."

"Why on earth would anybody put a note behind their paintin'? Ain't nobody going to see it, unless they know where to look."

Eisley lifted her gaze to her dad, the full implication of his words tingling through her. Her breath blew out in staccato. "That's right, Dad." Her gaze shifted to Uncle Joe. "A secret message hidden for someone to find." She swallowed through the lump forming in her throat. "But only if they know where to look."

Uncle Joe's lips tilted with uncertainty. "You don't think?"

"What are you two yappin' about? You ain't making no sense."

Eisley's voice trembled with her body. "We've been trying to figure out how Julia smuggled Scriptures into parts of Derbyshire, but we hadn't been able to figure it out." Eisley inched the note from canvas into the twenty-first century light. Other pieces slid into view from behind it. Her breath clogged tight.

Dad leaned over Eisley's shoulder. "Well, you can't read it. It ain't even in English – only some kind of scribbles."

Eisley tilted the slip of paper toward the light. "Dad, I think—" She looked closer, vision blurred from staring. "Those are Old English letters." She worked her dry voice around the words, slow and uneven. *"Reioyce in the Lorde alwaye and agayne I saye reioyce. Let youre softenes be knowen vnto all men. The lorde is even at honde."*

"That's a verse from Philippians, ain't it?" By this point, even Uncle Joe was on his knees on the floor by the coffee table.

"It's beautiful." Eisley's voice caught in her throat.

Uncle Joe nodded. "I think your story is coming together."

Her story? She met his smile with a hesitant one of her own. "I think you might be right."

"Lizzie's gonna be real pleased."

"I can't wait to share it with Wes, too." Eisley ran a thumb over the paper. Rejoice?

"Wes?" Her dad's question slipped in like a ten-foot grizzly. "Who's Wes?"

Eisley squeezed her eyes closed, a chuckle shaking her shoulders. Yep, her father was a great listener. "Someone I can't wait for you to meet, Dad."

Chapter Nineteen

*E*isley tucked Nathan and Pete into their beds with another round of questions regarding Santa Claus's impending visit. Thirty minutes and ten questions later, they finally calmed down enough to appear to be sleeping, but with the excitement buzzing off their bodies, she wasn't holding her breath.

She melted into her desk chair with a long sigh and stared at her computer screen, as the screensaver photo of her and Wes at the airport stared back at her. Wes had texted around 8:00 pm with a *Happy Christmas Eve, pet. My thoughts are with you tonight.*

Her attention drifted from those wonderfully intoxicating eyes to the stack of Julia-notes to her left. Eisley had sent a few chapters to Uncle Joe for a critique and then spent two days researching how to write a synopsis so she could send it to his editor by the end of the week. In three days, to be exact.

She dropped her face into her hands. What was she thinking, writing a novel? The first few chapters had been a test run, and the thrill of words emerging onto her screen had infused energy like a sugar rush. Her own experiences breathed life into the words on the pages as she wove in her journey through the secret tunnel, the amazing discovery of the hidden room, and the chill of the frostbitten British morning air. But write an entire novel? Could she do it? A restlessness urged her to dive into her craziness headfirst.

The little blue envelope at the corner of her desk teased her attention. It had arrived four days earlier from England with the words ***Do Not Open Until Christmas*** scrawled across the back.

As if Wes didn't trust her or something.

She pulled the card closer and checked the clock. Only 10:30 pm. She shrugged and fiddled with the edge of the card. Technically, it was already Christmas in England, about 3:30 am, but definitely Christmas morning.

The clock flipped to 10:31. Close enough. She peeked over her shoulder for any signs of awake children. A bump of something hid inside the paper. A gift? She squeezed out a quiet squeal. The last "romantic" Christmas gift she'd received had been almost five years ago, when Marshall tried to make up for his first stupid incidence of adultery. He'd given her some gaudy ring they couldn't afford, and she'd worn it like the crown jewels, in the hopes her joy on the outside would soothe the constant ache of his betrayal.

She broke the seal. On the inside flap another warning blazed in black ink.

If it isn't Christmas, pet, do not open it, yet.

What a poet!

Eisley worried her bottom lip and allowed her index finger to skim over the back of the blue card peeking from the package. 10:32pm. The beautiful tingle of anticipation spiked her fingers into motion. She slid her fingers into the paper and pulled out the card.

Something slid out from the middle of the paper and landed on her desk with a light metallic click. Sealed within a plastic bag rested a silver charm bracelet, simple and elegant.

Eisley gasped with delight and pulled the thin chain from the bag, caressing the cool links. The only charm fitted to the bracelet was a simple heart with a small inscription. She moved the bracelet closer to the light and her vision grew blurry. Engraved along the edges of the heart was the phrase, *Many waters cannot quench love.*

∞ ∞ ∞

Wes opened the large box from Eisley after all of his family members departed from the room. Inside the package nestled a spiral-bound book of all of Joe Taylor's research, a letter from Jonathan Taylor to Joe, and two photographs, both in black and white. Penned beneath the first photo of a dapper young man was *Jonathan Taylor before sailing to America.*

Wes stared into the dark eyes of the man in the snap. Serious. Determined, with a strong jaw and body to match the look in his expression. The next photograph showed a couple. Older. At the bottom read, *Jonathan and Laurel Taylor, 1948.*

Jonathan stared down at his bride with unabashed adoration, her head of long, light-colored hair tipped back in a full laugh. In 1948 they'd have been married about thirty years, with four children and a lifetime of heartache and healing behind them.

Laurel's uninhibited laughter reminded him of Eisley. He couldn't imagine ever growing tired of her joy, her exuberance for life. Her photo Christmas card rested at the bottom of the stack. Eisley sat in front of a Christmas hearth, her shiny blue blouse bringing out the deepest auburn in her hair. Emily curled up on her lap, a black bow barely hanging on to a loose strand of blonde. Nathan stood at attention to Eisley's left, white collared shirt buttoned to the very top, wearing a smile to match his mum's, with Peter to her right, attention in the distance, and hand scratching the top of his head.

Wes laughed and turned the photo over to read Eisley's note.

Loving this fairy tale with you. I hope we have many more chapters in this story. Here's hoping to see you much sooner than later. I miss you with my whole heart. A very Merry Christmas to your family from my crazy one.

Yours, Eisley

He rested his chin in his palm, wrestling with the sudden force of emotions.

With a glance to his watch and a second of mental math, he figured the time in Virginia to be mid-morning. Grabbing his phone, he pressed her number for a video call. He needed to hear her voice, see her smile. Merely forty-eight hours without a call and her absence tore into the silence of his family's house.

When her face came into view on the screen, his grin must have reached imbecile status. She was, quite simply, adorable.

"Hi, handsome. This is a pleasant surprise. I wasn't expecting a call until tonight."

"Texts and emails are quickly losing their charm, pet."

Her smile broadened, and she lowered her voice. "I know, but if I close my eyes and remember your kiss my lips still tingle a little."

His gaze dropped to her mouth, hunger of a different kind burning an ache in his chest. "It's good to know I can leave a lasting impression."

His words curled out on a growl and her eyes widened. *Derail the inner hunter, chap.*

"Oh heavens, I'm sufficiently branded, whew." She placed a palm to her chest and sighed. "By the way, Happy Christmas to you."

Her use of the British greeting brought another smile to his face. If love was for fools, he would happily stand first in line to don the jester cap. "And to you. I hope it will be the first of many. Thank you for the remarkable gift. I'm anxious to take its contents and apply it to my script."

"Oh good." She scrunched her shoulders with sheer delight. "What do you get the guy who has everything, right?"

"Your heart will do quite nicely, if I could make a particular Christmas wish."

Her gaze locked with his, her breath caught, and then she looked away, color rising into her cheeks. "Well, it was difficult to place that one in a package." She cleared her throat and lifted her arm to the screen, shaking the bracelet for him to see. "And thank *you* for this. It's beautiful—especially the message."

"I meant it, though I don't fancy those many waters at present."

She wrinkled her nose in a frown. "No, me either, but I'm so glad I can still see you." Her eyes glowed with addictive admiration. "I do love your emails. I never thought guys could write letters anymore. I mean *real* letters. I was pretty certain the only reason why Mr. Darcy could write anything was because he was a fictional character created by a *woman*. Please keep proving all my stereotypes wrong, okay?"

He started to answer when a commotion crackled from her side of the phone, followed by two faces peering into the screen.

Eisley's smile turned apologetic and she gestured to the intruders. "I believe I have some kids here who want to talk to you." Her brows rose in clear warning. "Ready or not. Here's Nathan."

After a short pause, Nathan looked into the phone, his round hazel eyes much more serious than his mother's. "Hello?"

"Hello, Nathan. It's a pleasure to speak with you."

"You too, Mr. Harrison..." There was a pause while Nathan and Eisley had some sort of conversation and then Nathan turned back to the screen with an uncertain grin. "I mean Wes."

His heart did a funny flop when the little boy said his name. "Have you enjoyed Christmas?"

"It's been great. You should see the Nerf sword Mom bought me." Nathan paused for a breath and the screen shook as he moved to pick up a flash of silver from the floor. "Can you see?"

"Brilliant."

"Mom is good with cool presents." He seemed to notice something nearby and then focused his attention back on Wes. His face lit into a grin. "Thanks for helping her pick out the remote-control dragon. It's really cool."

"Amazing creatures, aren't they?"

"Yeah, Mom found this picture of Smaug the dragon from *The Hobbit*. It looks so real."

"When I come to visit, I'll bring my brother's drawings he made from Tolkien's *The Lord of the Rings* series. Would you like to see them?"

Nathan gasped. "Sure. Yeah—" Another interruption and pause as he spoke with Eisley. "I mean, yes sir, I'd like it. Mom likes dragons and stuff too and she can make a really good Gandalf voice."

"Hmmm, that would be interesting to hear." Wes couldn't contain a chuckle. "It's been a while, but I used to be quite good at fencing. Would you like to learn?"

Nathan's brow puckered. "My Papa knows 'bout building fences. I'm sure he can teach me."

Wes squeezed his eyes closed and swallowed down another bubble of laughter lodged in his throat. "Building fences is certainly a skill worth having, but in England fencing is something like...um...let's see sword-fighting."

Nathan's eyes grew wide. "You know how to sword-fight? With real swords?"

"Indeed, I do. My family has a small sword which has been passed down through generations. If the airport will allow me to bring it along, I shall."

"It's a *real* sword?" The little skeptic's brow rose.

"Quite real, and if your mum doesn't mind, we could practice together."

"Pete! Hey Pete!" Nathan suddenly screamed and set the phone down so that Wes was left staring at the ceiling. His voice grew distant. "Wes has a real sword and he's going to bring it when he...."

"Can you hear anything after Nathan screamed in your ear?" Eisley looked him through the screen, another apology in her eyes.

"It's quite alright. He sounds delightful, really."

"He is delightful when he's not causing permanent hearing loss. And after all the dragon and fencing talk, you're his favorite person, I'm sure." Oh, how he wanted to land a kiss on her beautiful grin. She shifted her attention to her right, where a small, web-gloved hand appeared in the screen. "Are you ready to talk to Pete? He is certainly ready to talk to you."

"Put him on." A sense of belonging settled around Wes's heart. He was ready to bound across the ocean this very moment.

"Do you really have a sword?" Pete's face came so close to the screen, Wes couldn't see anything except his enormous blue eyes and a ream of freckles across his nose.

"I actually have a few swords. One from my great-great-grandfather."

"Whoa, that must be a *really* old sword." Pete paused to talk to his mother and then said in a rehearsed tone. "Thank you for the art set."

"You're welcome. I can't wait to see all the pictures you will draw with it."

"I'm a good draw-er," Pete added without hesitation. "I draw Spiderman and dogs and—"

"Emily!" The delightful trill of a giggle interrupted the conversation. "Get those leggings back on your body, little girl."

Pete continued his explanation, nonplussed by the disturbance. "And it was a good thing you helped Mom pick out my present. Last year she bought me two Web-Slinging Spiderman dolls and didn't even remember. She forgets sometimes. Says her mind is full of dumplings."

Dumplings? Perhaps he meant stuffing.

Pete focused his intense gaze, serious. "Do you like Spiderman?"

"Of course." Wes answered quickly, knowing the answer was a make-it-or-break-it with Pete. "I think it would be amazing to climb up walls, don't you?"

"I can climb up the walls on the stairway." He lowered his voice to a whisper and Wes had the sudden urge to grab the little boy in a hug and grapple him to the ground. "When Mom's not watching." He shot a look over his shoulder and moved with the phone, the room bouncing along with Pete's steps. "I put my hands on one side of the wall and my feet, with no socks on, up on the other side of the wall and then I do this." All Wes could see was Pete's mouth. "Watch." He placed the phone down at an angle so Wes could see Pete's small feet, edging up the white wall. "I'm good at it." He raised his voice to a proud boast. "See?"

"Quite remarkable." Wes barely contained his laugh.

"Peter Jonathan Barrett!" Eisley called from a distant place. "No more Christmas candy before lunch in this house. I have a naked baby tossing wrapping paper around like confetti and a little boy who is trying to scale my *clean* walls."

"Aw, man."

Eisley came back into view. "I'm sorry, Wes. It's a madhouse around here. Christmas morning and all." The little girl in Eisley's arms blinked big blue eyes at him and wrinkled her nose just like her mother. He fell in love on the spot. "Actually, that's just an excuse I'm using. It's pretty much a madhouse every day."

"I can't wait to meet them."

"You can't?" She looked at him as if he'd gone soft in the head.

Actually, he'd gone soft in the heart, and it had never felt so right. "Your boys are delightful."

The tension in her brow relaxed. "Yeah, as crazy as they seem, God's blessed me with two really good boys." She bounced Emily against her side. "And an adorable nudist, here."

"Adorable." Like her mother.

"You don't seem as far away when I can see you through the screen." Eisley stared at him in silence for a few moments, a tender smile in her eyes. Did he have the same look on his face? The sweet awe? He felt it. He attempted to make out the flakes of gold in her green eyes, but the blasted screen didn't do them justice.

She shook her head from her trance and grinned, a swell of auburn blush touching each cheek. "Um...so handsome, when are you going to risk the humiliation of meeting my father and trek across the Atlantic?"

"Soon, I hope. Dad gains strength every day, but I have a few interviews to complete in the next few weeks, as well as another audition. Don't fear, pet. I can't wait much longer."

"Good, because I need a refresher kiss for sure."

He loved the teasing sound in her voice, igniting another blast of certainty for him. It didn't make sense—such assurance, such intensity in a short space of time, but it was real. *Love.* "I assure you. I will make up for lost time."

Chapter Twenty

"Just as I expected." Lizzie topped off her comment with a nod from the other side of the truck. "As charming and lovely as our ginger-headed friend."

Wes couldn't agree more. A brick box-style house appeared around the bend in the road, where branching trees bowed to meet overhead and create a tunnel of frosted green up to the white-columned front veranda. He smiled for the hundredth time since his drive from the airport. Reading about the Blue Ridge Mountains in Jonathan Taylor's book painted a dim picture compared to the actual beauty of the surrounding landscape. Smooth, rolling mountains shaded with a misty hue welcomed his arrival into Virginia. The air held a sting of winter, but not as harsh as he'd expected, though snow powdered the ground in a thin layer of angelic white. *Beautiful.*

"Thank you for accompanying me, Lizzie."

"I'm so happy to have come. Do you realize how long it's been since I've traveled anywhere beyond Matlock? Ages."

"A good place to start, I would think." Eisley grew up in this cozy corner of the world. The openness, the far reaches of countryside, stirred a sense of belonging he couldn't quite explain. The front garden stretched to the surrounding wood and the drive curved almost to the house's steps. He tensed his fists against the steering wheel, preparing for one of the most important "auditions" of his life. As the truck slowed to a stop, two large dogs raced off the veranda in pursuit.

Lizzie patted his arm, one corner of her lips tweaked in mischief. "Ah, yes, time for the knight to prove his worth, isn't it?"

"Your encouragement is somewhat underwhelming, Lizzie."

"Humility is a fantastic teacher, my dear boy. I'm certain you're in for a healthy dose of it here."

Before Wes could respond, Lizzie slipped from the truck and slammed the door on his question. Brilliant. Humility? What on earth could she mean? The two phone conversations he'd shared with Kay Jenkins to plan this surprise visit were pleasant enough. Not one sign of trouble.

He ran a hand over his tight jaw, took a deep breath, and opened the door to join Lizzie around the front of the truck. A golden retriever bounded toward them. Wes stepped in front of Lizzie and took the full brunt of the dog's greeting, a jump that nearly knocked him over. The shepherd followed suit. At his firm *sit* command, both dogs obeyed at once. He rewarded them with a scratch behind the ears. Well, that wasn't so bad.

"You're here, you're here." A young woman, hair dancing about her face in smooth waves of caramel, approached him with the same enthusiasm as the dogs. Her red beret-like hat matched her shimmery blouse and boots to perfection, both adding a rosy glow to her smiling face. From the photos and zeal, he'd guess this was Sophie.

"Move over, boys." She tossed a nod to the dogs. "It's my turn to hug him." And she proceeded to do just that, golden eyes shining. "Oh gee, you smell good."

Sophie took Lizzie into a hug and then stepped back, her hands in motion with her words. "I don't know why they didn't tell me you were coming until today, as if I'd spill the secret or something. That's so rude." She rolled her gaze to Lizzie and produced a mock pout. "The boys think I'm an airhead, but I'm not. I'm just chatty. After all, I made the highest score on my GREs than anyone in the family, except Rick, but he doesn't count because he has a computer for a brain." She took Lizzie into another hug. "Oh, we're so glad you're here."

"It's a pleasure, dear." Lizzie chuckled through her words.

"Eisley's gonna be tickled to pieces when she finds out." Sophie's gaze fastened back on Wes. "She talks about you all the time."

"You must be Sophie." Wes tilted his head in greeting.

Her palm fluttered to her chest and she produced an audible swallow, eyes widening even more. "Oh! Could you say my name again?"

He quirked a grin and exchanged a look with Lizzie. "Nice to meet you.... Sophie."

Her hand waved to cool her face. "Please tell me you have some unmarried brother, cousin, or nephew, who desperately needs to sweep a Southern girl off her feet. I'm ready for a feet-sweeping, tower-kissing experience...."

"Stop your blubbering, girl. You're embarrassin' me."

Nate Jenkins lumbered toward them from the veranda, a grizzly bear in human form. Dark eyes narrowed, face void of emotion, with his moustache shadowing his upper lip from view. Was he smiling? Grimacing? Devising a murder plan?

He stood about an inch above Wes and his chest boasted hard labor from one massive shoulder to the other. Wes's throat tightened, but he straightened to his full height and offered his most charming smile.

"Nate Jenkins." The man extended his hand and gripped Wes's in an iron hold. "I gotta bone to pick with you, boy."

"P... pardon me?"

"Nice to meet you, Lizze." Nate's face softened when he looked at Lizzie. "Did you have a nice trip, darlin'?"

Lizzie's smile expanded to laughter size. "Lovely, Nate. Thank you for asking."

Nate turned back to Wes, expression darkening into a looming storm. "How dare you bring some Ford pickup truck up my driveway? Don't you know that's almost criminal? We're Chevy people 'round here."

Wes hoped for comprehension, but Ford and Chevy strung between the word driveway left him at a loss, and the half-furious look on Nate Jenkins' face didn't assist his clarification.

"Don't mind him. He's just teasing." A petite, light haired woman stepped forward with enough welcome in her eyes to chase a little of Nate's chill away. "We're real pleased to have you. I'm Kay Jenkins."

"You have a beautiful home," Lizzie interjected, giving the house another appreciative glance. "Perfectly situated on this hillside. And what a magnificent view of your blue mountains."

"Thank you, Lizzie."

"Ain't near as fancy as *some* people's houses." Nate directed the words at Wes. "But it's been just fine for us. Built the back addition myself."

"Eisley says you are quite the craftsman." Wes hoped the acknowledgement might soften the fierce crinkle of Nate's brow, but it only deepened. Wes turned to Kay, searching for some kinship on the battlefield. "It's a pleasure to meet you as well and thank you for allowing us to stay with you."

Nate's grin lifted viciously. "Best way to keep your eyes on the enemy."

Their gazes locked for a few seconds. "Well, I don't suppose you have any enemies within close proximity at present, Mr. Jenkins."

The corner of Nate's moustache twitched. "Mr. Jenkins? Oh naw, you can't go 'round calling me that. Only my wife can call me Mr. Jenkins."

Kay rolled her eyes and shook her head. "Among other very specific names."

"Hey, Daddy, did you see how the dogs took to him?" Sophie knelt down and ran her fingers through the retriever's golden fur. "You always say dogs know a good person when they see one."

Nate jolted Wes's entire body with a firm pat to his shoulder. "Even dogs can have an off day, huh Wes?" Nate shook from laughter and pointed to the younger men scattered across the front garden. "We was fixing to start up a football game now that everyone's here except Eisley. We have about an hour before she gets here." Nate's expression darkened with challenge. "Lots can happen in an hour, can't it, boy?"

"Oh, good grief." Sophie shook her head. "Give the man a break."

Wes hoped Nate didn't notice his tension. He'd never appreciated his acting lessons so much in his entire life. He was on a very different stage.

"Don't you worry, Wes." Kay lowered her voice to a whispered, "He's not as mean as he looks."

Wes's smile tightened, and he matched her volume. "That's comforting."

"But he's not going to make it easy on you."

Wes swallowed down his newfound confidence.

"Desserts here," Emma shouted, pulling Wes's attention from Nate's surly scowl to a woman stepping from a small blue car.

"No dessert 'til we finish football, men." Nate called to the others tossing the football and then turned to Wes, smile ruthless. "You too, Wes."

Wes's grin perched on one side. He had a good mind to believe Nate Jenkins wouldn't tease him if he didn't like him a little.

The dark-haired beauty walked from the car and handed Kay a white box. "Julia's bringing the rest. She's trying to keep Eisley busy at the shop for a little longer."

Wes watched the sweet exchange as Sophie took the box from her mom, shot him a scrunched smile, and nearly danced up the steps into the house. What a collection of differing personalities.

"She *is* beautiful, isn't she?"

Wes blinked his way back to the present and turned to see the brunette at his side, her dark brow raised. He drew in a deep breath and tried to collect some words to satisfy her curiosity.

"Don't be embarrassed. Everybody looks at Sophie that way...until they meet Julia. And then they're awestruck for a while."

Wes offered his hand. "Eisley said Julia was the pretty one, but it appears this family has a genetic disposition toward lovely ladies. It's a pleasure to meet you."

"Rachel." She took his proffered hand, smile guarded. "Impressive, Mr. Harrison. Words as smooth as that fancy voice of yours."

Obviously, Nate Jenkins wasn't the only one who had him on trial. He studied the defensive tilt of her chin and chose his words carefully. "I'm quite sincere. My words as well as my intentions."

Rachel's eyes narrowed, examining him. "I suppose you've figured out we're a close-knit bunch and pretty protective of our own. Especially the ones who have been hurt the most, so you're walking on some pretty precarious ground. I advise you to watch your step. My dad knows how to get rid of a body."

Wes shot her a look.

Her gaze softened. "Have I scared you yet?"

"Terrified."

"Healthy fear is a good thing, eh?"

Wes pushed up a fake grin and became distracted by some colorful design on the side of Rachel's neck. It was a curious tattoo: a small red dragon devouring a flaming sword.

"I'm the family's reformed pagan." Her lips twisted into a saucy grin that flickered with a touch of mischief.

"That would be all of us, wouldn't it?"

She measured him with her stare, and then a genuine smile bloomed. "Smart, too?"

"Intelligence by trial might be more like it."

She chuckled and crossed her arms, nodding. "It's nice to have a smooth talker among the pack of Neanderthals around here."

"Hey, boy, we're gonna introduce you to some country charm." Nate claimed attention and pointed toward the two men tossing a football. "There's two of my boys." He gestured toward a dark-haired man who offered a one finger salute in Wes's direction. "That's Rick."

The golden-headed youngest caught the ball and then sauntered forward, hand extended. "Great to have you, Wes. I'm Greg."

"You dress like you're goin' to church." Nate's gruff voice drowned out all others. "You can't play no football in something prissy like that. Didn't Kay tell you to bring your play clothes?"

Wes swept a downward glance at his navy jacket, beige slacks, and loafers. "You would wear this attire to church?"

Nate knitted his thick brows together. "A tire?"

"Well if you don't mind messin' up your nice duds, you could still play." Greg frowned and ended with a one-shoulder shrug. "Unless you're...well, chicken."

Nate slammed his hand into Wes's back again, sending him forward two steps. "Naw, he ain't chicken. What'd you know about football, boy?"

Wes studied the football flying overhead. "American football?"

"What other kind is there? Football is football."

Ahhh, the golden calf of American sports. "Back home football is what one refers to as soccer, but rugby is more akin to American football, I believe."

"Why don't they call football...football?" Nate challenged with hands to his hips. "Don't make no sense to call soccer...football."

"It seems in soccer one mostly use one's *feet*, thus the reason why the British refer to it as *football*. From my limited experience, in American football one tends to use one's *hands* for the most part." He donned a smile as a peace offering. "Thus the confusion."

"Naw, naw. Football's all about strategy." Nate pointed to his forehead. "You use your brain to really get the job done right."

"And a few three-hundred-pound linebackers help too." Greg started off at a run to catch the pass from Rick.

"Similar to rugby, but I notice you throw the ball forward, not back? In rugby, a forward throw is illegal."

"Boy, this ain't rugby, this is football." Nate spoke with the conviction of a preacher.

"Come on, Lizzie, I'll give you some tea and we can let the boys finish their testosterone-driven stand-off." Kay ushered Lizzie toward the veranda.

"Daddy, remember." Sophie took a seat on the steps and rested her chin in her hands like a little girl. "Be nice, he's not used to your way of playing."

Nate's head jerked up and he patted his chest. "Nice? I'm always nice." He called to the house. "You just ask my little wifey over there. I gotta heart of gold, right, honey?"

Kay turned from the doorway, brow tilted with pure innocence. "Did you say as hard as gold?"

"Hmmpf!"

"Are ya'll gonna talk all day?" Greg braced his palms on his hips "Or can we play some football?"

"You in, boy?" Nate pointed the football in his direction, a challenge in his eyes.

Wes pulled in some air through his clenched teeth, placed his hands on his hips, and grinned. "I'm in."

∞ ∞ ∞

The boy stayed plumb nice. Not one sassy word or dirty look. Nate rubbed his scruffy jaw and eyed Wes Harrison from top to bottom. He wasn't lookin' so prissy no more. Dirt slathered his pretty clothes and his hair stuck spiked from a healthy mixture of mud and sweat. Nate tried not to grin, tried not to show he kind of liked the city boy, but when his gaze met his wife's lifted brow, he knew...*she knew*. Daggone it. Why'd she always have to read his mind?

He growled. Well, just because the boy was fast at catchin' onto football and could kick a mean punt didn't mean he was a match for Eisley.

Wes caught Nate's pass and then made a run for the goal line with Greg and Rick in hot pursuit. The boy was quick, but his fancy shoes slowed his speed. Greg caught him around the waist and slammed him to the ground, with Rick landing on top of him for good measure.

Sophie hopped up from the steps. "Oh no. You've made a sandwich of a movie star. This is bad."

Greg helped the city boy up from the ground, no more worn for the wear and Nate nodded toward him. "Aw, he's all right. Tougher 'n I thought."

"That's comforting." Wes tossed up the ball, caught it and then kicked it out toward Rick. The ball sliced through the air in a clean spiral.

Nate pulled his jaw up from the ground at the pure beauty in the kick. "Where'd you learn to kick like that?"

Wes massaged one of his arms and that infernal grin returned. Nate just couldn't seem to wipe it off the boy's face. "I was the Fly Man in rugby and top kicker on the team."

"You take a lickin' and keep on tickin', don't ya, boy?"

Wes looked up through squinted eyes and let out a weak chuckle. "I suppose you could put it that way. One question, though, when I've watched American football, I don't recall seeing the players pull at each other's trousers to distract them from catching the ball? Is this an American ritual?"

Before Nate could decipher Wes's question, Greg answered. "Dad fights dirty." Greg shrugged and stepped past Wes to catch another pass from Rick before adding, "He's always looking for the weak spots."

"That's right." Nate winked. "It just keeps you on your toes." Nate held Wes's gaze for a second of healthy intimidation. "See what you're made of."

Wes didn't flinch, but an impressive southern accent toppled out of his mouth. "I'm made of a lot better stuff than I used to be, Nate. Since God got a hold of my heart, I'm a changed man. But in the future I reckon I'll keep a better hold on my trou...*pants*."

Nate's grin broadened until he tossed his head back and laughed. "Now you're talkin', boy. Now you're talkin'."

Twenty-One

*E*isley boxed up another dozen of Julia's red velvet swirl cupcakes, but her sneaky two-year-old kept distracting her. The scent of the freshly-baked combination of sugar, flour, and butter seemed to add pounds when Eisley simply walked in her sister's bakery, *Sugar and Spice*, and Emily's little fingers wanted to investigate the confectionary delicacies. It was a good thing all those tasty sweets were going directly to her parents' house or she'd succumb to the temptation of hoarding them away in her refrigerator...and then mourn the appearance of an extra ten pounds around her already cushiony waistline.

But at least she could indulge for today. Her birthday. One year older. She groaned and snatched Emily from a stool before her little acrobat made another chocolate chip cookie dive.

Julia emerged from the kitchen, white apron wrapped around her slender body and arms filled with a piping hot apple-raspberry pie. How on earth Julie kept her waif-like figure while cooking up these delicious masterpieces blew Eisley's mind. And seemed extremely unfair to the entire female population.

Of course, no one could be angry with Julia. She breezed into the room bringing a calming warmth with her. She'd always been the sister who eased away looming chaos with a gentle word. Always the optimist—until three months ago and Mack Richards. If the courts didn't prove next month that Julia had suffered a date rape and find Mack guilty, her dad might take the law in his own hands. Thankfully, for Julia's sake, the news had been safely tucked within the family's walls. Eisley shuddered. Julia had already suffered enough. The last thing she needed was her private horror splattered all over the papers for the whole south side of Virginia to read.

Rick's runaway-bride story from last year had already turned her brother into more of a hermit than he'd been before. Their family had its fair share of bad publicity. Julia's story needed to stay nice and quiet. For her sake.

"Would you mind locking up once you finish icing those?" Her powder-blue eyes glimmered with a smile that rarely made it to her lips now that Mack had left her with shadows of pain behind her gaze and a growing baby bump beneath her blouse. "I need to pick up a few other things on the way to Mom and Dad's."

"Sure." Eisley licked a frosting-covered finger and placed Emily down on the floor with an almost empty bowl of icing. "It shouldn't take fifteen minutes to finish up here."

Julia's eyes widened. "Um...Oh. Well, take your time, sis. Greg's always late to these family gatherings anyway, so we'll have to wait for him. There's really no rush."

"Ohhhkay." If she didn't know better, she'd think Julia was stalling. "I won't hurry, then."

Weird. If anyone else in her family sparked a question mark in Eisley's thoughts, it wouldn't have concerned her, but Julia? What was she hiding?

"Come on with me, Em." Julia gathered Emily's hand and tugged the toddler to the door. "Let's go see Nana and Papa."

Julia waved as she went out the door and Eisley went back to working with the cupcakes. The door jingled with an entrance.

"Forget some—" She looked up and caught her mistake. A high-class stranger walked through the door, impeccably dressed, with dizzying heels and enough eyeliner to shame Captain Jack Sparrow. Definitely a tourist. A rich one. "Can I help you?"

The woman pushed back a handful of silky blond hair and offered a toothy smile. "I think I'm lost."

Eisley rinsed off her hands and met the lady at the counter. "That's not hard to do this far off the interstate. Where are you headed?"

"Actually." Her eyelids drooped with an apologetic smile. "I'm a rather new reporter writing a story about small towns in the southwestern part of Virginia."

Her accent wasn't Blue Ridge. Her words formed in an interesting mix of something Eisley couldn't quite make out. Not northern, exactly. Refined, for sure.

"Well, Pleasant Gap is certainly one of those small towns. I'm closing up shop here in about ten minutes, but I'd be glad to answer any questions about our town. Would you like a treat while you wait?" Eisley gestured toward the desserts behind the glass.

The woman peered forward and tapped the glass container with her nail. "One of those chocolate chip bisc...cookies would be splendid."

Eisley paused, a sudden warning blasting through her middle. "Which paper did you say you were with?"

The woman's smile reappeared. "Southwestern Chronicle." She extended her palm across the counter. "Dana Lewis."

Southwestern Chronicle? The Southwestern Virginia Chronicle? From the sleek style of her suit, the Chronicle must pay much better than she thought. She took Ms. Lewis's hand. "Eisley Barrett."

"Now I will know who to reference. My piece is more about the people and culture of the towns, not the towns themselves. For instance, educational aspirations, family expectations, travel. From all I've read, many small-town Appalachian people rarely travel outside their sphere of birth."

The woman didn't pronounce Appalachian like she'd ever heard a native say it. Caution etched a little deeper in Eisley's stomach. "Well, I don't know if I'm the best person to interview for those questions. My brother studied veterinary medicine in Scotland for a semester. My sister lived in Italy with our aunt for six months, and I just got back from a trip to England." She frowned. "But my parents have never been north of West Virginia or DC, let alone out of the country."

"Lack of interest?" She rested her pen against her chin as she studied Eisley like a professor.

"Primarily lack of resources. There's no absence of dreaming, but most parts of *Appalachia*," —she emphasized the appropriate pronunciation— "are pretty poor. I'm sure you've learned about it from your research. It's a common theme."

"Yes." She tapped her pen against her lips. "Poverty and lack of educational opportunities." She shrugged and continued. "Would you like to return to England again someday?"

Alrighty then, let's not ponder on the big issues, like low socioeconomic status and hungry children. Ms. Lewis wasn't winning any favors here. "I'd love to go back, but apart from winning the lottery, I don't imagine it will be a common occurrence in my life."

Ms. Lewis's nose crinkled with her grin. "You could always marry rich."

"Oh yeah, that's what I'll do. Marry rich." Eisley laughed and then the implications of her statement clicked into place. She examined the woman. "Are you writing a fairy tale, Ms. Lewis, or a newspaper article?"

Nathan and Pete crashed from the back room into the main part of the bakery, with Nathan arriving at her side first. "Mom, we finished."

"All the boxes." Pete added.

"Are these your children?" Ms. Lewis's voice heightened into Disney princess pitch. "Oh, how adorable."

Pete and Nathan froze, staring up at her like she might blossom into something pink any minute.

"Excuse me just a sec, Ms. Lewis." Eisley turned to the boys. "Did you get the inventory from the crate by the back door? That was the last box of cans to stock on the shelves."

Nathan looked at Pete, who gave an exaggerated sigh. "I don't know."

"Come on, Pete. One more and Aunt Julia gives us three dollars each."

The boys dashed away and Eisley closed the lid on the cupcake container. "I think we're about done here, Ms. Lewis. Is there anything else I can get for you?"

"Are most people in town as helpful as you?" The gleam in her dark eyes appeared more mischievous than friendly.

"I'd steer clear of the Hardware Store. Russell Franklin doesn't take too well to strangers, but otherwise, you're pretty safe."

Strangers. The word resurrected Wes's wariness. Something didn't fit here. Eisley looked up from the cupcakes in time to catch Ms. Lewis taking a photo.

"What are you doing?"

She slid her phone into her purse. "Taking a snap for the article. You don't mind, do you?"

Snap? Where had she heard that word before? "I think I'd prefer no pictures, okay? I hate to rush you, but I need to go. Davis down at the shoe shop can talk your ear off about this place."

"Thank you for your help and the cookie."

"We finished, Mom." The boys came back into the room.

The door jangled alerting Eisley to Ms. Lewis's exit, but as she replayed the weird scene in her head, realization dawned. *British. The woman was British, though she was attempting to hide it.*

Eisley ran to the bakery door and swung it open, scanning the narrow line Main Street made between the quaint rows of shops. No one similar to Ms. Lewis moved down the lantern-lined sidewalks. This wasn't good. Maybe she was being paranoid, but she needed to tell Wes. He could help her sort it out during their phone conversation tonight.

"Mom, are you okay?" Nathan asked.

She smiled to the boys. "Yeah, buddies. Let's get these cupcakes to Papa and Nana's." She gave the street another glance, mind-weary. "And I really hope we don't have any more unexpected guests today. I'm ready for a nice relaxing evening."

Eisley pulled her jeep up her parents' driveway, still mulling over the stranger's visit. It might be her birthday party but what sounded more tempting was a long nap. Between trying to write Julia's story, late-night phone calls with Wes, the regular insanity of being a single mom, and the crazy events with Ms. Lewis, Sleeping Beauty's siesta sounded better all the time.

But naps lived in another world. With fairy godmothers.

The boys jumped from the jeep and ran headlong into the ensuing football game on the front lawn. The usual boisterous greeting followed with some quick redirection from her dad as Greg plowed forward, ball tucked beneath his arm, pulling her attention away from the strangely familiar addition on the field.

"Oh hi, Eisley." Sophie danced down the porch steps, her smile even bigger than usual. She clapped her hands together and did a little jump. "You're finally here."

Eisley's grin hitched, uncertain. "Thanks, Sophie. I'm glad to see you, too." *Obviously, she didn't go for the decaf this morning.*

Eisley walked toward the game, grinning at the way her Dad bossed everyone around, another sign of his fierce affection. Oh, poor Wes. When he did come, she hated to think what Dad's inner Papa Bear might do.

Greg had one of her boys on each arm and swung them around like a carousel.

"Heads up, Eisley." Dad called.

The football spiraled toward her, a perfectly placed pass. She hooked a grin and caught it against her body. Before she could ready herself for a sprint, someone swooped her up and took off in a dead run. *What?* She looked over at her assailant and a pair of smoky gray eyes greeted her.

Wes? Her mouth dropped open and she blinked, linking her arm around his neck to keep from falling out of shock. "Wh...what are you doing?"

His lopsided grin dimpled. "Interception."

Her brain swam through syrupy thoughts, searching for something solid to say, but from the touch of his hands at her back to the gentle warmth in his eyes, not one solitary word emerged. She just stared like an idiot until he placed her feet on the ground across the family-created goal line.

She had to be dreaming.

She steadied her palm against his shoulder, waiting to surface from her delusion, but he added reality's touch by sweeping a strand of hair from her face and settling the pad of his thumb against her cheek. He felt like Wes, looked like Wes, and even carried the faintest hint of cowboy cologne like Wes, but the mud-tinged hair didn't fit the norm.

Her father's voice broke in to confirm her living daydream. "Boy, that don't count. You can't pick up a player and make an interception." He marched forward, finger jabbing the air. "I don't care how love-struck you're tryin' to look. It just ain't right."

Wes kept his gaze locked on Eisley's, his familiar smile filling her shocked skull with all sorts of beautiful music. "I think it should still score as a Try."

She was pretty sure she heard *I love you* in the middle of that sentence, if looks said anything.

Dad's voice hammered into the hum of her gravitational pull toward Wes's lips. "If I've told ya once, I've told you a hundred times. It's not a Try, it's called a touchdown."

Eisley reached up and touched Wes's dirt-smudged cheek. "When...how...why?"

He narrowed his gaze, in mock contemplation. "When? About an hour ago. How? By plane. Why?" He leaned in close, breathtakingly close, his words honed to an intimate whisper. "I hope it's fairly obvious."

Breathe, Eisley, breathe. The pleasant warmth of his closeness played a serenade over her skin.

"Disgusting." Greg walked by, face scrunched like he smelled stinky socks, one boy tucked under each arm.

"Wipe that silly grin off your face, girl." Dad snatched the football from Eisley's hands and looked at the two of them as if he'd never seen anything so gross in all his life. Yep, maturity radiated off of the men in her family in gusts. "You're too old to be moonin' over some fancy pants like this."

"Dad, he's not some fancy pants and..." Eisley rolled her eyes. "Couldn't you have picked a less embarrassing nickname? Pants in England are..."

"Actually, it's quite funny." Wes's fingers trailed down her arm to braid with her hand and then he turned to Nate. "We've become well-acquainted with our different quirks, haven't we, Nate?"

"Hadn't met nobody who can kick a football better than Ray Guy." Nate sniffed, smoothed his thumb and forefinger over his moustache, and feigned indifference. "So, I've seen worse, but I can't get past that hoity-toity accent."

Wes's breath vibrated near her ear and encouraged a cascade of warmth down her neck. "I think he likes me."

Eisley swayed into his scent, familiar and missed. Her fingers fisted the sleeve of his jacket and pulled him to her. Their lips remembered each other pretty well, gentle and inviting, sending tingles down all the familiar paths they'd traveled in England.

"Ahem." Her dad cleared his throat and brought the football between their faces. "Let's get our mind on football, boy."

She shoved the ball away and kept her attention on Wes, reveling in the wonderful hum of satisfaction cascading over her body. "Where are you staying?"

"We set him up in the guest house."

Her gaze swung back to her father's. "The guest house Cousin Lacey used to live in?" Visions of pink carpet, lace curtains, floral wallpaper, and a princess bed infiltrated her star struck wonder. Her dad's self-satisfied grin branded the decision as his. Of course.

She squeezed Wes's forearm. "I'm so sorry."

"Sorry?"

Poor guy really had no clue the world he had unwittingly entered when he crossed the big pond. Yep, class took on a whole new definition...and accent.

"Hey, y'all," Sophie called from the porch. "Mama says you have time for one more game, then we gotta eat."

"You gonna play a game with us, girl?" A challenge flickered in her dad's eyes. "Or are you afraid you'll hurt your sissy boyfriend."

Heat soared from her cheeks to her forehead. "Good grief, Dad. Can't you tell that Wes is capable of handling any tackle you throw at him? He's certainly strong and—" Her gaze swept over Wes's chest, from shoulder to fabulous shoulder and her palm took on a life of its own by sliding up that muscular arm and drawing a little closer. Even beneath the cloth of his jacket, the flex of his muscle spiked her internal thermometer about twenty degrees. His smoky eyes sent a fire trail through her middle. She swallowed. "—sturdy enough."

Dad growled a warning. "Stop acting like a girl."

"I am a girl, Dad." She rolled an apologetic gaze to Wes, then grabbed the ball from her dad and shot a bullet-like pass to Rick. "I'm in. It'll give me a chance to *check out* our new player?"

Wes's smile paused, his darkening gaze making her feel very girly indeed.

She took her time examining his erratic hair and then let her gaze savored the journey all the way down to his muddy loafers. Yep, totally checking him out.

"This is making me sick." Nate grumbled forward and pointed his finger in Wes's direction. "I can tell you one thing right now. You and that boy are gonna be on the *same* team. You got it. *Same.* Come on."

Eisley ran for the huddle. She was playing all right, for keeps. *Happy Birthday to me.* Suddenly, her sluggish brain didn't bother her so much.

Wes jogged up beside her. "I suppose your father wants you on my team because he pities my poor English ways?"

"Nope." She slowed to a stop and turned to face him, wrestling with her smile. "It doesn't have anything to do with your lovely English ways."

Wes's brow shot high in silent question.

"He didn't want you to have an excuse to tackle me."

His smile eased up slowly as he took a small step forward. "I already have a rather substantial list of reasons. What's one more?"

"I aint' gonna be able to stomach Rick's chili if you two keep it up, and nobody should miss Rick's chili." Her dad's voice broke through the trance. "Get ready boys. You too, Fancy Pants."

She rolled her eyes so hard a twinge of pain twitched at her temple. If Wes could survive her father's merciless teasing, he could survive anything.

"Chili?" Uncertainty replaced the hungry look on Wes's face.

Eisley stared at him a moment, her vision blurring. *Okay, maybe she'd gotten a little carried away with the eye roll.* She blinked Wes's eyes back into focus, only to have it blur again. The fog traveled from her sight to her brain, spreading spots across her vision. She blinked again. "Not the best food for a British stomach, I'm afraid."

A tingle started in her right cheek and crawled toward her lips. *Oh no. Ignore it and maybe it will go away. Not today, not right now.* "I advise you to load up on salad and bread, okay?"

Eisley rubbed her eyes in a futile attempt to stop the white mist entering her periphery, but the bleary picture only became fuzzier, invading more of her sight. She'd fought off warning signs for the past hour. The familiar numbing of a migraine branched further over the left side of her face and even prickled in her left thumb.

"Eisley?" Wes voice came from a distant tunnel. "You don't look well."

The numbness grew along with the slow build of pain creeping across her forehead and leaving a nauseating ache. She pushed her right hand against her head. "I think I'm getting a migraine."

A brief moment of silence followed and then her father's voice reverberated over every aching bone in her skull. "Eisley's got a migraine, y'all. You know what that means."

"Snow!" Pete and Nathan screamed from the other side of the yard. "It's going to snow. Mama has a migraine."

*Oh, the love...*but even as she tried to grin, the pain intensified. She leaned forward with both palms against either side of her head to relieve some of the internal pressure. Her stomach convulsed. *No, no. Lord. Don't you think I've been humbled enough?*

"I think I need to get home, everybody." Her voice sounded strange, almost like it was detached from her body. Migraines were not fun, and thankfully fairly uncommon for her, but as her kids' reactions proved, usually weather-related.

"Aw Eisley," Dad's voice broke through the fog. "You'll miss your birthday fireworks. Greg smuggled 'em all the way from Tennessee."

"We'll watch them from the back porch, okay? Maybe I can take a rain check for tomorrow after church."

Dad nodded and then sent a glance to Wes. "You'd better take her home, boy." He stepped close to Wes, chin wrinkled with his frown. "And you'd better take good care of her, you hear?"

Eisley squinted up to Wes, trying to bring enough thoughts together for an apology, when Wes replied. "You have my word, Nate."

Twenty-Two

es steered Eisley's jeep down a winding lane and over a hill, following her whispered directions. He examined her disheveled profile. Pieces of ginger hair had worked their way out of her makeshift ponytail and curled about her face in a fiery halo his fingers ached to touch. Her head leaned back against the seat, eyes closed. How he'd missed her! A restless stirring in his heart settled at her nearness.

Take care of her, Nate had ordered. Not a problem. He gathered her hand into his and gave it a gentle squeeze. "Do you have something you can take for relief?"

"Home," she whispered and pointed a weak finger down the tree-lined drive.

A voice piped up from the back seat.

"You look different than you do on TV." Wes peered into the rearview mirror and found Pete's narrowed blue eyes examining him. "Like a normal person."

"Pete," Eisley muttered.

"I know." Wes turned a little to get a better view of the ginger-headed boy. "I think it's because they make me wear make-up when I go on the tele."

"Make-up?" Nathan asked, his face contorting into a horrified grimace. "Like a girl?"

Nate's influence ran a strong course through these boys' veins already. Wes stifled a chuckle.

"Whew, I'm glad I'm going to be Spiderman when I grow up." Pete sighed as he relaxed back into his seat. "I'll never have to wear make-up."

Wes lost all control of his laugh that time.

The boys had eased into conversation with him as if they'd always known him. Seeing them in person tightened the bond he'd developed over the past month of video calls.

"You can't be Spiderman, because he's not real." Nathan sent Wes a look that read *what do we do with him?*

"I hungry," Emily whined with a heart-wrenching wobble of her bottom lip.

Wes reached behind him to grab her little foot. She squealed, jerked her foot from his hand, and produced an effective pout. He had the sudden urge to nuzzle her neck until she giggled. "Peckish, are you? We'll get you something soon, chicken."

"Chicken?" Both boys said in unison, exchanging a look.

"She's never afraid of much except thunder." Nathan patted his baby sister's hand.

"Then she starts squawlin' like a banjo, Mama says," Pete added.

Nathan huffed. "Banshee, not banjo." He shook his head and then focused his attention back on Wes. "Why'd you call her a chicken?"

"It's a term of endearment, like darling, I suppose."

Pete wrinkled his freckled nose. "I'd rather be a lion. Could you call me a lion?"

"Turn here." Eisley murmured. "Duck." She closed her eyes again, but her lips tipped up at the corners. Her fingers tightened around his, kindling a slow heat in his stomach, a heat he'd kept in amicable control for their long month apart. Skin on skin ignited his senses.

"Mom called you a duck, Wes." Nathan snorted.

"Hmm, what do you suppose I should call her? Any suggestions?"

"How 'bout puppy? Or kitten?" Pete suggested. "She likes puppies. Our dog, Fritter, just had puppies last week. Five of them."

"I hungry." Emily repeated a little louder.

"We're here," Eisley whispered.

The road ended in front of a two-level white farmhouse trimmed in red. A white fence, overgrown with ivy, framed the front. The red front door emphasized the berries on the holly bushes at either corner of the porch and the rust-colored stones of the front steps. A haven of trees circled the edges of the front yard but opened behind to reveal a frosted expanse of countryside with blue mountains lining the distant horizon.

Wes ushered everyone inside, sent the boys upstairs to play with their Legos, and attempted to coax Emily away from Eisley, to no avail. Finally, after a near-argument and a snack for Emily, Eisley agreed to have a lie-down.

"What can I do to help you?"

The question seemed to take a moment to register. She studied him through squinted eyes. "I'm sorry for this."

He took her elbow and led her over to the bed. "Stop apologizing and lie down. Is there something I can do to quiet Emily for you?"

"You're wonderful." A sheen of tears emerged in her eyes.

He kissed her cheek and breathed in the minty scent of her hair. "I've missed you, pet."

She leaned into him, burying her head into his shoulder. "And I've ruined your beautiful arrival with my stupid migraine."

"You need to rest." He gave her a nudge toward the bed. Emily rubbed her eyes and yawned. "What can I do for Emily?"

Eisley curled up on the bed and pulled Emily close. "Maybe read to her?"

He tucked the blanket around them both. "Any particular book?"

"*Goodnight Moon* is her favorite. It's in the basket by the door." She nodded toward the door and lifted tired eyes to his. "Thank you."

Wes retrieved the book and stretched onto the bed, Emily tucked between the two of them. As he read, Emily snuggled up against his arm and the touch fisted in his chest with a protective and grateful grip. By the end of the story, both girls slept and he'd fallen in love all over again.

Eisley's hair fanned across the pillow, her lips slightly parted in sleep, with Emily curled against the crook of her body. He brushed a kiss over the soft curls of Emily's head and quieted the urge to lie down behind Eisley to curb his curiosity of how well her body would fit against his. Somehow, he knew it would. As well as this love for her fit into his heart. He'd spent a lot of years searching for a home for his unsettled heart, and now...he'd finally found it.

∞ ∞ ∞

Eisley woke with the light-headed remains of the migraine. At least her thoughts came in full sentences—full, *embarrassing* sentences. *Oh, what must Wes think?* From her Dad's annoying ribbing to a girlfriend who fell into a comatose state, it didn't look good.

The last thing she remembered was Wes's smooth voice reading *Goodnight Moon*. The man could make a children's book sound sexy. She peeked down at Emily, still asleep, and carefully slid her arm out from under her daughter's head, sneaking a quick kiss before slipping from the room.

Her stomach rumbled its need, so she shuffled into the kitchen and sliced an apple. Wes would really be better off without her and her rude, chaotic family. She popped a piece of the apple in her mouth and picked up Pete's jacket off the floor, scanning each room as she passed it. Where was he? She wouldn't blame him if he ran away and didn't look back. A choice like loving her wasn't for the weak of heart or will. Maybe she *had* been dreaming.

She flipped on the large hall closet light and looked for a vacant hanger.

"Feeling better?"

Eisley spun around. Wes leaned against the doorframe, thumbs hitched in the pockets of a fresh pair of jeans, his pale blue oxford bringing out the blue in his eyes. Her breath caught somewhere in the middle of such thoughts as *He's in my house* and *Kiss me and I'm yours forever.* She pinched herself. *He's still here.* She pinched one more time for good measure.

"You're still here."

His white teeth split his lips apart and his smoky glance skipped over her entire body, setting her skin on fire. "I thought I'd stick around." He winked and stood taller, his gaze darkened with a step forward. "Since who I came to see is right here."

Every bone in her legs softened to jelly. *Deep breaths, Eisley,* and she would do just that once she remembered how. She shrugged through a whimpered laugh. "I'm glad." She turned back to the hanger and sighed through a smile. *Thank you, Jesus.*

Feet shifted behind her. "Emily still taking a kip?"

"Yea, poor little thing seemed as pooped as her mom." She adjusted the jacket on the hanger and closed her eyes as teases of his scent reached her. A deep heat began to build in her stomach.

"The boys are occupied upstairs." Wes's voiced edged a bit closer, words slow, almost calculated.

"You're amazing. You brave my dad and brothers, tuck your pitiful girlfriend into bed, *and* entertain the boys for an hour. You're like Superman or something." She placed the hanger on the rod and turned in time to see him flip off the closet light.

"Superman?" The door clicked closed. "Then I think I've found my kryptonite, pet."

His silhouette moved toward her, outlined by the gap of light slipping underneath the door. Her sharp intake of breath slit the darkness. *Mama never told me there'd be days like this.*

"Oh?" She managed a whisper.

His hands cupped her arms and slid upward to cradle her face, thumbs caressing a soft line across her cheekbones. "Separation from you." His murmur breathed against her lips.

Mama Mia, what a man!

His mouth slowly found hers in the electrified darkness, first testing her upper lip then the lower one, like a gentle experiment between the two. He lingered, almost as if he savored the feel and touch of her as much as she did him. It was a slow, easy greeting, sweet and filled with longing. Neither of them seemed to be in a hurry.

One of his hands moved to cradle the back of her head, nudging it to the side so his mouth could roam her jawline. He inhaled her skin as his cheek smoothed against hers until he captured her lips again. His other palm caught her at the base of her spine, pinning her stomach against his. Tight.

"I'd prefer not to take such an extended holiday between our next kisses, if you don't mind."

Eisley cleared her throat, but her head remained foggy, and a thick English fog at that. "Wait, I don't think I can answer any questions right now. The steam from that kiss just clouded up my brain."

His smile stretched against her cheek and he took his time trailing his fingertips down her neck until every piece of her skin screamed with the need for more. Her hands slid around his waist, palms exploring the familiar territory of each contour of his back, strong and warm.

"Mmm...you smell like apples." He nuzzled just below her ear, igniting liquid fire in her veins.

She swallowed a big lump of *oh my goodness* and closed her eyes, drowning in a myriad of senses enhanced by the darkness—the feel of his soft, cotton shirt at her fingertips and the warm smoothness of his skin underneath. The earthy, intoxicating scent of his cologne and his deep voice filled every inch of space outside and inside of her.

Eisley palmed his cheek, tiny hints of scruff tickling her hand. "Why are you here?"

"It's fairly obvious, don't you think?" His voice reverberated deep and close. "I've always wanted to snog in a closet."

Tears scratched against her throat even as her grin spread. "No, I mean *here.* All the way here."

"Because *you're* here. Because everything I want is here with you. And there are so many reasons to be with you, pet. You are lovely." He swept her hair back and kissed her temple. "Funny." His lips moved to her cheekbone. "Honest." Her nose. "Sincere." His mouth hovered over hers. "Did I say lovely?"

"I come with such a big package, and I—"

The touch of his lips silenced her. "Just the way you are, Eisley."

The knotted fear in her heart began to unbraid. *Just the way she was?* The truth in his words rifted the wall around her heart and all she wanted to do was show him how much *he* meant to her.

She took his face into her hands and captured his open mouth, pouring out her appreciation and pent-up passion. His surprised moan fueled one hand to entangle into his hair, drawing him deeper into the kiss, closer. Her other hand slid from around his neck and moved slowly across his solid chest, his skin hot beneath his thin oxford.

Somewhere in the back of her mind, a caution light started blinking, but instead of pulling away, her body melted into his, requesting more. He groaned while one of his palms brought her hips closer against him. Good heavens. What had she started? His fingertips traced a fiery line from her chin down her neck to the small hollow point between her collarbones, pooling warmth across her chest.

She mumbled words on chunks of broken air. "Are you...trained in kissing...for films too?"

He murmured something unintelligible against her neck.

"I bet...you made...an A."

A robotic voice from a childhood movie sounded off in her brain: *Warning! Warning!* In rebellion against the voice, she lifted her chin to expose her neck to the beautiful sensations of his kiss.

"Eisley." His whisper tickled her shoulder blade and moved over to the skin peeking above the V-neck of her shirt. Need and desire weighed his voice down an octave. Every nerve in her body begged for just a little more.

Four weeks? Felt more like four years.

When his hot mouth captured her collarbone and continued a steamy descent along her shirt's neckline, her eyes flew open in surprise. "Oh, heaven help me."

Her muscles shut down, beginning with her wobbly legs. She stumbled back to steady her limbs and pulled Wes along, but the foot she placed her faith in landed on something small, soft, and slippery.

With an unladylike squeal, a painful grunt, and a resounding crash, Eisley succeeded in landing on her back and bringing Wes—plus a couple of coats—with her.

"Why do all my romantic scenes end in a commercial break?" She pushed herself up to a sitting position. A twinge of pain shot down her back and produced a groaned laugh. "Maybe break wasn't the best word to use."

"Are you all right?" Wes gripped under her arms, but before she made it to a complete stand she reached down to find the leg-splitting culprit...*or perhaps a providentially designed agent of rescue?* The soft object felt amazingly familiar.

"Yeah." She reached for his hand. "How about you?"

"Humbled, ashamed, and a bit disappointed."

Suddenly the closet door swung wide and two little silhouettes filled the entry.

Nathan flipped on the light, looking from one adult to the other. "Hey, what are you two doing in here and what was that big noise?"

Eisley exchanged a sheepish glance with Wes, thoughts stopping just a moment to appreciate his untidy raven hair and oxford with two buttons unhooked. Did she do that? She jerked her attention to the boys. "Well...um...I was hanging up Pete's jacket and eventually fell over..." Eisley looked down into her hand. "Emily's shoe."

"You finally found it, Mama." Pete's grin dimpled each freckled cheek. "Good job."

"Thanks, Pete." Eisley moved past him and out the door. The room temperature dropped about fifty degrees. She focused on the curious little faces in front of her and tried to ignore the handsome but somewhat guilty one standing with his hands in his pockets.

"You're faces sure are red. Are you mad?" Pete's bright blue gaze volleyed between them.

Eisley contemplated how to answer, but Nathan beat her to it. "It's hot in there, silly."

In more ways than one.

"Hey, did you two finish that Lego castle?"

"Naw," Pete drawled out.

"We are almost finished though." Nathan pushed Pete toward the stairs. "Wow, Mom, I thought Santa might have popped down the chimney again from the sound of that crash." He started up the steps. "You must be real heavy."

Eisley closed her eyes and moaned. *Reality check.* "Thanks, Nathan."

The boys disappeared back up the stairs and she lifted squinted eyes up to her closet-rogue. He'd probably think she was ridiculous, feeling guilty over a little momentary frisk. After all, she knew his past was filled with much more than making out in a closet. She cringed. *What had his elegant life resorted to?*

What a crazy world! She had the strongest urge to laugh. Out loud. A long time. Maybe with a few hysterical tears involved.

"Eisley." Wes voice sounded raspy. With a tentative step forward and a frustrated tuft of his hair, he drew one of her hands into his. "Forgive me for moving too fast."

Her mouth came unhinged. *Him?* She's the one who'd attacked him with the self-control of a rabid wolf. "You? I think I'm the one who got carried away."

He kissed her hand, the breath from his chuckle escaping over her knuckles. "Who entered the closet with you and turned off the light, then proceeded to taste those lovely lips of yours?"

His gaze dropped to her mouth and she gravitated toward him, drugged by Wes-smell and the sweet purr of satisfaction. She brushed her lips against his and then lowered her cheek to his chest. "I'd forgotten how hard it can be. Reigning in those desires, especially when you really care about someone, and that someone is particularly delicious." Eisley leaned back and lost her train of thought in the dark intensity of his stare. "I was completely intoxicated." She blinked from her trance. "But that's bad."

"Bad?" His countenance dropped like a seven-year-old who'd just been told his drawing received second place instead of first.

"But soooo good." Eisley lessened the blow with a sympathetic sigh. "I could—"

"Lose yourself." He rocked his head back and forth, his expression hardening with determination. "I can't. I won't lose myself with you...well, not until the right time." He looked toward the window and heaved a twenty-pound sigh. "You deserve better and I know my weaknesses." He tucked a loose strand of her hair behind her ear. "Kryptonite or not, I apologize. I had no conviction or foundation for patience before, but now—with you? Loving you makes it both easier and more difficult."

"You didn't hear me complain, did you? In fact, I was urging you to hit a home run." Eisley paused in mid-shrug. "Did you say *loving me*?"

His dangerous smile crooked up on one side. "I already told you I'm playing for keeps." He caught her other hand and drew both of them against his chest, gaze sober and intense. "I want to do much more than make your pulse race. I want your friendship and your confidence. I want to make you laugh and be your best secret-keeper. I want to capture your heart."

Her eyes stung. "You are totally chocolate pie. With chocolate icing, chips, and syrup on top."

He kissed her hand again and looked up through dark lashes. "Your weakness?"

"And then some."

He studied their braided fingers a moment and then met her gaze again. "You are worth the wait. Of anyone, you need to know a man can control his passions enough to honor you."

She buried her face into his shoulder to hide the tears. "Okay, I'll help you out when you're weak, if you'll help me."

"And who helps us if we're both weak?"

As if on cue, Pete screamed something indistinguishable at Nathan, followed by a resounding thud. Eisley looked up with a wobbly smile. "I think we've got it covered."

Twenty-Three

Wes didn't even have to open his eyes to feel *pink* crowding in on him. The guest apartment over the garage at the Jenkins' hadn't boarded a male in a long time- if ever. Eisley's apology over the sleeping arrangement became painfully clear—in neon. When Lizzie retired to one of the elegantly furnished front rooms of the Jenkins' colonial, Wes had entered a room which had suffered from a powder puff explosion. Pink and lace adorned every piece of furniture. Fuchsia rugs covered the hardwoods leading to a white sofa with rose pinstripes. The bathroom was the only place not infected by a combination of magenta and flora. However, the red-heart wallpaper and heart-shaped mirror looked as if Cupid took holiday there.

Nate Jenkins' brand of vetting bordered on terrifying.

Wes released a chuckle and stood, rubbing his eyes awake and taking his steps to the window. Once he pulled back the inches of lace, he stared in wonder at the winter scene. A fresh layer of frost covered the back garden in a soft white sheen leading all the way to the snow-covered mountains in the distance.

The forecast of Eisley's migraine? His smile softened. He'd spent the previous evening by the fireplace at their house playing Candy Land with Nathan and Pete, and as darkness fell, they gathered on the back deck and watched the fireworks from the Jenkins' house across the pasture. After tucking in the children, Eisley had gathered a quilt and snuggled close beside him on the couch while they watched a movie. They'd talked long into the night before she'd nudged him out the door so he wouldn't fall asleep at the wheel.

He closed his eyes, remembering the good-night kiss. Her soft lips against his, urging him to linger. Her hands on his back, coaxing him further into her embrace. Her smile.

A loud knock rattled Wes's door. He startled and turned in the direction.

"Hey boy." The door muffled Nate Jenkins's voice a little, but not much. "You gonna sleep all day? We got some guns to shoot."

Wes glanced at his watch and felt a growl rumble up from his throat. Only 7:30 am. He slid into some jeans and fumbled into his sweater, moments before Nate pushed it open with a thud. *So much for privacy.*

"Well, well, Sleepin' Beauty. I guess I don't need to douse you with cold water after all." Nate framed his scheming grin with a camouflaged cap and jacket. "Shucks, I was hopin'."

"Sorry to disappoint you, Nate. I wasn't expecting you to start so...early."

"Early? Kay talked me into waiting til now. I've been ready since 6:30. Come on, we gotta get this shooting contest in before my daughter comes back over here and makes you get all googly-eyed. Besides, church starts in three hours and I don't want to see you crying during the service 'cause you lost."

Despite his annoyance, Wes found a humored grin pushing its way up onto his face. He could see Eisley's personality in both her father and mother. Somehow, it made him like Nate Jenkins even more. "Give me ten minutes and I'll join you."

Nate's brow rose in doubt.

"Ten minutes, Nate. And then I'll best you at shooting."

Nate released a boisterous laugh. "Best me?" He walked to the door, his shoulders shaking. "You keep telling yourself that, Fancy Pants."

The door clicked to a close and Wes finished getting ready with an added pound of intimidation hot on his heels. Nate Jenkins certainly cut his own mold. Wes pulled on his anorak and scarf and started for the door as his mobile buzzed.

Andrew's number.

"Hello, mate."

"Enjoying your visit in the wilds of Virginia?"

Wes turned and sat on the edge of the bed, long legs extended and crossed at the ankles. "It's providing quite the education."

"Education, is it? A better acquaintance with some *ginger-headed angel*, as I recall?"

"Did I say that?"

"With stars in your eyes."

Wes ran a hand through his hair and chuckled. "I've fallen hard."

"Well, you're the type to settle down and grow old with a passel of American-bred children."

Wes stood, heat creeping into his face, took his cap from the pink mannequin-shaped hat rack and decided to change the subject. "Any news?"

"Diverting the conversation from your nauseatingly sweet romance, I see." Andrew's teasing tones fell away. "I'll humor you for now. The author of the article resigned soon after printing, but her name was Dana Lewis. No one seemed to know much about her. She hadn't been working there long, and we both know it isn't a reputable paper. It doesn't seem they were particular in their employees either."

"No reputable paper would post such bosh."

"Right." Drew's words held his own frustration. "I'm following a few leads, so I expect to have more sound information soon."

"Thanks, Drew."

"I wish I had more to share."

A door slammed outside. "Boy, are you comin'?"

"I appreciate all you're doing."

"You're not going to be a chicken about it, are you?" Nate's voice drew closer to the doorway.

"I need to go for now. Might I ring you later?"

"Any time. Cheers."

Wes placed his mobile in his jacket pocket and walked to the apartment door. He'd half expected to hear Vivian Barry's name associated with the paper, but she wouldn't descend so far as to ruin her own career, would she? His solicitor would make quick work of holding the culprit accountable for falsifying information, breaching privacy, slander. He opened the door and a cool blast of morning air nearly took his breath away.

Nate Jenkins met him and slapped his large hand on Wes's shoulder. "Now's the time to find out what you're really made of, boy."

Wes's cool and controlled attempts at reserve were no match for the jovial directness infecting almost every person in this home. Why should he be surprised? It was Eisley's family.

The thought tugged a broader smile. He shoved his hands into his pockets and wore the silly grin in place all the way to Nate's truck door. He didn't have to pretend here. He merely needed to survive the next hour or two without shooting Nate or being shot by him, right? However, trying to be a knight with the dragon-sized fury of an overprotective father stalking him might be the death of him.

∞ ∞ ∞

"Where did Lizzie go after church?" Eisley wiped some mustard from Emily's chin and tossed a look across the table to her mom.

"We dropped her off at Joe's. She couldn't wait one more minute to meet him, and he was nearly as excited. The two of them were cooing like a set of long-lost lovebirds when we left." Mom shook her golden head. "If God had given Joe a little more time, there's no doubt he'd have crossed the ocean to meet her. Aren't you headed over there with Wes after lunch?"

"That's right." Eisley exchanged a smile with Wes. He sat directly across from her, with Sophie to one side and her father at the head of the table to his left.

Pastor Rhodes probably didn't appreciate Wes's presence at church today, as he'd proven to be a tempting distraction to the well-planned sermon. Eisley stifled a chuckle, knowing there probably wasn't a woman in attendance, single or otherwise, who could recall a word the pastor said. Who was she to blame them? *Forgive me, Lord, for you've seen my thoughts.*

"Uncle Joe is going to love you, Wes."

"What makes you think everybody's going to love this city boy of yours? I'm still not too sure about him." Dad slit Wes a scowl to which her knight in a snug turtleneck merely grinned. Was the guy bulletproof?

"Dad. Be nice."

He ignored her. It really was a weak threat anyway. She needed something stronger. Like a chair. Or an anvil.

"He's eating french fries with a fork," Rachel whispered.

Eisley looked across the table at Wes, who was completely unaware of the effect his social graces were having on her uncultured family. She rested her chin on her hand. "Yeah, he's so great."

Rachel tilted her head to one side and surveyed her sister with a long-suffering eye. "Who eats their french fries with a fork?"

"British people do." Eisley picked up her fork and shot her dad a grin. "I heard Wes showed you up at shooting this morning, Dad." She pointed her fork at her father again, needling the victory a little deeper.

"Who went and told some big story like that?" Nate patted his belly and shook his head. "I figured it was a fair tie."

Everyone froze. Rachel spoke first, gaze locked on Wes. "You tied Dad with rifle shooting?"

Wes gave a one shoulder shrug. "And pistols."

"*And* pistols?" Greg slammed his palm to the table.

"Come on now, we don't need to make such a big fuss about it. I was being easy on him."

Eisley slapped the table as she laughed. "You just can't admit he's as good as you."

"Braggin' on the boy won't help him none." Nate took a large bite of his hot dog and then pushed at Wes's plate. "And what's this here 'bout eating your fries with a fork? Afraid you'll get your pretty fingers dirty?"

"Dad, don't change the subject to save face."

"Oh, Eisley." Kay shook her head and shared a comforting smile. "The two of them have been at it all morning long. You should have heard them during breakfast, one insult after another." She tossed Wes a grin. "Seems Wes can dish it out as well as he can take it."

"If I was afraid of getting my fingers dirty, I wouldn't have allowed you to slam me into the ground outside during football, would I?" Wes picked up his fork again and lifted a fry into his mouth with a defiant tilt of his chin. "And I think nudging me in the back as I made a shot was no accident. Were you getting nervous, old chap?"

Nate nearly spewed his orange juice out. "Nervous? You don't have the stuff in you to make me nervous, boy."

"Are you the ones over there who wear skirts?" The glint in Greg's eyes betrayed his otherwise serious expression. Most likely, her sneaky brother was trying to rescue their Dad's pride with distraction.

Wes coughed through his swallow. "Skirts?"

"You know and play those pipes or something?"

Wes's confusion cleared. *Poor guy. Couldn't everybody just leave him alone?* "Oh, you mean the Scots, my northern neighbors. Those *skirts* are called kilts." He took a sip of his water and stared Greg directly in the eyes, face awash with sincerity. "I only wear a skirt when I dance ballet."

An audible gasp filled the shocked silence. Silverware clattered to the table. *Oh great!* Eisley squeezed her eyes closed. He did *not* say that out loud to her family. She could almost hear the testosterone in the room screaming in protest.

Wes chewed another bite of fries as if he hadn't just dropped a bomb to rock her family into fasting and then he lifted his gaze. "I was teasing. Since you've been taking the mickey out of me all morning, I thought I'd have my turn."

Nate sighed. "I don't know about no Mickey, but I can tell you one thing. I like you a whole lot better now that you cleared up the confusion." He shook his head slowly and groaned. "A man in skirts and a ballerina too. That's just wrong."

Wes winked at Eisley and she grinned back. Yeah, he did fit in and the longer he stayed, the more she didn't want him to leave.

"We've talked for nearly four hours without a break, haven't we, Joseph?" Lizzie turned to Eisley's Uncle Joe and touched his arm. "It's been delightful."

"Best visit I've had in a long time. And the undivided attention of a beautiful woman? I can check it off my bucket list." Joe adjusted himself on the couch and gave Lizzie one of the most tender looks Eisley had ever seen. An expression so heartfelt and appreciative, she couldn't watch for long without getting teary-eyed.

A sweet blush swept over Lizzie's face and she shifted her attention to the floor. Wes reached over and took Eisley's hand, the gentle pressure telling her he recognized the bittersweet-ness of the moment too.

"It's been long overdue." Lizzie cleared her throat and her smile returned. "It's quite pleasant to share conversations in person with the man I've engaged in chats with online."

They shared another look, one that made Eisley feel as if she was intruding on something fragile and intimate. If she didn't know better, she'd question God's timing.

Lizzie blinked from her stare and turned to Eisley. "Now, dear, I can share with you my delightful findings. Discoveries of such magnitude, I could only show you in person."

Eisley leaned forward. "Did you find another painting? Another letter?"

Lizzie drew a small bundle into her lap, her amber eyes lit with contained excitement. "Much better."

"Better?"

Lizzie unwrapped her precious package of paper and string to reveal a tattered stack of papers bound by twine. "There are three letters, and one of them is exactly what you've been waiting for." Lizzie slanted a glance toward Joe. "I've become quite fond of letters over the past year."

His grin creased his eyes and the old twinkle burned to precancer brightness. Well, this looked like some good old-fashioned medicine.

"You mean Uncle Joe?"

Joe sat up straight, her question hitting him right in his defensive streak. "Now, Pippy, with the right motivation I can write a lot more than adventure stories." His fond gaze rested back on Lizzie. "And I've certainly had the right motivation."

Lizzie placed one thick stack of papers into Eisley's waiting hands. "This is the letter Julia wrote to her great-granddaughter. It's a concise account of her life."

Joe nodded. "I've already examined it, honey, and it's gonna crack the pages of your novel wide open."

"Oh my." Eisley peeled back a page, afraid to tear the fragile cloth-like pages. The first line revealed a long-awaited answer.

Sylvia,

As thou awaitest the birth of thine first child, I will give thee something for which to help pass the long hours. Within these pages is fulfilled the promise I made to thee upon thy last visit. Before I came to the Fels, or met my Beloved, or held the first bound pages of the Scriptures. Thou hast only known me as a woman long in years, but the tales of my past are true and God's good grace hast brought me thus. My own beloved Geoffrey took my barren life and pierced it with a love as fierce as steel yet gentle as the touch of snow. Many trials led us thus, yet I praise God for the harsh sword of suffering, for as He bound my wounds, He fashioned me stronger.

I will write to thee of mine own scars and the sheerest delights of human love, but these words are all bound within the grace of God. He makes the impossible possible and the crooked path straight. Mine eyes, though old and failing, look to an unseen world with clearer vision each day—a world God allowed me the opportunity to experience in mere glimpses from my early years until now. May these words fulfill their purpose to display God's handiwork to thy child and other children to come.

Eisley's vision blurred. "I think my fellow sleuth and I have an assignment after the kids go to bed tonight." She nudged Wes with her shoulder. "Letters and more inspiration for the novel."

"And to think you'd given up on writing," Joe added.

Wes looked to Eisley. "Given up?"

"It's a long story." She leveled Uncle Joe a warning look. "Not worth a recap."

Joe folded his hands together and leaned forward, completely ignoring her. "She let her brother steal her love for writing. Ain't written a story since high school." He stared at her, an I-told-you-so smirk lighting his dark eyes. "Until this one. She has a gift and somebody needs to force her to see it."

She rolled her eyes as warmth fused to her cheeks.

"What kept you from writing?" Wes asked. "The chapters I read were brilliant."

"Betrayal of the worst kind." Joe released a low whistle. "Her brother."

Eisley growled at Uncle Joe and turned her attention to Wes. "Literature was my thing in school. Some people had sports, others popularity. I was a Lit geek, and writing came naturally." She stared down at her and Wes's twined fingers. "I was good at it. The best in the class. So, when my senior Advanced Literature teacher announced a statewide contest where the winner received an all-expense-paid trip to Great Britain, I thought someone had handed me my dream. Writing *and* England?"

Even now the memory ached a little, which seemed petty after all this time. "I worked two months on my short story – a modern day retelling of Northanger Abbey with some Nancy Drew twists thrown in for good measure. My teacher raved about it and I could almost taste the British tea of success." Eisley tossed Wes a grin to douse some of the residual pain.

"Then Brice swooped in." Joe interjected. "Wrote his paper overnight and turned it in an hour before deadline."

"And he won," Wes stated, wincing for her.

"It's silly, really. Such a long time ago, but I lost some of the desire, or maybe it was plain old fear of another failure." She waved the thoughts away. "Besides, it's ancient history."

"It took a dying man, a beautiful Englishwoman, and a new opportunity." Joe nodded to Wes. "To find her dream again." His grin spread. "My editor is optimistic about taking it to pub board. For a new author, this is gold."

"Well, my dear sleuthing partner." Wes squeezed her hand. "This evening, you work on your novel while I see to the children."

Okay, he needs another closet reward, for certain. "You'd do that for me?"

"Tsk, that's a small thing, pet." He quirked a brow. "I know what it's like to try and create words on a page." His brows wiggled. "And I'll use whatever excuse necessary to spend extra time with you and your children. What do you say?"

"You don't need an excuse to spend time with me. If you haven't figured it out by now, this Jenkins family is a stubborn lot. Don't say you haven't been warned, Wes Harrison."

She was determined to keep him.

Twenty-four

T̶he boy followed every instruction without complaint, even though the wind chilled the hair on Nate's moustache and the steep pitch of the roof wasn't easy for an amateur to balance. Wes was a good fella. Nate didn't have to admit it out loud, though.

He felt like a prosecuting attorney, peltin' the boy with questions as quickly as Wes could pound nails into the thick asphalt of the cold shingles, but he already knew he didn't need to nurture worries about this one. Except for getting a black eye from bumping into Nate's elbow as they moved an eighty-pound bag of shingles, Wes had managed well. He'd talked about his childhood in the country, spent a heap o' time on his daddy and mama, and even opened up to Nate about some of his weaknesses as a Christian. Nate felt that warming feeling he always got when he connected with a new dog, so it must be good.

Daggone it! He liked the boy.

He stifled a sigh. He reckoned he'd have to overlook Wes's accent. Of course, the boy couldn't help it none. The gentlemanly behavior wasn't *so* bad, and it seemed to make Eisley happy. He could even ignore the boy's ignorance about football. Nate covered his grin with his hand. Nothing a few more lessons couldn't teach him.

Wes had what mattered most: an honest faith, a teachable spirit, and a sense of humor. But it was as clear as the nose on Uncle Herman's face that Wes struggled with his past.

"You mentioned bein' out in the world for a while before you made things right with God. Any young'uns from your past?"

At just that moment, Wes brought the hammer down, lifted his shocked eyes to Nate, and slammed the hammer into his thumb. "Ahh," he grabbed his hand, jerked off the glove and stuck his thumb in his mouth.

Nate felt his brows skyrocket. Smart boy. He'd have done the same thing.

"Well, you passed the cussin' test and I wasn't even testing you." Nate laughed and patted Wes on the back. "Here let me see."

He grabbed Wes's hand and inspected the discolored thumb. "Oh, that's a good one." He grabbed a handful of snow from a nearby eave and slathered it onto Wes's skin. "Not as good as the time I poked a screw through my finger, but you might lose your nail over it."

Wes swallowed, working hard to control his anger, and with the speed at which it came, it was gone. "No, no children."

The boy lifted sad eyes and Nate knew he still carried around guilt, a feeling he understood all too well. He'd accepted God's forgiveness for his past sins, but it had taken a long time and a lot of love from Kay to convince him God loved him anyway...and always. His youngest son, Greg, lived the life Nate used to know, and the sun never set on a day he didn't pray for his boy.

Wes heaved a sigh which must have cost a hundred bucks and met Nate's gaze head-on. "Nate, I love your daughter and I have every intention to marry her someday. Apart from the grace of God, she's the best thing that's ever happened to me. I can't change who I was, but God has changed who I have become."

Nate's chest deflated. *This boy was serious.* Guilt prickled through Nate's veins and finally gave his heart a tight squeeze. He examined this man as he would have one of his own sons. Wes's swollen left eye was the color of a Granny Smith apple, a bright red mark on his chin reflected a blow from the back of the hammer, and his thumb was beginning to bleed a little around the nail bed. He'd been teased, tackled, nearly poisoned by chili, introduced to a bunch of crazy people, and somehow, to beat it all, he still talked proper and never lost his temper. *If that ain't love...*

"Listen, *Wes*," Nate murmured.

Wes's eyes lifted at quick attention.

"Next to God, family is the most important thing to me. Watchin' Eisley's heart get broken was one of the hardest things I'd ever been through. She's always been the happy-go-lucky one, always looking on the bright side of things and helping others see it, too. I saw a part of her shrivel up and couldn't do nothin' to stop it."

Wes's jaw hardened. "Marshall was an idiot."

"And a load of other words I'm not gonna say." Nate growled.

They sat in silence for a few moments, nothing but the sound of tinkling icicles dropping off the eaves of the shed or chiming through the forest trees.

"Do you think she'll forgive me when I tell her the worst?"

Nate studied him and saw a reflection of himself thirty-four years earlier. To his disgust, a strange, warm mist filled his eyes. *Good grief.* "Eisley's got her mama's heart. She's the most forgivingest young'un I've ever seen." Nate dusted off his jeans. "And she cares a whole lot for you, so you got that in your favor too."

"I'm going to need it."

Nate placed a palm to Wes's shoulder. "We all do and she knows it, Wes."

Wes released a big sigh, as if he'd been holding his breath for a long time. He draped his arm across his bent knee, the tension on his face softened. "You called me Wes."

Nate leaned back on his hands and nodded. "I reckon I did, but everybody has a weak moment time and again."

They started back to work and Nate cleared his throat. "So, *Wes*, tell me about this rugby."

∞ ∞ ∞

Wes slung the towel over his shoulder and turned a thousand-watt grin on Nathan. "You're an expert at washing up, aren't you, mate?"

Nathan's smile reached near idol worship. "It's one of my chores."

"You're a pro. You might have to teach me some tricks."

Eisley watched the exchange, a fresh awareness of her children's need for a male figure searing her heart. The right kind of male figure. A gentle, generous, intelligent, Godly man. And here he was. Doubts crumbled to dust. Yep, she could trust him with her most precious possessions.

Add the bonus points that he was romantic and probably delusional, and she was in a state of perfect euphoria. Only a delusional man could have wanted to kiss her as soon as she walked in the door from work. She'd looked like a van Gogh, with paint on her shirt, a little pudding on her jeans, and hair in a frazzled array of dishevelment.

Her fingers danced over her lips at the memory. Yep, she was in love with this guy.

"I kind of like having you around." She bumped him with her hip, grabbed the towel from his shoulder, and took one of the plates to dry. "Great with kids, easy on the eyes *and* free labor? Sounds like an advertisement from a dating website."

He flicked water at her and followed the splash with a kiss on her cheek. "Where do I sign up? I've been looking for this sort of employment with a lifetime guarantee."

"I really like the sound of that, Handsome." She wrapped her arm around his waist. "It's kind of crazy how well you fit in. We're nothing like your family."

"I don't know about that. I think, at the heart, our families are very similar." His hand hit the side of the sink and he winced.

"Oh Wes." Eisley grabbed his hand before he could slide it back into the water. "What on earth happened to your thumb?"

"It's nothing." He tried to tug his hand free but she held tight. "Distracted while working with your father."

"Good grief. Did he do that to you?"

Wes laughed and succeeded in pulling his hand free to wash the next dish. "No, I missed the nail. No permanent damage, from what Nate tells me."

"Well, he should know. He's had more injuries than an NFL linebacker." She ran a hand along his back to smooth his muscles liking the way he felt. "You're going to be aching tomorrow. Your shoulders and thighs will kill you."

"You've done this sort of work before."

"My dad doesn't discriminate between sons and daughters. We *all* had to learn to"—she raised her fingers to make quotes— "work like a man. Dad would have thrived during Julia Ramsden's day as lord of the manor. Raw strength. Brute force."

"That reminds me. Did you finish studying the letters?"

"Yes!" Julia's true story still floored her every time she thought about it. "I'll have to change some of the names and places, but Julia's life is more spectacular than any novel."

"Mama." Emily ran into the room, shirt off, but thankfully her leggings held tight. She lifted her hand, her blue eyes wide. "Me has boo-boo."

Eisley handed the dry plate to Nathan to put away.

"Do you?" She picked up her little bundle and examined the perfectly fine hand. "What happened?"

"Pete web it."

Pete peeked around the corner of the door, his sneaky smile about as impressive as Emily's pout. "I didn't *really* web blast her, Mommy. It was only pretend."

"Let me kiss it, sweetie, and it will be all better." She brought the little hand to her lips.

Emily turned to Wes. "Wesh tiss it."

"Of course, chicken." He held out his hands to her and she snuggled right up to him. He did nothing to contain his look of pure adoration. Yep, Emily had him branded as a softie already. He kissed her hand and her head, and then she wiggled free from his hold and ran off.

Eisley only stared at him. He shrugged helplessly. "I know. I'm doomed."

"Oh, the cuteness factor will probably wear off after a while, and you'll toughen up. Until then, though?" She offered him a sad shake of her head. "You're in trouble."

His smile warmed her to her toes. "Now, continue with the story."

"Right." She grabbed another plate. "You remember that Julia's father and Geoffrey's family were enemies?"

"Geoffrey's family feuded with Lord Ramsden over a piece of land near the Scottish border, right?"

She nodded and handed another plate to Nathan. "Well, Geoffrey's younger brother intercepted Julia's caravan to meet the old withered guy her father was forcing her to marry. They kidnapped her, along with her dowry to hold as ransom. Somehow, in the process of her stay, she and Geoffrey fell in love."

"End of story?"

"Nope. Lord Ramsden captured Geoffrey's younger brother and offered a trade—Julia for Philip. To save Philip's life, Julia returned to her father with the plan to renew her previous wedding plans to the withered guy."

Wes had stopped washing and leaned back against the counter, arms crossed over his chest and gaze fastened on her. Really listening. Another slap of certainty hit her in the forehead. She loved Christopher Wesley Harrison. His eyes, his dimples, his feet—and everything in-between.

His lips curled up on one side. "But?"

She snapped back to the story. "Sorry, I got distracted."

He graced her with one dimple and rested his hands against her waist, teasing her a little closer. She placed her palms on his chest and tried to regain her train of thought. Tough job.

"Anyway, the priest found out about her smuggling Bibles, placed her under house arrest, and then tried to burn her at the stake for heresy. That's when Geoffrey and his small band of warriors arrived. He jumped into the fire. Julia described it as a *miraculous rescue.* That night he took her back to his home, married her soon after, and her father counted her as dead."

Wes studied her face, caressing her chin. "And to think all that courage and faith passed down to you."

She ducked her head. "I'm not brave."

He tipped her chin and waited. She met his gaze, his tender, loving gaze. "Yes, you are. Forgiveness takes a great deal of courage."

"You guys aren't going to kiss, are you?"

Nathan's question penetrated the gravitational pull Wes's lips had on hers. She stepped back, but Wes leaned down to Nathan's level. "Would you mind, mate?"

Nathan studied him a moment, then wrinkled his nose. "Seems kind of gross when Nana and Papa get all smoochy." He shrugged. "But grown-ups like gross things sometimes."

"And this from the kid who can't wait to dig for nightcrawlers with Papa?" Eisley ruffled his thick hair. "Or dissect poor defenseless bugs with a pair of scissors and a nail?"

His hazel eyes popped wide. "That's not gross. Besides, I'm too big for kisses."

"Oh really? Too big?" She took a step forward, hands grabbing for him. He backed away, but the open dishwasher stopped him. She snatched him up and buried her face into his neck, kissing him until he squealed.

"Mom's got Nathan." Pete yelled as he ran into the room, sliding his Spiderman mask down over his face, readied for battle, with Emily close on his heels. "Wes, let's get her."

She caught the glimmer in Wes's eyes before Pete jumped on her back and brought her to her knees. Her laugh joined Nathan's as Emily pulled Wes into the dog pile. Could she get used to Wes being a part of her family? A father to her kids? Definitely.

∞ ∞ ∞

"Wes, it's good to hear from you." His father's voice held a smile, health. He pictured him, sitting in his favorite chair in the library, the firelight playing off his features and sending a glow to his pale gray eyes. "Your mother tells me your trip is going quite well—educational even."

"Indeed. I've provided a bit of education too, I believe."

His father chuckled. "I look forward to making the acquaintance of more Jenkins family members, from the tales I'm hearing."

"Mother says you might be fit for a trip in a few months. The mountains are breathtaking and though the culture is quite different, the kindness in our families is very much the same."

"And Eisley? What of her?"

Wes smiled at the thought of her. "I think you've proven yourself to be a skilled matchmaker, Dad."

"Love?"

Wes paused a moment. "I expected it with Eisley, but not so quickly with her children. Not like this. It's as if I belong."

"Have you spoken to her about Jane and Vivian? The baby?"

"I plan to this weekend." He drew in a deep breath and released it slowly. "I don't want to disappoint her."

"Wesley," his father's voice breathed out his name like a prayer and he felt the comforting power of his care pour through him. "God has given you this moment to start again. He loves you and has made you whole."

Moisture gathered in Wes's eyes as his throat constricted, and though thousands of miles separated them, he felt his father's love with the tangibility of a hug. "Thanks, Dad."

"And I am certain of yet another thing." His father chuckled. "Even in the short span of time I've known Eisley, her full heart spills grace and joy over everyone in her wake. Should you become the benefactor of her love, imagine how great a love it will be. She cannot contain her heart, nor will she contain her grace."

"I've known her a little over a month and I love her. How can that be possible?" It continued to shock him. Love so encompassing exposed past fancies as shapeless and superficial.

"When you give your life to God, amazing things can happen, son, and with the right woman...?"

Wes laughed and pushed his hand through his hair. "It's all certainly unexpected, but I've learned from the best. I want to love her as I've seen you love Mum."

"I have every faith in you, Wes." He waited a few breaths and added in a raspy voice. "I love you, son."

"I love you too, Dad."

Twenty-Five

At 9:30 am, Eisley called Wes and he reassured her all was well. At noon, she contemplated returning home for lunch, but the teachers threw her a little birthday party celebration. When she finally walked into the house at four o'clock, everything was dangerously quiet—and a mess.

The paper towel roll hung crooked from its stand, half unraveled to the floor. Some strange sticky substance, which smelled a whole lot like grape jelly, stuck to the front of the refrigerator, and an Emily-sized handprint plastered to one side of the door. *Good grief, were there any survivors?* She followed a trail of water droplets into the living room.

Nathan and Pete sat together on the love seat, eyes focused on a movie, toys scattered around them. They looked fine, but where was Wes? Her gaze flitted to the couch and her breath stuck like the jelly in the kitchen. He lay on the couch with Emily sprawled across his chest, both fast asleep. Emily's little diapered bottom stuck up and Wes's strong palm covered her bare back in a protective hold. A rush of tears swelled like the heat in her chest. *Oh...*

"Hi, Mom." Nathan grinned up at her. "We're trying to be quiet. Wes *just* got Emily to sleep."

"He told us if we woke her up he'd make us watch one of your girly movies." Pete wrinkled his nose. "With dancing *and* singing on it."

"He actually said with "singing on it?"

"He said with kissing, too." Nathan visibly shivered.

Eisley crossed her arms in front of her chest and her grin grew. "So how tough were you on the poor guy?"

Nathan arms came up in defense. "Mom, it wasn't us, really. Pete and I only argued a few times."

"And I didn't mean to hit Nathan in the head with my helicopter." Pete's voice grew louder in his own defense. She raised her finger to her lips. He lowered his shoulders along with his voice. "He just took away my Spiderman web blaster—but he didn't bleed a long time."

Eisley rolled her eyes up to the ceiling and released a long sigh.

"Emily kept him really busy, though. Especially after lunch." Nathan's perfect ability to distract from his own questionable involvement came shining through. Blame it on the sister. Boys learned that skill at an early age. "You know how she gets when she's tired."

"She rubbed jelly all over the *whole* kitchen." Pete's voice rose again, and his arms stretched out to emphasize the vastness of Emily's destruction.

"Not the *whole* kitchen, just the refrigerator and a few cabinets and Wes's shirt." Nathan corrected.

"So, she climbed on the counter to get the paper towels?" Eisley asked, visualizing the entire scene, which she knew all too well from firsthand experience. "And dipped them into the sink water?"

"Yep," Pete chirped.

"We were really good this morning, Mom."

"I let my guard down," Wes murmured from the couch. "They were such well-behaved children, I didn't keep as close a watch on the little Houdini here." He opened his eyes and gestured with his chin to sleeping Emily.

"Did the head wound happen at the same time as Emily's jelly finger painting?" Eisley sat down at the bottom of the couch and lifted Wes's feet on her lap.

"How did you know?"

She shrugged, patting his legs. "It usually all happens at once, when you least expect it. I told you parenting was dangerous." She leaned in close and whispered. "More than you bargained for?"

He chuckled.... *chuckled.* "Despite the obvious destruction of your home, we've had a grand time. Since the temperature was quite warm, we spent most of the morning outdoors. We took a walk, played a bit of soccer, I gave some fencing lessons—"

"Until Pete started crying about not getting to hold the sword." Nathan interrupted.

"And we finally came inside for lunch." Wes placed his hand on Emily's head. "That's when all the trouble started. It was truly my fault. You warned me to let her put herself to sleep." He lifted stormy eyes filled with regret and her heart melted. "But I couldn't. She kept looking at me with those large, pleading eyes and well, I felt like a monster."

"Softie," Eisley teased, but her voice couldn't be trusted for anything more. She'd thought after last night nothing else could make her heart flip-flop as much as him kissing her boys goodnight, but today he caught her whole heart in a new way—

hook, line, sinker, and fishing pole. Shucks, she was even in the pond along with all the other fishing gear.

"I'm sorry about Emily's clothes. Her first two outfits disappeared and her third became covered in jam. The missing clothes must be somewhere between your bedroom and the loo, but I've not been able to find them."

"Oh, they'll turn up. Eventually." Eisley leaned back into the couch and turned her head toward him. "I don't think you could've given me a better birthday gift than to see how much you care about my kids."

Wes sat up slowly, keeping Emily as still as possible. He tucked her close in the crook of his arm, strong and secure. Eisley sighed at the sweetness of it.

"This doesn't count as a birthday gift." His lips tipped up in a gentle smile. "This was a mere bonus. I have dinner reservations Saturday night and a gift which is burning a hole in my pocket." His gaze brooked no refusal. "We have a date."

"But you already gave me a wonderful present." She shook her wrist at him where the Christmas bracelet stayed.

He winked. "Not a *birthday* present."

Pete shot up from his seat and produced an elfish grin. "Ooh, Mom, you love presents." He climbed up on the couch beside Wes and made a poor attempt at whispering. "Did you get her a web blaster?"

Wes flashed a two-dimpled grin, his smoky gaze sending her heartbeat off at a gallop. "Actually, it's something she'll like even better than a web blaster, I hope."

"Then it has to be the double Web blaster." Pete squealed and collapsed back on the couch.

Wes stared at his reflection in the gold-embossed full-length mirror and adjusted his tie. Though he'd only been with Eisley's family a week, every day confirmed the thought he'd had when he'd taken her hand from the creek fall. *Belonging.* It was as if he'd walked into a missing part of his life that had been waiting to be found.

His ridiculous grin reflected back at him but he couldn't tamp it down. He loved the way every broken piece of his life made sense when he walked through her door and the children met him, when he pulled her close to him on the couch, or when she pressed her cheek into his shoulder as they embraced.

Hopefully, his declaration tonight wouldn't frighten her away. He infused courage into his reflection. "You love her, mate." He swallowed against his tightening throat. "And she seems to fancy you."

He paused on the notion. She'd never voiced her love for him, but she showed it in so many ways. Did uncertainty or reluctance cause her hesitation? Of course, they hadn't known each other long, and he'd pursued her. His grin reemerged. Because he knew fairly quickly there was no one else for him.

He glanced at his watch, ran a hand through his hair, and retrieved the bouquet of papier mâché butterflies he'd found at a specialty shop on his drive back from his audition. The bright colors on the butterfly wings matched Eisley's bedroom as well as her personality. He drew out his phone to text his arrival time and noticed a missed message from Andrew.

Andrew's message was short and revealed the awaited information related to the photos. The name associated with the tabloid article was unfamiliar to him—Dana Lewis—however, the mobile number he knew as well as his own.

He stumbled to the chair and replayed the message. The number stayed the same. *Eisley's number.* How? Why? He squeezed his head between his palms, pressing out the news, the possibility. No, it couldn't be true.

He stood and marched to the door, opening it and then slamming it closed. *Think, think.* He couldn't have misjudged her. It was impossible for her to play this game so long without showing her hand. And bringing her children into it all? Unconscionable.

He swallowed down the rising fury and ripped the tabloid from his bag, reviewing the photos, sifting the information through the past month. They had been taken during father's first day in hospital, based on his appearance, and Eisley had been there? He reran the scenes from that day. Yes, Eisley had taken care of Simon. His throated tightened.

Wait. She was never alone with his father. Not once. Wes blinked. In fact, she hadn't even entered his father's room until two days later, when he brought her. The doubts ground into a knot of anger. Dana Lewis? Who was she and why was she trying to frame Eisley, because that was the only reasonable explanation to connect Eisley's number with his father's photos. He couldn't reconcile the woman he loved with a betrayer like Jane or Vivian. Until proof left no room for doubt, he'd believe in her.

He stood and strengthened his resolve. Hopefully that proof would never come.

∞ ∞ ∞

Eisley wore a little black dress. Lacy back and sleeves. Slimming V-neck line. And a little flirty ruffle at the knee. She even dared heels. Safe heels, if there was such a thing.

Wes had surprised her with dinner in the small neighboring city of Winston-Salem, at one of the more upscale restaurants. Everything should have been perfect, dreamy, but it wasn't.

Despite his typical swoon-worthy appearance, spicy-leather scent, open-collared green oxford, and black jacket, his smiles held an air of apprehension or caution—a look she hadn't seen since they first met. What was going on behind those gray-blue eyes? "Is your dad okay?"

His gaze shot to hers and he tilted his head. "He's well."

Her stomach twisted. "Has *my* dad done something to you?"

"Nothing out of character."

She had to grin at his perfect reply. "Were my kids too hard on you?"

His brows creased, and he looked completely confused. Well, at least that was better than distant and suspicious. "I adore your children."

"Then what's wrong? You've been extra quiet since we left my house."

He paused, drew in a deep breath, and slid a hand through his hair. "You're right. I should be honest with you."

She reached to grip his hand, a little bit of fear nibbling at her confidence. "I'm a big fan of honesty." *Except, maybe, right now. In fact, maybe he should resort to acting all lovey dovey again.*

"Yes, yes, you are." He spoke as if reminding himself and then covered her hand with his. "Andrew sent me some information today. The name and number of the person associated with the tabloid photos."

"Oh." She sighed away her concern. "No wonder you're distracted tonight. What did you find out?"

"Have you ever heard of the name Dana Lewis?"

Her mouth dropped open. "Yes. I mean, I met her once. Last week."

"Did you?" He watched her with such intensity, she wished she could read his mind.

"I meant to call you after it happened, but it was the day you surprised me from England." Her lips stretched into an apologetic smile. "And I kind of got distracted when you arrived in the flesh."

His shoulders relaxed, but his eyes still watched her with some reserve. What was going on? "Listen, you're making me a little nervous right now, so I guess you'd better tell me whatever it is you're not. I've been honest with you this whole time, and you're the one who came all the way over here to surprise me, so if you're having misgivings now?" She cleared the rising emotion from her throat and held his gaze. She'd tried to keep her distance from day number one, but *he'd* pursued her. If he didn't trust her, she wanted to know sooner rather than later.

"I'm sorry, Eisley." He tugged her hand between his warm palms and exhaled a kiss over her fingers. "Could you tell me what happened?"

She wasn't fooled by that sweet kiss, even if her fingers tingled all the way up to her wrist. Something was still wrong...very wrong. She slipped her hand from his and sat back, trying to pull her feelings away as much as her body. "It was strange. She showed up at Julia's bakery when I was getting ready to close up shop. She said she was doing an interview for the local paper, but then she started slipping out a few British words and I knew something was up. She got out of the restaurant before I could confront her."

He rested his mouth against her fingers, brow scrunched. "Hmm, this leads me to another part of Andrew's information."

Something in his expression spiked her concern.

"The photos were taken from *your* mobile."

She didn't hear him correctly. "I don't understand."

"Andrew was able to track the photos to the mobile number from which they had been sent. It was yours. You know what this means?"

"Whoa. How is that even possible?" She fisted her hands in her lap. "You don't believe I had something to do with it, do you?"

His gaze lingered on her face, taking its time examining her features. Not again. He wouldn't mistrust her after all they've discussed, would he? His expression softened, and he gathered her hand in his. "No, not you. But I'm trying to work out how your number is associated with those photos."

She released her tense breath into a sigh. "Right. How? And why my number? Who would I know in England besides Lizzie and your family?"

"Right. Can you think of any way someone would have had access to your mobile? Or...I don't know. Used it?"

She scanned through her memory, revisiting the day at the hospital. "I didn't even have my phone for part of the time, remember?" Her gaze shot to his. "I...I lost it in the elevator with Vivian the Vicious. We found it an hour or so later at the nurse's station."

A sudden flare of certainty came into his eyes, something she desperately needed to see. "Vivian?" He whispered the name and tapped the table. "Someone is attempting to frame you, Eisley."

"Why me? I'm not..." she waved a hand toward his very swoony self. "Famous. I'm not even popular."

He rubbed his thumbs over her knuckles. "If Vivian is involved then I think she might be using you to hurt me in some way. I don't know how, and what of this woman...Dana Lewis?"

"Do you know her?" This whole thing was getting more Nancy Drew than Scooby Doo.

"No but tell me everything and we'll attempt to sort it out."

She explained the entire exchange, but none of her information seemed to help in identifying who she was or why she was involved.

He slid his chair closer to her around the table as she talked, gaze softening with each detail of the story. By the time she'd gotten to the end of the tale, he'd gathered both her hands back into his and pressed them to his lips, holding her gaze. "We'll work through this, pet. Vivian is quite adept at manipulation, I'm afraid."

Vivian. Just her name left the scent of trouble behind. Beautiful, bold, a part of Wes' past. Eisley stiffened against the comparison. Nope. Wes had chosen her not Vivian.

"You've gotten quiet." He narrowed his gaze and leaned close. "Hey, don't worry about Vivian. I'll sort it out. She's out to steal my happiness out of spite, I believe, but I won't allow her to touch you. Not if I have the power." He placed a lingering kiss on her wrist as a promise.

She squeezed his hand. "How about we sort it out together? As a team. You and me." She teased him with a grin. "Besides, I want to steal something from you too."

"Do you?" He must have caught the intent because the smoky glint returned to his eyes.

"I'm after your heart."

"Well, you're a clumsy thief, my dear, because I've already placed it in your hands for safe keeping, and you can't give it back."

"Oh, I'm playing for keeps too. The happily-ever-after kind."

His attention dropped as he placed his napkin up on the table, brow crinkling in a serious way. "I want to give you that kind of happiness, Eisley." He stood, offering his hand. "Let's finish this conversation in a more private setting. I have some things I'd like to share with you. Things I need you to know, first."

Her stomach fisted against the suggestion. "Okay."

He tugged her close and brushed a touch across her cheek. "Besides, we have another appointment to make."

To her delight, they drove to Old Salem, a two-hundred-year-old restored Moravian village nestled near downtown. Christmas decor still clung to the brick and stone box-shaped houses, and the old-fashioned lanterns cast a magical glow across the street. A few couples walked arm-in-arm, snuggled tight against the slight chill in the January air.

"They have a performance of *Peter and the Wolf* tonight."

Eisley pulled her gaze from the tranquil town. "Oh wow, really?" She rubbed a hand over his jacket. "You're pretty great, you know that? And I really like having you around. Do you *have* to leave in a week?"

His grin tipped. "Actually, I'll be back in two months for an extended stay."

"The audition?"

He took her hand into his, thumb tingling a smooth caress over her knuckles. "They rang today and said I was the perfect fit. I think the chemistry between me and Sarah was the tops."

Eisley gulped down a strangle. Chemistry? With Sarah? Who the heck was Sarah? "So, what did you have to do to show chemistry, exactly?"

The rotten man's lips twitched like he was trying to reign in a smile. Torture really shouldn't be so cute. "Since I'm no longer making movies of questionable romantic content, all we had to do was go over a few scenes and kisses."

"Kisses?" She tried to pull her hand free, but he wouldn't let go. Okay, she'd assumed in his line of work he'd kiss other women, but the jerk was practically bragging about it. Eisley drew in a deep breath. Did he like kissing her? No doubt Sarah liked kissing him. She frowned. Bad thought. But hurt? To her surprise, not even a little. Which proved she was either insane or she actually trusted him.

"You can ask most actors. It's only part of the job. Fairly meaningless to the heart, pet."

Meaningless? When his kisses sent her spiraling into drool-mode? How on earth could it be meaningless? Maybe she should take back her forgiveness, just in case.

She stared at him, searching for any hint of deception, but his tender appeal only deepened her faith in him. "I know. I know." She sighed and leaned back in the seat, eyes pinched closed. "My head realizes it's not a big deal, but my heart kind of gave a twinge. Don't worry. My heart is sometimes slow on the uptake, but it'll catch up eventually."

"I understand that." He squeezed her hand. "Like earlier, my head knew to trust you. My heart was afraid."

"Old scars carry deep reactions."

"Do you know what?" His chocolate-rich voice edged close just before his lips warmed the skin beneath her ear, lingering to graze a trail down the side of her neck.

"Hmm?" She leaned into his touch, breath staggering an uneven rhythm.

"I think you've improved my auditions, especially the kissing scenes."

She pulled her mind out of the glorious haze. "How on earth could I have improved your kissing auditions?"

"I merely pretended she was you." His words breathed against her mouth, tempting her to bridge the gap, but she steadied the inner vulture.

Oh yes, she was getting the hang of this romance thing. "So, I'm your muse?"

"Without a doubt. That is fiction. You are quite real. I'll not confuse the two." His palm brushed across her cheek, thumb smoothing a slow trail over her lips. He dropped his gaze to her lips, eyes hooded. "If you want, I can reenact it with much more sincerity."

He took her in a lingering kiss, slow and gentle, caressing his mouth over hers until she felt the gentle ridges of his lips. Her hand slipped up his chest to palm the back of his neck, the slightest nudge for him to enjoy the journey. He deliciously obeyed. Their shallow breaths whispered into the darkness. He tasted of the crème brûlée they'd shared at dinner.

"I can safely say I have never been kissed the way you kiss me." She kept her eyes closed, her lips tingling. "I could drown in all of the beautiful warmth your touch leaves behind."

She opened her eyes and met his smile.

"I've never cared for any woman the way I care for you." His Adam's apple bobbed with his swallow and his expression turned pensive. "Which leads me to an important topic of conversation. I need to tell you about Jane and Vivian. The whole story."

Vivian's words from the elevator came back to gnaw on Eisley's inner peace. She gave them a mental shove. *Nope, over and done.* "You don't have to tell me anything. It's in the past. I trust the man you are *now*."

He gathered her hands back into his. "Thank you for saying so, but the past has a way of touching the present whether we like it or not. There will be enough challenges in the future; I don't want any secrets surprising us."

"Okay," she whispered. *The past is in the past.* No matter what he had to say it couldn't be worse than Vivian's claim.

"There were several things not known by the media surrounding Jane's death. Information which only the most intimate people in our lives knew." He looked away toward the misty Moravian street. "Four months prior to her death, she informed me she was pregnant."

Eisley released her clenched breath, gaze unswerving. "Oh, Wes."

"The news of the pregnancy wasn't what either of us expected, not with our growing careers, but I accepted it as a part of the choices we'd made, and I asked her to marry me."

Sounded like Rick's history—except his fiancée disappeared from his life without a hint to her whereabouts.

He ran his free hand through his hair and released a slow breath. "Three months later, she lost the baby."

"Oh, no."

"She fell into depression, withdrew from her current film, and wanted no one with her but me. We grieved together. I harbored my own sense of loss."

"It hurts the father, too."

"Right." His chin tightened, a clear attempt at controlling his emotions. "And there was this associated guilt, as though I'd failed to protect the child in some way. Was it punishment for my profligate life? My ruthless choices?"

"You know that's not the case."

"As you said earlier, one's heart and one's head aren't always in agreement. The news of our sudden engagement caused a backlash of new conflict. News of her infidelity of the past year came to light, which even put the parentage of the child in question. My reaction?" He winced. "I had every intention of making Jane suffer for her infidelity. I called off the engagement and separated myself from her. In a way, perhaps I severed her lifeline by doing that."

"No, Wes. It wasn't your fault."

"But…Vivian." He sighed and stared down at their hands. "Vivian remained. Feeding me the attention and the words of affirmation I thought I deserved, inflating my pride." His gaze sought hers, pleading for her to understand. "I was weak, Eisley. Grieving, selfish, and an easy target of manipulation. I see it now, the competition between the two of them. The impenetrable bitterness with everything. Their careers, the popularity, their love lives. I was merely another pawn." His brow creased and he looked down at their joined hands. "One night, after drinking away my sorrows, I slept with her."

The admission didn't hurt as much as she'd thought. Watching the remorse work its way out through his words added clarity to his choices. His wrong, painful choices. He'd beaten himself up over them for much too long. She knew the feeling. It was past time for both of them to live free.

His expression held such remorse. Pale moonlight highlighted his features, bringing a white sparkle to his eyes. At that moment, she saw him as a regular man, someone as flawed and stupid as she could be, but someone who also sought reconciliation and admitted his faults quickly. The realization melted her fears. She touched a palm to his cheek. "I know. Vivian told me."

"What?"

"In the elevator at the hospital. She tried to intimidate me, and it worked for about five minutes, until I realized what I believe about you and God and forgiveness." Her lips twitched crooked. "You're a new man, remember?"

He stared, eyes wide, until without warning, he took her face in his hands and kissed her. Everything sweet and tender between them melded into it. She gripped his jacket, holding him close, until she tasted salt. *Salt?*

She drew back and met his watery gaze. "Wes?"

"You're amazing," he rasped, palms keeping a gentle caress to her cheeks. "Even after I doubted you? You hear the worst about me and stay?"

"I don't want to be anywhere else, besides, I'm sure I'll need you to remember this moment the next time I screw up and you need to forgive me." She pushed her finger into his chest. "Because I'll give you plenty of practice too."

"I certainly hope you do so we can even the score. I'm at a distinct deficit." His smile spread to double-dimple gorgeous, even as tears glimmered in his moonlit eyes. He pushed her hair back from her face, staring at her as if she was the most beautiful woman in the world. Unbelievable....and completely addictive. "I never imagined God could—" He kissed her again. "I'll finish the full story so you'll know everything." He stole another kiss. "When I woke the next morning and came to the full realization of what I'd done, I left straightaway, determined to distance myself from the entire Barry family. But Jane had left a haunting voice message, telling me goodbye. I didn't understand until I arrived at her flat, with Vivian directly behind me."

"I'm so sorry, Wes."

"My father came to London to retrieve me. Otherwise, I have no idea how I might have harmed myself. I was so riddled with my own guilt over her death, but God had not forgotten this lost man." He brushed back her hair. "He rescued me in my darkest moment, gave me hope again, and sent you."

"Best Christmas present I've ever gotten." She patted the lapel of his jacket.

He shook his head and brushed the back of his hand over his eyes. "Speaking of gifts." He pulled a small box from his jacket and raised a brow. "Beware. It isn't a double web blaster."

She produced a mock pout. "Well, I guess it's the thought that counts."

His grin spread, and she slowly removed the lid. Inside were three exquisite charms for her bracelet, each much more elegant than anything a box store could provide. One was a mother and child, one was a house with *family* engraved across it, and the last was an open book. "They're beautiful."

"Three more amazing things about you. You're a wonderful mother." He pointed to the appropriate charm. "You love family." His brow tilted with his smile. "And you're an author."

Well, not technically an author, but she wasn't going to argue about a perfectly lovely birthday present. "Thank you. I love them." He helped her fasten them to her bracelet.

"Thank *you*." His gaze locked with hers as he adjusted her coat tighter around her neck. "For braving my batty world and not running away."

"Ditto, mister. In our lives, it's all the madness or nothing, right?

He kissed her forehead. "And, pet, I want it all."

Twenty-Six

*E*isley's phone rang as soon as she nudged Sophie out the door from babysitting and drifted into her house with the afterglow of Wes's goodnight kiss. Uncle Joe's number popped up on the screen. She glanced at the time. Eleven o'clock. *Crazy man.*

"Hello?"

"I saw Wes's truck leave."

Eisley groaned, stomped to the back porch, and flicked the light on and off. "Would you stop snooping?"

He chuckled. "It's real hard to break a good habit."

She narrowed her gaze to try and see the light from his house on the hill. The leafless winter trees allowed for more visibility. "What are you still doing awake, anyway?"

"I had my own date night."

Eisley paused at the comment. "Lizzie?"

"She won't stop coming by, and I've grown tired of trying to convince her that a dying man doesn't have a lot to offer a classy British lady."

Uncle Joe couldn't see her smile from all the way across the pasture, but he probably knew she wore one. A big one, with a few tears sprinkled in. Eisley knew Lizzie well enough to believe that when she made up her mind about something, she would be as stubborn as Uncle Joe. Nice match, for however long it lasted. Funny, after all these years of bachelorhood and spinsterhood, God would give the two of them this quirky opportunity.

"She's pretty smart."

"Yep, pretty and smart. Don't know why she's wastin' her time with a geezer like me, but I'm not one to complain about good things." He cleared his throat. "Besides, I didn't call you about me. I called you about your book."

"*Our* book," she corrected.

"Jack has a contract for you."

"A contract? For publication?"

"That's right, Pippy. You're going to be a published author."

Eisley legs weakened and she reached for the kitchen barstool. "Are you serious?"

"I don't have time to play games."

She coughed out her laugh. "Yeah, right. Evidently you have enough time for romance, spying on your niece, and convincing an editor to publish this story."

"It's all based on your talent. I'll forward the contract to you, and then the real fun...and work begins."

Uncle Joe ended the call, but Eisley knew she wouldn't be sleeping any time soon. Her brain buzzed with the news. Julia Ramsden's story was going to be a published novel. She was an author. She shook the book charm on her bracelet and then danced a happy jig, quietly so she wouldn't wake up the kids. Another reminder of God sprinkling pixie dust on her life. Maybe fairy tales weren't just on paper.

∞ ∞ ∞

Wes took the paper from Eisley's front step and knocked on her door. He'd grown accustomed to arriving after breakfast on her days off, enjoying as much of the day with her and the kids as possible. A rush of feet clambered from the other side of the door, jolting his heartbeat with welcome. The door swung wide, revealing two faces he couldn't quite get enough of.

"You're here," Pete screamed, as if he hadn't seen the boy every day of the week.

"Good morning, boys."

"We finished the X-wing fighter." Nathan grabbed his hand and pulled him into the living room. "Look, it has five guns."

"And the wings move." Pete yelled with excitement, demonstrating. "See?"

"Fascinating." Wes laughed and tousled the boy's ginger hair. "A bit quieter there, mate, but I love your enthusiasm."

Pete's wide-eyed grin looked a lot like his mom's. Adorable. Endearing.

"You're going to lose your hearing by the time you leave." Eisley walked in from the kitchen, drying her hands on a towel, her long ponytail swishing behind her. The tight hug of her green sweater paired with dark jeans forced him to keep his eyes on her face for fear of dragging her into the nearest closet.

"Not a problem. In fact, I could get used to a similar welcome every day." He backed her out of view of the kids, slid his arm around her waist, and kissed her until he trapped her against the kitchen wall. The kiss was decadent, flavored with the hints of butter and honey. Most certainly a breakfast of champions.

"I'd take a welcome like that every day, too." She tugged him forward for a few more quick kisses. "There's a good chance I'll go into withdrawal without a daily dose, mister."

He grinned and followed her to the sink, placing the paper down on the counter.

"Whatcha got there?"

"I'm not certain. It was on your doorstep."

"Oh, it's the Southwest Virginia Chronicle. Comes every Saturday." Her eyes shot wide. "Wes, that's the paper from the interview. Do you think—?"

He opened it and flipped through the pages as she nestled up close beside him. He almost tossed the paper to the side and visited her lips again, but a headline on the second page chilled his blood. "No, no, no," he murmured, setting the paper on the counter and reading over the piece. "Dana Lewis was exactly what we feared."

Eisley looked up at him, a question in her eyes, and then pulled the paper closer. Personal information about her was splashed across the page. Her initial gasp, her hand to her mouth, her uneven intake of breaths alerted him to each new thread of privacy unraveled. Her history with Marshall and a few unsavory details related to Marshall's choices. Rachel's stint in rehab for her drug addiction with a grueling quote or two from college mates. Greg's exploits, including a comment from his former fiancée and two disgruntled former patients.

"Why?" she whispered. "Why would anyone do this?" The pain registering on her face seared his conscience and broke his heart. What had he brought on her family? How could he promise never to hurt her if his life brought pain with it? She stepped from his arms and paced across the kitchen, stopping to review the article again and again.

"Someone's targeting us." His response was low, contemplative. "That sort of article doesn't happen by chance."

"Targeting us?" She slapped the paper against her thigh, fire lighting with the pain in her eyes. "Who would do this?"

"This Dana person, I fear, is not alone in her actions." He ran his hand through his hair and slammed both palms down on the counter. "It doesn't make sense. It's almost like she's trying to punish me or ruin us, and I don't even know the woman. This isn't typical. Not even close, Eisley."

"Whether it's typical or not, it's happened." She pointed the paper at him.

"Bad reporters can be very good at manipulating the truth." Wes tugged her into his arms and sighed into her hair. "It is an unfortunate possibility in my line of work. I've never witnessed anything like this. I'm sorry you must feel the sting of it, pet."

"My family." She stepped out of his hold and massaged her crinkled forehead, her breath catching on a sob. "They printed things about them—"

The implications dug into his chest. "Perhaps there's something we can do. I can have my solicitor contact the paper and—"

"Could it happen again?"

He steadied his hands on her shoulders. "I suppose there is always a risk, but there are many couples who make it work. Together."

She studied him for a long time, her face a wreath of pain, leaving a draining silence. The agony Nate spoke of when Eisley's ex-husband hurt her came to life with aching clarity.

"What if she digs deeper, Wes? If Rick's runaway bride story came out in the papers, he'd be mortified. Do you realize how reclusive he's become since Anna disappeared anyway?" Her eyes flicked wide. "And Julia."

Wes rubbed the back of his neck, another twinge tightening his clenched jaw.

"It's only been four months. We've just gotten her smile back. If someone splashed the controversy from her date rape across the papers—" Eisley put her hand to her mouth and pulled away. "I know the guy involved would have plenty of lies to tell, and the court case is coming up next month."

"Oh no, Eisley."

"It's one thing if the risk is only about me, but this hurts my family." Her gaze met his, watery and sad. "You understand how important it is to protect the people you love."

He did—and her statement crushed air from his lungs. *Worth almost anything.* "Eisley?"

"My family didn't sign up for this, Wes." She lifted the paper. "They didn't know the risks. They shouldn't have to suffer for them. And if it means the possibility of Rick or Julia reliving the pain, the nightmare—"

"Let's talk about—"

"I can't bear the thought of hurting the—."

"Listen to me."

"I'm not saying this is over, but it's much bigger than you and me now. If my family is going to suffer for my choices again, they have a right to be in the decision too."

She leaned into him, pressing her damp cheek into his shoulder, her hand smoothing over his chest as if to make a memory. Something precious and beautiful began to slide from his grasp.

"I'll give it up." He whispered against her head, fingers grasping her closer.

She pulled back and the tears blinked more visibly in her eyes. "It's a gift and a dream. A beautiful dream God created in you." She stood on tiptoe and kissed his cheek as if in benediction. "You can't give it up."

"That's not your decision, pet. Some things are more important."

"I'm not sure I could let you give it up for me."

His throat burned, clawing at his words. "Eisley, we can work through this. We can go to your family and sort it out together."

Her lips tilted into a sad smile and she touched his cheek. "I need to talk to them alone, so they can speak openly." She sighed. "They've been through so much, Wes. I need to protect them, if I can."

His fingers trailed through her loose hair, afraid to let her out of his sight. "I don't want to lose you."

Her bottom lip wobbled, much like Emily's, and pierced his heart all over again. "I don't want to be lost." She wrapped her arms around him and clung tight.

He ran his hand the length of her ponytail, over and over, as they stood in silence. He'd hurt her. He pulled her closer. He'd brought pain and embarrassment to her family. *Lord, what do I need to do to repair this?*

Wes offered to stay with the kids until Aunt Tilley arrived, but the fear in his eyes, the uncertainty, nearly had her turning her car around and taking back all the words about her family. Why would God bring him into her life only to take him away?

She loved them too much not to care about their reaction to this risk. Had she somehow sabotaged her family with her little fairy tale? No, that couldn't be true.

As she pulled into a parking place in front of *Sugar and Spice,* the full implication hit. She killed the engine and placed her head against the steering wheel.

She had to protect Julia and Rick, if she could. The agony of Julia's upcoming court battle sent enough stress to her little sister. What would a slanderous article do to her, to the outcome, to the ego of Mack Larson?

The sweet memory of Wes holding her baby girl pushed into focus. He was everything she'd prayed for and so much more. An unimaginable dream come true.

Kind, compassionate, tender, funny. He walked right into her kids' lives as if he'd been tailor-made for them, too.

God, please don't make me choose. Please.

Heat crept beneath her closed eyelids and a ping-pong match of emotions slammed against her rib cage. *I love him. Why would you bring him into my life only to take him away?*

Because she knew, if it came down to a choice between Wes and her family—she held back a sob—her family won.

∞ ∞ ∞

As soon as the sitter arrived, Wes phoned his solicitor followed by Andrew. There was no more time to lose. If Dana Lewis proved to be the culprit, then he'd make an example of her and anyone else who chose to slander his loved ones or invade his privacy. If Andrew didn't get through to the little Virginia publication and force them to print an immediate retraction, his solicitor would be certain to make the point clear.

But one thing he couldn't change was Eisley's pain. The look of anguish on her face at this betrayal seared deep, and worse was the knowledge that his presence had brought this hurt and embarrassment to her and her family. He massaged a palm into his chest where an ache throbbed. He didn't want to lose her, but even more, he didn't want to be responsible for another wound in her life.

"The little paper gave up no fight whatsoever. The editor promised a full retraction in the next print." Andrew said from the other side of the mobile.

"I was going to ring you later today, Wes. After some investigating and rather impressive threatening, the tabloid sent me a photo of Dana Lewis. "She seems familiar to me." I'll forward it to you once we end our call."

"A photo? Nothing else?" It wasn't very comforting, especially since Andrew had discovered nothing on the mysterious Dana Lewis. No address or phone number. He disconnected the call, but when the photo arrived on his mobile, all the pieces fell into place.

Dana Lewis was actually none other than Miriam Barry, Vivian's cousin, who basically idolized her more famous and wealthier elder cousin. Proof Vivian was behind it all—the photos of his father, the article about Eisley's family, and who knew what else. His past overshadowed his present, but should it cloud hers, too? Her family's?

He dropped to his knees. Only God had the answer, but the deep ache in his chest alerted him to the right choice...his only choice. He closed his eyes on the sting. He had to let her go.

Chapter Twenty-Seven

"I'm so sorry everyone." Eisley pointed to the paper on the middle of the counter at *Sugar and Spice* and turned to her mom and sisters. "Wes just texted me that the paper is going to print a retraction because he had his lawyer make a call. But I never imagined this could happen. Why would anyone have a reason to expose our family to this?"

"But you said even Wes was surprised by the article." Mom stepped forward and scanned over the paper again, grimacing at the contents. "It must be unusual."

"He thinks someone planted it to hurt him."

"By hurting you?" Rachel reached across the counter and grabbed a cookie from the plate Julia placed in the middle of their girl powwow. They always thought a little clearer when chocolate was involved.

"Whoever is doing this must think Wes cares a lot about me, so by hurting me, it will automatically hurt him." She shrugged. "It's the only reason I can conjure up."

Julia kept her gaze down, a sorrowful pull to her bottom lip making her look like a sad, porcelain angel.

"This could happen again." She focused all her protective instincts on Julia's bowed head. "I can't let it go further and hurt anyone else."

Julia's head came up. "Further?"

"Wes is trying to stop it, but he can't make any promises." Eisley drew in a deep breath to gain strength, keeping her gaze focused on Julia's. "I can end it now. Then there won't be another risk for anyone else."

"End what?" Realization dawned in her expression. "Wes?"

No, please God, no. Her throat repelled against forming the words, so they emerged in a rasp. "You're my family. I'll do anything for you."

"Oh, Eisley." Mom shook her head. "You care about him, honey."

Eisley's fist tightened with the muscles in her stomach. "That article brought up so many hurtful things. What if someone tries to dig up even more?" Her gaze zeroed in on Julia, who quickly returned her attention to the counter. The ache in Eisley's chest surged deeper, pulling her in two directions, right down the center of her heart.

"I know my dirty laundry isn't worth your relationship with Wes." Rachel said landing a hand to her hip. "I made my choices and these are the consequences." She looked over at Julia. "But not everyone had a choice in what happened to them."

Julia traced a finger over the rim of her glass, her lips pierced tight as if she worked to control her emotions. She settled a palm to her belly. Eisley's stomach turned, remembering those first few months of anger and fear when Julia grappled with the indescribable betrayal of being raped by her date. Having the ugly news spread back across the minds of the county would reawaken the hurt all over again. Julia was strong, right? The answer seemed simple until Eisley actually realized the cost. Wes. Her little fairy tale started to crumble.

"Julia, honey?" Mom placed her hand to Julia's shoulder.

Julia wiped a tear from her cheek and shrugged. "I'm okay." She lifted her gaze to Eisley. "Really, I am. The papers can't do anything worse to me than what's already happened."

A male voice broke into the conversation.

"Some people are getting cold coffee around here." Blake Connors, their dad's younger partner in the carpentry business, lifted his mug and shot them an impatient glare.

"You're interrupting, Blake," Mom answered and added such a stern mother look, that Blake wilted back into his booth.

"I can wait."

"Yes, you can."

"Look." Sophie raised the paper. "I know none of my dirty laundry was aired out in the article—"

"That's because you haven't done anything worth the papers." Rachel rolled her eyes.

"Fine." Sophie's golden eyes brightened with purpose. "But it isn't like any of this is *new* news. We're from a small town. Everybody already knows all our junk. It's part of the territory."

"I already knew it all," Blake offered from across the room.

All the ladies silenced him with a unified glare.

"But to have it blared in front of the whole world?" Eisley's asked.

"The whole world?" Rachel laughed and settled back down on a barstool. "The paper's circulation might be a fifty-mile radius, Eis."

"But what if it turns into something more. What if—."

"The world is full of *what ifs*, sis." Rachel shrugged. "Getting lost in the *what ifs* steals your peace and future."

"And we can't live in fear." Julia lifted her chin and nodded, as if to herself. "We can choose to live above it."

"Wait a minute." Sophie stood and placed her hands on her hips, tossing the paper to the counter with enough force to make a little slapping noise. "So, what if some stupid paper posts lies about us, or even old news about our family? *We* know the truth. I thought that was what mattered."

Rachel breathed out a long sigh. "The kid's right."

"Amen," Blake added, and then ducked his head.

"And you know what else?" Sophie's head started to move with her words, like a zealous preacher, no doubt fueled by Blake's interjection. "We don't have a slew of secrets in our family. But even if something bad happens, we always have each other." Her hands moved along with her words. "If people want to twist information around, well, we've never had the power to control what they think, anyway."

Eisley stared at her baby sister, shocked. "Sophie, I think that's the most grown-up thing you've ever said."

She wrinkled her nose with her grin. "Don't get used to it. I still prefer make-believe." Her face sobered. "I know I'm not in this stupid paper, so I can't speak to the embarrassment, but I don't think anything they could print in here is worth *your* fairy tale, sis."

"Do you love him, Eisley?" Julia asked.

An ache swelled up through her chest and pinched at her breath. *Love him?*

She bit back the tears, everything within her fighting to keep her focus away from her breaking heart. "That doesn't really matter. What matters is—"

"Actually, it does matter." Julia stood, periwinkle eyes taking on a bit more steel. "You're trying to protect us. Me. But we want to protect you, too. Your heart is just as important."

"Julia—"

"Sophie's right. Everyone who matters already knows what happened to me, but more importantly, the people who love me most are here to give me comfort and to protect me from making a wrong decision when my fear or my bad thoughts tempt me." She rounded the counter and placed her palms on Eisley's shoulder. "And we're here to do the same for you. Do you love Wes, sis?"

Eisley stared into Julia's searching gaze. She'd not spoken those words to any man since Marshall. It seemed almost dangerous to say them out loud. "Yes, I do."

"Well then, that means Wes is a part of our family now." Julia's smile grew. "Why wouldn't we shelter his heart as much as we would each other's?"

"And we'll deal with whatever happens." Mom wrapped her arm around Julia's shoulder and smiled to Sophie. "As we've always done."

"Every small town needs a little conflict now and again." Rachel grinned. "Livens up the place."

Julia's smile grew to light her pale eyes. "Family sticks together, no matter what."

"Great." Blake's deep voice rumbled from the other side of the room. "Can I have some coffee now?"

***

Two days. It had taken Vivian two days to find the small town of Pleasant Gap. The hired taxi only took her to another small city, and then she sat through the hideous ordeal of travel by coach before arriving in an inconsequential place called Mt. Airy. From there, for an exorbitant amount of money, the taxi driver agreed to take her the hour north to Pleasant Gap, through a maze of nauseating twists and turns, and finally left her at the edge of a rustic downtown street. Stone walkways lined each side of the garland strewn main street but were practically empty.

She hated the ginger-headed boiler for all the trouble.

If only Miriam hadn't gone silent and left her with little more than the name of Eisley's sister's bakery. No doubt Wes's solicitor was snooping, examining the tabloid and following the leads she'd carefully placed for his discovery.

She rolled her eyes. Who would ever want to live in such a miniscule part of the world? It all should be over soon enough. Before Miriam disappeared for fear of being caught, she'd confirmed Eisley's mobile number had leaked. Vivian had given up everything for him, so if she couldn't live in peace and happiness, neither would he. They didn't deserve happiness unless it was with each other.

She shoved back her hair and started a brisk walk toward the closest shop, a brick building with a green door and a sign overhead reading *Deals on Wheels*. Someone in this small place had to have directions to the Jenkins family's home. Her grin etched up on one side. And finding a chauffeur to her destination shouldn't be too difficult. A groan curled from her throat as she pushed open the heavy door, the jingle of bells announcing her stumble into the shop. She smoothed her jacket, sweeping the room with an impatient glance. The filthy scent of oil swirled so thick she felt as though it covered her skin. Bicycles hung from the ceiling, tools lined the walls, and wheels of various sizes and shapes sat in stacks on the floor.

No, this was not the place for her.

A deep baritone voice stopped her turn. "Can I help you?"

A pair of dark eyes met hers from across the room. His green t-shirt was rolled up to reveal muscular arms braced against the counter. He caught her unhidden perusal and his brows rose in question, then he returned the examination.

Well, well, perhaps this was the perfect stop.

She made the inspection worth his while, straightening to highlight the best of her figure.

His grin took an easy trip across his face as he rounded the counter, an arrogant swagger to his moves. Oh yes, he was perfect. "You look lost."

She tucked her chin and gave a shy smile. "I'm afraid you're right. I've traveled all this way to meet someone and have no idea how to find him."

The man drew close, smile twisting in a flirty turn. "Maybe you're looking for the wrong man."

She nibbled her bottom lip to add to the allure of a damsel in distress. "I'm willing to consider those possibilities, Mr.—"

"Barrett." He offered his hand. "Marshall Barrett."

Oh, this was even better than she could have hoped.

She slid her cool hand into the warmth of his palm and produced a gasp, as if his touch awakened the reaction. His grin inched wider.

"Vivian Barry, and the man I'm looking for gave me the wrong address where I could meet him. Being English, like me, I assumed he might stand out in your little town."

Marshall tilted his head, his eyes narrowing as he examined her. "I don't know of anyone visiting from England."

"He's visiting a family here, I believe. The Jenkins family. Do you know them?"

His frown furled. "I know them."

She squeezed his hand again and donned her most brilliant smile to draw his attention back to her. "We have an important business decision to discuss."

"Business?"

"Of course." Her hand fluttered to her chest. "I'm currently unattached."

The man's flirty smile regained control of his lips. *Amateur.*

"Well Ms. Barry, what if I treat you to lunch and then give you a ride out to the Jenkins' farm. Most likely they're keeping your friend in the guest apartment."

She inwardly groaned, but her smile never wavered. There was no time to waste. She'd planned out her strategy and was a day later than she'd hoped. Wes should have discovered Eisley's mobile as the one in which the photos were taken yesterday or the day before. She needed to encourage his doubt, though Marshall Barrett made a tasty distraction. "Lunch? I'm not certain I have time."

He took her arm, knowing the game, but he'd met his match with her.

She leaned her body into his, sliding close for only a moment. "Mr. Barrett, I'd much rather have something more intimate, especially as a thank you for all your trouble."

His brow shot high.

She covered his arm with her hand, looking up through her lashes. "Perhaps dinner? After I've finished my business with Mr. Harrison?"

"It's a date, Ms. Barry." He slid her body another look and stepped back. "Let me get my keys, close up for lunch, and we'll be on our way."

∞ ∞ ∞

Eisley hadn't returned home yet, and despite Lizzie and Joe's reassurances, Wes couldn't shake the look of pain he'd seen in her eyes. Pain his presence in her life had caused. He didn't want to lose her, but neither did he want to hurt her, and there was no assurance her family's privacy wouldn't be breached again.

And again.

He pulled up to the apartment and shot a look to the main house. No sign of Eisley's car or the Jenkins'. A different scent hit him as he entered the apartment. Lavender? He shrugged. With as many feminine motifs in his rooms, he wouldn't be surprised if artificial flowers didn't start growing out of the floral print wallpaper, let alone another flowery scent or two.

Eisley had been gone for two hours. Two excruciating hours. What would her decision be? He knew the choices he'd made to protect his family. Moving away from his beloved home. Cutting off any person who dug too deeply into his private life. He groaned and ran a hand through his hair. Except Vivian. Guilt fueled his blindness and idiocy with Vivian.

Wes tossed his mobile onto the flower shaped coffee table and sat down on the couch, elbows resting on his knees. *Lord, I would do anything to protect her. To keep her from hurting the same way she'd been hurt in the past. Help me.*

Pain squeezed his breath closed, his prayer grinding to an excruciating halt. *Even give her up.*

The thought hurdled through him, singeing a direct line to his heart. The best way to protect her from the ill effects of his life would be to leave her alone. He stood and paced the floor, a growing ache throbbing deep in his chest. She'd never wanted him in her life. He'd pursued her all along, selfishly, with the cravings of a starving man, hunting the fruit of a second chance.

He'd thrust her into his world, and now—

The sound of an approaching vehicle drew him to the window. Eisley's jeep came into view up the drive. It would be the right thing to let her go. If he loved her, or even cared for her family, he would do it. She'd not signed on to the insanity accompanying his profession. Her anonymous world played a comforting song to her. He couldn't promise privacy, ever.

For her. His chest constricted again. *Or for her children.*

She stepped from the jeep and met his gaze through the window, her beautiful eyes lit with her answer. She'd choose him. His smile froze on his face. And he shouldn't let her.

He met her at the door.

"Hey," she whispered.

He couldn't get his voice to work. Perhaps it was in protest for the words he needed to speak. The choice he must convince her to make, because if she didn't and more of his past crowded into their lives, he'd only continue to hurt her and her family.

But how could he let her go?

Because you love her, mate.

She stepped into his arms, burying her face into his shoulder the way he loved. The way which brought the deepest surge of protectiveness. With strength forged from his decision, he placed his hands on her shoulders and drew back.

"We need to talk." He almost added 'pet' but couldn't pair the sweet endearment with what he needed to say next. "Things have changed."

She searched his face. "Changed?" Her palm caressed his cheek. "It's only made me more certain."

He took her hand from his cheek and cradled it in his. "My life poses challenges you shouldn't have to face."

"I'm not afraid. Not anymore." Her smile glowed with a naive confidence. "If you love me, we'll work out all the crazy stuff. You trust me, and I trust you."

"Your first mistake, my dear." The glacial tones from behind him identified its author. Eisley's face paled as she glanced over his shoulder and confirmed his fear. Turning, he took the sight like a punch to his stomach.

Vivian Barry stood in the bathroom doorway wearing nothing but a dangerous smile and a thin, red towel.

Twenty-Eight

*E*isley's brain turned in agonizing slow motion. Hadn't she mistaken Vivian for being in a red towel when they'd first met? At the Christmas gala? And now, in her family's powder puff apartment, the woman literally stood in a red towel. This had to be a horrible nightmare.

It didn't make sense. Why would Vivian be in her parents' apartment with—

The thoughts moved faster, painfully clearer. *No!* An internal protest rose from the pit of her soul. Impossible. She looked from Vivian to the man she loved, who stood wide-eyed and pale at her side.

"Wes?" Her voice sounded pitiful and small. *Weak, just like before.* Memories crushed in on her. *This couldn't be happening. Not again. Not with Wes.*

He pulled his gaze from Vivian. If she didn't know the lying actor so well, she'd have thought he was shocked to see Vivian too, but it didn't make sense. How could Vivian have found him in her family's apartment if Wes hadn't told her where to come? Hadn't Wes ended things with her?

The same emotions from Marshall's betrayal, the devastating scenes, flickered through her mind and slashed over her heart with a deeper burn. Wes? Not Wes too. No.

"Eisley, I didn't know she was here."

She swallowed down the useless tears and rolled her burning gaze to his. "I've...I've heard that line before."

"I swear to you, it's the truth."

"That one, too." She pressed a palm to her queasy stomach. "Twice."

"Not from me." His stare held a conviction she wanted to believe, but how? Proof positive stood grinning in her skivvies across the room.

Wes shot Vivian a steely look. "I don't know how you got here, Vivian, but I see your plan and it won't work. There is nothing between us and never will be."

Vivian took her time looking over Wes from shoes to forehead and then a feline smile slid into place. "Do you truly think she'll believe you, darling?" She sent a cobalt glare toward Eisley. "I did try to warn her about our...bond."

Wes growled and stepped forward, blocking Eisley from Vivian's gaze. "There is nothing you have that I want." His turned back to Eisley. "It has only been you since the first day we met. Can't you see that Vivian's been behind everything? The tabloids, the article, even *this*." He ushered his hand toward her. "Please believe me."

Eisley's attention was drawn against her will back across the room. The little towel dropped a teensy bit lower to show off the perfect twin curves at the top of her chest. Eisley's throat pinched against the bitterness rising into her throat.

"Right now, I'm having a hard time seeing past the naked woman in your apartment." She took a deep breath, pulling up her strength. She would not be weak now. No matter how badly the scene confused and hurt her. No matter how much she wanted to close her eyes and wish it away. "Is this why you wanted to end things with us? She fits better into your life, I guess." Eisley blinked the realization into place. He'd tried to tell her. Warn her. But she'd forged ahead with her Pollyanna hope right into the freefall. *Fairy tales weren't for her.*

"I wanted to prevent this." His fist slammed against the side of his leg.

"Getting caught?" Her question hardened against a sob.

Pain flashed across his expression and collided with a fresh sting to her chest. "Hurting you."

She squeezed her eyes closed and stepped back, trying to weed between her past, the present, her thoughts, and her feelings. They all crashed together into a myriad of blinding confusion. "I'm tired of playing pretend, and I'm really sick of being an idiot." Tears closed off her throat and she took another step back, toward the door. "You're right, Wes. This *won't* work. I don't share well when it comes to the man in my life." She braced her hand against the doorframe, vision burning. "I've gotta go."

Wes called after her, but she ran—from Wes, from her own stupidity, from the confusion of the scene as it replayed in her mind, but she couldn't outrun one thing.

Her lacerated heart.

∞ ∞ ∞

Wes tried to run after Eisley, but Vivian clutched his arm and conveniently dropped her hold on her towel at the same time. Fury surged through him and exploded in his head like a battle horn. He jerked away, leaving her to regain her balance on her own, and then raced down the stairs.

He ran up to Eisley's jeep as she started the engine. "Eisley, please listen to me. You must believe—"

"Don't." She raised her palm to him, tears floating in her emerald gaze. "Just let me go."

"Eisley."

The expression on her face, the hurt, ripped through him with the precision of a bullet. She shook her head and put the jeep in reverse, peeling down the drive.

Wes lowered his face into his hands. *No, no, no.* He'd wanted her protected from his life, but not like this.

His gaze moved back to the apartment window and a fresh scorch of anger set his feet in motion. He wouldn't allow Vivian Barry to stay in Pleasant Gap near the Jenkins family any longer. He marched back up the stairs, walked Vivian to the bathroom, grabbed the pile of clothes from the counter and shoved them into her hands. "Get dressed and get out. You've done your worst today."

She took the clothes with a shameless grin, proving his point. His past came in the form of Vivian Barry and broke Eisley's heart.

He turned away and began tossing his belongings into his bag without thought. "Gather your things, Vivian. I'm going to ensure you leave the Jenkins family and Pleasant Gap before you cause any more damage."

"Don't play the wounded party here, darling. The game of fame and fortune comes with its rules and risks." She tsked and then glared at him. "I risked *everything* to win." Her gaze darkened. "And in this game, winner takes all."

"No, Vivian. You've lost everything." He ran his gaze down her crumpled clothes, certain to allow his disgust to show on his face. "All of this because of jealousy for your sister? Why? Why ruin me and yourself because of it?"

"You haven't the foggiest what it was like. Jane was the favorite, and I was never good enough. She had everything. Beauty, talent, you." She sneered. "If father hadn't forced her to have the abortion, she would have given birth to the perfect child too, no doubt."

Wes choked at the declaration. "Your father forced her to have—"

Vivian released a long line of expletives and averted her gaze. "Don't worry your tender heart about it." She recovered her look of feline satisfaction. "The only reason Jane mourned for the child was because she couldn't use it as leverage to keep you anymore."

He'd carried all the blame for so long, and yes, he still hurt her, but her deep depression? Could it have been from this? He couldn't find words to respond.

"The baby would have ruined her career. Father wouldn't abide it." She looked back at him, the guilt lacing her expression proving she didn't believe her own words. "It's old history."

That sentence rekindled his fight. "So, you've given up your self-respect, and once I speak to my solicitor you'll likely lose your reputation too, over some vendetta against your sister? Did you think that would free you from your jealousy?"

She looked away, words grinding an octave lower. "I can't be free. Not after all I've done. The price I paid." She focused back on him, a fresh intensity tensing her expression. "For you. I deserve you. Don't you understand? I gave my *soul* for you."

Tears, true ones mingled within cobalt blue. Something dark waited behind her words.

"What do you mean? Vivian—"

"It was a game. Only a game to prove to her I could best her by sleeping with you. I never meant—"

"Jane knew about us?" Wes's jaw slacked, and his words formed in slow motion. "Did you speak to her the night she died?"

Vivian pinched her eyes close and turned her face away, lips clamped together.

"You did." His gut roiled. "What did you tell her? Tell me, or so help me, Vivian...."

"I have nothing else to say to you."

Wes reached for his mobile. "Then I'll learn it from your father."

Vivian's hands were on his arm in a moment. "No, no, don't bring Father into this." Her eyes rounded, pleading. "He...he doesn't know."

"Doesn't know what?"

Her expression turned vicious again. "You were so trolleyed that night you could have slept through anything. I knew it was the only way I could have you." Her words coursed through clench teeth. "I could finally claim a victory over my sister, though. She'd betrayed you, and you came to me."

"So, you phoned her? And she believed you?"

All emotion fell from her expression. "I sent her a photo from my mobile of you in my bed."

Wes opened his mouth, but no words, no thoughts could battle the atrocity of her confession. He closed his eyes, blotting out her face, her bitterness. How could he have been so blind?

Her rasped words scratched at his fury. "If I must suffer with the sins of my past"—she pointed her shaky finger at him, her eyes taking on a misty hue— "if I am not free of her, than I won't let you be either."

The desperation, the fear in her voice pushed him back a step. A haunted look took over her expression, a vulnerability he'd never seen before and somehow, an unexplainable compassion curbed his anger with a touch of grace. "I know the guilt you suffer, but it doesn't have to master you." He gentled his voice but didn't move closer. "There is a way to find peace for your heart."

Her eyes grew wide, desperate for an answer.

"Forgiveness. The end to the consuming anger and wrenching guilt is forgiveness."

She jerked back as if he'd slapped her. "I will never forgive her for lording her perfect life over me, and I will never forgive you for rejecting me." The haughty look returned, coupled with a wicked smile. "No, darling, forgiveness has never been my forte, but I excel in retribution. When you rejected me, you forced me to strike back and teach you a lesson with the pain you so carelessly inflicted." Her smile spread, eyes alight with a sinister glow. "To watch your world, your dreams, ripped from your hands by the plans of another."

She was beyond his reach. Lost and hard. "I'm sorry for you, Vivian. Bitterness is stealing your life. Forgiveness—God's forgiveness—is the only way you will find freedom."

Her lips tilted into that same, heartless sneer. "Save your sermon for yourself. You'll need it when your little American rejects you. And she will, Wesley dear. No woman wants a betrayer." Her brow rose like a dagger. "Especially a woman who's known this wound before. She'll never be back."

And in Vivian's world, it was probably true, but Vivian couldn't understand the beautifully generous heart of Eisley Barrett. She couldn't comprehend the forgiving grace of God. His heart accepted the chill of his decision. Nor would she understand how he would give Eisley up because he loved her. "Get in the truck, Vivian. You're leaving."

They drove in silence. Each time Vivian attempted to begin a conversation, Wes closed it. A second chance wasn't worth the risk of Eisley's heart—or her family—and his past kept haunting him. How could she want to risk everything for this?

No. By the time they'd made it into town, he knew the right choice. The selfless one he should have chosen on the night of the Christmas gala. Protect Eisley by keeping away from her.

Wes phoned Lizzie to make her aware of his plans to leave and ask if she'd accompany him, but she wanted to stay with Joe. A mist filled his vision. At least one of them could hold on to their relationship. Wes's heart pulled against leaving, but he refused to weaken. This was the right choice for Eisley and her family. No doubt, time would lessen her affections and help her move on with her life.

But he'd never recover. The experiences with her and the children would remain in his heart forever.

He wrote a note to Nate and Kay with apologies for his hasty departure, leaving it in their front door, and then he hired a taxi for Vivian's direct trip to the airport by way of coach.

With one last look down the long stretch of Main Street, gaze fastening on the pink flag from Julia's bakery, Wes slipped into the truck and put it into gear. *Goodbye, Eisley.*

Chapter Twenty-Nine

*E*isley stumbled into her house, blinking through her tears, and grateful for time alone before picking up the kids. How could she have been so wrong again? Hadn't the past three years taught her anything about rotten jerks? Everything felt so...so wrong.

But Wes wasn't a jerk. Everything he said and did proved him true and...good. Marshall had given off signals to his duplicity long before she'd caught him in the act, but not Wes. Her heart squeezed painfully in her chest.

He couldn't have been acting all this time, could he? With her family? With her children? She swallowed down a sob. With her?

She slumped down in her office chair and buried her face into her hands, reliving the scene with Vivian. On the heels of the great article debacle, when her emotions were still reeling from the rift in her family's privacy, Vivian's presence hit a weak spot, but as she replayed the scenes holes emerged.

Why didn't Wes try to get her to leave the apartment if he knew Vivian was there? With her mom's hawk-like eyes, not to mention Aunt Tilley's next door, wouldn't they have noticed a stranger in the guesthouse if Vivian had been there for any length of time? Wes's look of pure horror and pain appeared sincere, and he'd run after her, begging her to listen to him, not to leave.

Marshall didn't even try.

Besides, what did he get out of all of this anyway? Pleasant Gap and the Jenkins' family certainly weren't a one-way trip to fame and fortune.

She massaged her aching forehead. Her heart and her thoughts wrestled for the right answer. Something wasn't right.

A stack of research stared back at her from a pile on her desk. One of the shortest letters from Geoffrey MacLeroy sat on the top, begging her to give in to distraction. She blinked back a new rush of tears and focused on the timeworn page.

Beloved Julia,

Do not fall prey to the lies surrounding my delay. And do not forsake hope. Hope cannot cease because God does not cease. I come for thee on the morrow. If thine eyes fail thee, trust in thine heart, for it speaks the truthe of mine affections and constancy. Thou knowest me as none other. I will come for thee. Hold to hope and look for me.

My heart is in thy hands always,

Geoffrey

Eisley placed the letter down. So short yet filled with such assurance. Doubt waited in the far corners of her mind, but hope? Even if it led through pain, it also paved the path to love. She pressed her palm to her chest. The love she clung to for Wes Harrison.

Help me, Lord.

She sucked in a noisy breath and glanced over the letter again. Her love for him urged her to weed through the possible hurt and focus on what she knew. He *loved* her. He was not the man he used to be. He left England to visit her middle class, anonymous, and somewhat strange family and to spend time with her *because* he loved her.

A liar and cheat wouldn't do something that crazy.

He'd trusted her even when her number came up as the one that took the photos of his father. That proof seemed pretty incriminating, but he'd trusted her. She stood from her desk. She needed to talk to him...because she trusted him too.

Noise erupted from the kitchen as the back door opened and slammed against the wall, followed by a rush of voices. Eisley found her dad holding Emily in the kitchen, surrounded by all three of her sisters, her two boys, and her mom pulling Greg by the arm through the back door.

"What is going on?"

"Triage." Rachel, the nurse, tossed the word at her. "You're in desperate need of intervention."

"Wes went to the airport."

Her dad's announcement had her gripping the counter for support. "What?"

"He left a note at the house. Tilley said she saw him pull out of the driveway about an hour ago. I went to grab your mama so she could talk some sense into you."

"But I had to come too, because you're making a horrible mistake, Eisley," Julia said, tugging Emily out of Dad's arms.

"I just came along as a witness," Sophie added. "Family drama is better than prime time TV any day."

Eisley was still trying to follow along. Her gaze shifted to Greg.

"I just happened to be coming to check on Fritter's puppies and they pulled me inside." Greg's hands came up helplessly. "This is the reason I like animals over people, by the way."

"Why did you ask him to leave?" Julia's eyes rounded with concern. "He's perfect for you."

"I didn't—"

"What did you do to that poor boy then?" Her dad shoved a letter into her hands.

"Me?" Eisley scanned over the words, her heart pinching at his evident concern for her. "I was actually on my way—"

"Your Aunt Tilley saw Marshall drop some fancy woman off at the house a couple of hours ago and she got worried 'cause nobody was at home." Her dad continued.

"Marshall?"

"If anybody's going to find a pretty woman in town, it's going to be Marshall," Rachel added with an eye roll. "It sounds like that Vivian woman you've talked about stumbled upon the perfect idiot to help her get to Wes."

"His note said something about never wanting his past to hurt you or our family." Mom intervened.

"He said it'd be easier for you if he left you alone." Dad's finger nudged into her shoulder. "You need to do something to fix it. Any boy who would leave the woman he loves to protect her, now that's a real *somebody*."

"You have to go get your man," Rachel announced, both hands planted on her hips with the same conviction as her voice.

"To know what is right and to not do it is the worst cowardice." Sophie grinned. "Confucius."

"Who's Confusion?" Nathan asked from the center of the circle of adults, his poor little head swiveling from one excited person to the other.

Eisley wanted to raise her hand. Confusion. Right here.

No. She shook her head. She wasn't confused. She knew exactly what she wanted...and needed to do.

Tears swam into Eisley's eyes before she could stop them. Faith, hope and a whole lot of true love shocked her into motion. She grabbed her purse. "I was on my way before you guys barged in here. It took me a little while to catch up with the truth." She grabbed her car keys. "I kind of got distracted by the naked woman in his apartment." The statement sounded horrible.

Greg's head perked up. "There was a naked woman in the apartment?"

Mama slapped him on the shoulder.

"I know I should have put locks back on those doors," Dad murmured.

"He's in love with *you*, Eisley." Julia raised a honey-colored brow. "You have to go after him."

"A true romantic encounter, though prevalent in fiction, is not as common in the real world and therefore must be valued for the uniqueness of its opportunity," Sophie added.

All heads turned to the youngest Jenkins. She dazzled them with her infectious smile and shrugged. "That's what Chris Lucas writes in *The Idiot's Guide to Finding Your Prince Charming.*"

Rachel squeezed her eyes closed. "You actually read something with that title?"

Eisley pushed through her family toward the front door, taking out her phone to dial Wes' number. If they kept talking she'd never get to Wes. "Let me get on my way—"

The kitchen door slammed open and Lizzie walked in, her face flushed from exertion. "What are you still doing here?"

Eisley sighed. "I was going to call Wes and tell him not to leave and then—.""

"No." She waved Eisley toward the door. "You can leave a voicemail on the way to the airport. Don't waste time, Luv. I've learned a great deal about not taking chances when one should, about the brevity of life and love." She gave each face in the room a severe look. "Who is the most efficient driver in this house?"

Everyone's attention fastened on Greg.

"Whoa, wait a minute." Greg backed away, his movements slow, like he was retreating from a wild herd. "I'm just here to check on the puppies, remember?"

"Can I go, Mama?" Pete asked. "I want to see the airplanes."

"We can help you catch Wes, Mom. We're good searchers." Nathan added.

"Spit, spot, people." Lizzie rushed them forward. "You haven't all day."

Eisley shoved her keys into Greg's hand. "Come on, Greg. I have a Prince Charming to catch."

∞ ∞ ∞

An hour and a half later, they bounded through the doors of Charlotte-Douglas International Airport, Greg's frustrated voice carrying into the cavernous entrance. "If I hear any more of that singing vegetable music, I think I'm going to shoot the CD player. How can you listen to that stuff all the time?"

Eisley barely heard him, too busy searching the crowded room for a miracle. Any miracle would do, but she preferred one with a British accent and some heart-stopping dimples. "I'm going to the information desk."

"I need to go to the bathroom, Mama," Pete whined, beginning an impressive potty dance.

Greg sighed. "Listen, I'll take the boys with me down this way and meet you at Information."

"Thanks, Greg. And please pray."

A young woman stood behind the information desk, phone to her ear, white uniform blouse perfectly starched. Eisley tapped the counter, talked to Emily, and tried not to worry that Wes might never want to talk to her again. She had to find him.

The receptionist hung up the phone and pressed the intercom mic. "James Lincoln, please report to the information desk in the baggage area. Your party is waiting for you. Thank you." She turned to Eisley. "May I help you?"

Eisley sat Emily up on the desk and leaned forward. "Yes, I need to get a message to someone quickly. He's probably trying to board a flight to London, England and—"

"England?" She checked her computer. "We have one flight boarding for New York as a connection to London and another with a connection to Chicago-O'Hare." She typed something into her computer. "Then there is one to Atlanta boarding now."

"Now? Which way do I go?"

Her face registered compassion. "Unless you have a ticket, you can't make it through security, honey." She picked up the phone and spoke to someone, then returned her gaze to Eisley. "They just gave the last boarding call for Atlanta and New York won't be far behind."

Eisley leaned forward, one arm hooked around Emily. "There's got to be something I can do. The man I love is getting on one of those flights." Eisley stretched so far over the counter she lifted to tiptoe. "He thinks I don't care, or at least that leaving is the easiest way to protect me, but he's wrong. I've got to stop him. Please, can you get a message to the people on the plane? Or something?"

The woman lifted a curious brow. "What is his name?"

"Wesley Harrison."

She took the microphone and gave her head a little shake. "Wesley Harrison, please report to the information desk at the front of the building, Terminal B entrance." Her voice echoed through the airport. "Your party is waiting."

She clicked the microphone back into place on the counter.

Eisley stared at her. "That's all?"

Greg and the boys came up to her side. "What's going on?"

"The receptionist says there's nothing we can do." She sighed. "He's not answering his phone and I've got to talk to him. Maybe if he knows how much I want him to stay, then he won't leave."

Greg looked over at the information desk and then back to the crowd, a very sneaky grin rising into the pattern of his face. "You think the intercom will work for your message?"

"What do you mean?"

Greg winked and walked over to stand in line next to a few people. He looked around, touched the handle of a suitcase nearby and then tried to take it. The business man nearby turned. "Take your hands off of my bag."

Greg looked shocked. "Your bag? This is my bag. You get your hands off of it."

Oh, good grief! Was he serious? He was going to add *arrested* to his resume—no wait, he'd already been arrested once for picketing an inhumane dog shelter.

"It is not yours." The man's voice rose. "I'll call security if you don't unhand it."

"Call them, then." Greg shouted. "Better yet, I'll call them." He turned to the desk. "Miss. This man is trying to steal my bag."

The plan worked. Unbelievable.

The receptionist left her spot to try and resolve her brother's master plan. Greg sent Eisley another wink and nodded toward the information desk, propelling her forward. Could she be arrested for this? Did it really matter at this point?

Eisley's attention landed on the intercom mic. She chewed on her bottom lip for a second and then sent a glance toward the crowd. On tiptoe, with Emily in her arms, she rounded the desk, both boys trailing behind.

"What are you doing, Mom?" Nathan's voice interrupted her stealth.

"I really need to use this microphone to get in touch with Wes."

"Are you supposed to be back there?"

His question paused her forward momentum and she cringed. "Not technically. This is an emergency." She turned and pointed a finger to the boys. "But you're never to do something like this okay? Never."

Pete's eyes rounded. "Oh, is this one of those *pretend we don't see it moments?*"

"Or *do what you say not what you do* times?" Nathan added.

She squeezed her eyes closed and sighed. *God, please protect them from their mother.* "Yeah, buddies, something like that."

With a little fumbling, she picked up the microphone, fingers moving to the button she'd seen the woman push. She took a deep breath, shot one last look at the gathering crowd in the center of the room, and then pushed the button. "Umm...hello...um..."

The information desk lady's head swiveled like an owl's, eyes wide with surprise.

Might as well fully commit now.

"Wes Harrison, if you can hear me, don't you dare get on that plane." Her voice echoed through the cavernous expanse around her and carried right toward the woman's reddening face. "Um...please. I...I...know that what happened wasn't your fault and I'm sorry I didn't listen to you."

The woman pushed through the crowd, her progress slow, eyes narrowed with purpose. Greg tried to intersect her with a question, but it barely stunted her forward momentum.

Emily giggled, and the trill resonated like surround sound.

"Please don't leave. You are better than any fairy tale."

The woman rounded the counter, eyes furious, and grabbed for the microphone.

Eisley leaned back as the woman pulled against her. "I love you, Wes."

The microphone jerked free and the woman stumbled back. "I should have security called. What were you thinking?"

"I'm sorry, but I had to try."

Emily giggled again, and the woman's expression softened a little. "If you remove yourself at once, then I'll overlook this." She pointed toward the doors. "Go."

Eisley gathered up the kids and followed the direction of her pointing finger.

Greg ran to catch up with her. "Who'd have thought it was that guy's bag after all? My bad." He shrugged and grinned. "What are you going to do now?"

"I'm not sure." She stopped in the middle of the room, at a complete loss of what to do next, except maybe cry.

The buzz of her cell stopped her descent into the depths of despair. She adjusted Emily in her arms and put the phone to her ear. "Hello."

"I'm on number thirteen of your seventeen messages."

"Wes." Tears of relief clogged her voice. Calling him every ten minutes as they careened toward the airport at record speed saved the day? *Oh please, say yes!*

"Hi Wesh." Emily pulled at the phone. "I talk Wesh."

"No honey, not right now, Mommy needs to talk to Wesh, I mean Wes." She placed Emily down and followed her busy little feet across the glossy floor while Greg sat down on some nearby chairs with the boys. "Where are you? Are you on the plane?"

"The intercom announcement was quite...impressive."

Heat rushed to her cheeks and she laughed. "Well, whatever it takes to get a guy's attention, you know?" She lowered her voice. "Seriously, please don't leave. Obviously, I'm not afraid of what people think, right? I just announced my undying devotion to you throughout all of Charlotte-Douglass International. So, no more worries about those nasty tabloids. I can handle them, which means you should probably stay here."

A brief silence had her checking her connection.

"I'm sorry about Vivian, pet."

The endearment washed over her. She breathed it in. "Vivian doesn't matter to me, or the tabloids or the articles. What does matter is you, me, and you staying *with* me. So, where are you?"

The phone clicked to silence. "Wes? Wes?" *Full roaming coverage, my eye.*

She scanned the flight display for the next flight to London.

"Wesh!" Emily squealed and took off at a run.

Wes parted the crowd at full speed, phone in hand, bag over his shoulder, and smoky gaze sifting through the distance directly to her heart. Eisley nearly squeezed her phone to mush in her hands. Every word she tried to form stuck to the roof of her mouth and a knot of tears crowded against her vision.

He dropped his bag at his side and swept Emily into his arms, giving her a little swing. Her giggle played the mamba all the way through Eisley's quivering middle. *Oh, how she loved this man.*

She stepped forward, blinking through tears. "You...you didn't leave."

His gaze found hers and held. "I didn't leave."

She moved closer, swiping at her fountain-eyes. "I'm so sorry. I should have seen through Vivian's scheme, but...but I was distracted by the whole towel-scene. I figured it out after I got home, but I was too late and then you were gone. I promise, I'll do better next time."

"Next time?" He gave a ferocious shake to his head, which Emily imitated to perfection, even with the crinkled brow. "I'm trying to prevent a next time. I can't bear the thought of anything of this nature hurting you again." He smoothed a palm over Emily's crazy sprigs of hair. "Or your family." His expression hardened. "You were right all along. You didn't want a romance with me. I chased you and brought all of my past mistakes with me."

"But if I have to take all of them to have you too, then so be it. My family were up in arms to get you back." She gestured toward the bench where Greg and the boys sat. "You care more about me and my family than for yourself." She stepped closer. "And I can assure you, Mr. Harrison, I want a romance with you and a whole lot more."

He produced a crooked grin and narrowed his smoky eyes. Yep, she was making good progress, so she went in for the win. "Listen, you have your baggage from the past and I have mine."

"Yours are much cuter." He stared down at Emily, a tender look washing over his features. "My life isn't easy or simple."

"Life isn't simple, not when you really live it. And easy?" She shrugged away his words and moved close enough to touch his arm. "If you leave, I'll hurt more from missing you than I will from what happened today. You'll hear my breaking heart all the way across the Atlantic." She pointed her finger at him and put on her most intimidating look.

"I don't ever want to break your heart, Eisley. I'd break my own first."

"Okay, you need to understand two things, buddy. One, I'm not a wimp. I might be a little slow putting the pieces of Vivian's arrival together, but I'm strong enough to handle whatever comes our way. So is my family. They believe in us." She pointed another finger at him. "And two, I would rather take the risks or pain and have the comfort of your love through it all, than to let the fear of the past, or of things we can't control steal this beautiful—" She waved her palm between them, waiting for his reply.

His smile spread to two dimples and he bridged the small gap between them. "Relationship?"

"Exactly." She pressed her palm against his cheek and noticed the tears in his eyes. *Oh, sweet heaven, he was remarkable.* "I don't want to lose you."

He swept back her hair with his fingers. "I don't want to be lost."

"Then don't leave. Ever. Not from here." She placed her palm on her chest. "I've become a lot stronger since knowing you, but I don't want to have to be strong enough for that." She took hold of his jacket lapel and pulled him closer, squeezing Emily in between them. "I love you right now and I'm choosing to love you for tomorrow and the next day and the next, no matter what comes." She caught his protest with her finger. "Just the way you are, Christopher Wesley Harrison."

His gaze roamed her face, caressing over all of the last remnants of uncertainty with a fresh touch of faith. He pulled her deeper into his embrace, one arm hooked around her waist, the other holding Emily on his hip. With the gentlest of movements, he brushed his lips over hers.

"Wesh have boo-boo?" Emily took his face in her hands and pulled his attention to her. "Me tiss it." She proceeded to plant a loud kiss directly on Wes's mouth.

"Thank you, chicken." He jostled her against his side. "I'm feeling much better now."

"Mama tiss it." Emily ordered and pointed to Wes's mouth.

"Well, okay." Eisley exaggerated a sigh and then placed both hands on either side of his face to kiss a very severe boo-boo away. Twice.

"Oh gross, do you guys have to kiss in public?" Greg's voice broke through the tender moment like a clap of thunder.

"You kissed him *on the mouth*, Mom." Pete's face wrinkled into a hundred creases, all screaming *disgusting*. "Why would you do something like *that*?"

Nathan nudged his brother and smiled with a hidden knowledge his seven years and love for his mom seemed to understand. Obviously, Greg hadn't matured to that level yet.

"I love your mom, guys. I love her more than—" Wes looked up at the ceiling in search of the right description.

"Spiderman?" Pete asked, his lips wide in complete disbelief at the possibility.

Wes kissed Eisley's cheek and chuckled. "Yes, I love her more than Spiderman and even more than Aunt Tilley's chocolate pie."

"Wow," the boys shouted, including Greg.

"Chocolate and kisses." Eisley snagged his rolling bag from the floor and shot him a wink. "Two pretty powerful things."

"I know of something even better." He breathed the words near her ear and she sank into the heady scent of spice and leather and Wes Harrison.

Adult-rated scenes started a freefall of heat from her cheeks down. *Whoa, girl.* "What could possibly top chocolate and kisses?"

His lips warmed her cheek, his words taking a breathy detour to her ear. "I can think of a few very specific ones to add to your list, pet."

Great googly moogly. *Where was the nearest closet?*

"But I know what's at the top of the list for me."

She pressed her forehead against his shoulder as they walked. "And what's that?"

He paused and turned his lovely gaze on her. "Your love, Eisley. Apart from God's love, I've never experienced anything as sweet and disarming in all my life."

She swallowed past her dry throat and squeezed him to her side. "I have enough to share for an entire lifetime. Are you up for a happily-ever-after with me? It's certain to be a wild ride."

He buried a kiss into her hair and walked toward the doors of the airport, Emily giggling on his hip. "It's the perfect happily-ever-after and it's more than I could have ever imagined."

Eisley sighed against him. "I really think we should celebrate all of this sweet love, you know?"

He held the door for her to pass. "And exactly what do you recommend?"

She paused in front of him, leaned close for a quick kiss, and then wiggled her brows. "Oh, I think it starts with chocolate, ends in a closet, and has a whole lot of hope sprinkled in along the way."

"I'll take it all, as long as it's with you."

His arm around her and the sweet tenderness in his gaze promised something much greater than chocolate or kisses. They promised a love of a lifetime from a God who loved them both just the way they were—apart —but knew they would be much better together.

Acknowledgements

Despite popular belief, a writer really doesn't create these books on her own. A wonderful crew of family, friends, and professionals roll up their sleeves and get involved in the process through encouragement, directions, occasional bouts of chocolate, and a whole lot of motivation.

Krista Phillips, you are a Rockstar! Thank you for helping me navigate this new world of publishing by sharing your expertise, friendship, kindness and long-suffering. Wow! I could NOT have done this without you.

Carrie Booth Schmidt, God knew exactly what I needed in my life when he sent you my way. Thank you for being such an encourager – for putting up with my craziness, indulging in my endless messages, and reminding me (so often) that I have stories in me worth telling.

Katie Donovan, thank you so much for your editorial eyes and fabulous encouragement! You are definitely on your way to becoming an excellent editor some day.

Diane Gage, thank you for taking time to read one of the early copies of this story!

Rel Mollet, you rock! Thanks for being such an encouragement

Linda Attaway, thank you for taking a chance on my story and using your experience to make this book the best it can be.

Dream Team, you guys make this journey SO. MUCH. FUN. Having you on my side, sharing sneak peeks and seeing how you get excited about what's next, is like riding on a tour bus with a bunch of friends. Thank you all so much!

AlleyCats, I am ever grateful for God bringing you into my life, and for sharing the joys and challenges of this writing with you. Thank you for always being such a support.

This is my dad's favorite book I've ever written, and you might even find some of his personality on the pages. Thanks to my parents for always encouraging my writing and for celebrating stories with me my whole life.

To my family. I am beyond grateful to my husband and children, who support, love, and inspire me in this story-writing business. Writing children into my books makes me smile so much because I'm blessed with some of the very best ones on the planet.

And, of course, I am grateful to God for loving me just the way I am—and giving me the gift of story. Thank you for helping me create word pictures of your love for others to read.

A Note from the Author

This is my favorite book I've written so far because it holds so many of the things I love best—romance, mystery, humor, Britain, Appalachia, big families, adorable kids, fun banter, swoony heroes, lovable heroines, and God's grace—within its pages. Some people might even find glimpses of characteristics resembling some of my own family members from my wonderful Appalachian family.

In Appalachia, storytelling is an important part of the culture. I grew up listening to my Granny Spencer tell family history stories from five generations back—some stories more amazing and unbelievable than fiction—but what I love most about my culture is the importance of family. There's a bond, solidarity, and 'bigness' to how we view our families.

Thankfully, my big Appalachian family also understood the power of God's grace to transform generations. I've loved researching my family history and discovering the thread of God's redemption woven throughout hundreds of years to make it to my generation, my life. Now *that's* a story!

I'm so thankful I got to bring the sense of family, from both sides of the Pond, to life in this book. I hope you enjoy this lighthearted Britallachian romance—a combination of two amazing cultures and the fun and romance that we can uncover.

If you'd like to know more about me and my books, check out my website at www.pepperdbasham.com or visit me on Facebook, Instagram, or Twitter.

If you enjoyed this story, please leave your thoughts on Amazon, B&N, and/or Goodreads. Authors appreciate hearing from you.

Blessings,

Pepper Basham

Want to Read More from Pepper?
Pepper writes both Contemporary and Historical Romance.

ALSO BY PEPPER D BASHAM

Historical Romance
The Penned in Time Series
The Thorn Bearer
The Thorn Keeper
The Thorn Healer

Historical Romance Novella
Façade

Contemporary Romance
The Mitchell's Crossroads Series
A Twist of Faith
Charming the Troublemaker
A Pleasant Gap Romance
Just the Way You Are

Contemporary Romance Novella
Second Impressions
Jane by the Book

About the Author

Pepper Basham is an award-winning author who writes romance peppered with grace and humor with a southern Appalachian flair. Her books have garnered recognition in the Grace Awards, Inspys, and the ACFW Carol Awards, with *The Thorn Healer* selected as a 2018 finalist in the RT awards. Both her contemporary and historical romance novels consistently receive high ratings from Romantic Times, with *Just the Way You Are* as a Top Pick. Most recently she's introduced readers to Bath, UK through her novellas, Second Impressions and Jane by the Book, and taken readers into the exciting world of WW2 espionage in her novella, *Façade.* The second novel in The Pleasant Gap series, *When You Look at Me,* arrives in October and her contribution to Barbour's wonderful My Heart Belongs series hits the shelves in January 2019 with *My Heart Belongs in the Blue Ridge.* Her books are seasoned with her Appalachian heritage and love for family. She currently resides in the lovely mountains of Asheville, NC where she is the mom of five great kids, a speech-pathologist to about fifty more, and a lover of chocolate, jazz, hats, and Jesus.

You can get to know Pepper on her website, www.pepperdbasham.com, on Facebook, Instagram, or over at her group blog, The Writer's Alley.

Made in United States
Orlando, FL
24 March 2022

16119645R00159